ANN GRANGER

RACK, RUIN and MURDER

headline

First published in 2011 by
HEADLINE PUBLISHING GROUP

First published in paperback in 2011 by
HEADLINE PUBLISHING GROUP

1

Cataloguing in Publication Data is available from the British Library

ISBN 978 0 7553 4911 1

Typeset in AGaramond by Palimpsest Book Production Limited,
Falkirk, Stirlingshire

Printed and bound in Great Britain by
CPI Group (UK) Ltd, Croydon, CR0 4YY

HEADLINE PUBLISHING GROUP
An Hachette UK Company
338 Euston Road
London NW1 3BH

www.headline.co.uk
www.hachette.co.uk

Ann Gran... ...world, since for many years she ...ice and received postings to British e... ...far apart as Munich and Lusaka. She is m...ed, with two sons, and she and her husband, who also ...d for the Foreign Office, are now permanently based in O... rdshire.

Rack Ruin and Murder is the second novel in the brilliant new Cotswold crime series, featuring Superintendent Ian Carter and Inspector Jess Campbell. Ann Granger is also the author of three other hugely popular crime series: the Mitchell and Markby novels; the Fran Varady series and the Victorian mysteries featuring Scotland Yard's Inspector Benjamin Ross and his wife Lizzie.

Ann Granger's previous novels have all been highly praised:

'A good feel for understated humour, a nice ear for dialogue'
The Times

'Th... engrossing story looks like the start of a highly enjoyable ser...'
Scotsman

'A... ntriguing tale, with period detail interwoven in a satisfying wa...'
Oxford Times

'E... yable crime featuring credible characters in a recognisably real world'
Belfast Telegraph

To Tony and Pat Davey,
remembering many travels together,
and looking forward to many more

Chapter 1

Monty Bickerstaffe lurched along with his distinctive gait, his arms swinging by his sides. The movement endangered the bottle-shaped bulge in the sagging plastic carrier bag dangling from his right hand.

His presence in the supermarket had emptied the drinks aisle of any other shoppers. A very young junior manager had eventually come up to him. Prefacing his request with a polite, 'Can I help you, sir?' he had made it clear Monty's presence in the store was not welcome.

'Snotty little twerp!' observed Monty to himself now in a growl. 'I'm a customer, same as any other!'

He'd told the young man that. He'd told the senior fellow who'd come along to back up the young one. He'd told the store's security guard. He'd told this last one rather more.

'I shall lodge a claim of wrongful arrest!' he'd threatened. 'You don't know I'm not going to pay for it! I haven't left the store. Until I leave the store, the presumption is I fully intend to pay for it, which I do. What's more,' he concluded, '*you* can't search me, even then. You're not a copper. You have to fetch a proper copper.'

'I know the law,' said the store security man wearily.

1

'Not as well as I know it, old son,' said Monty to him.

'Yeah, I know, Monty. Give us all a break, why don't you?'

They stood over him while he paid. The girl on the till shrank from him when he handed her his money as if she didn't want to touch it. It was contaminated by contact with Monty's hand.

'Don't he ever take a bath?' he heard her ask her colleague in the adjacent aisle as he moved away.

'All right, don't shove!' he'd ordered the security guard. 'I need a plastic bag. I'm entitled to a plastic bag and I'm not paying for it. I've paid enough for my whisky.'

'Store policy,' chipped in the young manager unwisely, 'is for customers to pay for bags. It's not much, only five pence. It helps the environment.'

'How?' snapped Monty.

'It cuts down the number of bags out there.' The youth – he was, in Monty's eyes, little more than a schoolboy, or looked it – waved towards the plate-glass window. 'People throw them away anywhere.'

'How do you know I'm going to throw mine away? I should like to point out,' continued Monty, 'that should this bottle slip from my hand – due to my not being provided with a plastic carrier bag – then it will smash, leaving broken glass and causing a lot more problems for the environment.' He bared his teeth in a smile from which they all recoiled. 'What's more if, when I try to pick up the pieces of the broken bottle because I want to protect the environment, I should cut my hand . . .'

'Give him a carrier, Janette, for crying out loud,' the senior manager said wearily.

They escorted him outside and stood there in a row, watching, as he set off homewards. Monty made his way out of the shopping precinct, then past a scattering of small businesses, through one of the town's untidy residential areas, then through a slightly better later development of cottage-style homes ('rabbit hutches!' snorted Monty), and eventually came out, via a hole in a hedge, at the side of a petrol station on the ring road.

He ambled past the garage forecourt, ignoring the friendly wave from a man by one of the petrol pumps, and veered off across the road, this time oblivious of hooting car horns and yells of rage from drivers. Now he was heading into the countryside and it always made him feel better. He walked along the verge until he came to the turning and set off on the last leg of his journey down the lane known as Toby's Gutter.

No one knew any more who Toby had been, but the lane had been called that since time immemorial and was even marked as such on an eighteenth-century map. It ran downhill to join the main road. To this day, when it rained very heavily, excess water drained from higher ground and ran down the lane in a stream, just as it would in a gutter. At the point where it met the road, a sizeable pool formed in particularly wet months and spread right across the highway. Motorists, caught out unawares, wrote to the council about it every winter.

Monty passed the road sign bearing the name. It lurched drunkenly to the right, having been knocked sideways in a collision with Pete Sneddon's tractor two or three years earlier. Since then it had been slowly sinking earthward and would, eventually, fall flat.

3

'I'll write to the council myself!' announced Monty to a horse in a field alongside the lane. He owned the field and adjoining one but didn't use the land. It was part of his buffer against the outside world. The horse belonged to Gary Colley. Pete Sneddon occasionally moved some sheep down to graze the other field. As Monty saw it, this was quite enough use for the land and allowed him to give short shrift to anyone enquiring about it.

The horse snickered amiable approval or was, perhaps, only laughing at him, because even it knew the council had higher priorities than Toby's Gutter Lane (and Monty).

In this way, the whole walk taking him almost an hour, Monty reached his own home. Time was, he reflected, he could have done it in half the time or less. He fancied the arthritis in his knees was getting worse. Even the whisky didn't dull the pain now. But the last time he'd visited the doctor's surgery, the receptionist had been worse than that young fellow at the supermarket. What was more, a slip of a girl in jeans and showing a bare tattooed midriff, had accused him of bringing in diseases.

'This is a doctor's waiting room, my dear,' he had informed her. 'This is where you come to catch diseases.'

At that, every other patient had shuffled along the rows of chairs to put a good distance between himself and the next sufferer. They'd all put a good distance between themselves and Monty.

'Live and let live!' said Monty aloud, cheering up now he was home. He pushed his way through the rusted iron gateway. The hinges were set solid, so the gates no longer either shut or opened any further than the gap big enough to allow the passage of a single human being. Convolvulus twined over the bars obscuring a fine example of nineteenth-century wrought-ironwork. They obstructed access to a weed-infested drive to the front door of Balaclava House, which had once been an attractive house in Victorian Gothic revival style. Its brickwork was now crumbling. Above the front porch a crack shaped like a lightning bolt ran up to the first floor. It split in two an armorial shield invented by Monty's great-grandfather to suggest some entirely imaginary noble connection.

Monty had not climbed the stairs to the upper floors in years. His knees didn't like it and he wasn't interested to see the degree to which the bedrooms had fallen into ruin. He lived on the ground floor. He certainly had enough space there. A cloakroom was attached to a spacious entry hall, there was a well-proportioned drawing room, a large dining room, a butler's pantry and a vast kitchen, together with a back lobby and a small room off that, called by Monty 'the gunroom'. It no longer housed any sporting guns. The police had taken those away some years previously because he held no licence. They'd been his father's guns and Monty had resented being deprived of what he considered to be family property. Now Monty kept his empty bottles in the former gunroom and, lacking the transport to take them to the bottle bank, he had pretty well filled it.

His family had lived in this house since they had built it, way back in the late 1850s. But its slow decline had begun in the 1950s, long before Monty had inherited it, when domestic help had become hard to find and expensive. At about the same time the family business became less profitable. Monty remembered both his father and his mother resorting to surreptitious little economies. On his father's part, this had meant emptying cheap wine into bottles with better labels, occasionally adding a slug of port to help things along. His mother had her own ways of saving. Meals concocted from leftovers dominated Monty's memories of holidays at home. They'd also figured large in term-time at school. As an adult, Monty had occasionally reflected that he had grown up entirely fed on rehashed scraps. The cotton sheets on his bed had often been turned 'sides to middle' when they began to wear out. This had resulted in a long seam down the centre of the sheet, which chafed any bare skin coming into contact with it. The house had always been cold. But in Monty's opinion it had 'toughened him up'.

He limped down the echoing hallway, oblivious of the dust lying thick on all the furniture, pushed open the door to the drawing room and headed for the sideboard in which he kept his glassware. Monty opened one of the doors and, finding no clean glasses in there, tried the other side. Still no luck. He'd have to do some washing-up again and he'd only cleared the last lot three or four days ago. Considering he was the only person here, you'd think once a week would be enough.

Monty set down the newly acquired bottle with great care, sighed and set off back towards the door into the hall and the kitchen at the end of it. It was then he saw he was no longer the only person there. He had a visitor, and a stranger.

At first he thought it was his imagination. Hardly any stranger had come here since early in the year when some woman claiming to be a social worker had turned up. It seemed some interfering busybody had reported that there was 'an elderly gentleman, not quite right in the head, living in squalor all on his own in an unheated house.'

To be fair, the woman had not used the words 'not quite right in the head'. What she had actually said was, 'Perhaps we are getting a little confused?'

'I was not aware I was getting a visit from Her Majesty,' had been Monty's reply. 'I take it you are using the royal plural, referring to yourself when you speak of being confused? You may well be so. In fact, you give every sign of being it, if you think you are the Queen. I, however, am perfectly clear in my mind.'

'But you are all on your own, dear,' said the social worker, 'in this great big house, and you don't appear to have any central heating.'

'I like my own company!' Monty had thundered at the wretched woman. 'That I am alone is the only detail in which you are correct, madam! My mind, I repeat, is perfectly in order. I do not consider the state of my housekeeping to be any of your concern. My home looks all right to me. I have heating. I have a fire in the drawing room. I have plenty of wood around my garden and outbuildings to feed it. It costs me nothing and means I pay less for electricity. I am not connected to the gas mains any more. They replaced them in the lane a few years ago and wanted to dig up my garden to run the new pipe to the house. I refused so they routed the main pipeline right past my front door –' he pointed beyond the woman's shoulder – 'but cutting me off. I do pay an extortionate amount for something called council tax for which I receive virtually no council services. Go away.'

She had gone away, leaving behind a selection of leaflets about help for senior citizens. Monty had promptly thrown them on the fire to join the crackling remains of his garden shed.

Few people had passed this way since. But today was different. Today there was yet another uninvited interloper.

Monty was outraged. Was a householder to have no privacy? At least the intruder had not made himself comfortable on the chaise longue further back against the wall, which Monty used as his bed. That was a small consolation. But the stranger had taken possession of the Victorian horsehair-stuffed sofa, not so much sitting on as flopped out on it, propped up on the mouldering cushions at one end. He appeared to be fast asleep. Monty didn't know him from Adam. He was a well-nourished fellow in mid-brown corduroy trousers, an open-necked blue-checked shirt and a suede leather jacket. He wasn't a youngster but he wasn't that old. He looked, in Monty's opinion, a flash type.

'Who the blasted heck are you?' snapped Monty. 'This is a gentleman's private residence!'

The chap didn't answer. Monty edged a little closer, but not too close. He noticed to his disgust that the fellow had been dribbling and the spittle had dried on his skin. It had left a narrow silvery trail such as snails made. What was worse, the chap had had an unfortunate accident. It had all but dried off, leaving a damp patch at the crotch from which rose a distinctive smell.

Monty wrinkled his nose. 'Been drinking, have you, old fellow? Believe me, I understand. But you can't stay here, you know.'

There was no response. Monty cleared his throat loudly and ordered the visitor brusquely to wake up. The visitor slumbered on.

Monty, growing anger overcoming his caution, reached out and shook one suede sleeve, to no avail. The figure remained still, far too still. Movement of the clothing had increased the sour smell of dried urine.

Monty let out a long, low whistle. He glanced towards the door and saw with a spurt of relief that it was open and he could, if his knees permitted, make an escape. At the same moment it occurred to him that the door was always open. He never closed any internal doors because it only meant he had to open them again. But the drawing-room door had definitely been closed, shut fast, when he'd come home. He remembered opening it to come in here, just five minutes ago. The fellow sitting there must have closed it.

Or possibly someone else had done so, after depositing the man on Monty's sofa, because this chap showed worrying signs of being dead. The dribble-stained shirt-front didn't rise and fall as if he breathed. He seemed to have vomited a little, too, and that had also dried.

'Hey!' he addressed the visitor once more, without much hope of a reply.

His voice echoed emptily around the room.

'Bloody hell!' he muttered, edging away.

9

This put a different complexion on the whole affair. If the fellow had been alive, Monty could have told him to bugger off. But he couldn't do that with a stiff and he couldn't ignore the blighter. Monty sidled past the blank face and out of the room. He hurried down the corridor to the kitchen, grabbed a dirty glass and rinsed it under the tap, and then returned, at rather slower speed.

He had secretly, and quite illogically, hoped his visitor might have disappeared as inexplicably as he'd appeared in the first place. But no, he was still there. Monty skirted the sofa and reached the whisky bottle. He poured himself a generous measure and sat down on a chair facing the corpse to think over what he should do.

He toyed briefly with the idea of dragging it outside and burying it in his overgrown garden. But apart from the labour involved and his dratted knees not letting him do anything even mildly athletic, he knew he had to inform the authorities. He could walk back into town . . . but his knees gave a sharp twinge just at the thought of it. Or he could try and use that damn mobile phone he'd been nagged into buying in the spring. It was young Tansy, on her last visit, who had done the nagging. She'd turned up one day as unexpectedly as that fellow on the sofa there, driving up in a rattling old car, and strolled in.

'Blimey, Uncle Monty,' she'd said. 'How can you live like this?'

'Perfectly well,' Monty had growled back. 'What do you want?' He wasn't displeased to see the kid, being rather fond of her. But he had lost the knack of welcoming people.

'I was in the neighbourhood and I thought it would be fun to drop in on you.' Tansy's expression as she looked round suggested the idea was becoming less amusing by the minute. 'Mum's always saying she wonders how you are doing.'

'How is she doing?' asked Monty, not that he really gave a damn how the woman was. Although she'd always called him 'Uncle', Bridget was in reality a cousin once or twice removed; Monty could never work it out. She was, at any rate, a Bickerstaffe by blood and that, she seemed to think, gave her the right to interfere in his life.

'Your mother,' growled Monty to Tansy, 'has never been able to organise her own life, but she's never given up trying to organise mine! I've tried being rude to her,' he added gloomily, 'but she never gives up.'

Tansy grinned.

'You seem to be a nice girl,' he told her grudgingly. 'But don't end up like your mother, that's all.'

'Mum's getting married again,' said Tansy in reply to his original question.

'What number?' asked Monty.

'Four,' said Tansy.

'Woman wants her head seeing to,' muttered Monty. 'You see what I mean? Surely she must have realised by now she isn't any good at being married.' He paused and admitted, 'Neither was I. It must run in the family.'

The upshot of it was that Tansy had made a fuss about no one being able to communicate with him. He suspected Bridget was trying a new tactic in sending the kid to see him. But to please Tansy and because he was sorry he hadn't greeted her in a more kindly way, he'd listened to her then.

As a result, Tansy had driven him into town in that awful old banger of a car. They'd gone to a shop full of these mobile phones and Tansy had talked it all through with the salesman. No, her uncle didn't want to take photos or send emails with his phone. He wanted something really simple to operate. So they – he supplying the money and Tansy still doing the talking – had bought a mobile phone and a gizmo called a charger. They had then taken a further twenty-five pounds off him and explained it was a pre-pay phone and it now had that amount of money in its account. Monty had hardly used the thing. It sat on the kitchen dresser plugged into its charger. Occasionally he took it for a walk, putting it in his pocket when he went into town, but not today.

He returned to the kitchen, pushed the pile of unanswered mail surrounding the mobile phone on to the floor, and called 999. He asked for the police.

'Send a couple of your chaps over, would you?' he requested politely. 'I've got a dead man on my sofa.'

They asked his name and his address and, after a pause during which he heard some voices in the background, the woman asked him if he was sure.

'Pretty sure,' said Monty as politely as he could, considering it was a damn stupid question. 'He's not breathing.'

'Has someone there had a heart attack? Perhaps you want the ambulance service . . .' began the woman.

'No, I don't!' Monty was starting to have had enough of her.

Officials were all the same. They never listened to anything you said. 'Send a couple of your men or send an undertaker with his wagon. Take your pick.'

She said someone would call by as soon as possible but it was a busy day.

'*I'm* having a busy day,' snapped Monty. 'And a dashed unpleasant one. Look here, I don't particularly like having him in my house, so get a move on, will you?'

He dropped the mobile into his pocket and, after a moment's hesitation, took a swig from the glass of whisky in his hand and sidled back into the drawing room to check on his uninvited guest.

'They'll be coming for you soon,' he informed whoever it was.

He didn't, of course, expect any response. He just wanted to hear a human voice, if only his own. But he got an answer because it was at that moment that the dead man yawned and opened his eyes.

Chapter 2

It gave Monty such a shock that he dropped his whisky glass.
The air was filled with the peaty scent as the contents drained
away into the stained carpet. The man's yawn was accompanied
by a clicking noise from his jaw and at the furthest extent of it,
when it seemed his mouth could open no wider, the yawn froze.
The eyes bulged unseeingly, glazed in death.

'Now what am I supposed to do?' Monty muttered. 'Chap's
stiffening, rigor mortis must be setting in. Where are those
blasted coppers?'

He must have persuaded the woman on the phone that he was
in earnest because before long there came the sound of a car
drawing up at the gate. Footsteps crunched on the weed-strewn
gravel of his drive.

'Front door's open,' commented a male voice in the hall,
presumably to a companion. Then it called out, 'Anyone at home?'

'In here,' called back Monty.

They came into the room – two of them in uniform.

'Were you the gentleman who phoned?' asked one of them.

The other one had gone to the sofa and was bending over
Monty's visitor. Before Monty could reply, this one said sharply,
'No kidding, Trev, this chap is a goner.'

After that, things happened at bewildering speed. Monty sat and watched them come and go. Another police officer, apparently slightly more senior, arrived and then a doctor. 'I told them it was too late for that,' muttered Monty, remembering his emergency call. But he supposed they had to have official confirmation that the fellow had croaked.

Eventually, when the more senior officer and the doctor had departed, one of the remaining coppers remembered him and came across to where he sat. He asked again if Monty was the householder and if he was the person who'd called to report a death. Irritably Monty replied 'yes' to both questions. 'I told you I was!'

'Just checking, sir. Is there perhaps another room where we can have a chat?'

'A chat?' asked Monty. 'What the hell do you want to chat about?'

'We'd like you to tell us just what happened, sir,' said the constable. 'Was the gentleman taken ill? Did he live here with you?' The young man gave a doubtful glance at the surrounding jumble of dusty old furniture and worn carpets that filled Monty's drawing room.

'No, of course he didn't,' said Monty.

'Then we'd like to know his name and address. His next of kin will have to be informed and the coroner's office. Have you rung anyone besides us?'

'No use asking me any of that,' Monty told him. 'I haven't a clue. I don't know who he is or how he got here. I came home and there he was. I thought he was asleep at first. It goes

16

without saying I haven't rung anyone else. Who the devil would I ring?'

But he led the man into his kitchen where they sat at the table and the constable got him to repeat what he'd just said so that he could write it down. Monty watched him in resignation. This was officialdom all over: ask you the same thing twenty times and then write it down.

'Now, sir,' asked the constable at last, 'did you touch the body?'

Monty stared at him. 'What the hell for?'

'To try and find out his identity, sir. Looked for his driving licence, perhaps? You say he's a stranger to you. You must have wondered who he was, when you saw him lying there.'

Monty frowned and gave his answer some thought. 'I didn't worry who he *was*,' he said at last. 'I was more worried where he'd come from and how I was going to get rid of him. It didn't *matter* to me who he was – is. I don't know him. If I'd found someone I *knew* dead on my sofa, of course I'd have rung his home and told someone there to come and get him. I didn't know him, so I rang you.'

The constable sighed. But in the distance there was the sound of other vehicles pulling up before the gates. New voices sounded in the drawing room. The kitchen door opened and, to Monty's horror, his late wife walked in.

If finding the dead man had been a shock, this was worse. Monty's eyes widened and his jaw dropped open like the fellow's on the sofa. He felt the blood draining from his face and his head swam briefly. 'Bloody hell,' he muttered. Were there dead

17

people everywhere today? First one stiff in the drawing room and now a ghost strolling into the kitchen . . .

'Sir?' asked the constable in concern. He reached out and touched Monty's arm.

'No,' said Monty aloud firmly. 'This isn't possible and you're imagining it.'

'I'm afraid there is a corpse in the other room, sir. You haven't imagined it.'

Monty waved his words away irritably. He hoped the wave would also dispel the figure that had just come through the door. Penny had been gone from his life this past ten years; and quitted life altogether some four years ago. Bridget had driven over to tell him of her death and ask him if he wanted to attend the funeral. Of course he hadn't, he'd replied. Bridget had thought that churlish of him, suggesting, with some asperity, that even an ex-wife deserves last respects. But Penny had walked out of his life because he had been selfish and foolish and too obstinate to make things up, and, in any case, he had left it too late to change anything. Gazing at her coffin would have done nothing but remind him of his own short-comings. So he had simply told Bridget it was out of the question for him to attend the funeral. His knees wouldn't allow it. They had parted, as the old saying went, 'brass rags', not for the first time and certainly not for the last. But you could be as direct as you liked with Bridget; it didn't put her off. He knew; he'd tried. She always popped up again ready to interfere if he'd let her.

Now common sense told him this new arrival was not a spectre,

18

but a young woman who bore a remarkable resemblance to his late wife. There had been a wedding photo that showed Penny looking just like the newcomer. (He'd hidden all the photos after Penny left; and burned them after she died.) Penny had worn a wedding gown, of course, in the picture he had in mind, and this woman wore what, on a man, Monty would have called a business suit – striped trousers and matching jacket. But, oh boy, she was a double for Penny when younger: just above middle height, slightly built but wiry, a terrier of a girl, with short dark-red hair, a pointed chin and widely spaced grey eyes that sparkled with intelligence.

Under the severe mannish jacket she wore a flamboyant ochre shirt with a wide collar. That, with her red hair and elfin haircut, turned her into the spirit of autumn. He wished he had pencil and paper to hand and could sketch her. It had been years since he'd drawn or painted. Time after time he'd painted or sketched Penny in the old days, when they were young, so long ago. Now he was giving way to a stupid fancy.

'Who *are* you?' asked Monty humbly.

'Inspector Jessica Campbell,' the young woman replied. To the constable she added, 'All right, I'll take over now.'

The constable got up, not hiding his relief, and left them alone together.

'Do you feel unwell?' Penny's look-alike was bending over him in concern. Could she really have said she was a *police inspector*?

'Would you like a cup of tea?' she went on.

Monty rallied and made a great effort to pull himself together.

'I'm as well as I can be in the circumstances, thank you,' he told her. 'I don't want tea. I want another whisky.'

'How many have you had already?' she asked. (Now she also sounded like his late wife.)

'Only the one,' he replied, as he'd replied to Penny so many times in the past. 'And I spilled most of it when that dratted thing in there yawned.' He pointed at the kitchen door and the distant sofa with its occupant.

'Nasty shock,' said Inspector Campbell. 'But I think tea might be better.'

It was not only shock; it was the accumulation of unforeseen and inexplicable events that led Monty to explode. 'I don't want *tea*! Drat it, why have I been surrounded my entire life by women who know better than I do what I need? I need a whisky!' He glared at her.

She looked back good-humouredly. 'I think you're coping with this all right,' she said.

Monty's anger drained away. 'Sorry for the outburst,' he apologised. 'But a small whisky wouldn't hurt, would it?'

'No, Mr Bickerstaffe, I don't suppose it would.'

A few minutes later when the whisky had been brought to him, she began to ask questions. That's what coppers did. He prepared himself for going through it all yet again.

'Live here all on your own, Mr Bickerstaffe?'

'Yes, and you might as well call me Monty,' he told her. 'Everyone does.'

She smiled at him. 'Have you got somewhere you can go and stay tonight, Monty? A relative living nearby, perhaps?'

'Why can't I stay here, in my own home?' he asked.

'Well, you surely don't want to stay here alone tonight after – this?' She nodded towards the drawing room.

It occurred to Monty that his chaise-longue bed was in there and she was quite right. He didn't fancy sleeping there tonight.

'Perhaps you've got some friends nearby?' Inspector Campbell was saying.

'No,' said Monty grumpily. 'I haven't got friends anywhere.'

'We can put you in a hotel for tonight, then,' she said.

Monty gave a snort. 'If you can find one that'll take me.'

Her face showed that she appreciated that objection, but she made no comment on it.

Instead, she said, 'I understand that the deceased is a stranger to you. That's what you told the constables when they got here.'

'Never seen him before,' Monty confirmed.

'You weren't in the house when he came?'

'No, I was out – in town. I go every day, more or less.'

'So how long were you away?' she asked.

Time meant little to Monty. He looked vague. 'Oh, I don't know. Three, four hours? I had a bite to eat in a pub – sausage and mash – and sat there for a while reading the paper. The pub was the Rose and Crown. They always put a couple of daily rags in the bar for anyone to read. Nothing of substance, mind you. No *Telegraph* or *Times*. Usually it's something with more pictures than text, but it's better than nothing, and it's free. Then I went shopping. You can ask them at the supermarket. They know me. They'll tell you I was there. Same with the Rose and Crown.' He frowned. 'I hadn't long got home, only a few minutes, before I found him.'

'When you left to go shopping, you left the house empty? How did he get in?'

'Through the front door, I suppose,' Monty said.

'How did he open it?'

'It sticks,' explained Monty. 'The wood's swollen. It's a job to open it and to close it. I close it at night, before I go to bed. But during the day I just sort of wedge it shut. It opens if you give it a good shove.'

'That isn't a very good idea, is it?' She gave a reproving shake of the head. 'Leaving your house unlocked like that?'

'Nothing here anybody would want,' said Monty. 'Nobody comes to see me, well, hardly ever. Who's going to walk in?' Then the irony of his question struck him and he gave another snort. 'Well, that fellow did, I suppose you'd say.'

'It's a large house for one person,' she said.

'Always lived here, most of my life at any rate,' Monty explained. 'Family home, you know. I only use the downstairs now. My knees don't like the stairs – arthritis.'

'Is there a bathroom down here?'

Monty thought this rather an impertinent question, but perhaps she was a lady in distress.

'By the front door, on the left as you go out,' he said. 'Cloakroom. It's got the usual offices. No lock on the door, by the way. You'll have to sing or something.'

Her cheeks reddened. 'I don't need it, I just wondered how you managed for baths.'

'You mean,' he said, with a sudden gleam in his eyes, 'do I bath? Answer, no, I don't. There isn't a bath down here. I wash down in here, in the kitchen.' He nodded towards the huge old stone sink.

'You have plenty of room to have a bath or shower room installed,' the inspector suggested. 'What about that cloakroom, could it be converted? You might be able to get a grant from social services.'

'Meddling women!' said Monty, remembering his last encounter with a social worker. 'No, my dear, not you, social service people. Nearly all meddling women. Besides, I couldn't have workmen here. They'd be marching all over the place, whistling and making tea and getting under my feet. Couldn't be doing with it. Anyway, I like it as it is. What's all this got to do with the dead fellow on my sofa? Precious little, as far as I can see.'

He was growing combative. He hadn't asked the chap to walk in and die in his drawing room, for crying out loud! Anyone would think he was responsible. He was a man who'd spent his life avoiding responsibilities. Penny, were she still alive and here, would have confirmed this.

'True,' the red-haired inspector admitted. 'Well, Monty, we don't know what your visitor died of. But it's a puzzle to know how he got here, isn't it? There's no car outside except police vehicles. It doesn't look as if he walked from anywhere. His shoes are very clean.'

'Are they?' Monty was startled.

'Yes, I looked.'

At this Monty grew thoughtful. 'Well, I'll be damned,' he said at last. 'You're a cool one, aren't you? But you're right. There was no car outside when I got here.'

She smiled again. 'I need to be observant. His clothes are also clean for the most part.' She paused fractionally to glance over Monty's scruffy jacket and shirt, both with frayed sleeves. 'He's quite well turned out, isn't he? That's a real suede jacket he's wearing and they're expensive.'

'Looked to me like the sort of fellow who hangs around racecourses,' mumbled Monty.

The look in the grey eyes sharpened. 'Are you a racing man?'

'No, it was just an observation.' Damn, he thought, you had to be so careful what you said to the police. They jumped on every word and twisted the meaning out of all recognition. Penny had been the same, reading a subtext he'd not intended into every blessed sentence. Name, rank and number, Monty! Just answer the lady's questions.

'The thing is, Mr Bickerstaffe – sorry, Monty – it does seem incredible that you should walk in and find someone you'd never set eyes on before, lying on your sofa, dead.'

'Thought he was asleep,' Monty said. 'Until I realised he wasn't. I couldn't wake him up.' Hastily he added, 'I did give his jacket a bit of a twitch. I wouldn't say I shook him. I shouted at him. I thought he'd got drunk and come in to sleep it off. He'd wet his pants. I smelled it. I suppose you noticed that, too?'

'Yes, I did. Sorry to keep asking, but are you absolutely certain you haven't *seen* him anywhere?'

'Never.'

'Were you expecting *anyone* to call today?'

Monty was about to reply in the negative when they were

both startled by tinny notes playing the opening bars of Mozart's Rondo alla Turca. The tune appeared to be issuing from the pocket of Monty's jacket.

He stared at her wildly.

She said, 'I think it's your mobile phone.'

'What, oh, dratted thing . . .' He fumbled in his pocket and took it out, pressing it to his ear.

'Hello, Uncle Monty!' said a cheery voice. 'It's Bridget here. I thought I'd give you a call to see how you're getting on. Tansy told me she insisted you got a mobile but you've never called us on it.'

Monty gazed at the phone in dismay and then held it out to the policewoman. 'It's my— a family member,' he said. 'She insists on calling me "Uncle". I'm not her ruddy uncle. She's my cousin Harry's daughter, Bridget. You seem a capable sort. You'd better talk to her.'

'What's her surname?' she asked, reaching out with her hand.

Monty scowled. 'Last time I knew of it, it was Harwell. It's constantly changing. She keeps getting married and is just about to have a shot at it for the fourth time. Try Harwell. That was the last one. She probably answers to it.'

He sat glumly watching the young woman inspector and listening to the one-sided conversation.

'Yes, Mrs Harwell, it's a mystery, I agree. But there is, or was, a body on the sofa in your uncle's living room. We shall be removing it in due course, but he can't stay here tonight. Yes, he's in pretty good shape, but a little shocked. No . . .' The inspector glanced at Monty and at the empty whisky glass. 'No, he's not.'

'Wants to know if I'm drunk, does she?' growled Monty.

'I see, Mrs Harwell. That sounds an excellent idea. I'll tell him. Yes, I'll wait until you get here.'

'What?' shouted Monty, as the inspector broke the phone connection. 'What's all that about good ideas and Bridget coming here?'

'Mrs Harwell has kindly offered to take you home with her and put you up for a bit,' said Inspector Campbell. 'She says she'll be here in twenty minutes or so.'

'Bloody hell! Don't you think you might have asked me about that? I am not going home with Bridget. You might as well throw me into a prison cell, lock the door and chuck away the key.' Monty waved his arms in distress and knocked over the empty whisky glass.

'We have no reason to do that, do we?' she pointed out, at the same time neatly grabbing the glass before it could roll off the table and smash on the floor. 'Perhaps you'd better stay with Mrs Harwell, if only for tonight. I think you are rather shocked and you can't stay here. We've already agreed that.'

The kitchen door opened and a stocky, youngish man appeared and caught Campbell's eye. She excused herself and left the kitchen, the heels of her little pointy-toed black boots tapping briskly on the stone flags like a male flamenco dancer building up to a thunderous *zapateado*.

She'd closed the door behind her. He could hear the murmur of their voices but wasn't interested to know what they were saying. Bridget was coming. He had to go back with her to her place. He'd thought, when he'd realised the fellow on the sofa was dead, that things couldn't get worse, but they just had.

Chapter 3

'This is really weird,' said Sergeant Phil Morton quietly to Jess Campbell. They had retreated to the hall and Monty couldn't have heard them; but something churchlike about the empty vault of the stairwell encouraged whispers. 'I've had a quick look in our corpse's jacket pockets, and I can't find a thing to identify him. No wallet, car keys, driving licence, nothing. There's only some loose change. I'd say someone's been ahead of us and removed everything.'

'I don't like it,' said Jess. 'I'll bet my boots this isn't a natural death. Why try and hide his identity? I'll take Mr Bickerstaffe outside. He can wait in a police car until his niece, Mrs Harwell, gets here.'

'There's no sign of violence on the body,' said Morton doubtfully. 'At least, I can't see any. No sign of a struggle. Mind you, the whole place is such a tip it would be hard to tell if anything was out of place or untidier than usual.'

'So we'll have to scout round outside and see if we can find any tracks or any signs of activity out there. There may be a puddle of vomit. He's been sick. He didn't fly in here like Mary Poppins, Phil! He came here by car, so where is it? He didn't walk, not in those shoes. Anyway, he's not a tramp,

29

looking for a handout. He's a well-dressed, well-nourished male in his early forties at the most, would you agree?'

Morton nodded. Then he looked at the closed kitchen door with the invisible Monty behind it. 'The old fellow might have gone through his pockets, looking for cash to buy his whisky.'

'He wouldn't take car keys or a whole wallet, just the cash. But I don't think he did take it. I agree with you. Someone intended to delay identification and emptied our dead friend's pockets. I think it more than possible that person – or persons – brought him here by car and abandoned him.'

'Why here?' Morton asked promptly. 'You think whoever it was knew about this house?' He glanced round him. 'They chose the right place, didn't they? It's already a dump and as cheery as a morgue.'

Jess thrust her hands into her jacket pockets and hunched her shoulders. Phil was right. It was like a mausoleum: chilly, dank, dusty and musty-smelling. It must be Victorian. The flight of stairs to the upper floor was wide enough to allow for the passage of crinoline skirts. Above, the gloom of the landing was unexpectedly broken by light from a stained-glass window. Patches of red and yellow fell incongruously across the carved wood and blackened oil paintings. It added to the atmosphere; she felt she was in a memorial chapel. She missed only the smell of stale flower water and smouldering candles.

She gave herself a shake and said briskly, 'I'll take Monty outside. Then you and I had better take a look up there . . .' She pointed to the landing. 'To make sure there are no more dead bodies lying around.'

When she got back to the kitchen, Jess found Monty apparently sunk in depression. It was difficult to know what to do with him. He clearly didn't want to go and stay with Bridget Harwell although the woman had sounded very sensible over the phone. But he couldn't stay in the house until they were sure it wasn't a crime scene and he needed company. Whether he realised it himself or not, he was deeply shocked.

'Come along, then sir,' she said to him in as encouraging a manner as she could. He rose obediently and followed her outside.

Jess gratefully took a deep breath of fresh air. Monty shoved his hands in his pockets and hunched his shoulders, sulking. Outside the main gates one of the constables who'd first arrived on the scene was standing by his car, talking to a newcomer, a young man in jeans and a scuffed leather jacket.

'Hello, Monty!' the unknown hailed Bickerstaffe. 'What's going on in your place? This copper won't tell me!'

Monty opened his mouth to reply but Jess forestalled him. 'I'll answer any questions, Mr Bickerstaffe. You say nothing, all right!' She bundled him into the rear seat of the police car and shut the door firmly on him. Inside, Monty sank back into the seat and folded his arms like a truculent toddler.

She turned to the officer and the young newcomer. Jess looked him over carefully and judged him to be about twenty. His sunburned complexion indicated he spent most of his time outdoors. His hair was long, curling over the greasy collar of the leather jacket. Hair and jacket needed a wash. In a way he was quite good-looking, but the looks would soon coarsen. He met her gaze boldly. A real Jack-the-lad, she thought.

'You are?' she asked briskly.

'Gary Colley.' Despite the gleam in his dark eyes, there was caution in his voice and in his manner.

'This gentleman,' said the officer with some irony, nodding at Gary, 'lives a couple of hundred metres or so further down this lane. There's a sort of smallholding, apparently, belonging to his father. He lives there, with his family.'

Gary scowled at him but addressed himself to Jess. 'He won't tell me what's going on.' He took a hand from his jacket pocket and pointed at the officer.

'No, and neither shall I,' said Jess. 'You'll have to wait to find out. But I would like to ask you a couple of questions.'

Gary hadn't finished asking his own. 'You've not gone and arrested poor old Monty, have you?'

'No. Now then, were you here earlier today?'

'No,' said Gary promptly.

'Where were you?'

'Home, looking after the stock and doing odd jobs around the place. We farm a bit, like this copper said. Pigs, mostly.' He hid a grin.

He was the sort who normally referred to the police as 'pigs' and in his own mind he was being witty. Jess wondered if he had a police record.

'What brought you out here now?'

'On my way into town, thought I'd get in an early pint or two.'

Jess glanced at her wristwatch. 'Very early, it's only ten to five.'

32

'It'll take me half an hour to get there,' Gary said simply. He stared at her. His face wasn't laughing but his dark eyes were.

'Who lives at your farm besides you and your father?' she asked.

'Me mum,' he told her. 'My sister, her kid, and me grandma.'

Four generations of Colleys under one roof. Jess knew the set-up: a local family of the sort that was probably known to everyone, and mistrusted by most. They themselves would know everyone and everything that went on hereabouts. Not crooks, but not entirely honest. Poachers, probably, involved with illegal dogfights perhaps, that sort of thing. They might even store stolen goods at their remote smallholding, supplementing their income by obliging bigger, more professional crooks than themselves. It might be worth taking a look if they could think of an excuse for a search warrant.

'How old is your sister's child?' Suspicion of child neglect might be a way to investigate the Colleys.

Gary thought about that and then offered, 'About four?'

'And his – or her – father?'

He grinned. 'You a detective?'

'Yes,' she told him.

'Well, you might be able to find out who Katie's dad is. None of us know.'

Jess drew a deep breath. 'Have you seen any strange vehicles travelling along this road today?'

'Not much comes down this way,' said Gary. 'If it does, it's mostly coming from, or making for, Sneddon's Farm. That's about half a mile further on.' He pointed down the lane. 'I haven't seen any cars I didn't recognise. If we ever get a stranger it's probably someone lost.'

'Sure about that?'

He nodded confidently. 'I'd have noticed. Usually they stop and ask the way. I send them back to the main road. You can get across country this way but it's all lanes and bits of tracks going down to the woods. There aren't any signposts and the surfaces are all full of potholes. You can't pass another vehicle, neither. One of you has to back up and find the entry to a gate to pull off the road and there's not many of them. So a strange driver, he's pretty noticeable.'

'How about walkers?'

He shook his head. 'No. We don't get walkers as a rule, not on this road.' Gary turned and pointed with raised arm past the house and towards the rise of the land behind. 'There's a right of way across Shooter's Hill. We see a lot of walkers up there in good weather. But I can't say I noticed anyone up there today and I know I didn't see anyone down here.'

Gary squinted at her and tempered his statement with, 'But then, I wasn't out front of the place all day. Pigs are mostly in the field at the back. They're destructive blighters. They broke down the fence and got into Pete Sneddon's field alongside ours. He'd have kicked up a fuss, Pete, if he'd seen them; so my dad and I, we rounded them up. Then I had to mend the fence.'

'Thank you,' Jess said. 'Someone will come to your home and talk to your whole family. Try and remember if you saw anything unusual or anyone you didn't know around here today, either on the road or off it.'

Gary looked over her shoulder towards the house behind her. 'You lot staying around here for much longer, are you?'

'Off you go!' growled the constable.

Gary shrugged and walked off jauntily towards the distant sprawl of the town. Jess wasn't fooled. Gary was smart enough not to turn back to his home immediately, but she doubted he was making his way into town and the pubs, as he'd said was his intention. He would take himself out of their sight and then double back over the fields, carrying a warning to his clan. Any search warrant they obtained would be useless. If there were dodgy merchandise at the farm, it would be cleared out pronto.

'When Mrs Harwell gets here, let me know,' Jess told the constable. 'Keep her out here.'

Jess turned back to the house and saw Morton standing by the front door and talking to the constable. Both were peering at the ground. As she approached them, it struck her that there was a pungent animal smell in the air, something she'd not noticed before. She remarked on it, adding that it must be the nearby pig farm.

'They're clean animals, on the whole, pigs,' said the constable. 'But if you get a lot of them together . . .'

'OK, Farmer Giles,' said Morton to him.

'Carry on looking around,' Jess told the constable. 'Time for you and me to take that look at the upstairs rooms, Phil. Let's hope there are no more unpleasant surprises up there!'

They returned to the house and paused briefly in the cavernous entrance hall. Morton's habitual expression of gloom turned to one of wonder as he gazed upward.

'To think,' he said, 'that the old chap lives here alone. Wouldn't you think it would give him nightmares?'

'He's always lived here,' Jess replied. 'He doesn't notice the state of it, probably.'

'I reckon the family must have had money at some time,' Morton went on as they cautiously ascended the staircase in single file, keeping to one side. 'I wonder what happened to it. Hey, do you think the old boy is an eccentric millionaire? What are we going to find up here? Mouldering banknotes stashed under the floorboards?'

They had reached the landing and the stained-glass window loomed over them. It appeared to show a biblical subject with robed figures. Jess and Morton stood side by side and studied it. It was an action-packed scene. A crowd milled angrily outside a building, looking up at it. Above their heads, vengeful faces grimaced from a window aperture as a female form, with long yellow hair, plummeted earthward. Her braceleted arms were flung out in a mix of entreaty, despair and a doomed effort to save herself. At the very bottom of the window, a pair of hounds looked up expectantly.

Facing it, across the landing, was another window. It had probably been a companion piece with another Bible story depicted, but it had apparently suffered some accident and was partly boarded up in a rough job using sections of plank. Only a few pieces of coloured glass at the top remained visible.

'What do you reckon's going on here?' asked Morton, gazing up at the undamaged window.

'The death of Jezebel,' said Jess promptly. 'I've seen pictures

36

of it before and when I was at school, our RI teacher was very keen on the story. Jezebel was the queen of King Ahab and under her bad influence he committed all kinds of crimes. He was killed in battle by a stray arrow.'

'Like that chap, King Harold, at the Battle of Hastings,' said Morton, not to be outdone in general knowledge.

'Right. When people got news of his death, they took their revenge on wicked Jezebel and threw her from a palace window, as you can see there.' She pointed up. 'And the stray dogs ate her body. You can see a couple of dogs at the bottom there.'

'Nice,' said Morton, 'just the sort of thing to have in your home. Now, who in his right mind would want to get up every morning and walk past that on his way down to breakfast?'

'The Victorians liked stories with a strong moral,' Jess offered. 'It encouraged people to do the right thing. They saw it as uplifting.'

Morton wasn't accepting that argument. 'It's about violent murder and there's nothing very uplifting about that, just the usual blood and guts. If that blonde female is anything to go by, a good dollop of sex as well. People have always liked that kind of story; but not because it makes them feel better. Because it gives them a kick.'

The upstairs landing formed the short crossbar of a letter H. On either side corridors ran towards the back of the house and also towards the front.

'I'll take this side, you take that,' Jess suggested.

Morton, with another mistrustful glance up at Jezebel's death plunge, set off along the corridor leading towards the front of the house on the left-hand side. Jess took a parallel route on the right. Doors opened on to a depressing line of abandoned bedrooms with dust sheets thrown over the beds and some pieces of furniture also shrouded. Unshrouded pieces had their own powdery veil of dust. The damp had got in everywhere. Once-fine curtains hung in mouldering shreds. The remains of jackdaw nests littered the fireplaces. In a bathroom taps had rusted; and a huge Victorian iron bath on claw feet held part of the ceiling above it that had fallen down.

She turned back and began to make her way down the corridor to the rear. She had only opened the first door, discovering a large linen cupboard with yellowed sheets still stacked inside, when she heard Morton call.

He, too, had begun to investigate the rear corridor on his side. He was standing in an open doorway at the very end of the corridor, waiting. Jess joined him.

'What do you think of this?' Morton asked her. He gestured into the room.

Jess drew in a sharp breath of surprise. Then she stepped forward into the room and stood, looking around her.

In startling contrast to the rest of the house, this room showed signs of having been cleaned recently. There was not a speck of dust anywhere. All the wood surfaces gleamed. The bed had no dust sheet on it but the mattress was covered with a blanket of synthetic material, garish pink in colour. Its newness shrieked and its presence in this room with its antiquated fittings jarred as a false note.

There was something else, too, not something visible but she felt it powerfully. It was human presence. She sniffed. The air was fresher than elsewhere on the upper floor.

Slowly Jess said, 'Someone has been using this room. It's been aired out. That blanket was never put there by any Bickerstaffe. In any case, Monty says he never comes up here. So who's been in here, what for and when?'

'And does old Bickerstaffe know?' Morton added. He was prowling about the room, peering into corners.

'I'd guess he doesn't. We'll have to be careful how we ask him. Think about it, Phil. Here's a huge, empty rambling house with an owner who never comes upstairs and habitually leaves it unlocked. Local druggies, tramps, schoolkids, travellers, anyone familiar with the area might know about it. It might provide the ideal hideaway for someone. Monty would never find out. It's making more and more sense that someone left the body in this house. We need a fingerprint team up here.'

'No drugs paraphernalia,' pointed out Morton, completing his tour. 'No empty beer cans, food wrappers or other rubbish, like you'd expect.'

'Someone's cleared it all out. Let's suppose,' Jess went on, 'whoever left the dead man downstairs knew about this room, came up here and had a lightning tidy-up. But whoever it was couldn't have had much time. Call in and request a Scenes of Crime crew to come out. I want them here before the body's moved.'

Morton shuffled his feet unhappily. 'You're sure about this?'

'I'll justify my decision and the expense!' Jess said sharply. 'And it is my decision.'

Phil flushed and looked mulish but accepted that argument was pointless. 'Well,' he said, 'with luck, Scenes of Crime will be able to pick up a fingerprint or two here, as you say. Maybe we'll get really lucky and there will be some DNA on that blanket. There should be if it's been used for what I think it has.'

They went back downstairs and outside. One of the two constables came across to them.

'Inspector Campbell, perhaps you ought to look at this, ma'am.' The young constable's voice was excited and they hurried towards the spot. He was pointing into the overgrown shrubbery.

On their way they passed a long furrow scored in the gravel drive.

'New, that,' said Morton, indicating it.

A short distance further on another similar mark showed in the disturbed gravel, ending at the edge of the shrubbery.

The constable pointed at the jungle of overgrown bushes and unpruned trees. 'There are some broken branches and trampled grass, Inspector, making a trail or a path. I didn't want to disturb it any more but it seems to lead to a gap in the perimeter wall, on the road side.'

'Good work!' Jess exclaimed. 'We'll need a search team in there, too.'

'No expense spared,' muttered the unhappy Morton.

'I know all about budgets, Phil, thank you. They are the detective's ball and chain! But I don't think Superintendent Carter will argue over this one. Quite apart from an unidentified body where no body should be found, this whole scene bristles with unexplained oddities.'

Morton nodded reluctant agreement. 'What do you think?' he asked, as they made their way back to the main gates. 'Do you think someone brought chummy in that way? Not via those gates, but through the gap in the wall, dragged or carried him through the shrubbery, on to the drive and up to the front door, his heels dragging along in the gravel?'

'Well, to get him through those would have been nearly impossible.' Jess pointed at the rusted front gates. 'They haven't been opened properly in years and must be stuck in that position. One or two people, encumbered with a corpse or a dying man, couldn't have done it. There has to be a different way in. Yes, almost certainly they came through the shrubbery. I doubt one person could have carried him so far. I reckon we have a murder scene here and we're looking for either two murderers or one murderer and an accomplice.'

Morton opened his mouth to answer but before he could, a blue two-seater roadster, driven by a woman, came bouncing along the uneven surface of Toby's Gutter Lane. The constable at the gates stepped forward and flagged it down. The woman driver had already braked. She came to a halt and called out, 'Who's in charge? My name is Harwell.'

Jess hadn't expected Bridget Harwell to turn up in a sports car. It seemed too carefree for the occasion. The constable was bending down and explaining, Jess knew, that Mrs Harwell couldn't bring her car on to the property because more tracks would confuse the scene and, in any case, the gates didn't open. The driver got out and began to walk briskly towards Jess.

'You can't go in at the gates on foot, either! You can't go on to the property!' the constable said loudly, intercepting her.

'I know, I know! You've made it clear.' Bridget Harwell waved him aside.

From inside the police car where he still waited, Jess saw Monty gesticulating wildly. The contortions of his mouth suggested he was uttering curses. His niece hadn't noticed him. Jess hurried down to the gates and slipped through the gap to meet the newcomer. She couldn't help but feel curious.

'I'm Bridget Harwell,' the new arrival said again for Jess's benefit. She spoke courteously but her eyes assessed Jess at the same time as Jess was assessing her, and she kept her no-nonsense manner. 'Where's my uncle? Is he OK?'

She had a nervous, brittle way of speaking and Jess didn't know whether this was due to the unusual circumstances or just a habit. Bridget Harwell was in her mid forties with a slightly faded prettiness. She was a small woman, neatly built, with thick, expertly bobbed ash-blond hair. Standing before her, Jess felt gawky and unfeminine. She pulled herself together and told herself she was here as a police officer and this wasn't the moment to worry that she couldn't have afforded the designer jeans and cherry-red sweater that looked like, and probably was, cashmere.

'I'm Inspector Campbell!' The words reminded both herself and the newcomer that she was, here, in charge. 'Your uncle is over there, in the police car.' She walked up to it and opened the door. 'Come on, Monty, you can get out now. Your niece is here.'

'Thank you, I am perfectly all right where I am,' retorted Monty, arms folded.

Bridget Harwell descended on the police car and took effortless control. 'Now, stop that, Uncle Monty! Be sensible for once. How are you feeling?'

'Feeling?' Monty gaped at her, speechless for the moment. 'Bloody furious, if you want to know. Some bugger has dumped a corpse in my house. The cops are crawling all over the place. You've turned up to kidnap me and you ask me how I *feel*?'

Bridget turned to Jess. 'He seems to be OK,' she said with relief. 'Just the same as usual, anyway.'

Her exasperation bubbled beneath the surface of her practical manner but, thought Jess, she's controlling it well.

Bridget continued briskly, 'He's always a cantankerous old horror. Still he is getting on in years and I don't think he ought to hang about here in the circumstances. I'll take him with me, all right?' She fixed Jess with an enquiring look.

Jess found herself annoyingly distracted by the thought that either Mrs Harwell had taken a couple of minutes before coming here to fix her mascara, or she always walked round all day immaculately made up like that. Why, Jess asked herself, does mascara invariably run when I apply it? Is it because I buy the cheap stuff?

'Don't want to go with you,' yelled Monty to his niece, from within the police car. 'I want to go back in my own house.'

'We've been through all that, Mr Bickerstaffe,' Jess called patiently. 'Come on, you know you can't go back indoors.'

'What about his things?' Bridget asked. 'He'll need at least an overnight bag.'

Jess grimaced. 'Sorry, we've got experts coming out to look the place over. We can't remove anything until they've been.'

Mrs Harwell accepted that with a sigh, putting up her hand to one wing of bobbed hair and patting it absently. 'I suppose I can drive him into Cheltenham and fix him up with some togs.'

'There's nothing wrong with the clothes I've got on!' argued Monty, but there was a note of defeat in his voice.

'You can't sleep in them, Uncle Monty, and you'll need soap and a razor and so on. It's all right, leave it to me.' To Jess she added confidingly, 'He's been a bit of a worry to us for years. It's a good thing this didn't happen yesterday. I was up in London all day and wouldn't have been here to help.'

Monty's features had twisted in distress at the mention of the soap and razor. He opened his mouth to protest but then surrendered and hauled himself, muttering, from the police car.

'I've written down my address, my home phone and my mobile numbers,' Bridget went on to Jess, producing a sheet of paper. 'So, if it's OK with you, I'll just put my uncle into my car, and then nip back for a word, is that all right?'

Jess was beginning to understand how Monty felt. She watched him being led away and chivvied into the little sports car where he sat wedged in the passenger seat, scowling. Bridget secured his safety strap, rather as she might have buckled a toddler into a buggy. She returned at the same businesslike pace.

'You can't tell me exactly what's going on, I suppose,' she said to Jess, 'and I quite understand. But who is the stiff in there?' She pointed at the house.

'We don't know, Mrs Harwell, and your uncle says he doesn't know him. I have to be honest and say that it's difficult to believe the dead man could be a complete stranger, apparently dropped from the sky. Why in this house? There must be some connection, surely?' She hesitated. 'I suppose you wouldn't oblige us by taking a look?'

'I shouldn't think *I* know him!' objected Bridget Harwell at once.

It seemed that was going to be the cry from the whole Bickerstaffe clan. Jess felt herself growing obstinate and less sensitive to any delicate feelings Mrs Harwell might have.

'*Someone* has to know who he is. He might be a passing acquaintance and Mr Bickerstaffe may have forgotten him. It could be someone he hasn't seen for a while. That and the shock . . .' Jess hoped she sounded persuasive.

'Uncle Monty isn't forgetful but he is contrary. He may have decided to be awkward.' Bridget sighed. 'You're in a fix. You have to put a name to – to the dead man, I understand that. I admit I'd like to know who he is and why he's in my uncle's home. Lead on, then, I'll take a look – a brief look, mind! I'm not hanging about in there.'

On their way indoors Jess apologised for the request. 'I know it's not a pleasant thing to ask you to do.'

Bridget only waved the apology away. In the living room, she looked down at the dead man and murmured, 'Cripes!' She studied him a further moment, and shook her head.

'Can't help you. I don't know him from Adam. How did he get there?' She wrinkled her nose fastidiously. 'He whiffs a bit. Can we go outside before I throw up, too?'

'Of course, thank you for trying to help. We appreciate it.'

'Fair enough.' Bridget was already heading for the door.

Outside she drew a deep breath of air. 'I hope no one is going to ask me to do anything like that again. You'll be in touch, I dare say?'

They watched the little blue car roar away.

'Poor old fellow,' said the constable sympathetically.

Jess agreed but couldn't say so aloud. In any case, there was a distraction.

'Someone else coming,' observed the constable.

A red car was making stately progress along Toby's Gutter Lane towards Balaclava House. It had just passed Bridget Harwell's two-seater and now drew up outside the gates. The new vehicle wasn't unfamiliar.

'It's the pathologist,' Jess informed the constable, and went to greet the newcomer.

A stocky young man with a shock of black hair had clambered out of the car and made his way to the boot, where he stooped, head down beneath the opened lid, to rummage among the contents.

'Hello, Tom,' Jess called. 'You got here quickly.'

Tom Palmer emerged backwards from the boot, clasping a disposable protective suit. 'As it happened, Inspector Campbell, I got a call from your boss telling me you had a suspicious death. I was just settling down to a well-earned mug of tea, too.

He said you were out here and you'd requested SOCO and a pathologist. His tone of voice indicated some urgency. Well, I'm here – though I see no sign yet of the scenes of crime officers . . .' He glanced around.

'They'll be on their way,' Jess said. 'To be honest, Tom, I don't know how urgent it is. All I know is, it looks a very suspicious set-up. There's a dead man in there . . .' She pointed towards the house. 'And nobody knows who he is. The elderly owner of the house found him on returning from a trip into town. He says he's never seen him before.'

'Where is he now?' Tom asked, struggling into the suit. 'The old bloke, I mean.'

'He's left with a relative who has taken him to stay with her.' Jess hesitated. 'They were in that blue Mazda that passed you in the lane.'

Tom grunted. 'The woman driver glared at me through the windscreen as if I was trying to push her into the ditch.'

'It was a bit irregular, I know,' Jess said awkwardly, 'but I asked her (she's a Mrs Harwell) if she'd take a look at the corpse.'

Tom raised an eyebrow. 'How many people have been trampling over this scene?'

Jess pulled a wry expression. 'Probably far too many. But I wanted to make sure the dead man really was a stranger to the house owner. I thought perhaps the relative might recognise him, even if Mr Bickerstaffe says he doesn't know him from Adam.'

'Mr Bickerstaffe being the owner?' Tom asked and when she nodded, he added, 'If he's elderly he might be confused.'

'Oh, I don't think he's confused, Tom,' Jess assured him.

'But Mrs Harwell said he might have decided to be contrary. She didn't recognise the dead man either, though.'

'OK,' Tom said resignedly, 'Point me in the direction of this mystery stiff.'

As he spoke, an unmarked van came rattling along the lane and joined the now-sizeable queue of vehicles outside the gates.

'Here are the forensic boys,' said Tom, watching the occupants of the van come out and begin to unload their equipment. 'I'd better go and say hello to them first.'

For the moment, things were largely out of her hands. Jess went back to her car and got in. She sat watching the activity outside, until all the newly arrived experts had disappeared inside and then, a little hesitantly, rang her boss, Superintendent Ian Carter.

'How's it going?' Carter's voice asked in her ear.

'Everyone is in there, sir.' She paused. Morton had emerged from the shrubbery with one of the constables and they were coming her way. 'That includes Tom Palmer. He might be able to confirm whether or not it's as suspicious as it looks. But there are several odd things. Nothing indicates how the deceased got here. He's carrying no identifying documents. Mr Bickerstaffe still insists he doesn't know him and Mrs Harwell, his niece – or near relative, I can't quite sort it out – has also confirmed the man is unknown. There are some other puzzles, too.'

'Who exactly is Bickerstaffe?' came Carter's voice. 'How reliable do you judge him?'

'He's a very elderly recluse, sir. Certainly eccentric but he's quite clear about what happened, as far as he's concerned. His first name is Monty – I imagine that's really Montague. He's lived in this house, Balaclava House, all his life. There must have been money once, but I'd guess it's all gone. The building outside and inside is in a terrible state.'

'Definitely sounds a suspicious death. Keep me informed,' said Ian Carter and rang off.

Morton was bending down by the car and Jess let down the window. 'Was that the super?'

'It was, Phil, and he's quite happy to treat this as suspicious.'

Morton looked relieved.

A crunch of footsteps on gravel heralded the return of Tom Palmer.

'Well?' Morton and Jess chimed together.

Palmer scratched his mop of hair. 'I can't tell you more until I've got him on the slab. He hasn't been dead long, a matter of hours. Don't ask me to be more exact. Don't ask me what killed him, either, but outer signs indicate a possible poisoning.'

'Poisoning?' Morton exclaimed.

'I'll let you know later.' Tom looked uncertain. 'There is something about him that struck me . . .'

They waited eagerly to know what this might be. But Tom had changed his mind.

'Let me get a proper look at him. No point in me letting my imagination take over.'

They watched him go back to his car and begin to divest himself of his protective clothing.

'What was all that about?' asked Morton.

But Jess could only shake her head. 'No idea, just Tom being cautious, I suppose.' But cautious about what, exactly? Rather crossly, Jess added, 'What's Tom noticed that I've missed?'

Chapter 4

'Well, Ian,' said Monica Farrell, 'here's a turn-up for the books. None of us has seen anything of you for a very long time!'

The words were reproachful, but they were uttered in a comfortable tone that took the sting out of them. To underline they were meant as a welcome, she patted his arm.

'Come into the parlour, as the spider said to the fly. I've put out the sherry bottle ready.'

There was nothing spidery about his ex-wife's Aunt Monica, thought Superintendent Ian Carter ruefully, as he followed her into her cottage. She was built on solid, generous lines, broad in the beam, and dressed in a baggy skirt, old cardigan and sensible shoes. Her long grey hair was pinned on top of her head in a knot, insecurely held by a large tortoiseshell pin. To his eye, the pin looked Victorian.

He quelled his feelings of guilt. Now that he had moved from the other end of the country to this new area to take up his present post some months ago, he had been within easy visiting distance of Aunt Monica. There was no excuse for not having called before at her home in Weston St Ambrose, except for a certain natural diffidence about visiting one's former wife's relations. He couldn't be blamed for feeling that. Not that he and Sophie had broken up in a mass of recriminations, causing a division along family lines. Instead it had been a slow drift towards the inevitable. She had been unhappy and he had not known what to do about it. They'd bickered, rather than quarrelled. His job meant he often kept unsocial hours. Hers, for an international company, meant she travelled abroad a lot. In the end, they'd seemed to be always passing one another in the hall, one on the way out and the other on the way in. Then a new man had come into her life and Sophie had asked for a divorce. She'd taken their daughter Millie with her. He had raised a mild protest about that. But, as Sophie had pointed out in her usual way – reasonable with an underlying touch of exasperation – Millie was perhaps only ten at the time, but would soon be a teenager. Surely he didn't see himself bringing up a teenage girl? He'd capitulated.

Seeing Monica brought all this back with painful bitterness. If that didn't make the situation difficult enough, a further uncomfortable truth was that he'd underlying motives for seeking Monica out this mild evening. He wanted something from her, if she were able to provide it.

He passed a black cat sitting on a lichen-encrusted paving stone in the last of the evening warmth, and paused, before ducking his head beneath the low lintel of the front door, to look round the garden. It was bathed in a mellow rosy glow that would disappear within a few minutes as the setting sun finally sank below the horizon. He could hear busy twittering from nearby trees as the starlings settled for their nightly roost. The cat yawned, curling a bright pink tongue to meet sharp white teeth. It then looked studiously away from him.

Inside the cottage, it was just as he remembered it from the last time he'd been here with Sophie – and Millie. Millie had been jumping around full of excitement. The memory caused a sharp ache in his chest. The living room was still cluttered, untidy and cosy. He watched as Monica removed another cat, a surly-looking ginger one, from a chair and gestured to Ian to take the seat. The cat gave him a look that spoke volumes. He tried to make amends by bending to stroke it. It hissed at him and stalked away.

'He doesn't know you,' explained its owner. 'If you came more often, you'd soon be his friend.'

'I'm sorry, Monica,' Ian apologised. 'I know I should have come before, or even just telephoned. It's just—'

He broke off.

'Oh, I understand, we all understand,' Monica said. 'But we were all of us very fond of you, Ian. I was hoping very much that you'd look me out. Of course you mustn't come just because you feel obliged to.'

'It's not obligation,' he said frankly. 'Partly it's that I don't want Sophie thinking I'm hanging around like some sort of stray animal hoping to be taken into the family circle – again.'

'You and Sophie have a child,' Monica said firmly. 'And whatever your differences, Millie has a right to some sort of continuity in her family life.'

'Millie writes to me once a fortnight, more or less,' he told her. 'But she hardly ever mentions her mother. She's well aware that something is broken and can't be repaired. It's hard for her. She is only ten.'

53

'She'll have to come to terms with it.' Monica smiled. 'Children do. They're very resilient.'

'But hard as I try – and I know that Sophie tries hard too – Millie is paying the price for something she didn't bring about.'

Her wise gaze rested on his face. 'There's always a price to pay, Ian, for everything, in the end. Even happiness can have a price on it.'

'I just don't want Millie to resent what we did – break up, I mean.' He didn't intend to sound wretched and suspected he did. That would never do.

'If she does, then that's something you and Sophie will have to accept and make the best of. It's no use agonising over it, Ian. You just have to get on, all of you, and make a good job of a new set of circumstances.'

She poured out two generous glasses from the sherry bottle waiting on an unpolished silver tray on a coffee table. Monica Farrell wasn't a person who kept antiques in a display cupboard. She used them. 'However, listening to you, it rather makes me wonder why you did telephone out of the blue and ask if you could drop round at short notice!' She handed him a sherry schooner.

'I was hoping to persuade you to let me buy you dinner somewhere,' he said sheepishly.

'I never eat after six o'clock,' was the firm reply. 'You should remember that. It plays hell with my digestion. Cheers!'

Presumably the sherry didn't trouble her stomach. He watched her sip hers with appreciation.

'I'm driving,' he protested weakly.

'How many have you had today?'

'Alcoholic drinks? None.'

'Then one small sherry won't hurt.'

He sipped politely; his eyes straying round the room to see if there was any flowerpot or similar receptacle into which he could pour some of the sherry when she wasn't looking.

'Ian!' said Monica loudly, 'You look like a little boy caught with his hand in the sweet jar.'

Her disconcertingly direct gaze was fixed on him. It was always well to be honest to the point of bluntness with Monica, Carter reflected ruefully. He set down the sherry.

'I do have another reason for contacting you,' he admitted, 'apart from wanting to see you and apologise for not coming sooner. I've been settling in to a new house . . .' he heard himself add lamely and cursed himself. 'I recognise that's no excuse.'

'Do you think you'll like it in this part of the world, now you've made the move?' she asked.

He nodded. 'Yes, I do.'

'So, I'm all the more curious . . .'

'We're investigating an incident that occurred earlier today.'

'When you coppers say "incident",' she remarked, 'you can mean almost anything. Go on, Ian, I won't interrupt again.'

'Right, OK, it's a suspicious death. It occurred at the house of someone I thought you might know. You've lived here most of your life. Sophie always said you knew everybody—' He broke off.

'Sophie probably said I knew everybody's business.' Monica's promise not to interrupt couldn't resist his embarrassment. 'Well, once upon a time I did, though far less so nowadays because I don't get out and about so much. But in the old days, well, in a village news gets around. Besides, don't forget I taught at the primary school here for over twenty years. The village school-mistress does learn every family's secrets!' Her voice took on a grim tone. 'The old school is now a private residence; tarted up beyond recognition and lived in by a bally awful couple of townies who can't control their dogs! The man is a property developer and I suppose the poor old schoolhouse is an example of what he can do.'

'Have you registered a complaint about the dogs? If you have, then failure to control them—' the policeman in Carter responded automatically.

'They chase cats!' interrupted Monica fiercely.

'Ah . . .' Carter met the scornful gaze of the ginger cat. He could understand any self-respecting dog being annoyed.

'Of course I've complained. Not to the police. We don't have a police house here any longer, just as we don't now have a school or a post office. Instead I've complained to Hemmings, the owner, and his bottle-blonde wife. They say I should keep my cats in. But you can't control a cat!' She took a good swig of sherry to calm her nerves.

'True,' Carter agreed. 'A cat is a natural wanderer and there isn't the same legal requirement to keep it under control as there is on dog owners.'

'Exactly! I told the wretched Hemmings that. We had a row about it.'

Arguments between neighbours could take a nasty turn,

especially in small communities, and even more so when one party to the dispute was an old resident and the other party a newcomer. Carter made a mental note to keep track of this story.

'But you didn't come to ask me about Hemmings, I suppose,' Monica said regretfully. 'It wouldn't surprise me, mind you, to see the cops turn up on his doorstep. He's got a very shifty look about him. His wife is no better, nor his friends. However, who is on your mind, Ian?'

'I wondered if you ever knew a family called Bickerstaffe?'

She gave a great hoot of laughter. 'Bickerstaffe! I should say I do – or did. There's only one of them left living locally – at least, I suppose old Monty is still alive. I hadn't heard he'd died.' She frowned. 'Suspicious death? You don't mean Monty's dead, do you?'

He shook his head. 'No, although the body was found on his premises.'

'Balaclava House?'

'That's the one. Mr Montague Bickerstaffe found the deceased, by his own account, on his return from a trip into town. He claims not to know the dead man's identity.'

'Old Monty found a stiff, eh?' She drained her sherry glass. 'Well, well. He was half potty when I last saw him, quite a while ago. This must have sent him right over the edge.'

'Actually he seems to be coping rather well. He's gone to stay with a sort of niece, Bridget Harwell, while we're conducting enquiries.'

'Is that her name now?' Monica asked. 'I heard she'd married again.'

57

'And divorced again, I gather. I believe she's about to get married for the fourth time.'

'Humph! She was a pretty girl, Bridget Bickerstaffe. You're right, she's not a proper niece. Her father, Harry Bickerstaffe, and Monty would have been cousins. But Harry's side of the family didn't ever live at Balaclava House, although they visited often up to the time Penny Bickerstaffe packed her bags and moved out. So you want to know about the Bickerstaffes, do you? You've never come across Bickerstaffe's boiled fruit cake?'

The look on his face gave her an answer.

'No. Well, you're too young. You were spared one of the horrors of my childhood. My mother always bought one for Sunday teatime. I can see it now, a great dark brown lump of stodge, packed with dried fruit that got stuck in your teeth. It tasted more bitter than sweet and sat in your stomach like a lump of lead. But the history of that cake is pretty well the history of the family. By the way, I ought to tell you I knew Penny, Monty's wife, better than I ever knew Monty. He was always an awkward blighter. I don't know how Penny put up with him for so long. Eventually she decided that, having squandered the best years of her life on the old sod, she might as well spend her declining years in comfort and peace. She bought a little flat in Cheltenham and left him to stew on his own in that gloomy mansion.'

'She's still alive?' he asked eagerly.

Monica shook her head. 'No, I'm afraid. Died, oh, four years ago. She didn't have much time to enjoy her freedom. Sad, that. I managed to get to her funeral. Do you know, that wretch

Monty didn't have the good manners to turn up? The other members of the clan did. It was the last time I saw Bridget. What was her name then . . . ?'

Monica frowned. 'Let's see, she wasn't married to little Tansy's father. Peterson, that was *his* name. He was her first husband, ages ago. She'd already divorced him *and* divorced the chap she'd tied the knot with after Peterson. I'm blowed if I can remember the second one's name, not that it matters because that marriage didn't last long. Yes, of course, she was still married to Freddie Harwell, husband number three. He was definitely there; and half cut, breathing alcohol over everyone. As a matter of fact, even Peterson flew in from Jersey where he lurks, I understand, in tax-haven splendour. It was very odd, seeing Bridget perched in a pew between two spouses. Tansy, Peterson's daughter, was there too. She was only a kid at the time, oh, fourteen or fifteen years old. She'll be a young woman now, getting on for twenty. Peterson probably turned up to see her, rather than say goodbye to Penny. At any rate, pretty well *everyone* was there but Monty.'

'Did Monty and Penny produce any children?'

She shook her head. 'No, perhaps Penny found looking after Monty enough. He's something of a child himself. I don't mean he's simple. He was always a bright chap and could have been a success. But he never stuck to anything. He was a dreamer and would go wandering off on the track of anything that took his interest. Penny would have no idea where he was or when he was coming home. Perhaps being a Bickerstaffe didn't help. I'll explain.'

Monica gathered herself up to recount the tale, faintly taking on the manner in which, Carter imagined, she must once have addressed her primary class.

'It all started in the eighteen thirties when an enterprising baker by the name of Josiah Bickerstaffe found his biscuits sold rather well and went into business producing them en masse. By the middle of the century Bickerstaffe's had branched out, making other baked goods. They did rather well out of a contract to supply the army with hard tack during the Crimean War. Following that stroke of good luck Josiah's son built Balaclava House, on the proceeds.

'The firm then had a second bit of good fortune. They began to produce "Bickerstaffe's boiled fruit cake". They set about despatching this goody, sealed in a tin with a fake coat of arms on the lid, around the Empire. Their boast was no spot was too far-flung or too awkward to reach. Everyone from district commissioner to humble clerk could sit beneath the tropical sun, eating Bickerstaffe's boiled fruit cake with his afternoon tea. It makes a nice image.'

She chuckled. '"A Taste of Britain", the cake was called. It continued to be a best-seller right up to the Second World War when they had to suspend making it because they couldn't get enough of the ingredients. They relaunched it after the war, but tastes had changed, and the Empire was disappearing fast. Just when it seemed things were looking bleak, the family had another stroke of luck. A big American-based multinational company offered for Bickerstaffe's. They were keen to acquire such an old and reputable name in the cakes and biscuits world. The family were still the sole shareholders and did rather well out of the deal. Even Monty did, although he was still only a schoolboy, because he had inherited a large number of shares from his grandfather. So from scraping along they went to quite wealthy. But it didn't last, of course. Monty's father died soon afterwards. Inflation took care of the windfall money, plus their being saddled with that crumbling old house.'

'So Monty is the last Bickerstaffe to carry the name?' Carter asked.

She nodded. 'To my knowledge, he's the only one. There are other family members but they're all female, like Bridget, and have acquired other surnames on marriage. Monty must be, oh, I'd say seventy-six. He did National Service in the army; and after that he did have a brief career as a draughtsman. He didn't stick at that, either. There might still be a small amount of money coming in from investment of the windfall money, enough to keep him going, with his pension.'

'Thank you, Monica,' Carter told her. 'All that is very helpful.'

'I can't see how,' she returned. 'Well, I never had much time for Monty, but I'm sorry he's had such a nasty shock. What a strange business. So you're in charge of sorting it all out?'

'In overall charge, yes, but the case is actually being handled by Jess Campbell, Inspector Campbell.'

'Do you think she'll get to the bottom of it?' Monica's bright gaze rested on him.

'Yes, let's hope so, anyway. In the little time I've worked with Inspector Campbell I've learned that she's nothing if not thorough! She'll leave no stone unturned.'

He'd meant his last words as a casual reassurance. But Monica Farrell seemed to take them seriously.

'Then tell your Inspector Campbell to watch out,' she said quietly. 'When you turn over stones around the Bickerstaffes, you never know what might crawl out.'

Dusk had fallen while he'd sat talking with her and now it was almost dark enough to qualify as night. Lights were on in all the buildings around them when Carter left. He drove slowly away, raising his hand in a salute to acknowledge her farewell wave. In his mirror, he saw her turn and go back into the cottage. Both cats, ginger and black, twined round her ankles. He hoped they didn't trip her up. He would come and see her again before too long, a proper friendly visit; not one seeking information.

Eventually, after they had drunk their tea and eaten some brittle pieces of pastry with currants in them, called Shrewsbury biscuits according to his hostess, they had talked more about Sophie and what she was doing at the moment. He had known they would. It was inevitable. Not to mention her at all would be more awkward than talking of her, but it hadn't been easy.

Monica Farrell's approach to the subject had been typically simple and direct.

'How are you getting on, Ian? I don't mean work-wise or in moving house. I mean being on your own.'

'Well,' he replied slowly, picking his words. 'I'm doing all right. It did seem strange at first, being a bachelor again. I was only ever average at household chores. But I am learning to cook at the moment, in a rather hit or miss way.'

'No one else on the horizon?'

'Not so far. That's another thing about being thrown back into the bachelor pond. I have to learn to date again. I haven't even tried yet. I won't have another biscuit, thanks.'

'Don't blame you,' Monica replied. 'They are teeth-crackers, aren't they? I didn't make them. Our church had a fund-raising coffee morning and one of our congregation brought them.'

He smiled wryly at her. 'I wish I'd come at once to see you, when I moved down here. I was being a wimp.'

'Oh, I knew you'd come, sooner or later, when you felt up to it,' Monica said comfortably. 'Old Monty finding a body in his drawing room gave you the excuse you'd been searching for . . . even if you didn't know you were searching. The divorce hit you hard; we all knew that. But you're making progress, Ian. That's what matters. You have got your life together again; not completely, perhaps, but the framework is there in place. You are making a new life, without Sophie, starting to move on. I'm cheering you on from the sidelines, if that's any help.'

She gave him a surprisingly wicked grin, making him laugh aloud.

Now, alone in the car, he told himself: Monica's quite right. It's time you got your life together. You came down here to begin again, so get on and do it.

But you couldn't help looking back at a lost age as you drove around Weston St Ambrose. Mindful of Monica's words about the changes wrought by the years, he was curious to see the signs of them. He noticed, as he made a slow tour of the few twisted streets, where the post office had once stood. It was now a small restaurant, called, logically enough, The Old Post Office. There was the pub, still plying its trade but alarmingly gentrified in appearance. Here was the former schoolhouse where Monica Farrell had spent so much of her working life. Carter braked and sat, looking at it, remembering that Monica had fallen out with the owners.

It stood opposite the old church of St Ambrose, which now had a sadly neglected look. The ex-schoolhouse was a compact building of late Victorian design, probably one of the National Schools built after the education reforms brought in by Gladstone's government with the Education Act of 1870. Then there would have been plenty of children in the village to fill its classrooms. The number of young families living here had dwindled over the years, driven out by lack of good jobs and shortage of affordable housing as affluent town-dwellers sought holiday homes. The result had been closure of the school and its sale and conversion to private dwelling.

And an impressive private residence, at that! Carter thought. There was nothing neglected about the schoolhouse. On the contrary, a good deal of money had been spent converting it. Evidence of a garden could be seen to the side and rear, trees and bushes showing darker against the gloaming, but the front area – where infants had once raced noisily about the playground – had been brick-paved to provide plenty of parking spaces. They were needed this evening. The owners must be entertaining. Light beamed from the uncurtained downstairs windows, allowing him glimpses of people within, moving about, drinks in hand. A party was just getting under way. There was a home caterer's van tucked away in the corner of the parking area. The glimmer of a street light let him see the painted legend *Dine in Style*. So they'd be sitting down to dinner soon. It reminded him that he was hungry.

At that moment, the front door was unexpectedly thrown open and a woman was outlined against the hall lights. She came hurrying towards his car.

'Jay!' she called eagerly. 'We'd about given you up! What happened? Why are you—'

Her voice faltered and she stopped, almost right beside the car now, realising that this wasn't the expected, delayed, guest.

Carter was embarrassed and cursed his clumsiness in just sitting here, staring at the place. He could see the people inside. They, therefore, could see him – or see his car apparently parked out front. He let down the side window and switched on the interior light so that she could see him.

'Oh,' she said. 'You're not Jay. He's got that make of car . . . I thought . . .' A touch of panic was entering her voice and her manner changed from uncertain to hostile. Any moment now and she'd ask him what the hell he meant, sitting there, watching them.

'Forgive me,' he said. 'I've just been visiting an old friend, Mrs Farrell. She lives in the cottage at the end of this street, near the church. She used to be schoolmistress here when this place was a school. She told me it was a private house now and I was curious enough to stop and take a look at it.'

'Oh, Monica . . .' she said slowly, relaxing. 'Yes, she used to be a schoolteacher here. She's always talking about it.' She still wasn't quite sure, watching him carefully as if memorising his features.

Probably so that she could describe him to the police if necessary, thought Carter wryly. These were wealthy people; a stranger casing the place would be noted and reported. He could see her better now. She was a buxom blonde in her forties, heavily made up but attractive. Her taste in jewellery was flamboyant and her chandelier earrings trembled, glittering like Christmas tree decorations in the light from his car.

'It's all right—' he began. But he was interrupted.

A man came out of the house, a squat, beefy figure, and strode towards them. 'Terri? What are you doing out here? They're all waiting for their grub and the caterers want to serve up. Who's this bloke?' He peered angrily at Carter.

'I was just explaining to your wife,' Carter said, wishing he'd driven straight past this place. It was all getting complicated. 'Look,' he said, reaching into his jacket for his police ID, 'I'm not a suspicious stranger, I'm a police officer . . .'

This was worse.

'Police?' squeaked Terri, jumping back as if he had said he was the Grim Reaper. 'I thought he was Jay, Billy. He's driving a Lexus, just like Jay's . . .'

Hurriedly Carter began his explanation about having paid a visit to Mrs Farrell – but he was not allowed to finish.

The man, Billy Hemmings presumably, exploded. 'What? That old biddy's reported us to the police? I suppose this is about the ruddy cats!'

'No,' Carter said patiently. 'I've been paying a purely social visit to Monica Farrell. She's by way of being a relative.'

'Oh?' This was plainly disbelieved. 'She didn't complain about our dogs, then?' The tone was sarcastic.

'Well, yes, she did,' Carter admitted. 'But only in passing . . .'

'She wants to keep her ruddy cats indoors!'

'It's not our fault!' whined Terri. 'Ours are lovely dogs, but they're, well, dogs . . . Dogs chase cats, don't they? It's in their nature. You can't go against nature, can you?'

Carter had had enough of the pair of them. 'Where are the dogs now?' he asked. Not that he cared twopence, but with so many visitors on the premises, he would have expected the animals to be making a hell of a noise, barking.

'Penned in the shed, round the back,' snapped Hemmings, 'just till everyone's left tonight. My dogs only chase her moggies because they stray on to our property.'

'The law recognises that cats roam,' Carter said. 'But I am surprised they come on to your property when you have dogs loose.'

'She's told you about the time I was walking Benji and Rex in the churchyard, I suppose,' Terri began, 'and they spotted her rotten cats, who were doing their business right there among the graves . . .'

'Shut up, Terri,' said her dearly beloved brusquely. She shut up.

'I'm keeping you from your guests,' Carter said, 'Goodnight.' He switched off the interior light and pressed the button to raise the window.

The Hemmingses watched him drive away.

'Well, well, well,' murmured Carter as he drove back to town through the twisting lanes. 'I wonder if friend Hemmings is on the police computer? I think I recognise a shady operator when I meet one! Monica's a shrewd old bird. "Shifty", she'd called Hemmings. How did you make the money to buy the old schoolhouse and entertain lavishly, Billy, I wonder?'

Unprompted, a thought suddenly leaped into his head. Where was the missing guest, Jay, who owned a Lexus?

'Is it possible?' he mused, then shook his head. No, couldn't be.

Chapter 5

'He's not bonkers,' said Jess firmly. 'He's just different.'

'And unwashed, I understand,' said Ian Carter.

'That's not altogether his fault. He's been living on the ground floor of Balaclava House. There is no proper bathroom down-stairs, only a cloakroom with a loo attached. It's a very old loo, incidentally. The pan is probably Victorian, of an age with the house. It's covered in willow pattern, blue and white. The bath-rooms upstairs have cobwebs all over them and rusty taps. But Monty never goes upstairs. He's got bad knees. He "washes down", as he puts it, in the kitchen and hasn't had a bath or shower for years. The grime has sort of – built up.' Jess gave a rueful smile.

'Charming,' said Carter. 'Couldn't he have had the downstairs cloakroom converted to a shower room?'

'It would have meant having workmen in,' she explained. 'Anyway, he likes the house the way it is. He doesn't want it modernised.'

'Sounds like you've got a soft spot for him.' There was a warning note in his voice.

'It won't colour my judgement, sir.'

'Good!'

She tried not to let him see how much that irritated her. She turned her head away so that he shouldn't see it, and glanced at the window. It was the following morning, promising a mild late summer day. Rain had been forecast within the next twenty-four hours, but there was little sign of it. It was a pity about the spell of dry weather from a detection point of view. It meant they'd found no tyre or footprints on the road past Balaclava House; just some in old, dried mud, recognisably made by a tractor, presumably from Sneddon's Farm.

She turned back to her boss. Now that they'd worked together for a while, he usually called her 'Jess', particularly when no one else was around. When he called her by her surname, he really was put out about something but not, usually, anything she'd done. He wasn't the critical sort. He didn't breathe down an officer's neck. On the other hand, he had a way of making you realise you had to get it right. So far, Jess had got things right. But he would expect progress and she hoped she'd make some that afternoon.

The superintendent was still new here and the truth was, they hadn't quite got used to him. Not, thought Jess, that he was a person you got 'used to' very easily. She always had the feeling there was something going on in his mind he wasn't saying aloud. On the other hand, he had a way of getting other people to say out loud what was on their minds – even if originally they had not intended to. Jess, having sussed this out, was ready for it and had begun to phrase her answers accordingly. He probably realised that, of course. And this morning he'd sprung another surprise, wrong-footing her again. He was ahead of her in finding out more about Monty Bickerstaffe. He'd just recounted the information learned on his visit the previous evening to Mrs Farrell.

She knew that Carter was right to warn her about developing 'a soft spot' for Monty. She had already begun to feel protective towards the old man and it was a step from that to becoming possessive. It rankled that Carter had been telling her all about the Bickerstaffes and not the other way round. The family fortune had been built and lost, as far as she could gather, on a type of fruit cake. Well, people had made fortunes from equally odd things. She really wished she could have found out all this for herself and been the one to tell Carter. But she couldn't have done it half so well, because she hadn't had the necessary contact. He did have, in some old lady who was a mine of information. Would you believe it? He was supposed to be a newcomer to the area and it turned out he'd got a relative here – or rather his ex-wife's relative. She knew he was unmarried, but had supposed that at some point he'd been in a long-term relationship or a marriage. She'd also assumed, as they all had, that it had ended in break-up or divorce. Now she'd had confirmation of the fact, she had no idea how recently all this had happened. How warily did she need to tread? Was that why he had moved down here from the other end of the country? Making a break, beginning again . . . didn't people often try and deal with the situation like that? Presumably he'd no children. She couldn't even be sure about that.

Jess met the quizzical gaze of his eyes. Depending on the light, they either looked greenish or brownish. Today, she thought, they were brownish. She had the uneasy feeling he'd been reading her mind. No, she told herself next, that's just me feeling guilty. Pull yourself together, Jess!

'You believe someone has been using one of the upstairs bedrooms,' he said with sudden briskness as if he, too, were shrugging off some unwished-for frame of mind. He frowned, drumming his fingertips on the top of his desk. 'That's very odd. Bickerstaffe didn't mention anything about that? You're sure he doesn't sleep up there himself?'

'Absolutely. I told you—' She corrected herself hurriedly. 'I was explaining to you earlier that he doesn't go upstairs. I saw a bed of sorts made up on a chaise longue in the corner of the drawing room. That must be what he uses himself. But someone has been up there in that one bedroom, and cleaned surfaces and so on, before Morton and I saw the room. It's definitely been in use. You can tell just from the atmosphere. It's not so stuffy as the other rooms; windows have been opened recently. It feels lived in. Scenes of Crime couldn't lift any usable fingerprints.'

'That thoroughly cleaned, eh?' Carter murmured.

'Yes, polished to a shine. Makes you think. There is the blanket left on the bed. We don't know yet if we can get any DNA from that. It's out of keeping with everything else in the house. Whoever has been using the room brought it in. The thought of any Bickerstaffe buying something synthetic and bright candy pink is just impossible. Anyway, there is a linen cupboard up there full of old sheets and blankets. Why not use one of those?' Jess answered her own question, 'Because the person using the room didn't know about the supply in the linen cupboard. By the way, I checked out the contents of that cupboard. The blankets in the cupboard are all woollen and some of them have Second World War period utility labels in them.'

'I'm surprised you recognised those,' Carter said with a smile.

Jess bridled. Why the heck shouldn't she? 'I've seen the mark before,' she told him stiffly. 'My mother's branch of the Women's Institute organised an exhibition called the Home Front. You'd be surprised what people dug out of their attics for it. Someone brought in a gas mask. Some families just don't clear out old stuff. Bickerstaffes are that sort. You can bet your boots they have never thrown anything away or bought anything new, unless it was absolutely necessary. Monty's always lived in that house. He's inherited ancestral junk and gone on adding to it. Whatever has been going on in that bedroom, I'm absolutely sure Monty's blissfully ignorant of the whole thing.'

'Because he claims never to go upstairs.' Carter sighed. 'We can't take everything he says as gospel. He may wander up there occasionally and has just forgotten the last time he did so. It's his home. Why shouldn't he take a walk round it now and then?'

'If Monty saw a candy-pink nylon blanket on one of the beds, he'd notice that and he'd remember it!' Jess argued.

Carter held up a placating hand. 'You're probably right. I just find it very odd. But then, everyone seems agreed Monty *is* very odd, even if he isn't, as you describe it, quite bonkers. Well, you'll have to ask him outright about it. It's still possible, what-ever you feel, that he may just not have been volunteering information he thinks is none of our business. I've dealt with the type before. Bickerstaffe isn't a social animal. He isn't going to open up to you or anyone else and tell them his innermost thoughts. He probably thinks the less he tells the police, the sooner we'll go away and leave him in peace. You'll have to make it clear to him the reverse is true.'

'I plan to drive over to Mrs Harwell's home and interview him again there this afternoon. But I'll have to be awfully careful how I tell him he's had an intruder. I don't want to frighten him. He is very elderly.' Jess knew she was sounding stubborn.

'All right, let's suppose Monty is quite ignorant of his visitor or visitors. The next question is: are they connected with the dead man in the drawing room downstairs? And when did the thorough cleaning of the room take place? If the phantom visitors did put our corpse on that sofa, they would have been keen to get out of the place before Monty came home and found them. So, are we to believe they sought out dusters and brushes and spent anything up to half an hour polishing upstairs?' Carter shook his head. 'No,' he said firmly. 'That definitely doesn't make sense.'

This time Jess had to agree. 'Sergeant Morton thinks the room was used for assignations.' Feeling for some reason ridiculously embarrassed, she added, 'Romantic ones. Junkies would have left needles. They always do. Drunks leave beer cans. Schoolkids leave empty cider bottles and sweet wrappers. These visitors didn't bring booze or drugs. They just brought themselves.'

'Why bother to clean up so thoroughly after themselves and yet leave a bright pink blanket in place to tell the tale?' he countered.

'I don't know.' Jess thought about it. 'The blanket would be bulky when folded up. Perhaps it wasn't convenient to remove it each time? This wasn't a one-off visit, sir. That room has been aired regularly. It's got a real atmosphere of regular use.'

'They were careful to remove their fingerprints, these regular lovebirds, if that's indeed what they were up to. They weren't so carried away by passion they forgot about that.' Carter drummed his fingers. 'Yet leaving the blanket tells us they were confident Monty wouldn't walk upstairs and find it. It suggests they may have chosen the house because of the assured privacy. They knew the owner's habits. So why so careful not to leave any prints if there was little risk of discovery?'

Carter leaned back and folded his hands. For a moment they regarded one another in silence. Then the superintendent asked, 'Where's Sergeant Morton now?'

'He's gone to interview the neighbours. There's a family called Colley that keeps a small pig farm next door to Balaclava House, although you can't see it from the house because of a bend in the lane. You can smell it, though.'

'Nice neighbours,' commented Carter.

'I don't suppose the smell of the pigs bothers Monty. There is also another, larger, farm further on, belonging to a Pete Sneddon. I don't think the Colleys will be helpful. If they know anything, they won't tell us. They're not the type to cooperate with the law. Morton might have more luck with Sneddon.'

'I'd like to meet Mr Bickerstaffe,' Carter said.

Jess opened her mouth but he forestalled her protest. 'Don't worry. I'm not proposing to accompany you this afternoon. Bickerstaffe knows you. A stranger turning up with you might

75

upset him. I'll get a chance to make his acquaintance before too long, I dare say.'

While Jess's conversation with Superintendent Carter was taking place, Phil Morton was carrying out the job of interviewing the Colley family. He stood at the gate barring the track leading into their property and surveyed the hand-printed notice that read 'Beware of dogs'. He had parked his car in the road and had intended to walk up to the house, but not if ferocious dogs were on the loose. He could open the gate and drive through. He put out a hand and at once, as if they knew a stranger was about to invade the place, the dogs in question began to bark. They set up a deafening racket, but they didn't appear.

As Morton hesitated, someone else did. A figure came plodding down the track towards him and stopped on the other side of the gate. She was an elderly woman and appeared, to Morton, to be quite square. Short, broad, with straggling grey hair framing a sunburned face, she stood on stumpy legs, slightly spread to balance her weight. She wore a grimy tent-like patterned frock and carried a bucket.

'Who are you, then?' she asked. The question startled him, not because of the words themselves, but because of the timbre of her voice. It was as deep as a man's, with a hoarse quality that suggested a lifetime's addiction to gin and strong tobacco. Before he could reply, she went on, 'Copper, I dare say, come about that business at Balaclava.' She jerked the grimy thumb of her free hand in the general direction of Monty's home.

Morton produced his ID but she barely glanced at it. 'Are you Mrs Colley?' he asked.

'I'm one of them,' she said. 'My daughter-in-law, Maggie, is the other.'

'I'd like to talk to your family,' said Morton. 'Are they all at home?'

'They're about the place. You can come in. I'll take you.'

Morton opened the gate and looked past her apprehensively. She had already turned away from him and was stomping back down the track. She looked over her shoulder without pausing.

'Dogs is in their pen,' she said.

Morton followed her, curious to see the place the Colleys called home. It appeared as he turned a shallow bend in the track and he was surprised to see it consisted of several buildings. What a jumble they made! Something of everything, Morton told himself. Without knowing much about architecture, he realised the various parts had been constructed at different times and in some cases probably for different purposes.

The smallest construction, and the nearest to him, was the dog pen. It was a large cage made of chicken wire attached to rough wooden posts. Probably it had started out as a poultry run. In one corner of it stood a ramshackle hut, serving as a kennel. The dogs themselves were three in number, Alsatians with, Morton judged, a touch of something else in their blood-line. They were big, powerful creatures and he doubted that the wire run would hold them for very long if they really wanted to get out. They crowded together, snouts pressed against the wire, watching him with unfriendly yellow eyes. A slight shift in the breeze brought him the rank smell of pack animals kept out of doors. Morton turned his gaze away deliberately, recalling that staring a strange dog in the eye can be read as a challenge.

Mrs Colley, he was not altogether happy to see, had disappeared into the house that lay directly ahead of him, leaving him alone. It had originally been a honey-yellow stone cottage typical of the area. But over the years it had been added to in a piecemeal fashion, bits in brick, some in a different sort of stone, and a lean-to in wood tacked on the far end.

To his left were empty brick pigsties. He wondered where the pigs were. To his right, beyond the dog pen, stood a building of quite a different class. It was larger, both long and higher, brick-built with care, decorated with a fancy pattern of different colour bricks at intervals along the façade. The far end had dusty windows and a stable door. The nearer end, windowless, was pierced by a large doorway, closed now by wooden doors of a more modern and rougher construction than the rest of the building. It was two-storey; the upper floor showed twin openings, about the height of a man, beginning at floor level. A rusted pulley system protruded from the wall by one.

Old hayloft and stables, thought Morton, now a general storage area. I wonder what happened to the original doors? I suppose they use some of it as a barn or farrowing shed. Even in these reduced circumstances, the whole building was a cut above the rest. It was like seeing an elderly, tattered but dignified gentleman tramp, sitting on a bench with a group of less distinguished winos. It made him think of Monty Bickerstaffe himself.

While he had been studying his surroundings Mrs Colley had gathered her clan. They emerged now, some from within the house; others came round the corner of it from some area to the rear. They moved in a solid mass towards him and stood silently, waiting for him to open any conversation.

Mrs Colley senior no longer held her bucket but her fingers were still curled as if a handle rested in them. Next to her stood a belligerent-looking woman in early middle age. Her features and figure were lumpy and her skin weather-beaten and prematurely lined. Her lank, badly dyed black hair was dragged back from her face and fixed in a ponytail. She wore gold hoop earrings, but no make-up, and her bare arms were decorated with tattoos. She glared at Morton with small dark eyes as she drew on a cigarette. That must be Maggie, the daughter-in-law, Morton thought. Fancy waking up every morning and seeing that on the pillow beside you!

The husband who had that honour stood next to Maggie: a burly, bearded man in grimy jeans and quilted body-warmer worn over a plaid shirt. Then came the younger members of the family. There was Gary, with a wary grin on his face and, beside him, an overweight blonde wearing tight black leggings that did nothing to disguise her plump thighs and bulging calves. A loose garment draped the top half of her body. Lastly, a small child emerged from behind the blonde and stood staring unblinkingly at Morton. It was female, and between three and four years old, so Morton guessed. Her hair was uncombed. She was dressed in pink leggings and purple top, and grasped a grubby stuffed toy Morton thought he could identify as a Teletubby, though he couldn't have said which one.

'Mr Colley?' Morton asked the bearded man briskly.

The man stepped forward and nodded. 'Dave Colley, that's me.' He indicated the woman with the cigarette. 'My wife.'

Morton acknowledged the introduction with a nod. The woman ignored it and drew silently on her cigarette, still glowering. The expression was probably permanent.

'You've already met my mother,' continued Dave Colley. 'This is my son, Gary. You've met him, too, I reckon, yesterday. And my daughter, Tracy. That little 'un is my granddaughter, our Katie.'

'Hello, Katie,' said Morton to the child, since none of the others had moved a muscle.

''Ello,' said the child and sniffed noisily. She rubbed the Teletubby across her nostrils.

'Where's Mr Monty, then?' asked Dave Colley. 'What have you done with the poor old bugger?'

'He's staying with relatives,' said Morton. 'I'd like to ask you all about yesterday. You've probably heard by now that a dead body was discovered in Balaclava House by Mr Bickerstaffe, when he returned from a shopping trip to town.'

They showed no surprise at the news so they had heard about the existence of a body. Now, *where* had they heard it? That was another question that needed an answer.

'None of us know anything about it!' growled Grandma Colley. She had taken up a defensive stance, head lowered, shoulders hunched. Perhaps she thought that Morton, for some inexplicable reason, was going to rush her and tackle her to the ground.

'All right, Mum,' said Dave to her.

She wasn't so easily silenced. 'Old Mr Monty, he wouldn't know anything about it, either. Not his fault he found it. Anyone can find anything, doesn't make 'em responsible, does it?' She had a grievance now and having found voice, was getting into her swing.

There was an odd moment in which Morton and the Colleys were united in trying to ignore her. It was quickly over. The Colleys stood together, literally and metaphorically.

'You've been neighbours all your lives, you and Mr Bickerstaffe,' said Morton, more in dismay at the thought of anyone having to live next door to this bunch than anything else.

'That's right,' said Dave. 'My granddad, old Jed Colley, he knew Mr Monty when Mr Monty was a kid. Bickerstaffes and Colleys been living here for years.'

'You've always kept pigs?'

'That's right,' agreed Colley. 'This is our place, passed down father to son.'

'I see,' said Morton. 'Were you all here yesterday?'

'Off and on, I reckon. Gary went into town.'

Dave Colley was either telling the truth, or smart, thought Morton, and wished he knew which it was. Gary had told the inspector yesterday that he was on his way into town. Now his dad had backed his story.

'We particularly want to know if you saw any strangers, or even one stranger, in the area. Or an unknown car, in the lane out there.'

Colley shook his bushy head. 'No, no one. Pretty quiet down here, most of the time.'

'What about the rest of you?' Morton asked the family, since they seemed happy to let Dave do the talking with occasional contributions from Grandma Colley.

'Never seen nothing,' they chorused.

'How about you, Katie?' Morton asked the child suddenly, stooping to her level. He was aware of a rustle among the crowd of Colleys, perhaps surprised at his questioning a small child.

'Did you see anyone you don't know yesterday, Katie? Someone in the lane? A man or a lady, or lots of people?'

'No,' said Katie.

Morton fancied a collective relaxation of tension among the assembled Colleys.

'You can see for yourself,' said Dave. 'The track bends round from our gate. You can't see the lane directly from here. You'd have to be down there.'

It was a fair point. 'Where are the pigs?' asked Morton.

Dave blinked and surveyed him for a moment. 'I'll show you,' he said. He turned away and gestured Morton to follow. They set off towards the corner of the house. The other Colleys, with the exception of Gary, melted back indoors. Gary followed his father and Morton.

The smell of the pigs increased as they rounded the cottage. There, before him, was a large field full of the animals. They rooted about happily, pigs as far as the eye could see. Little corrugated iron huts were dotted about the field as shelters. They all looked in very good health. The house and other property might be ramshackle, but the pigs were well cared for. Morton supposed they had to be, or they wouldn't fetch a good price. In a further, smaller, enclosure, two horses grazed side by side, tail-end on to the pigs, as if blocking out the indignity of being kept alongside them.

Morton turned his attention back to the pigs. 'What sort are they?' he asked.

Gary, who had been silent until now, answered. 'Large white.'

'It's the kind of meat shoppers want,' his father explained, 'on the lean side, not too much fat. My old granddad, Jed Colley, he wouldn't have touched bacon that wasn't mostly fat, but tastes have changed.'

'I'm not keen on fat bacon, myself,' said Morton.

'Ah . . .' chimed both Colleys, shaking their heads.

'So, easy to rear, then?' asked Morton. If the Colleys were willing to talk about pig-rearing, it might make them chattier on other topics.

'Straightforward enough. You have to watch them in a hot summer. They can get sunburn.' Morton must have looked as though he thought his leg was being pulled, because Dave continued, 'It's those pink skins of theirs.'

Morton eyed the nearest pig. Its skin, beneath its white hair, was certainly very pink and vulnerable-looking. 'So,' he said, 'good business?'

Both Colleys immediately made noises of dissent. 'You've got your work cut out to make a decent living,' said Dave. 'But we keep afloat.'

It was time to bring the conversation back to the body found in Balaclava House. 'You see,' said Morton, 'our problem is this. There must have been someone – or some persons – around yesterday. The dead man was carried into the house, so we think. He may not have been dead at the time, but he was almost certainly dying and was very unlikely to have walked in there unaided.'

'Is that a fact?' asked Dave Colley. 'Well, none of us saw anything.'

'Nothing,' corroborated Gary. 'First we knew of it was when I walked past Balaclava on my way into town. I saw you lot outside the house and poor old Mr Monty being pushed into a police car.'

'But you walked on into town? You didn't turn back and come here to tell your family about the disturbance?' Morton didn't give up easily.

'I rang 'em,' said Gary. 'On my mobile.' He fished in his pocket and held up a phone. It looked like one of the latest models. 'This one, here.' Gary gave Morton what could only be described as a triumphant grin.

Morton made one last effort. He turned to Dave Colley. 'None of you was curious enough to walk up the lane to Balaclava House and find out what all the fuss was about, after Gary phoned you?'

'We were busy,' said Dave. 'And things had got behindhand. The pigs broke out earlier on the far side of the field there and got on to Sneddon's land. My boy and I had to round them up and fix the broken fencing. Then young Gary, he went off into town, and I got going on the paperwork. I should have been doing that when I was chasing the bloody pigs. Any kind of farming now is snowed under with paperwork. When Gary phoned in the news, I told my wife, but we didn't have time to go running round to Balaclava. We reckoned we'd hear all about it sooner or later.'

'Yes, that makes me wonder just where you did hear about the body, Mr Colley,' Morton said blandly, 'since Gary, your son, only saw Mr Bickerstaffe getting into a police car.'

The two Colleys exchanged glances.

'Well,' Dave said slowly. 'Later that evening, my mother walked up the lane and took a look. She wanted to check on the house and Mr Monty, you see, in case he needed anything. She saw the undertaker's vehicle just drawing away. There were still cops there. Ma came back and told us about it. So that meant someone had died, hadn't they? And it wasn't Mr Monty because Gary saw him with you lot.' Dave looked pleased with his own logic.

Gary's smile had broadened. Whatever Morton asked them, they'd have an answer.

Morton fixed Gary with a look to let him know the smile hadn't gone unnoticed. 'I'll probably be round here again. In the meantime, if you think of anything at all, let us know, will you?'

The Colleys mumbled indistinctly.

'By the way, whose are the horses?' Morton asked, nodding at the further enclosure.

'My lad's,' said Dave Colley. 'He's always kept a horse or two, since he was a nipper. Sometimes he grazes them in the paddock there and sometimes down in the field by the road.'

Gary Colley struck Morton as being more a motorcycle person than a horse one. He wondered if there was gypsy blood in the Colleys.

They walked back, all three, to the main area in the front of the house.

'That building.' Morton indicated the large brick-built block. 'When was that built?'

'Oh, the old barn there,' said Dave dismissively. 'That's been here longer than any of us here now. That was built when Balaclava House itself was built. It used to be the coach house and stables for the big house. This . . .' He waved a broad callused hand at his surroundings. 'This was originally the stable yard. Our cottage there was for the use of the head groom. The Bickerstaffes gave up the carriage and the horses after the First World War. They bought a motor car. They had money in those days, Bickerstaffes. They had a new garage built nearer the house and a flat for a chauffeur over it.'

'I didn't notice a garage with a flat over it near the big house,' objected Morton.

'No more you would. It fell down years ago. I went up and took the bricks away to build our pigsties, doing Mr Monty a favour, like.'

Doing yourself a favour, you mean, thought Morton.

'Well,' Dave began again, showing signs of impatience at the interruption, 'my great-grandfather had been their coachman and head groom since before Queen Victoria died, but now he was out of a job. He reckoned he wouldn't find work again, times having changed. He wasn't so young, either. Motor cars were coming in everywhere and he didn't see himself learning to drive one. The story goes that he did try, but he could never remember not to turn his head and talk to his passengers. After he'd driven a whole car full of Bickerstaffes into a ditch, they told him they'd get a younger man.

'So he went to the then Mr Bickerstaffe and asked if he could rent the stables, the yard, his tied cottage and the two paddocks between Balaclava and Sneddon's land. Then he could start a smallholding, since he was about to lose his job. After all, the family had no use for them any longer. Old Bickerstaffe agreed. Felt he owed it to him, I suppose. Later, my grandfather, Jed Colley, got the money together to buy it all. Bickerstaffes let him have land and buildings for a knock-down price. Land was cheaper in those days. No one had started putting brick boxes all over the countryside. Bickerstaffes weren't doing so well with their biscuit business by then, and even a bit of money, cash in hand, from my granddad was welcome.'

Morton walked past the dog pen on his way out, still avoiding the baleful yellow gaze of the penned animals. But he was aware of it, as he was aware of the gaze of Dave and Gary Colley watching him leave. From inside the cottage, he was sure, the women watched him, too. He was equally sure they knew something but they weren't prepared to tell him whatever it was. He just had to hope he had better luck with Peter Sneddon, the farmer.

Chapter 6

Monty sat in Bridget's back garden where he'd found a secluded spot, shielded from the wind by the junction of high dry stone walls. There was a white-painted metal seat here. It wasn't any more comfortable than the average church pew, but he was glad to be out of the house. He could relax, as he couldn't indoors: nobody could be at ease with Bridget hovering over him. He felt uncomfortable even out here, probably because of his new clothes. They had been bought during a humiliating visit to the nearest Marks and Spencer's in Cheltenham. Bridget had marched him around like a harassed parent of a six-year-old, ticking off items on a list. His only original possessions left were his shoes. He had pointed out to Bridget that it took time to break in shoes to the shape of his feet. She'd given way on that, but on nothing else. Everything else had an obstinate newness about it, fighting his shape. So the waistband of his trousers was too tight. His shirt collar was too stiff. The sleeves of his woollen sweater were too long. It was reliving his first day at his new prep school, wearing a uniform intended to 'let him grow'. He didn't feel he was himself but someone else. Perhaps that was why, when he dozed off, he began to see himself as a boy. Events unrolled in his dream world as if he watched a film and actors played out the story. Monty was a young boy in shorts and an Aertex sports shirt. He toiled up the steep rise of Shooter's Hill and Penny followed behind, complaining that he went too fast. He was carrying a brown paper bag containing a hardboiled egg, with a pinch of salt in a screw of paper to season it. The bag also held fish paste sandwiches made with a lot of bread and very little paste filling. To supplement this unappetising fare, he had a box of broken biscuits from the Bickerstaffe factory.

Penny, whose mother was more experimental in culinary matters than his, had brought banana and jam sandwiches cut into triangles with crusts trimmed off, and wrapped in grease-proof paper. Bananas were still a novelty in the shops after the war years and Penny's sandwiches were something special. Mrs Henderson was clever at creating little treats for the children. It would never have occurred to Monty's mother to take the trouble. Penny also had two sausage rolls and a bottle of dandelion and burdock.

They reached the summit and flopped down with relief after spreading out the threadbare green plaid travelling rug that Monty had also been obliged to carry uphill, rolled up over his shoulder. His shirt, where it had rested, was soaked in sweat and its rough woollen texture had rubbed an angry red mark on his neck. He hadn't wanted to bring it but Penny had insisted. Sneddon's sheep grazed up here from time to time and left their calling cards on the short dry grass. Penny, like all women, was fussy about that sort of thing despite being only ten years old.

In silence they proceeded to lay out their joint stock of provisions on the rug. This was the usual drill. It was followed by a ceremonial exchange of items. Monty swapped his boiled egg for one of her sausage rolls and they agreed to share the broken biscuits and dandelion and burdock. Monty had started out with a bottle of weak orange squash but had drunk it on the way up. Secretly, he would have liked one of Penny's jam and banana triangles, but he hesitated to offer one of his fishpaste monstrosities in exchange; so in the end he didn't.

This whole area of high land was known as Shooter's Hill. From up here you had a spectacular view, miles and miles of undulating countryside, patched with fields, divided by the meandering river and roads, dotted with cottages. It meant Monty could see his whole world, laid out at his feet like a tapestry carpet. Balaclava House looked like a toy building. Further along lay the Colleys' untidy yard and their ramshackle cottage, even tinier.

Way over there, behind the woods, lay Sneddon's Farm and the doll's house of a cottage where Penny and her widowed mother lived. Mrs Henderson eked out a precarious existence for herself and her daughter by writing children's stories. Their home was a former farm worker's hovel, no longer required. Mr Sneddon let Mrs Henderson have it for a peppercorn rent because it had an outside privy, and also because he felt sorry for her, being a war widow. You couldn't see cottage or farmhouse but you could see Mr Sneddon's sheep two fields away, mere white dots.

Beyond the farm was the quarry. You couldn't see that, either, but occasionally you'd hear a muffled roar. Down below to the right lay the dark stain that was Shooter's Wood. Sometimes there was shooting down there and you did hear gunshots exploding into the quiet air. Generally it was Jed Colley after pigeons. But not today. Today the woods lay dark, mysterious and silent. Now the only sound was the distant twittering song of a skylark high above. Not so long ago he'd have heard the drone of aircraft. But it had been a peacetime sky for over a year now. Monty fell flat on his back and squinted up into the bright light. He could just make out the fluttering black dot.

'If you look straight into the sun like that,' said Penny, 'you'll go blind.'

'I've got my eyes shut,' countered Monty, closing them to prove it.

'You didn't just now. You had them open and you were pulling a horrible face.' She paused. 'My grandma says, if the wind changes while you're pulling a face, you'll stay like it.'

'That's childish tripe!' said Monty indignantly. 'It's what they tell little kids like you . . .' (He was only twelve years old himself, but he knew that would annoy her.) 'You don't believe that now, do you? You must be potty.'

'Of course I don't!' Her face turned red with fury and it clashed with her carroty hair. To let him know how much he'd offended her, she didn't speak again.

He was glad of her silence because it meant he could just lie there, feeling the warm sun on his face, smelling the grass and earth, hearing the buzz of nearby bees on the clover and letting his thoughts drift along any route they chose to take. He was dimly aware that the pattern was already set for the adult relationship that still lay some years ahead of them. Penny would still be telling him what to do, when they were grown up, and generally she'd be right. He would find ways not to take her advice, or appear not to. Penny would be chattering and he longing for silence. She would ever be the practical one and he the dreamer.

Penny already said, 'When we are married . . .' and she was almost certainly right about that, too. Monty knew he was temperamentally lazy and accepted it would be easier to marry Penny, one day, than go out and find someone else. At least he knew Penny's faults and that was preferable, he reckoned, to marrying another girl and finding out she had a score of unexpected failings.

He pushed himself up on his elbows and peered at the back of her head through narrowed eyelids. The sun sprinkled her hair with gold dust. He liked her hair. The sun made her freckles darker but he didn't mind those. He quite liked the blue-check cotton dress she wore. He wondered how many years of relative freedom he'd got before Penny carried out her resolve to marry him. He was twelve now and he ought to be able to put it off for another twelve at least, surely? That was a lifetime. If he obliged his parents in their wish to send him to university, he wouldn't be able to marry Penny for ages. What a relief!

'What are you grinning at?' asked Penny suspiciously, turning round and speaking at last, if only to accuse him. She must have eyes in the back of her head.

'Nothing,' said Monty promptly.

'It has to be something. Is a beetle crawling up my back?'

93

Alarmed, she began to reach behind her and make awkward brushing gestures.

'No, honestly, Penny, I wasn't thinking of anything special.' To distract her, he added, 'Let's go down to Shooter's Wood.'

'No,' said Penny, grumpy now because she still didn't know why he'd been grinning and suspected a private joke at her expense. 'My mother doesn't allow me into Shooter's Wood.'

'That's only because she's afraid Jed Colley will blast you with his shotgun. He's not firing down there today. We'd have heard him.'

'I'm not going!' snapped Penny.

'Then I'll go on my own!' Irritated, he jumped to his feet.

He scrambled and slithered down the hill. Once he thought he heard her call after him. He half hoped she would follow, once she realised he really would leave her sitting there. But he couldn't hear her puffing behind him and male pride would not allow him to look back. He knew, of course, that he would be in trouble with both their mothers if they learned he'd left Penny all alone on the hillside. But Penny wasn't a sneak.

At the wood's edge he did stop and look back up the hill, shielding his eyes against the sunshine. Penny was still sitting where he'd left her, a lonely figure in blue with a red topknot. He waved to her. She didn't wave back. She, too, had her pride.

Monty turned back to the first line of trees and the mass of bramble bushes that fringed the track. He hunted around to see if he could find one of Jed Colley's expelled shotgun cartridges. He was rewarded with just one and put it in his pocket to take back to Penny as a peace offering. Then he plunged into the trees and felt the shock of the change in temperature. After the heat of the hillside, he shivered in the cool air. It was creepy in here. He wouldn't stay long; just long enough to show Penny she couldn't be boss all the time. He followed a narrow track probably made by deer. The wood closed around him shutting out all but its own noises: the rustles and fluttering in the branches above; the sudden crack of a twig as something living moved unseen by him. A dip in the track, filled with rain a week ago, had still not drained and he skirted the smelly green sludge. He picked up a nice undamaged magpie's feather and added it to the collection he was making to take back to Penny.

It was then, as he was thinking he could now return without loss of face, that he heard the other voices. At first he feared it might be Jed Colley who, though an amiable fellow, was likely to fire off his shotgun at pretty well any sound. He opened his mouth to call out and let Jed know he was there. But before he could, he realised that one of the voices was female. Jed would never take a woman along with him shooting. The Colley women all busied themselves around their smallholding and rarely went anywhere. They were always pegging out washing or scrubbing pots or feeding chickens.

A man's voice joined in the conversation. Curiosity led Monty to make his way quietly towards it. He made a game of it, imagining he was a hunter tracking a prey. The conversational sounds changed and it was as if no humans made them, as if there really was some animal ahead of him. The invisible pair were making strange, disturbing noises, the like of which he'd never heard before. Someone was grunting and panting. He heard the woman give an excited little cry and then there was silence.

Without warning, he came upon them. They were in a small clearing and he almost walked right into them. He drew back in the nick of time; although they were not paying attention to anything but each other. As he and Penny had done, they'd put down something on the ground to lie on. It looked like an old raincoat. What shocked Monty most deeply at first was their nakedness. They'd taken off *all* their clothes and lay on the flattened raincoat still entwined in each other's arms. It was like coming upon Adam and Eve, as illustrated in the stained-glass window of their local church.

Then realisation struck him. This, then, was the sexual act! He was both appalled and thrilled. His heart thumped and he broke into a sweat. This was *it*: the subject of the whispered conjectures and imaginative boasts made among the boys at school. For accounts of this they avidly devoured the occasional 'dirty book'; smuggled in (or purloined from an older boy at great risk) to be passed around the dorm. Before him now wasn't myth or invention, this was the real thing and he, Monty, had seen it. What a tale he'd have to tell next term! How his stock would rise among his contemporaries. Excitement gripped him and made his head spin. It found its way down into his shorts in a way both disturbing and pleasurable. He could hardly breathe.

Then they sat up and he saw their faces. This was not Adam and Eve in the Garden of Eden. This wasn't a badly printed Continental magazine or postcard. This was Shooter's

Wood and the couple consisted of his own father and Penny's mother.

It was as if a cold shower had drenched him. It was all he could do not to cry out. He pressed his hand over his mouth to stop the sound. He wanted to run away, crashing through the undergrowth, but he had to be silent; they must not know he was there. They must never know he'd seen them. No one must ever know of it. He crept back the way he'd come, hardly daring to breathe, avoiding the smallest twig lest it snap and betray him. Then he ran, far enough away at last, bursting out of the trees into the bright sunshine as if he'd been pursued by a band of cannibals.

Penny was still up there, waiting for his return. He climbed laboriously up the steep slope towards her and she watched him draw nearer, stony-faced and silent.

He threw himself down on the rug and put the shotgun cartridge and magpie's feather down on the rug between them.

She glanced down at his peace offering disdainfully. There was the dried track of a tear on her cheek.

'I've drunk the last of the fizz,' she said. 'So if you're thirsty, too bad. Serves you right!'

He didn't say anything because she was correct again. He ought to have stayed here with her and then he wouldn't have seen what he had seen. He wouldn't have to carry this awful secret inside his head; carry it for ever.

'Uncle Monty?'

Monty opened his eyes with a start. Someone was standing

in front of him. The sun dazzled him and at first he couldn't make out who it was. His mind was confused, too, still half back there in Shooter's Wood.

Seeing his bewildered expression, she said: 'It's Tansy.'

'Oh, Tansy, my dear,' said Monty. 'So it is. I was having a little nap.'

'I'm sorry to wake you up.' She sat down on the garden seat beside him.

Monty thought the kid looked wretched. She had always been slim but now looked skinny, all bones and angles. Her face was drained of colour except for the dark blue patches under her eyes.

'What's up?' he asked.

'That police inspector woman has just rung up. She wants to come out here and speak to you again. Or else, she says, you can go in and speak to her at the police station or headquarters or whatever it is. She wants to come today. Mum's annoyed.'

'What's new?' muttered Monty.

'Mum says, they're harassing you. She wants to have a solicitor here when the inspector comes. She suggests Mike Heston.'

'Lawyers?' said Monty fiercely. 'Bloodsuckers!'

'Or, Mum says, we can ask Dr Simmons to write a letter saying you are suffering from shock and can't answer questions. Mum thinks that would be a good idea for you to have a little time to recover and consider what you are going to say.'

'What on earth have I to consider? Tell your mama,' said Monty loftily, 'that I am certainly capable of talking to Inspector Campbell and I don't need a solicitor there. Let the woman come. I'll see her here. I don't want to get back into that midget's car and be driven miles to see her.'

'I'll tell Mum, but she won't be happy.'

Tansy didn't look very happy, either. She brushed back a strand of long, fair hair. 'This is a rotten business, Uncle Monty.'

'Unexpected, certainly,' said Monty, 'and inconvenient. Oh, I am grateful to your mother for bringing me here, and so on. She means well. But I want to go home.'

'When you can do that will depend on the police, won't it?' The strand of hair fell forward again and she began to twist it round her forefinger. 'When I said rotten business, I meant it was horrible for you to find that – to find it – and in your house.'

'Fortunately I had that mobile phone you made me buy. Anyway, it's not the first horrible thing I've ever found,' said Monty.

'Not – not someone else dead, surely?' She gazed at him with appalled blue eyes.

'There are other horrors,' said Monty. 'Death isn't the worst of them.'

'I've never had anything to do with death before,' said Tansy almost inaudibly.

Monty glanced at her and then patted her arm. 'Cheer up, young lady. You can go back and tell Bridget what I told you to tell her. Don't worry about me. I'm tough. But there is one thing . . .'

'Yes?' Tansy looked up quickly with the finger still entwined in her hair.

'Be a little love and smuggle me a glass of whisky out here?' Monty gave her a pathetic look. 'Please?'

A smile broke the strained expression on her face. 'OK, Uncle Monty.'

He watched her hurry back to the house. Poor kid, only a child, really. She couldn't be more than eighteen or nineteen and that, to Monty, seemed unbelievably young. She was coming to the end of what she and her mother called 'a gap year' before going to university somewhere to study some subject he'd never heard of. He couldn't say Tansy had had an uneventful life, not with Bridget's habit of serial marriages. But Tansy had been packed off to some girls' boarding school for most of the time. The job of those establishments, as far as Monty could make out, was to shelter the young ladies from bad influences, unsuitable friends and the wicked ways of the world. All the things, in fact, that made existence interesting. Now, for the first time in her young life, real unpleasantness and the outside world with all its grubby nastiness had burst in.

Perhaps it wouldn't do her any harm. She'd have to face it sooner or later. She'd get over it, lucky if life threw no worse at her. She'd make a career eventually, or meet a nice young man or . . . just do whatever young people did nowadays. Blowed if he knew anything about it.

He couldn't worry about Tansy. The police inspector, Jessica Campbell, was coming to see him here. The idea made him uneasy, though not because he had any hidden information. He'd told her all he could about the dead man. He wished he could tell her something else, something useful. Then the whole business could be sorted out and settled and he wouldn't be troubled by it any more. Until then, he'd be getting continual visits from Inspector Campbell. As a person, he'd nothing against her at all. But she did bear a remarkable resemblance to dear old Penny. No wonder he'd dreamed about his childhood and Penny sitting up there on the hillside alone, brave, angry, determined and terrified.

'Sorry, Pen,' he whispered now. 'Sorry for all the times I let you down. You're always lurking at the back of my mind, you know. That's why I got such a helluva shock when the police female walked in.'

And later on this afternoon she was going to walk in again. 'Damn, damn, damn . . .' muttered Monty. 'Are you having a laugh at my expense, Penny, wherever you are?'

Chapter 7

Jess climbed out of her car before the Harwell home and stood for a moment assessing the scene before setting off towards the front gate. The house, she'd been warned by its owner, was located 'rather in the middle of nowhere' and it did stand alone on a country road. It was called, so the wooden engraved sign on the gate told visitors, The Old Lodge. From the look of the place it might once have been exactly that, a gatekeeper's lodge standing at the entrance to a substantial estate. Both the drive and the gates it had guarded were long gone. Any great mansion to which they had led had also been pulled down or lay out of sight sinking into ruin. But, if the land beyond had been sold off, it remained as yet undeveloped.

Trees formed an untidy backdrop to the lodge. They looked like the remnant of native woodland, left to its own devices. Perhaps Bridget didn't own that scrap of land, or perhaps she did and had let the trees stand, not only to shield the house from the wind, but also to reduce the appearance of it having been left behind when the world moved on. The house itself had a curious Grimm's fairy-tale look. Its eaves were fringed with carved wooden boards. It had little casement windows and wooden shutters, painted dark green. The path that wound its tortuous way to the front door was paved with mossy stones. The property was surrounded by a dry stone wall.

Lonely at any time of year and I wouldn't like to be shut up out here in winter, thought Jess. She frowned. The house did not seem to match the sophisticated woman she'd met. She imagined Bridget Harwell liked company, the bustle of city life, shops and bright lights.

She entered through the gate and set off towards the front door. It opened as she got to it, before she could knock, and a very young woman faced her. It must be Bridget's daughter. She was pretty in a wan sort of way. With the exception of her large, pale blue eyes, she resembled her mother, having the same sharpness of feature but without the worldliness. A waterfall of long straight fair hair framed her face and the blue eyes were reddened and dark-circled, as if she'd been crying. She was dressed casually in jeans and sweatshirt emblazoned with a sportswear logo. She held, in her hand, a tumbler of whisky.

'You've come to see Uncle Monty,' she said, ignoring Jess's proffered ID. 'I was just going to take him his whisky. Keep Mum talking for five minutes, will you? So that I can smuggle it out to him. He's in the back garden.'

'Tansy?' a woman's voice called.

Tansy slipped past Jess and disappeared round the corner of the house, carefully shielding the whisky from view.

A second later, Bridget appeared. Seeing Jess, she heaved a theatrical sigh. 'It's you, then. I know you said you'd be coming. You had better come in. I should tell you that my uncle is a bit confused. I think all this has rattled him badly. I'm not sure it's a good idea for you to talk to him today. Must it be now?'

'Yes,' said Jess simply. 'I understood from your daughter that Mr Bickerstaffe is in the back garden. Perhaps I could just walk round there?'

'Was Tansy here? I thought she was on her computer.' Bridget frowned. 'This has upset her. She has a vivid imagination. She always liked Balaclava House when I used to take her over there, when she was a little kid. Aunt Penny still lived there then and made a fuss of her.'

Bridget paused and squinted at Jess. 'Funny thing, you look a bit like Penny – in photos I've seen of her when she was young. I suppose it's the red hair. Monty was kind to Tansy in the old days, too, letting her rampage around the place. Aunt Penny eventually walked out on him, with every good reason to do so. She should have gone years earlier but she stuck it out like a heroine. Finally even she had had enough. It gave Monty a helluva shock,' Bridget added with grim satisfaction. 'He'd never believed she'd do it. After that, he decided to shut us all out. I have tried to maintain contact, over the years. Tansy has, too, but . . .'

Bridget shrugged in despair and shook her head. 'Well, go and talk to him if you must. But honestly, we could all of us do without this hassle. None of us can help you. I know you can't say how long this investigation will last, but at least, perhaps you could tell us – give *me* some idea – how long Uncle Monty will be involved. He wasn't there, after all, when the – the dead chap found his way into Balaclava. He doesn't know who he is – was.'

105

'He may still be able to tell us something of interest,' Jess persisted calmly. 'Often people don't realise that some small fact may be very important to us. They judge something trivial. We see it as an important link.'

Bridget folded her arms and studied Jess. The movement brought the large diamond on her ring finger into view, sparkling in the sunshine. 'This is very inconvenient for me, you know,' she said with sudden energy. 'I'll be putting the house in moth-balls at the end of the month when Tansy goes off to university. I'm going over to the States.'

'To live?' Jess asked, surprised.

'I'm getting married again. I'll be living in New York.'

Oh, yes, Monty had said Bridget was remarrying; for the fourth time, if Jess remembered rightly. 'So Tansy will be left all alone here in the UK, except for Mr Bickerstaffe?' Jess raised her eyebrows.

'There are other family members dotted around,' Bridget said irritably. 'I'm not abandoning her. She is just coming up to her nineteenth birthday. She's not a child. If you must know, Max – my fiancé – and I tried to persuade her to go to college in the States. But she wanted to stay here in the UK.' She shrugged. 'The problem is more with my uncle than with my daughter. I can't alter my plans because of him. He can't stay here in this house alone. He can't go back to Balaclava. It's out of the ques-tion. He won't accept it, but he's got to sell the old museum piece, if he can find a buyer for it, and move into sheltered accommodation. The old boy could live the rest of his days in relative comfort. But you try telling him that!'

She shrugged. 'You'll find him in the far corner of the garden. There's a seat.' She walked back indoors and Jess was left to find her own way.

Jess was pleased Bridget hadn't accompanied her into the garden. She didn't want Monty annoyed when she, Jess, was trying to start a conversation. She was irritated herself by Bridget's self-absorption and lack of sympathy for the old man.

She turned the corner of the house and the afternoon sun struck her face, blinding her for a moment. She put up her hand to shield her eyes.

There was no sign of Tansy. She must have slipped back into the house through the rear. The garden had been carefully laid out for low maintenance, mainly lawn with a surrounding border of shrubs. In a far corner, there appeared to be a flagged patio and a sort of bower with a seat. A pair of legs stuck out into view past intervening shrubbery. She walked towards it. 'Monty?'

Monty was sipping his whisky. He was almost unrecognisably well scrubbed and his hair had been trimmed professionally in a 'short back and sides' style. This had spruced him up but had the unintended effect of making him look both older and frailer. His previous well-worn and begrimed appearance had been both a kind of disguise and an armour. Now, stripped of it, it was as if he was sitting inside the wrong skin. When Jess's shadow fell across him, he sat up with a start and placed a protective hand round the glass.

'Oh, it's you,' he said with relief. 'I thought it was Bridget,

come to boss me about and stop me enjoying my one consolation in life.'

'Mind if I sit down?' Jess asked.

'Please yourself,' said Monty. He shuffled along the painted
metal seat and indicated the space created beside him.

'How are you?' Jess asked, when she'd sat down. 'How are
you feeling?'

'Bloody awful. But not because of that dratted stiff in my
house. Look at me!'

'Very smart,' said Jess, taking note of all the new clothes.

Monty uttered a ferocious growl. 'Smart? Why on earth
should I want to be smart? I'm not going to a wedding or a
funeral. I'm sitting in a garden. It's not my own, but it is still
a garden . . .' He paused and surveyed the view. 'Of sorts,' he
added.

He sipped his whisky and his manner mellowed. 'Have you
taken him away?'

'The deceased? Yes, he's gone.'

'So I can go back?'

'Well,' Jess hesitated. 'We're still looking round the grounds.
You have a lot of land there and it's all – um – rather overgrown.
Searching through it isn't easy.'

Unexpectedly Monty chuckled. 'Grounds? What do you think
you're going to find there? Of course it's overgrown. I can't do
any gardening. Know yet who he is?'

'No, not yet. We'll get there.'

'What did he die of?'

Monty was gazing studiously ahead, avoiding eye contact;

but the question had been crisply put. He does want to talk about it, thought Jess with some relief. He doesn't want to appear curious, but naturally he's eager to find out all he can.

'I hope we'll know that soon, too. A post-mortem examination is being carried out.'

'Seems to me it's going to be a slow business,' observed Monty. 'I can't stay here indefinitely, you know. Bridget's going to America, getting married.'

'So she has just explained to me.'

'And young whatsit, Tansy, is going off to some university or other. Bridget's not selling up. She's keeping on the house for when she and the new man come over to the UK . . . a little place in the Cotswolds!' Monty snorted. 'But it will be all locked up. I suppose Tansy might come down and use it from time to time. But I can't stay here on my tod. Bridget wouldn't let me, anyhow, in case I wrecked the place with my dissolute lifestyle!' He snorted again.

It's not for me to mention sheltered accommodation, thought Jess. I'd like to be a fly on the wall when Bridget does suggest it to him. But the sad fact is, she's right. He can't go back to Balaclava. He's getting older, less steady on his feet, less able to take care of his day-to-day needs. Then there's all the drink he puts away. It has to have affected his health. His liver must keep going on borrowed time. Monty himself is on borrowed time. The thought made her very sad.

'Mr Bickerstaffe,' she said. 'You told me that the dead man looked, to you, as if he might be a racing man. "The sort of fellow who hangs around racecourses", you said.'

'Did I?' Monty frowned. 'I suppose I must have done, if you say so. Yes, he did look that sort. Well, more or less. I didn't spend that much time looking at the fellow, not after I realised he'd snuffed it.'

'There was nothing else about him that put that idea in your head?'

'No,' said Monty. 'Didn't he have a driving licence or something on him?'

'He had nothing on him at all to identify him. No keys, house or car, no credit cards, nothing at all.'

Monty twisted slowly on the seat so that now he faced her. 'Rum, that, isn't it?'

'Very rum. We think someone, whoever brought him to your house and left him there, cleaned out his pockets.'

'Ah . . .' said Monty, watching her face closely.

Now that she had his full attention, Jess tackled the awkward subject of the bedroom that had been in some sort of use.

'Monty, we think that you may have had a visitor you were unaware of, apart from the dead man, I mean. We looked round upstairs. We checked all the bedrooms. One of them showed signs of a recent presence. It was tidied and dusted. The air was fresher, as if a window had been opened in there. You say you never went upstairs?'

'Not for years,' Monty said slowly. 'Well, I'll be jiggered. Who would want to use a room in Balaclava?'

'We don't know. Nor do we know if it's connected with the dead man. But someone has been spending some time up there and, we think, on a fairly regular basis. A tramp or a

110

druggie would have left rubbish, used needles, beer cans, some kind of debris. This person came and went, not making any mess. Also, before we – Sergeant Morton and I – entered, surfaces appeared to have been carefully wiped of fingerprints. Someone went to great lengths to hide his tracks. That leads us to suspect whoever it was could – just possibly – be the same person who brought the dead man to Balaclava.'

Monty shook his head. 'Don't make sense, m'dear. If my unknown visitor didn't want you, or me, to know he'd been using one of the rooms upstairs, why dump a dead man downstairs for me to find? The police were bound to come. They would search round, as you did. No, no, you're on the wrong track, I'm sure of it. But good luck, anyway,' Monty concluded.

'Thank you, Monty,' Jess said with a wry grin. The point he'd made was a valid one. The drink hadn't addled his brain. His next question proved it.

He turned his head to look closely at her again. 'Think it's a murder, then, do you?'

'Yes, Monty, since you ask me. We don't know yet how he died, of course, so it's not yet official. It's still an unexplained death. But it's shaping up that way.'

'That'll rattle Bridget's cage,' said Monty with satisfaction.

It wouldn't suit Jess if Monty upset Mrs Harwell so much that she refused to continue to have him under her roof, and turned him out before the investigation was concluded.

'I understand that family members don't always get along,' Jess began tactfully, 'but don't you think you're being a little hard on Mrs Harwell? She has made you comfortable here—'

'Comfortable!' squawked Monty, tugging at the sleeve of his new pullover. 'You call this comfortable?'

'She has obviously *tried*,' persevered Jess desperately.

'She's been *trying* . . . I grant you that,' was the reply, 'but that's not the same thing!' He chuckled at his own joke.

'It's a difficult situation for everyone,' Jess reminded him. 'I met Tansy earlier.'

Monty's merriment died away. He nodded. 'Yes, it's got to her. Well, death, the first time you meet it, does come as a shock. When you're her age you think you're going to live for ever. She's a nice kid. I hope she has a happy life. I wish I could do something for her, but I was never any good at making money. I haven't a bean to leave her. It's too late for me to have regrets now. Doesn't mean I don't have any, though.'

On that cryptic note, Monty sighed and gave a little nod of dismissal. The conversation was over.

Jess left him on the garden seat, his hands folded over his new pullover, staring meditatively into space. He didn't appear to be studying the garden. She wondered what he did see. Increasingly, the impression she was getting of Monty was that he had ceased to find the present relevant and spent much of his time in the past. Perhaps that was why the whole business of the discovery of the dead man in his own drawing room appeared to have made so little impact on him. It was as if he'd brushed it off. It didn't matter to him because other things, in his memory, mattered much more.

She rounded the corner of the house, her footsteps silent on the grass, and was startled to hear the sound of voices raised in anger. The window was open; in the room beyond Bridget and her daughter were in full flow of a mother-and-daughter spat. Jess's natural instinct was to move out of earshot. But that impulse only lasted a moment and then her detective instincts kicked in and she stayed to listen.

'I really don't know why you're so set against going to college in the States. Max and I would be delighted . . .'

'Nice of you to say so,' snapped Tansy. 'Max doesn't want me hanging round.'

'Rubbish. I realise you don't like Max, for some unaccountable reason!' was Bridget's brittle response.

'Whether I like him or not is neither here nor there. He won't be around long enough for it to make any difference, will he?'

'And just what does that mean, young lady?' Bridget's repressed anger burst through her controlled façade.

'You know damn well!'

'Don't swear at me! I'm your mother!'

'Well, *Mother*, none of your previous marriages have lasted long, have they?' Tansy, too, had been repressing her feelings. A fountain of bitterness welled up with the accusation.

'Things don't always work out in life, Tansy.' For the first time, Bridget was defensive.

'Don't I know it!' yelled Tansy.

There was the sound of a door slamming.

Jess hurried away before she was caught eavesdropping. She reached the front gate just in time. The front door opened and Tansy erupted from the house, pulling on a long knitted jacket of vaguely Andean pattern and jangling car keys.

'Hallo, haven't you gone yet?' she asked when she saw Jess.

Jess indicated the car keys. 'If you're getting behind the wheel, Tansy, I suggest you calm down first.'

'Certainly, Officer!' said Tansy sarcastically. She pushed the car keys into her pocket and came up to Jess. 'It's good you're still here. I want to talk to you.'

'OK, we can walk a little way down the lane, if you want.'

They set off together, Tansy with her hands thrust into the pockets of the knitted garment and striding out, jaw set.

'You must think we're a bloody weird family!'

'I don't know a lot about your family . . .' began Jess.

'You've seen enough. We *are* a weird family. Are your parents alive? Are they still married?'

'Yes, to both those questions,' Jess told her.

Tansy stopped abruptly and turned to face her. 'How do you find someone who wants to spend a whole lifetime with you, just because he loves you? Someone who isn't just passing through, like this guy my mother's set on marrying at the moment, or doesn't turn out to be a total deadbeat like the last one she was hitched to?'

'I don't know,' Jess confessed. 'I'm not into giving advice about love, life, the universe and all that. I haven't taken the plunge myself yet. I'm a police officer. It's surprising how many police officers marry another officer. You have to marry the job, you see. It's very difficult.'

'You wouldn't perhaps find a different job, if you got married?' Tansy was watching her face carefully.

'No, of course not, it's my career.'

'My mother seems to think I ought to have "met somebody" by now.' Tansy's voice was unexpectedly sad. 'You know, somebody wealthy and the right sort. That's more important to her than a career. I don't know what she'd do if I said I was going to join the police. She'd have hysterics, probably. No offence. My mother lives in a very narrow world.'

'I expect she worries about your future,' Jess told her. 'Have you got your mind set on anything particular you'd like to do?'

'No,' said Tansy. 'I've never felt the urge to be a doctor or a teacher or a – a pop star or any damn thing. Most people do have some idea what they want to do by my age. I bet you did. How old were you when you decided to be a cop?'

'I was in my last year at school,' Jess confessed. 'The head teacher cornered me one morning as I was scooting along the corridor, late for a class as usual. "Are you always going to be late for everything you do?" he asked.'

'He'd no right to say that!' Tansy was indignant on Jess's behalf.

Jess smiled an acknowledgment but said, 'It was a good question and he followed it up with a better one. "What are you planning to do when you leave here?"'

'Aha! A trap!' said Tansy.

'Yes. I hadn't really fixed on anything. I think he knew that or suspected it. But I was determined to give him a firm answer, just to make it clear I'd given thought to my future. I picked the toughest thing I could think of and told him, "I'm going to join the police force!" It did take the wind out of his sails a bit. After that, he didn't let me forget it and he told other staff

115

members. So eventually I got used to saying I was going to apply to join the police. They began to ask me, why? So I started to read it up and find out more about it. That's when I got really interested. I thought, yes, it *is* what I want to do. So, here I am. I've never regretted my choice. It is a tough job but it's a worthwhile one. I don't see myself doing any other. I'm satisfied I'm in the right one.'

'At least you had the wits to think of something when he asked you. I couldn't pick a career if you held a gun to my head.' Tansy hunched her shoulders despondently inside the knitted jacket.

Jess smiled. 'What are you hoping to study at university?'

'Oh, media studies, but without any long-term aim. I told you, I've never had an aim in life, not one more than six months ahead. I'm not that interested in going to university, to be honest. But I've got to do something, so I thought I might as well do that.'

Jess heard herself say something she immediately regretted. 'You're pretty well off, I suppose. No financial worries?'

She had not meant this to sound either sarcastic or ill mannered but somehow it did.

Tansy replied robustly. 'None. Yes, I'm what you call "well off". I've got a wealthy father. He's very generous. He's also the only decent man my mother ever married and she couldn't keep hold of him! My mother is a loser, you know. That's her problem. But if you think that money makes life easier, then let me tell you, it bloody well doesn't.'

They had reached the end of the lane where it joined a bigger road and by mutual consent turned back towards the house.

'When you said you wanted to talk to me,' Jess began, 'I hoped it was about this case. I'm not much use as a careers adviser or life coach, I'm afraid.'

'I didn't mean to bend your ear about my troubles,' Tansy said. 'What the hell do you care, anyway? But I do want to talk to you about the case, or rather, about Uncle Monty. You're not going to badger him, are you? I don't often agree with my mother, but I do agree about this. He's old and he's pretty well pickled in booze.' Tansy stopped and turned to face Jess. 'Look, he really doesn't know anything about that body.' She leaned forward earnestly.

'The dead man came from somewhere, Tansy, and he wasn't alone when he got to Balaclava House,' Jess told her gently. 'Someone, at least one person, had to be there to help him inside.'

'Then it was someone driving through. Toby's Gutter Lane is hardly used but it joins a main road, which is really busy. It means Balaclava House isn't even as off the beaten track as The Old Lodge is here.' Tansy pointed down the road towards her home. 'Even Uncle Monty with his dodgy knees can manage to walk into town from Balaclava. He does it almost every day except Sunday.'

'We are bearing all that in mind,' Jess told her. 'In fact, it seems other people did know about Balaclava House. Someone has been using one of the bedrooms.'

She intended the question to come as a shock and it did.

'*What?*' Tansy stared at her in disbelief. 'That's rubbish. Upstairs at Balaclava is a ruin.'

'Nevertheless, there are clear signs that someone has been using one of the bedrooms on a fairly regular basis, unknown to your uncle.'

'*Someone has been hanging round Balaclava?*' Tansy put up both hands and pushed back her untidy long hair from her face. 'But that's – that's awful.' An expression of panic crossed her face. 'While Uncle Monty was *there?*'

'More likely when he wasn't at home. He has a habit, you know, of leaving the place unlocked.'

'Then someone could have been in the house . . .' Tansy's voice trailed away in horror. She went on, 'Could have been there when poor Uncle Monty was downstairs, absolutely at their mercy, whoever it was. They might have murdered *him*. Mum or I could have called to see him and found *him* lying on that sofa.'

She stared down at the ground, apparently collecting her thoughts. 'Mum says he ought to be in sheltered accommodation,' she said, looking up suddenly. 'I've always thought it would kill him. But perhaps she's right – if he's not safe at Balaclava. What did he say when you told him? I wish you'd told Mum or me first. Then we could have broken it to him.'

'He didn't say a lot. Your uncle is quite tough, Tansy. I don't think my visits worry him. He doesn't appear worried by the idea of someone using the house. As you were saying, someone could have been upstairs while he was downstairs. Or, if he'd come back early, he could have met up with whoever it is, any sort of mishap like that. Perhaps he hasn't quite thought it out that far yet.'

They had reached the gate again and Tansy took out the car keys.

'Taking your mother's car?' Jess asked.

'No, my old wreck.' She pointed.

Jess looked in that direction and saw an elderly Ford Fiesta parked by some bushes.

'Dad wants me to buy a new one. But I'm sort of attached to that one.'

'Your first car?' Jess smiled, Tansy's words sparking a memory.

'That's right. I'll drive carefully,' Tansy said. 'Honestly.'

Phil Morton was driving carefully, too, down Toby's Gutter Lane from the Colleys' towards Sneddon's Farm. The surface of the lane became progressively more potholed and narrow with hedges or stone walls to either side. If he met an approaching vehicle, one of them would have to back up or pull over awkwardly into the entry to a field for safety. He was also getting nearer to Shooter's Wood. It loomed darkly ahead, both beckoning with its mystery and repelling at the same time.

He reached a track off to the left. A wooden signpost indicated it led to the farm. On the corner stood the ruins of a tiny cottage, roof collapsed, foliage sticking through the frameless windows and the shell of an old privy standing like a lonely sentry guarding the jungle of a former back garden.

Toby's Gutter Lane itself ran directly on towards a bend and the woods. Eventually, he supposed, via links with other lanes zigzagging across the landscape, a traveller would reach a main road. But it would be a slow and hazardous route. He understood why motorists who mistakenly turned down Toby's Gutter Lane were advised by the inhabitants to go back to the main road and not try to cut across country. He turned into the track past the sad ruin of the cottage, wondering if this heralded what he'd find ahead.

However the farm, when he reached it, presented a neater, far more prosperous scene. The house was a rambling but well kept old building of mellow local stone. Geraniums still bloomed in pots by the front door. The outbuildings were well maintained and there were no penned guard dogs, he was relieved to see. But as he got out of his car, a black and white Welsh collie ran round the corner of a barn and came towards him, barking, but wagging its tail at the same time.

'Hello,' said Morton to the sheepdog. He reached out his hand for the animal to sniff.

The collie stretched its nose and then looked up at him, panting happily.

'Where's your boss, then?' asked Morton. Generally he liked dogs, and they liked him. This was an honest working dog and he respected that.

The Colley dogs, on the other hand, were of a type familiar to him from breakers' yards, scrap metal dealers' premises and various undertakings not keen to have outsiders taking an interest. Such dogs, like their owners, usually had an unfailing nose for the law and regarded it as the enemy.

A man had appeared, tall, slightly stooped, with long, sinewy arms, and a flat cap atop thick greying hair. He stood in silence, watching Morton and the collie.

He's judging me by the dog's attitude to me, thought Morton. If the dog decides I'm a friend, so will the owner.

'Mr Sneddon?' he called out.

Sneddon came towards him. 'You a copper?'

Even out here, they knew the law when it appeared.

'Yes,' admitted Morton, producing his ID.

Sneddon barely glanced at it. 'You didn't look like a lost motorist. We get 'em from time to time. They think they can get across country, but it's better for them to turn back.'

'So I gather,' Morton said. 'One of the Colleys was telling me that.'

He was interested to see how Sneddon reacted to the name of his neighbours. The farmer eyed him again and then commented, 'Been there, have you?' He might or might not have been amused at the idea. It was hard to tell. But his mouth twitched as if he repressed a smile.

'We're making enquiries,' Morton told him, 'relating to a dead body found at Balaclava House yesterday. You've heard about it, I suppose?'

There was a chance that Sneddon hadn't if he'd been on his own land for the past twenty-four hours.

'My wife heard about it,' Sneddon said. 'And she came and told me.'

'Oh? Who told her?' asked Morton.

'She took her car down to Seb Pascal's petrol station, on the main road, to fill up. Seb had seen the police cars go by. Later on, he saw a little blue sports job go past with old Monty Bickerstaffe sitting in the passenger seat, and a woman driving.

121

He reckoned the woman was Mr Monty's niece. So he picked up the phone and rang one of the Colleys, young Gary. Seb reckoned they'd know what was going on. They did.'

Morton thought about this, working out the timetable in his head. 'It was after Mrs Harwell left with Bickerstaffe?'

'It's what I said.'

I'll have to talk to this Seb Pascal, thought Morton. Seems to me those ruddy Colleys were creeping about all over the landscape, spying on us at Balaclava House and spreading the news. And how did Gary . . . ? His thoughts were interrupted by Sneddon.

'I was all set to ring you lot myself this morning,' Sneddon said in a growl. 'Not you, exactly. You'll be CID, I suppose. I was going to phone the local cops. Not that it would have done me any good.'

'Oh?' Morton asked sharply. 'Why was that?'

'Because they'd have sent a bloke out who'd have taken a look, made a note of it, and then done nothing, most likely.'

'Note of what? *What has happened?*' Morton was getting exasperated. 'What led you to think about calling the police?'

'I heard a car being driven past my farm last night, very late it was. It was coming from the direction of the junction with the main road, and heading towards Shooter's Wood.' Sneddon pointed. 'I thought it was odd. There's no one wants to drive down there, not in the middle of the night, leastways. If it was a lost tourist or summat, it'd have been in the daytime, wouldn't it? So I listened out –'

As he spoke, a woman appeared in the doorway of the

farmhouse, wiping her hands on a towel. 'Pete?' she called anxiously.

Sneddon turned his head towards her. 'It's nothing to bother you, Rosie.'

Disregarding this reassurance, she came towards them, her eyes on Morton. He saw that she was attractive in a mature way and possibly a few years younger than her husband.

'Sergeant Morton, madam,' Morton introduced himself. 'About the – the events at Balaclava House, just down the road.'

'Oh, that . . .' She looked worried. 'I couldn't believe it when Seb Pascal told me. I'd called in his garage, you know it? Just to get a couple of gallons of petrol in the car. The price is going up again, they say.'

'Yes,' said Morton, with feeling.

'And Seb, he said he'd spoken to Gary, Gary Colley, that is, who lives down the lane there.' She pointed in the direction of the Colleys'. 'He said something really weird had happened at Balaclava House. Someone was dead. He said Mr Monty was all right. That was the first thing I asked, you know, was it poor Mr Monty? But Seb said he'd seen Mr Monty go by in a car driven by Mrs Harwell. That's Mr Monty's niece . . .'

'Stop rabbiting on, woman!' ordered her husband. 'I've told him all that.'

'It's a worrying thing,' protested his wife. 'Things going on just down the lane and us none the wiser.'

Sneddon heaved a gusty sigh.

'You all call him "Mr Monty",' Morton said curiously. 'Sounds a bit odd to me.'

The Sneddons exchanged glances. Sneddon hunched his shoulders.

'Sneddons, Colleys, Bickerstaffes, we've all been here generations. My family was farming here when the Great War broke out. Colleys have been here as long if not longer. They worked for the Bickerstaffes before they took up the smallholding. Bickerstaffes, they were important then, a family that mattered hereabouts. We know times have changed. But our feelings haven't, see? Besides, Mr Monty saw me grow up from a nipper. He saw Dave Colley grow up. He's seen our two girls and Dave's kids grow up. He's owed some respect, I reckon. You can make what you like of it. Now, if you're interested in that car I heard, come along with me, I'll show you.'

'Show me? Show me what?' asked Morton, startled.

Sneddon heaved a deep reproachful sigh and looked at him as if Morton was being deliberately obtuse. '*The car*. It's what I'm telling you about, isn't it? We can go in your vehicle, if you don't mind me getting in it?' Sneddon pointed to his boots. 'It's only honest dirt.'

The collie ran alongside them to Morton's car but Sneddon sent it back to where his wife still stood. The dog settled down, nose on paws. Dog and Rosie Sneddon watched as Morton did a three-point turn in the yard and drove, with the farmer alongside him, back down the track to Toby's Gutter Lane.

'Turn left,' said Sneddon, 'down to the woods.'

Morton followed instructions. Sneddon was going to give his information in his own way. Any attempt to hurry him would result in his digging in his heels like an obstinate mule.

They rattled over more potholes and came to the first trees. Sneddon stuck to his policy of saying nothing, so Morton drove on slowly until they had reached almost the farther roadside limit of the woodland.

Abruptly Sneddon ordered, 'Stop here. You can park up on that bit of grass. We walk from here.'

Morton did so, but growled, 'I hope this is worth all this effort, Mr Sneddon? I'm making enquiries about a suspicious death. I hope you're not wasting my time.'

Sneddon snorted. 'Well, this is a bit of a mystery too, if you want to call it that, and you can make enquiries about it at the same time.'

He got out of the car and set off down a wide track, Morton on his heels.

'Like I was telling you, I heard a car late last night after we'd gone to bed.' Sneddon resumed his story, speaking over his shoulder. 'Must have been well after midnight. I said to my wife, if that's some bugger taken the wrong turning, he's going to have a job getting back on the main road. But she didn't answer me anything because she was asleep. She sleeps like a log, always has done. After that, I was sort of listening for the car coming back. But it didn't come back before I fell asleep again meself. I'd had a hard day and I couldn't worry about people driving round the countryside at night, getting themselves lost. If I'd stayed awake, I'd have seen the light in the sky from the fire.'

'Fire?' exclaimed Morton.

'Mind out, now,' Sneddon advised him, putting out a

sunburned hand to warn him. 'We're just about at the edge. There is wire round it, but it's not much.'

The remaining trees had thinned yet more while they'd been walking and now they were again in open land that rose towards the top of Shooter's Hill. Ahead of them, a wonky notice at an angle showed the legend 'Danger. Quarry' in faded paintwork. There was a fence of sorts composed of tangled wire and blackberry bushes that had grown up round it. Sneddon led him to a wide gap where wire and bushes had been broken down. He pointed downwards.

'Bloody hell!' muttered Morton.

The quarry was long disused and overgrown. No one had worked it for almost half a century. The wide path they'd walked along must originally have been the access road before that, like the quarry, had been left for nature to recolonise. But someone had been here very recently. The grass at the edge of the steep descent, where the fence and bushes were destroyed, was scuffed and torn up. At the bottom of the excavation, resting among the debris of the old workings, was the blackened, burned-out skeleton of a car. A haze of dust and smoke still rose from it.

'Stolen, could be,' suggested Sneddon. 'Or someone just wanted to get rid of it. Plenty of townsfolk think they can dump anything in the country. It'll be the car I heard last night.' He gave a satisfied nod. 'This is where the blighters were taking it. They got out at the top here, gave it a good shove and sent it careering down to the bottom there. Either it caught fire or whoever drove it here climbed down and torched it. What are the police going to do about that, then? And who's going to come out and take it away? Reckon no one will. That'll just be left there to rust, along with all the rest, one more bit of junk in the countryside.'

'Can we get down there?' Morton asked, ignoring Sneddon's grumbles and scouting round for a path.

'This way,' said Sneddon.

Together they scrambled to the quarry floor. When they reached it, Morton saw why Sneddon felt so strongly about rubbish dumped in the countryside. Fly-tipping had been going on here for some time. Old black plastic rubbish sacks lay around, their motley contents bursting out. There were the smashed remains of a wooden child's cot, still showing scraps of the original painted decoration of teddy bears; a Radiation gas cooker such as he remembered his grandmother cooking at; and an old-fashioned pushbike. More recent domestic history was marked by a smashed television set.

The burned-out wreck of the car smouldered amongst all this. Morton saw that, before abandoning it to its fate, someone had taken time to remove the number plates. They'd change hands in a pub for ready money. The next time anyone saw those, they'd probably be fixed to a getaway car. A shimmer of heat came from the scorched metal frame and made his face tingle. He took out his mobile phone.

Sneddon, watching him impassively, observed, 'You won't get no signal for that down here in this bowl.'

He was right.

'I'll phone in when I get back to the lane. Someone will come out and secure the area. It may have something to do with the incident at Balaclava House,' Morton told him. 'I'm sure the wreck will be taken away.'

'How did that chap die, then?' asked Sneddon, after nodding in a satisfied way. His only real interest was the wreck of the car. The dead man at Balaclava was a secondary matter. He probably only asked for details so he could tell his wife.

'We're not sure yet. We're awaiting identification and the post-mortem.'

'Don't know who he is, eh?' That did puzzle Sneddon, who put up a hand to push his cap back on his head. 'Old Mr Monty not know him?' He squinted at Morton, his sunburned skin wrinkling.

'Apparently not.'

Sneddon nodded again slowly. 'He'll be a stranger, then.'

The farmer turned and began to climb the slope of the disused quarry.

Chapter 8

Morton dropped Sneddon off at the turning to the farm and continued down Toby's Gutter Lane towards the main road. He was a thorough man by nature and it made him good at his job. He wasn't gifted with a great deal of imagination, but he did doggedly track down every detail. Now he sought out the petrol station belonging to Seb Pascal.

It was clear which one it must be. There was only one such establishment near the turning to the lane. The forecourt was empty except for a young man with a shaven skull. He was wearing stained blue work overalls and was polishing up a maroon hatchback that had apparently just been through the car wash. He looked up curiously as Morton pulled in, checking whether this was a customer requiring any service. But when Morton parked in a corner and set off towards the building, the young man's expression sharpened. He returned to his car polishing.

Once through the automatic doors, Morton found himself in a minimart. The shelves were stacked with a variety of goods, ranging from sweets and biscuits to tinned soup. In a far corner a separate unit held fresh snack food behind a glass shield. He glanced through the plate-glass window and saw that the youth outside by the maroon car had stopped work and taken out a mobile phone. He was talking earnestly into it, and looking towards the minimart. Catching sight of Morton watching him through the window, the youngster turned away quickly.

Hah! thought Morton. You know I'm a copper, too, don't you? Why does that worry you and who is that you're calling to warn on that phone of yours, eh?

It was probably nothing to do with matters in hand and would have to wait. Morton turned to where a tall, olive-complexioned, black-haired man stood behind the counter. He was talking to a middle-aged woman assistant and watching the newcomer at the same time.

'Mr Pascal?' Morton asked, holding up his ID.

'That's me.' Pascal gave him a suspicious look. 'What's the problem?'

'We're making enquiries about an incident at Balaclava House yesterday.'

Pascal relaxed. 'Oh, that, yes.' He glanced at his assistant who was showing signs of lively interest. 'Best come into the office, then,' he said. 'Keep an eye on things, Maureen.'

The assistant looked disappointed.

The office was tiny and cluttered. Pascal took a pile of motoring magazines from a chair and indicated Morton should sit down. He himself perched awkwardly, like a large bird on a fence, on a small, low filing cabinet. It was so dented it looked as if someone had been kicking it with a strong boot.

'What can I do for you, then?' asked Pascal affably, but his dark eyes remained watchful.

'As I said,' Morton began again. 'We're making enquiries into certain events that happened yesterday, at Balaclava House in Toby's Gutter Lane.'

'I wouldn't know anything about all that,' Pascal interrupted. 'Not to help you, like. I would if I could,' he added virtuously. 'But I never left here all day.'

'Nevertheless, you do know something, Mr Pascal, because you spread the news of what had happened to others. For instance, you told other parties that you'd seen Mr Bickerstaffe being driven away by a relative, driven past this petrol station. So, why don't we start there? Or better still, let's go back and start a bit earlier. Why don't you tell me exactly what you saw yesterday, especially anything *before* you saw Mr Bickerstaffe being driven past here.'

'Before that, nothing much.' Pascal shrugged. 'Trade's been quiet. Maureen and I were in here chatting for a bit. I did a bit of my paperwork.' Pascal looked disconsolately at the litter of paper on his desk. 'It gets away from me a bit,' he confessed.

It gets away from me, too, thought Morton in sympathy. There wasn't so much difference between his desk and Pascal's.

'But I did see old Monty Bickerstaffe walk past here earlier on his way into town. He goes most days, though I don't pay much attention to him, normally. He's like part of the landscape. You've got to hand it to the old blighter. He walks all the way there and back and it can't be easy for him. A couple of times, when we've been really quiet here, I've gone out and called out to him, offering him a lift in. But he's an obstinate old so-and-so. Unless it's raining or really cold, he'd rather walk. He says,' Pascal grinned with a flash of white teeth, 'it keeps him fit!'

'What time was this?' Morton took out his notebook.

'Oh, about eleven fifteen, morning break time. Maureen had just made us all a cup of coffee.'

'All?' Morton asked.

'Well, me, her and the boy.'

Ah, yes, the car polisher with a guilty conscience. 'Your son?' asked Morton.

'Maureen's nephew,' said Pascal.

'Would Maureen be Mrs Pascal?'

The idea appeared to alarm the garage owner who replied pithily, 'Not bloody likely!'

'What was the next thing you saw?'

Pascal shrugged again. 'Nothing or nothing much, not what I'd call unusual. Suddenly it had got busy, so I wasn't watching. Trade is like that, one minute dead and the next you're rushed off your feet. A couple of lorries pulled in. We sell hot pasties and sandwiches, so lorry and van drivers stop by around lunchtime. Then there was a chap who'd got some problem with a rattle under the bonnet. People came by for petrol. It didn't quieten down again until mid-afternoon.

'That's when I saw Monty coming back. It must have been around half past three. He stays in town for what he calls his lunch. It's mostly liquid and usually he has it in the White Hart. Sometimes in the Rose and Crown. That's how he spends his day, see? Mid-morning go into town. Mid-afternoon come back. He was carrying his supply of whisky in a plastic carrier bag.

I did wave to him yesterday, as it happens, but he didn't wave back. He's not sociable, as you might say.

'Next thing was, a couple of police cars went past and turned up there. So after that, I kept an eye out. That's how, later, I saw Mrs Harwell drive by in her little Mazda MX-5. I recognised the car first of all, because there isn't another blue one like that around here. I saw Mrs Harwell was driving and old Monty was sitting alongside her, looking pretty fed up. I thought, hello! Something's wrong. He wouldn't be leaving the place, otherwise. Monty and that old ruin of a house, it's like a tortoise and its shell. Take him out of it and he'll likely die. So then I decided to ring Gary Colley. Colleys are his neighbours and they might know something. I got young Gary on his mobile. He told me someone had found a stiff at Balaclava. Well, the dead 'un wasn't old Monty, because I'd seen him alive and well. So someone else had croaked, but don't expect me to tell you who.' Pascal thrust out his jaw pugnaciously.

Morton frowned. Gary, if he'd been telling the truth, should not yet have known anything about a dead body when Pascal rang him. Gary had told Jess Campbell he was on his way into town. According to Dave Colley, it was much later, early evening, long after Monty had been driven away, that Grandma C had walked up the lane and seen the hearse leave; and returned with the news to the rest of the family. That, so Dave reckoned, was the first they'd heard of a death. Blasted Colleys, fumed Morton silently, you couldn't rely on anything they said.

'Go on,' he said to Pascal.

'That's it,' the garage owner replied. 'Except that later on I saw the cop cars go by again, back into town.'

'Did you pass the news on before or after that?' Morton wanted to get his mental timetable straight before he tackled the Colleys again.

Pascal looked puzzled. 'Pass it on? Why do you keep saying I passed it on like I was the bloody town crier? I told Maureen and the boy, if that's what you mean.' He pointed to the window and the garage forecourt. 'That one, out there.'

Morton wondered briefly if 'the boy' had a name. 'No one else?' he prompted.

Pascal's brow cleared. 'Rosie Sneddon stopped by for petrol and I told her. Sneddon's Farm is further down the lane. I reckoned they'd want to know if anything odd was happening down the road from them. They're pretty isolated on the farm and if I hear someone is wandering around up to no good, or I see a dodgy-looking vagrant or two, well, I naturally let the Sneddons know of it. It's the neighbourly thing to do. I can't remember exactly what time I told her. But it was before the cop cars went past back into town. A quarter past six, something like that? Don't ask me to give you a closer guess than that.'

'Fair enough,' agreed Morton. There was no reason why Pascal should have checked the clock when he spoke to Rosie. His telling her the startling news was understandable, too. In country terms, the Sneddons were neighbours of the garage, itself quite isolated here on the roadside. 'They'd let you know, too?' he suggested. 'If they saw anything suspicious?'

Pascal nodded. 'Reckon they would.'

134

'Is your petrol station here open at night?'

Now Pascal shook his head firmly. 'No. We close at nine p.m. sharp weekdays, five p.m. on Sundays. If I were to stay open later than that I'd have to employ extra staff. My outgoings for wages are high enough already. I have to pay a chap to mind the till after Maureen's taken herself off home. Nine to five, she works, days. He works evenings, five to nine. That's only half the hours but he seems to think he ought to be paid the same as her. He says it's because he works unsocial hours. But there you are, nobody works for peanuts these days. Even that lad out there expects a decent wage, for all he's learning a trade here, too. Besides, we wouldn't do much business after that time of night. It wouldn't be cost effective. Sundays I have to manage on my own unless my sister-in-law can come in for a couple of hours.'

'You don't live here, or near here?' The business did not appear to have any accommodation attached but there might be a cottage tucked away at the rear.

But Pascal was shaking his head. 'I live five miles away in Weston St Ambrose; so does Maureen – and the boy. Nobody lives around here except down in Toby's Gutter Lane and that's only Colleys, Sneddons and old Monty.'

'You say,' Morton began, and Pascal began to look a little apprehensive again, 'that you and the Sneddons operate a sort of neighbourhood watch scheme. You phone them, or let them know, of anything unusual hereabouts, and they'd do the same for you. Neither Mr or Mrs Sneddon has phoned you about a car?'

Pascal shook his dark head slowly. 'No. What car would that be?'

'Last night Mr Sneddon woke to hear a car being driven past his farm, on Toby's Gutter Lane, very late. It was going towards Shooter's Wood. Then he fell asleep again. This morning he discovered someone, joyriders or others, had pushed a car down into the old quarry, just beyond the woodland, and torched it. I've been down in the quarry and had a look at it myself. It's still smouldering.'

'Is it, now?' said Pascal, after a pause. 'Little buggers, those joyriding kids. No, they didn't call me about that. They might have done any other time, mind you. Any funny business with cars is of interest to me! But very likely they didn't bother, not with the other news to think about, the business at Balaclava.'

'Probably,' Morton agreed amiably. 'Mrs Sneddon apparently didn't hear the car during the night. Only her husband did.'

The garage owner was showing signs of impatience. 'I don't know what all this is about. Asking me about Balaclava makes sense, yes. Asking me about a car that was torched in the middle of last night when I wasn't here and no one told me about before you came in here, that doesn't make sense to me at all. Yesterday I told Rosie – Mrs Sneddon – I'd seen poor old Monty driven off by that tough cookie of a niece of his, and that there was a stiff found at his house. That's what I knew. Now you tell me about a burned-out car, dumped by some joyriders from town, and expect me to know about that, too. Well, I don't.'

'If they were joyriders,' Morton went on imperturbably, 'and they torched the car they'd taken in the quarry, they had a long walk back home, didn't they? Assuming they came from town?'

'They'd have to come from town,' said Pascal immediately. 'They didn't come from Weston St Ambrose. I'm not saying we don't have our tearaways there, but I'd know if someone had had a car stolen yesterday. It's only a village and news gets around. Someone would've told me about it last night when I got home, or this morning, as I was getting ready to leave.'

He paused and screwed up his face in thought. 'You're right, though. Whoever took it, had to get home.' His expression brightened. 'Here, perhaps they had two cars. Pete thought he heard one car but he was half asleep, you said, so perhaps there were two? The thieves torched one and they all piled into the other and drove it back to town, where they dumped it somewhere else. Why don't you ask your uniform lot if any cars have been reported stolen or if any other car has been found dumped?'

'We'll be doing that,' Morton told him. 'Well, that's all for now, Mr Pascal. Thank you very much for your help.' Morton closed his notebook, to Pascal's evident relief. 'If I think of anything else, I'll be in touch.'

Pascal stopped looking relieved. 'It's nothing to do with me,' he said.

Outside the boy had disappeared. 'Don't worry, my son,' murmured Morton. 'I've got an eye on you. You needn't bother hiding away!'

Pascal watched his visitor go from within his minimart. After a glance to check that Maureen was safely busy, he went back to his office and quietly closed the door. He picked up the phone. A brief conversation followed, finishing with Pascal saying irritably, 'Of course I didn't say anything! Do you think I'm daft or something? No, I can't do anything about it. I can't get in there. The police will have sealed it off. I'm not breaking in, if the cops come back, they'd realise it. No – *no* – we'll just have to hope no one finds it.'

He replaced the receiver and stood, staring down at it. 'Damn . . .' he said softly.

They had ended the day still not knowing the identity of their corpse but Carter had been cautiously optimistic that they soon would.

'Probably someone will come forward tomorrow or the day after,' he said to Jess as they left the building that evening and headed towards the car park. 'A well-dressed, well-set-up bloke like that, someone's got to miss him.'

Jess hadn't mentioned to him that Morton had been far less optimistic.

'He might be a foreigner,' the sergeant had said gloomily earlier.

'His clothes look as if they were bought here,' said Jess, 'although, I admit, it's hard to tell from the labels nowadays. Everything's made abroad. But they look English.'

Morton had stuck to his theory. 'He could still be a foreigner. The country is full of people who've arrived fairly recently. So he's bought himself a set of togs since arriving. He decided he wanted to blend in.'

'Is this your idea or Milada's?' asked Jess, referring to Morton's Czech girlfriend.

'I don't discuss my work with Milada,' retorted Morton loftily.

Jess had grinned and Morton stalked off homeward in a huff.

Now she was home herself, letting herself into her Cheltenham flat with a sigh of relief. Sometimes she regretted living a solitary life. One of the drawbacks was having to defend it constantly to her mother. But then, her mother couldn't understand Jess's wish to join the police force. When she moved to CID and announced it proudly down the phone in a call home, her news was met with a wail of dismay. Her promotion to inspector was grudgingly approved but only to be followed by, 'It's all very well getting to a senior position, Jessica, but it will frighten a lot of men off.' Jess's reply, that 'they must be pretty insecure sort of men, then', did not find favour. 'You were always one for the clever answer,' said her mother, adding, 'and see where it's got you!' It was easy, Jess thought, to sympathise with Tansy.

But tonight, coming into the quiet flat, with everything just as she'd left it that morning, she savoured her pressure-free solitary home life after a busy and often frustrating day. Her pleasure was cut short when she saw the red light on the phone blinking an ominous welcome.

'Not work . . .' she groaned, pressing the 'Play' button. It wouldn't be the first time she'd been called out again straight away.

'Hi, Jess!' said Tom Palmer's recorded voice cheerfully. 'Fancy going out for a pint and a curry? Or, failing that, a bowl of pasta and a glass of wine?'

She could easily ring and tell him no. Tom wouldn't be offended. Theirs wasn't that sort of relationship. But maybe Tom had had a gruesome day's work and needed to unwind. He, too, lived alone. A friend in need is a friend indeed, as the saying went.

Jess called the pathologist's mobile number. 'Got your message,' she told him. 'Yes, I would. I'd prefer Italian tonight, I think. Where?'

'Meet you at the usual place in The Promenade in about an hour?'

An hour later, Jess had showered and changed. Generally revitalised, she was sitting opposite Tom at an outside table, studying the menu. It wasn't quite as warm for outside dining as it ought to have been, but it was still a fine evening. People were strolling by and the little tables under the trees looked so attractive, they'd decided to go for it. Tom, his mop of black hair tousled as he rubbed it as an aid to concentration, was inclined to a pasta option. Jess, who ate quite a lot of pasta in her flat, this being one of the few things she could cook (and in a hurry), was tempted towards the *pollo alla griglia*.

Most people, seeing them, would have assumed them to be a couple. But they weren't. They were, as Tom had once put it, 'fellow refugees'. The brutal fact was that Jess's occupation (face it, her mother was right) made a lot of people uneasy. So did his. Both of them found it stymied social chitchat to a remarkable degree.

'I can understand it, in my case,' Tom had confessed. 'What do you do for a living? they ask me merrily. "I dissect corpses,"

I tell them. That's when they start sidling away from me and reaching for the garlic.'

'In my case,' Jess had explained, 'they think I'm hell bent on ferreting out their secrets. I've come to the conclusion that half the population harbours guilty knowledge.'

The result had been a friendship of colleagues that worked extremely well. The one thing Jess was determined on was that her mother should never find out about it. Seeing them here for example (God forbid!), she would scent romance. But it's not romance, she thought wryly; I only hope it never becomes desperation. (Although that was unfair to Tom, who was excellent company.)

When they'd ordered, Tom raised his glass of wine. 'Cheers!' Jess responded.

'I'm not going to talk shop.' Tom set down his glass. 'But with regard to that stiff you called me out to yesterday . . .'

Jess groaned. 'Go on . . .' Then she brightened. 'Hey? Do you know already what he died of?'

'I'm not certain yet. But I think – I am fairly sure – it was from a combination of pills and alcohol. Also there are early signs of heart disease. He probably didn't know about that himself yet, but it would have made him vulnerable. I've sent some samples over to the lab and I'll have to wait for them to come back to me. But all the indications are there. He'd had a really good meal very shortly before he died. Beef and vegetables in a wine sauce, boeuf bourguignon or something like that. He hadn't had any time at all, hardly, to begin digesting it. The whole thing was sitting in his stomach—'

'Tom!' begged Jess. 'We are going to eat soon.'

'Sorry, well, what I mean is, something with a strong flavour. If it were doctored, he wouldn't have noticed. I toss this in as an observation rather than a suggestion. I'm not attempting to do your job.'

'Aha!' Jess looked thoughtful. 'He was poisoned, is what you're saying. You thought that when you first saw him.'

'Thought you'd be interested, Sherlock. He could, of course, have taken the pills himself.'

'He'd probably have gone to bed with a bottle of whisky and the pills, if he meant to do that. I don't see him sitting down to French cuisine,' Jess objected. 'Although I realise that, if he wasn't thinking straight, he might have done almost anything.'

'Well, you work it out. But there's another thing . . .' Tom looked slightly embarrassed. 'I've been turning over in my mind whether to mention this to you. I think I recognise his face, well, sort of.'

'Tom!' Jess squawked. 'Why didn't you phone through earlier?'

'Hold on, it's not so simple. As soon as I saw him on that sofa, I thought, Hello! I've seen you before, chum. But I don't know where, that's the problem. I can't place him. You know how it is with a face that seems familiar but you can't put it in context. It was recent, or fairly recently. I've run through in my mind all the places I've been and haven't been able to come up with a location. It's definitely not work-related. It's been nagging at me. But all I can say is I've seen him but I don't know where. As for his name, I don't think I ever knew that.'

'Was this sighting local?' Jess pressed.

'Well, maybe. It would still have to be somewhere I don't usually go. That narrows the field. I hardly ever,' said Tom phlegmatically, 'party. Being jammed in an overheated room or club in a press of people who are all getting steadily drunk, yelling to make myself heard over horrible music, and totally unable to make out what's being said to me – it's not my idea of fun.'

'The mind boggles, Mr Palmer, at the idea of the sort of party you get invited to!' she told him.

'OK, if you're hell-bent on going upmarket, I don't like standing around in my one and only decent suit and a tie, holding a glass of plonk and being offered nothing to eat but peanuts and canapés that have been in the fridge all day and gone soggy. I dislike crowds. It's one of the reasons I go on walking holidays and it's one of the reasons I actually like my job.'

'The corpses don't answer back or spill beer over you?' she suggested. I must be getting light-headed, she thought. It's the wine on an empty stomach. Bring on the food!

'I'm not a nutter,' he argued, 'I don't talk to the subjects I'm investigating. I examine them at the behest of you and others like you. I try to find out how they spent their last hours and I try, as far as it's possible, to treat their mortal remains with respect.'

'Sorry,' she apologised. 'So you haven't seen our victim – when he was alive – in a social context.'

'I don't think so . . .' Tom still sounded uncertain. More firmly he added, 'I haven't seen him in a work context, for sure. I can't

143

think, for the life of me, where I *have* seen him. But I do know I have seen that face recently, so there.'

The food arrived and Tom's attention slipped away.

Jess couldn't dismiss the subject so quickly. 'Seen him on television?' she asked eagerly.

He paused in painstakingly twirling spaghetti round his fork. 'Nope. Don't think so.'

'In the newspapers?' Jess cast about furiously for where Tom might have spotted a similar face.

He frowned. 'Ah . . . no . . . don't think so. Pretty sure not.'

Jess made a last throw of the dice. 'He's not someone you've met up with on one of your hikes?'

Tom shook his head. 'No, I did think of that and decided he wasn't. He didn't look like a rambler or walker of any sort. Too flabby. All I can say with reasonable certainty is: I saw his mug recently. I'll keep trying. It will come to me. But not right now. How's your chicken?'

Jess recognised the subject of the victim was closed. 'Let me know,' she said, 'the moment you remember, won't you?'

'Um . . .' was the reply through a mouthful of pasta, accompanied by vigorous nodding.

With that, she had to be content.

Chapter 9

They gathered in Carter's office the following morning to discuss their progress, or lack of it. It was the third day of their investigation and a critical moment. From now on, the trail would grow colder.

Jess set the ball rolling, describing her visit to Bridget Harwell's home. Morton then contributed a breakdown of his activities the previous day, his conversations with the Colleys, Sneddons and Seb Pascal, the discovery of the burned-out wreck in the quarry, and gave his conclusions.

'I don't trust any of the Colleys. That doesn't mean they've got anything to do with this case. That sort never gives you a straight answer and, because of that, you can never rule them out of an investigation. Time wasters, probably.'

Morton snorted. 'Take young Gary. He says he went into town after he left us outside the gates of Balaclava House. He also says he phoned his family on his mobile to tell them something was going on involving Monty Bickerstaffe, whom he'd seen sitting in a police car. His dad, Dave Colley, says that in the early evening his old mother went snooping around up the lane and saw the private ambulance leave, so they learned someone had died. But Seb Pascal, the garage owner, says he saw Monty being driven away by Mrs Harwell, long before that. He immediately phoned Gary who told him about the death. But that must have been before Mrs Colley senior went to spy out the land. Gary shouldn't have known about a body at Balaclava. All he saw was Monty being helped into a police car. He stopped and asked one of the uniformed men about it and, when we came out of the house, spoke to me and to Inspector Campbell. We sent him on his way.'

'For my money,' said Jess, 'he didn't go into town. He doubled back over the fields and watched what was going on at Balaclava. He made his own deductions and took the news to his family. That would explain the discrepancy. His grandma doesn't come into it.'

'So Gary bends the truth,' Carter had commented. He rubbed a finger over his chin thoughtfully. 'The Colleys, as a family unit, bend the truth. Does it, in this case, matter? Or are we being led down a road going nowhere?'

'Probably,' was Morton's prompt reply. 'It's what I said about the Colleys. They just can't tell you the simple truth; and because you know they're not telling it straight, you waste time on them. I'll talk to Gary again, try and shake him up a bit. If he's messing us around, he'll find out he made a mistake!'

'Have we got anything on any of the Colleys?' Carter asked.

'Organising illegal hare-coursing,' said Morton. 'Both Dave and Gary were fined. Plus, in Gary's case, driving with an out-of-date tax disc. Someone ought to check whether either of them holds a valid gun licence. If they do, perhaps they shouldn't. The daughter, Tracy Colley, was selling pirated DVDs around the pubs a couple of years ago. She was helping out a man friend. The man friend was convicted. She was cautioned. Mrs Maggie Colley has twice been up before the magistrates for being drunk and disorderly in local pubs. Even the elder Mrs Colley's got a record. She punched another old woman in a post office queue. The police were called; she refused to leave, became abusive and then threw another punch at one of the constables. It took two burly coppers to haul her out. Remarkable for her age. They're a lovely family, all round, and well known to the local police. But they're not the Mafia.'

'Sneddon?' asked Jess.

Morton shook his head. 'Hard-working, law-abiding local farmers. I looked up Seb Pascal, the chap who keeps the petrol station, for good measure. Nothing is known against him, either. He did seem uneasy when I walked into his garage minimart and showed my ID. But a lot of people do. It doesn't mean they're guilty of anything. He's got a shaven-headed yob cleaning cars for him. He didn't like my turning up, but I doubt he's into anything big time.'

'So,' Jess said, 'we're looking for joyriders who went down Toby's Gutter Lane very late the night before last. The police had left Balaclava House and the Sneddons had gone to bed. It's quite possible the car has nothing to do with our dead man. On the other hand, it seems a bit of a coincidence. We do need to find whoever was driving it. Local police are helping, but so far without luck. No one has reported a car being stolen and that, in itself, is odd. You know, Tansy Peterson, Bridget Harwell's daughter, said something to me about whoever was responsible being someone driving through. As she pointed out, Balaclava House is tucked away on that narrow lane, but it isn't remote from civilisation. The lane is just off a main road. Plus we have yet to establish how our dead man got to Balaclava House.'

'The burned-out car has to have come from outside the area,' agreed Morton, nodding. 'The wreck's being examined and I'm waiting on a phone call. If you'll excuse me a tick, sir, I'll call the forensic boys and ask how they're getting on.'

He went outside the room into the corridor. They could hear his voice murmuring into his mobile.

'The dead man must be missed somewhere by now,' Carter fretted. 'What about appointments, business meetings? Hadn't he a wife or partner, a secretary, anyone at all?'

The door opened and Morton stuck his head through. 'Not much joy yet. They are pretty sure the car is – or was before someone got happy with a box of matches – a Lexus.'

'A Lexus!' exclaimed Carter so loudly that the other two stared at him in surprise.

'It is just possible,' he said more calmly, 'that we might have a lead at last.'

Sometimes hard graft got you a little further on in an investigation: endless interviews, routine elimination of possibilities, and meticulous reconstruction of events. Sometimes, just very occasionally, you had a bit of luck.

So Ian Carter was telling himself as he drove, once more, towards Weston St Ambrose, this time with Jess Campbell for company. Neither of them had expected to be making the journey this morning, but that was detection work for you. The identification of the wreckage as belonging to a Lexus might be the key to open the door. It might be leading them up the garden path. There was only one way to find out and they were taking it.

'Hope for the best and prepare for the worst,' he informed Jess. 'William of Orange is supposed to have said that,' he added helpfully.

'And did he really?' asked Jess.

'It's disputed.'

'Oh.' They were progressing at a crawl, slowed by a tractor making a stately progress ahead of them along the narrow twisting road.

'That room upstairs at Balaclava,' Jess reminded him. 'The one so nice and clean but used recently. That ties into the mix somewhere. I mean, I know it would be good to know who the owner of the burned-out car is. But somehow or other, we have to find out who has been using that room and exactly when.'

The tractor turned off at last into a field. Carter accelerated. 'We do need to find out about the mystery visitors, I agree. But let's get this car business sorted first. Perhaps this is a wasted journey. But it's got to be made and the Hemmingses have to be questioned about it. What's the worst? They may know nothing about it and their missing guest may have contacted them to say he had to fly to New York at short notice, or some such reason for his absence. Then we can rule him and them out.'

'The worst would be, I suppose, if neither of the Hemmingses is at home this morning,' observed Jess. I'm beginning to sound like Phil Morton, she thought. I mustn't start being negative.

'Billy might not be, but we might strike lucky with Terri. That's why I've brought you along.' Carter added hastily, 'It is your case and if this does lead to identifying our corpse, you need to be there.'

'I'm not coming along to protect you from Terri Hemmings, then, sir?' Jess risked asking. Carter had given her a brief but vivid description of the lady.

'No!' he said sharply. Then he relaxed. 'Although it is just possible that she might get the wrong idea if I turn up alone.' He allowed himself a smile. 'Or worse, Billy might.'

'Yes, sir.'

Carter cleared his throat. 'Of course, I'm aware it could just be coincidence that the wreckage is that of a Lexus. Some coppers don't believe in that sort of luck. In my experience it happens all the time, and usually turns out not to be quite as coincidental as it first looks. The Hemmingses expected a guest driving a Lexus at the old schoolhouse the evening of the day the body was discovered. The guest didn't turn up. Nor, by the time I arrived outside the house, had this mysterious guest sent any message. Of course, he may have turned up at the party twenty minutes after I left, although I didn't pass a Lexus being driven towards Weston St Ambrose. Or, as I was saying, he may have sent a message or phoned to explain his absence. In either case, he's not missing and we can cross him off the list. But, I repeat, we have to check it out.'

*   *   *

The dogs were Jack Russell terriers. As Jess and Carter got out of the car before the old schoolhouse, they set up a noisy barking that brought Terri Hemmings, in tight white jeans and clinging T-shirt, to her front door. The terriers rushed past her to the gate and began jumping up at the newcomers. Terri peered towards them in a way that made Jess wonder if she were just a little short-sighted but too vain to admit it.

'Oh,' she said at last, recognising Ian Carter, 'it's you again.'

'Can we come in and speak to you, Mrs Hemmings?' he asked politely.

'If you must, I suppose,' was her unenthusiastic reply. 'Although I don't know what you want. Hang on; I'll shut the dogs in. They won't bite but they get under your feet.'

She called the two terriers and, with some difficulty, chivvied them indoors. She then disappeared and returned a few minutes later.

'You can come in now,' she invited. From behind her muffled, frustrated barking indicated the dogs had been shut in a back room.

'She's phoned her husband to let him know we're here, what do you think?' whispered Jess.

'I think you're right. I wonder how long we've got with Terri before Billy comes storming in?'

Terri was beckoning them indoors with scarlet fingernails. She had decided to be gracious, or had received instructions down the phone to be so.

'We'll go into the sun lounge,' she suggested. 'It's nicer there on mornings like this, when it's a bit cool, but sunny. We spend a lot of time in the sun lounge, Billy and me. We like the sun. We've got a little place in Marbella and we'll be going there soon for a couple of weeks, now the evenings are turning so chilly here. We're going to retire there one day. I can't wait.'

She teetered ahead of them on stiletto heels ill suited to country living and they followed, both taking a good look around them.

Jess thought the house fascinating. Like many an old building adapted to residential use from something quite different, the old schoolhouse was full of oddities. The doorways were wider than normal, to allow for the passage of a mob of little bodies. The windowsills were too high and the windows themselves reached nearly to ceiling height. There was a solidity to the inner walls quite unlike anything in a modern construction. They were as good as soundproof. It wasn't difficult to imagine a lingering whiff of chalk and sweaty gym shoes. As regarded colour schemes, Terri's liking for white and pale colours generally extended to the walls, paintwork and furnishings. They glimpsed white leather sofas, oatmeal shades of carpet and floor-length curtains of ivory damask.

The sun lounge, when they reached it, turned out to be a huge glass extension running along almost the whole width of the building. The floor tiles were of mottled grey and white. The bamboo-framed furnishings were upholstered with thick cream-coloured cushions only faintly patterned in rose pink and pale turquoise. There was a white-painted cane lounger. A few pot plants were dotted around but theirs was a token presence. The whole effect was curiously sterile.

'Coffee?' asked Terri brightly and, before they could refuse, went on, 'Make yourself comfy, won't you? Won't be a tick!'

She disappeared again, clacking across the tiles on her stilettos.

Jess and Carter took seats on the fat pale cushions and looked at one another. 'She's playing for time,' Jess whispered.

'That suggests to me that Billy isn't far away,' he returned. 'What's the betting he'll come barrelling in here in –' he consulted his wristwatch – 'about fifteen minutes' time.'

The Jack Russells were still setting up a noisy protest at being shut in. They could hear Terri calling out to them. 'All right, boys, it won't be long.'

Five minutes later, during which time Jess noticed that Carter was getting increasingly restive, Terri tottered back, bearing a tray with the coffee things. She set it down on a glass-topped table.

'Here we are!' she announced.

As she spoke, they heard the sound of a car drawing up outside. They were not even to get fifteen minutes with Terri. Carter showed his frustration.

'Well, isn't that nice?' said Terri, without bothering to go and see who the new arrival might be. 'Here's Billy, just in time for coffee. *We're in the sun lounge, darling!*'

The last phrase was unexpectedly yelled full volume. Both her visitors jumped and the invisible terriers started barking again. Terri poured coffee and passed them a cup each, smiling serenely at them as she did so. Thus they were both at the disadvantage of balancing a full cup of hot liquid when Billy Hemmings appeared.

153

Jess saw a large, red-faced man. He was a good few years older than his wife, as testified to by his balding head and the grizzled grey fringe of remaining hair surrounding the shiny, sunburned area. His jawline had lost its youthful tautness, jowls forming. His stomach protruded in an arc above the tight band of his jeans. His shirtsleeves were rolled up to reveal hairy muscular forearms and a very expensive-looking gold wristwatch; but the backs of his hands were wrinkling and showed age spots. He was annoyed.

'So, what's all this, then?' he demanded, standing over his visitors. 'I can't have the cops drawing up to the house every five minutes! What'll the neighbours think?'

Carter had already passed on to Jess Monica Farrell's opinion of the Hemmingses. She repressed a smile.

'Have a biscuit?' invited Terri then, proffering a plate.

'This is Inspector Campbell,' Carter introduced Jess. 'My name is Carter, Superintendent Carter. You remember me from the other evening, of course. We don't want to take up much of your time. Mrs Hemmings has been most hospitable . . .'

Terri beamed above the rim of her coffee cup.

'But this shouldn't take long. The evening before last, when I stopped for a moment outside here to admire your home . . .'

'It is nice, isn't it?' said Terri.

Her husband glared at her.

'You appeared to be expecting a guest who would be driving a Lexus. Is that right?'

Terri opened her mouth, intercepted another hard look from her spouse, and closed it again. She took a biscuit and bit into it. Apparently, her part in the conversation was over.

154

'So what? What's it got to do with you?' asked Billy Hemmings.

'We're wondering if your visitor arrived safely.'

'Police matter, is it?' Hemmings was sarcastic now. 'Worried about one person missing from our dinner table?'

'No, concerned about a missing Lexus. Did the guest arrive?'

Hemmings surveyed Carter, glanced briefly at Jess, and then turned his attention back to the superintendent. 'As a matter of fact, no, he didn't. But I want to know why *you're* so curious about it; and I'm not answering any more of your questions until you explain yourselves a bit better. Neither is my wife,' he added.

Terri, with a mouthful of chocolate digestive, could only nod her agreement.

Carter nodded. 'Fair enough. The burned wreck of a Lexus car has been found in a disused quarry about five miles from here, on the other side of a local landmark called Shooter's Hill. We believe, from a witness's statement, that it was dumped and torched there the same night as your dinner party, but much later, around midnight. We want to trace the owner.'

'Jay's car!' squeaked Terri. 'Don't say poor Jay has had an accident! Is that why he didn't turn up for our party? Oh, Billy, isn't it awful?'

Hemmings turned to her. 'Why don't you take the dogs for a walk across the road, in the churchyard,' he suggested. 'It's distracting, having them barking away all the time.'

'Oh, all right,' said Terri resentfully. She departed and the terriers were heard making a noisy exit from their prison. Shortly thereafter the front door slammed.

'Now then,' said Hemmings. He lowered himself heavily on

to the chair vacated by his wife. 'What's it all about? Is the wreck Jay Taylor's car?'

'We don't know. But it's a coincidence. You say Taylor didn't arrive that evening. Did he phone? Send a text message or email? Anything to explain his absence?'

Hemmings shook his head. 'No, and it is odd, I'll admit that. I've been trying to get in touch with him, but no joy. He's not answering his home phone or his mobile.' He pulled at the lobe of one ear and squinted at them appraisingly. 'He might have gone up to London, business reasons, or decided to take a few days off, like anyone might.'

Jess took out her notebook. 'The gentleman's name is Jay Taylor, you say?'

'Yeah . . .' Hemmings frowned. 'His real name is Gerald, but everyone calls him Jay.'

'You've got his address? You say you have contact numbers for him?'

'Got his business card, somewhere . . .' Hemmings lumbered towards the door and disappeared. A few moments later he was back, holding out a small white card. 'There you go. Got all his details on that.'

Jess took the card and tucked it safely away. Hemmings seated himself again and leaned forward, resting his hairy forearms on his knees.

'There's more to it than a burned-out car,' he said. 'A couple of senior coppers like you two don't turn up checking out something like that. Local police do that. Joyriders, probably. If you think that car might be Jay's – and it's the only thing on your mind – you'd go chasing after him. You wouldn't come bothering us. You've got something else worrying you. What's up? Can't you find him, either? Why are you looking for him?'

Jess glanced at Carter, who said, 'Yes, we do have something else worrying us. We have an as-yet unidentified body. That's why we'd like to know if Mr Taylor turned up at your dinner party in the end, or whether you'd heard from him with his excuses, anything at all. But you say you haven't been able to make contact and that, naturally, fuels our interest.'

Hemmings let out a long, low whistle. He leaned back and the bamboo chair creaked beneath his weight. 'So that's it.'

'Have you known Mr Taylor a long time?' Jess asked.

'A couple of years.' Hemmings answered her question but he was still looking at Carter.

Carter was examining the business card. 'This doesn't actually state Mr Taylor's line of work.'

Hemmings grinned. 'Yeah, well, Jay writes those books, don't he? For the football stars and people you see on the telly.'

There was a puzzled silence. Then Jess had a brainwave.

'Do you mean, Mr Taylor is – possibly was – a *ghost writer*?'

'That's it.' Hemmings nodded approvingly at her. 'All these well-known people who write books about themselves, well, they don't always *write* them in the sense of doing the actual work. Someone else does that. I can understand that. I sometimes think I've got a lot of good ideas for a book. But I know I couldn't put the thing together. That's where Jay comes in. Jay can write you anything. You just tell him what you want; he does his research and writes the book. He started out as a journalist, he told me once. But then he found there was work a-plenty for ghosts. Literary ghost, he called himself.'

'Mr Hemmings,' Carter said, 'I wonder if we might ask your help. We're hindered considerably by not knowing the identity of the body—'

Hemmings interrupted him. 'I've got a photo of him, if you want to wait. I can look it out easy enough. Terri keeps a big album and sticks snaps in it all the time. Don't know why she bothers, myself. I'll fetch it.'

'He's being quite helpful . . .' Jess murmured to Carter as Hemmings disappeared yet again.

'He wants to know what's going on. He hasn't asked us *where* Jay Taylor's body was found – if our corpse is Jay. I didn't say the body was *in* the car and he hasn't asked if it was yet. Don't you think that would be the obvious question? Something's been going on . . .'

Hemmings was back carrying a large white leather photograph album. He opened it out and held it towards them. 'There you go. Cheltenham Races, last year. That's Jay with Terri. He's looking pleased with himself because he's had a good win. He took us off to dinner that evening on the strength of it.'

So Monty was right, thought Jess, about the dead man looking as if he belonged on a racetrack.

'Jess?' Carter turned the album towards her.

Terri, in the photograph, wore a large and no doubt expensive hat. She was smiling happily and held a raised champagne flute towards the camera. The man standing beside her was so obviously full of life that it was difficult to connect him with the stiffening corpse on Monty's sofa. Death drains away all personality. Features lose their expression and become just a nose, a mouth. The person who dwelt in that body has quitted the outer husk and gone on somewhere else. Yet this could well be the same man, here in this photo, as he'd once been. The face was beaming, the hair slightly dishevelled; he'd obviously had a drink or two. The expression 'flushed with success' couldn't be better illustrated. Moreover, although boyish good looks had given way to a mature solidity, he was still a handsome man.

'This does look like him.' She hesitated. 'But not enough for me to swear to it right now. May I keep the photo for a while? You'll get it back.'

'Feel free,' Hemmings said. He leaned back in the creaking chair and folded his hands on his ample stomach. 'Jay Taylor, eh? Who'd have thought it?'

'We can't be sure, not just from comparison with this photo,' Jess warned.

'What sort of state is this body of yours in?' asked Hemmings suddenly. He squinted at them. 'Burned or what? Was he in the car?'

'Not in the car, not burned and in a good state.'

Hemmings sighed. 'Then I'll come and take a look at the poor bloke.'

Carter quickly masked his surprise. 'That's very good of you, Mr Hemmings.'

Carter is right to be surprised, thought Jess. Few people volunteer to view a corpse. Hemmings is worried about something and it's not just the possibility of a racing crony having died. He wants to be sure; he wants to see that body for himself.

'So, if you're free, we can go now?' she suggested.

Hemmings nodded. 'I'm doing this voluntarily, right? There'll be no nonsense about cautioning me.'

'It doesn't apply in these circumstances,' Carter assured him.

'I'm doing my duty,' said Hemmings virtuously, 'like, being a good citizen.'

Jess, removing the photograph carefully from the album, avoided Carter's gaze.

Later they were all three standing outside the morgue in the welcome fresh air, away from the chemical smells that never quite disguise the odour of death. Hemmings had lit a cigarette and was pulling on it thoughtfully. Beneath his tan his skin was pale. He looked older.

It had not been a wasted journey after all. The Lexus had been the key Carter had hoped for. Thanks to Billy Hemmings, they had learned the dead man was Gerald, known as Jay, Taylor, professional literary ghost and now, in one of those macabre twists of fate, departed to the great beyond to be an unseen presence for ever.

Hemmings had identified the body at once and confidently. Then his confidence had evaporated and he'd muttered, 'Bloody hell . . .' before turning away, and blundering out of the door.

'A nasty business for you,' Jess said sympathetically to him now. 'But we're very grateful. Thank you.'

Hemmings expelled smoke in her direction and looked her

up and down as if seeing her for the first time. 'Right,' he said.

'Could you tell us a bit more about Mr Taylor? Do you know if he had any steady girlfriend? There must be someone we can contact.'

Hemmings rallied. This was a question he was happy to answer. 'Girlfriends? Jay had dozens of them. Don't ask me to name any. They came and went. He was strictly a love-them-and-leave-them man. He always had some piece of totty on his arm.' Hemmings gestured with the cigarette in a wide arc through the air. 'No tarts, mind you. No "models" or "actresses" or whatever they usually call themselves. He moved in racing circles and you meet every sort, doing that. High and low in society.' A jab of the cigarette, this time in Carter's direction. '"I look for breeding in my ladies like I look for breeding in a racehorse," that's what he used to say.'

Charming guy . . . thought Jess sarcastically.

'The day the race meeting photo was taken, did Taylor have a companion with him, at the races?'

'No, he was on his own that day. I think Terri did ask him about his girlfriends and he made a bit of a joke about having split up from the last one and being a free man again. But that was Jay for you.'

Hemmings had paused for a decent moment of grief. 'Poor bugger, and there he is, cold as a cod on a fishmonger's slab. It makes you think.'

It makes *you* think, thought Jess. Thinking is what you're doing now, on your feet.

'The girlfriends?' she prompted rather sharply. Carter gave her a warning glance.

'What? Oh, yeah. Well, we would all pull his leg about it, mind you. "One of these days you'll meet your match," I used to say. You ask Terri. She'll remember me saying it. "Then," I'd tell him, "it'll be down the aisle with pictures of the happy day in one of those celebrity magazines."'

Hemmings shook his head mournfully. '"Not me, Billy-boy," he'd answer. "They won't pin me down." Well, he's pinned down now, as you might say. Poor devil, he won't be watching any more winners pass the post.'

'Did he gamble heavily at the races?' Carter asked.

Hemmings shrugged. 'He liked a flutter, like anyone does. Well, all right, since he's gone, I can tell you he used to put quite a packet on a horse he fancied. Then it was win some, lose some. But look, that was the advantage for him in not having a wife and kids. Any money in his pocket was his to spend however he wanted.' A note of bitterness entered Hemmings's voice. 'There was no one wanting a ruddy great conservatory built on to a house, that sort of thing.'

They murmured understandingly and Hemmings finally came round to the questions he had been careful not to ask so far.

'How did he die? Was it in a car smash or what? Where did you find him? Was it near Weston St Ambrose? Was poor old Jay on his way to our dinner party?'

Jess answered. 'We don't have the results of the post-mortem yet. Nor do we have any kind of timetable for his actions that day. But the body was found well away from the car at a place called Balaclava House.'

She and Carter both waited.

There was a silence. Hemmings dropped his cigarette stub on the ground and stepped on the glowing end. 'Never heard of it,' he said.

'He's lying,' said Jess firmly, when Hemmings had driven away. 'He didn't ask where Balaclava House is, or what kind of place it is. He's heard of it before, all right.'

'He's a tough nut, our Billy-boy,' mused Carter. 'But this has shaken him. There's certainly something he could tell us, but won't.'

'I could tackle the wife on her own, if I can work it,' offered Jess.

'She won't talk unless he gives her permission and as soon as he gets home now, he'll be telling her to keep shtum. I doubt she knows anything about his business deals, in any case. I wonder where he and Taylor met? On the racecourse, probably. Well, we know where our man lived from his business card. We'll have to get over there and take a look at the place.'

There was a movement behind them and they turned to find Tom Palmer had come out of the building and joined them.

'I was waiting until that bloke had gone,' he said. 'Bit of a thug, wasn't he? I do have results back from the lab. It was as I suspected. The victim was killed by a massive overdose of painkillers and booze. They would have knocked out a horse. He had a creaky heart as well.' Tom pulled a face. 'If you ask me, someone doctored his last lunch.'

Chapter 10

This time, when Phil Morton arrived at the five-barred gate marking the frontier between the Colleys and the rest of the world, no one appeared. When he got out of his car and listened, not only was there no Grandma Colley to reassure him the dogs were penned, no barking could be heard either. Morton opened the gate, got back in his car and drove on to the property. He halted so he could close the gate, all the while listening, at first in nervous anticipation and then in puzzlement. Where were the faithful hounds? He drove on slowly along the track until he reached the jumble of buildings, glancing at the dog compound as he passed by. It was empty. Wherever they were, the dogs were loose and it wasn't a comforting thought. But they weren't in this yard. That appeared as eerily deserted as the *Marie Celeste*.

Morton tapped the horn lightly twice. In response, Tracy Colley appeared at the cottage door, scowled in his direction, and plodded across. She was dressed as before in unflattering leggings and a voluminous smock top. She had done something to her hair. It was now streaked with scarlet. She surely didn't imagine it made her look any better? They ought to get Tracy on one of those make-over programmes on the television, thought Morton. She'd present them with a real challenge.

'What do you want this time?' enquired Tracy inhospitably.

'To see your brother, is he here?'

'Whaffor?' demanded Tracy.

'Just a chat. Is he here?'

'Round the back with his horses,' Tracy admitted. She indicated the rear of the cottage with a backward jerk of her thumb.

'Thanks,' said Morton drily. 'And the dogs?'

A malicious grin flickered across Tracy's doughy features. 'You don't have to worry about them. Dad's taken them for a run across Shooter's Hill. They wouldn't hurt you, them dogs. You don't need to be afraid of 'em. They only bark. That's their job, innit? To let us know we've got visitors.'

Morton wondered how many visitors the Colleys got. No one who didn't need to come here on business as he had, he fancied. Under Tracy's scornful gaze he got out of the car for the second time and made his way to the rear of the property. Gary was feeding his horses some fodder in a bucket.

Morton called his name. Gary turned and, identifying him, came towards the fence. Both horses followed: when he got there, they formed up to flank their owner on either side so that the trio stood in a row to stare at Morton enquiringly.

'Got time for a word, Gary?' asked Morton pleasantly. One of the horses blew noisily down its nostrils at him.

'What's up?' Gary showed no sign of leaving the field and the conversation was obviously to be conducted across the fence. The effect of this was to put Gary very much on his own ground, with his equine supporters. Morton was an outsider in every sense.

'I've been making a timetable of events that day when Mr Bickerstaffe found a body at Balaclava House.'

Gary said nothing, his dark eyes watchful.

'And it doesn't quite work out,' Morton went on. He paused for comment.

'How's that, then?' mumbled Gary.

Morton took out a notebook and flipped it open. He didn't need to consult it, but the action made Gary visibly nervous. Good, that was what Morton had intended.

'Let's see,' he began. 'Following the discovery of the body, the local police arrived first on the scene, uniformed officers. Then the police doctor. A little later, Inspector Campbell and myself arrived.'

'The red-haired bird.'

Morton ignored this though he did slightly emphasise Jess's rank when he continued, 'Inspector Campbell took Mr Bickerstaffe outside to where you were talking to one of the uniformed officers. You had asked what was going on and added that the officer wouldn't tell you. Is that correct?'

Gary frowned. 'Yeah, I guess so. It looked to me like you were arresting poor old Monty.'

Morton, still ostensibly consulting the notebook, went on, 'You then left the scene, claiming you were on your way into town.'

'Yeah, that's right.' The horses sensed their owner's unease. They tossed their heads and moved a little away from him, ready to flee any threat.

'So . . .' Morton was beginning to feel a glow of satisfaction.

There was something particularly annoying about Gary and it was good to know he was rattled. 'At that point of time, you knew nothing of a dead body in the house.'

''Sright,' Gary agreed.

'About an hour later, Mr Bickerstaffe was driven away by a relative. They passed a petrol station on the main road, owned by Sebastian Pascal –'

'Old Seb . . .' Gary sounded resentful, perhaps sensing his present predicament was in some way due to the garage owner.

'Mr Pascal recognised the occupants of the car. He phoned you on your mobile number to ask if you knew what was happening. You told him a body had been found at Balaclava House. This is where I have a problem.' Morton closed his notebook. 'You see, Gary, how did you know that? The body was still inside the house. No one had told you it was there. It was not until very much later that, according to your father, your grandmother walked up Toby's Gutter Lane and saw a private ambulance with its darkened windows leave Balaclava. That, according to your dad, was how you all learned that someone had died. But *you* knew much earlier. You see my problem?'

Gary didn't meet his gaze. After chewing his lower lip for a second or two, he burst out, 'OK, look, I'll tell you what happened.'

Morton opened the notebook again. 'You're making a statement, right?'

'Well, yes, if you like. After I saw old Monty put in the cop car, I didn't go into town, like I said I was going to. I did mean to, right? I was telling the truth to your inspector. But I changed my mind. Anyone can change his mind, can't they?'

He paused hopefully for confirmation and, when Morton said nothing, was obliged to go on. 'I started off to walk down the lane towards the main road, just like I said, and then I thought I ought to find out what was going on. Old Monty's a neighbour,' Gary added virtuously. 'I was watching out for him. After all, you lot wouldn't say why you wanted him. I had to find out myself, didn't I? I doubled back over the fields and came up at the rear of the gardens, Balaclava House's gardens. Only they're so overgrown you can hardly call them that. Anyway, I climbed over the wall there and sneaked up through all the bushes to the house. It wasn't difficult. There's plenty of cover. I could hear the two coppers outside talking. One said, they ought to look for tracks because the body must have been carried or dragged into the house. A dead man is quite a weight, the other one said. So I knew they'd got a stiff on their hands. I didn't want them to catch me, if they were planning to search, so I set off home to tell Dad and the rest of the family what I'd heard. Before I got there, Seb rang me. It was lucky he didn't ring me five minutes earlier, when I was snooping around in them bushes. The coppers would've heard the ring tone and come looking for me.

'A lot later, Grandma went up the lane, just like she said she did. She saw the van leave, with its blacked-out windows. She knew it for a hearse. That's the truth. But I couldn't tell you, could I? I couldn't tell you I'd been eavesdropping on the cops?' Gary ended on a plea.

Jess Campbell will be pleased to learn she was right about Gary doubling back, thought Morton. But the question is, is the blighter telling the truth this time?

'You're not going to change this story of yours again, are you?' he asked Gary.

'No, that's what happened. I swear it.'

'Prepared to sign your statement?'

'Yeah, if you want.' Gary eyed the notebook as if it might explode.

'You realise that by your actions, creeping about the grounds, you were possibly contaminating the scene of a suspicious death?'

'I didn't know anything about a suspicious death, did I? How could I know when you wouldn't tell me about anything?' countered Gary.

He scored a point but Phil continued over it, ignoring it.

'Plus, by not coming clean about this straight away, you've made it necessary for me to make a second trip out here to interview you. Think I've got nothing better to do? You've been wasting police time, Mr Colley, and that's an offence.'

'What?' yelled Gary. Both horses wheeled away and cantered off to the far end of their paddock. 'You're not going to charge me over this?'

'It will all be reported to Inspector Campbell, and it will be up to her.'

He left Gary Colley a very unhappy man. A few minutes later, as Morton prepared to turn out of the Colleys' gateway into Toby's Gutter Lane, he was forced to wait and let a vehicle coming from Sneddon's Farm drive by. He recognised the driver as Rosie Sneddon. Morton followed her car down the lane. Rosie joined the main road and Morton, at a discreet distance, did the same. Rosie's car didn't travel far, just to Pascal's petrol station, where she turned in.

Morton drove on past the place, frowning. Now then, Rosie, he thought, you told me you bought petrol the day the body was found. It was Pascal who told you the news. So, why are you stopping there again? Unless you've done a heck of a lot of driving in the last couple of days, you shouldn't need to fill up again.

There was probably an innocent explanation. Perhaps Rosie wanted the minimart. The petrol station was the nearest place she could shop. She might emerge carrying a packet of biscuits and a newspaper. Phil had other things on his mind than Rosie Sneddon and drove on.

Rosie had been aware of a car following her down the lane but she, too, had other things on her mind. She drew into the forecourt of Pascal's garage and switched off the engine. As she got out of the car, the shaven-headed boy who worked for Seb saw her and came towards her, wiping his hands on a rag and grinning in a way she didn't care for.

'Want some help?' he asked. His front teeth were chipped. She'd never noticed before. But she'd never taken much notice of him before. She wondered vaguely if the damage was the result of a childhood accident or an adolescent punch-up.

'I can manage, thanks.' She flipped open the cap on the tank and unhooked the nozzle. But the youth was still there, grinning in that disconcerting way.

'Something bothering you?' she asked sharply.

'Police have been here,' he said. 'They came about that business at Balaclava House. You know?' he prompted.

'Yes, of course I know. They came to the farm as well and spoke to my husband.' Rosie was trying to concentrate on the reading on the pump. She didn't need fuel. She should have gone straight inside and bought some grocery item, then she would have avoided this encounter altogether. She wasn't thinking straight; she needed to get a grip and not do anything stupid.

'Seb reckoned he didn't have anything to tell them. Seb's not here,' the garage hand was saying.

If Seb had been there, this lout wouldn't be hanging round, wasting time, and bothering her. Rosie thought she remembered the lad's name as being Alfie. She said firmly, 'I don't need to see Mr Pascal and haven't you got any work, Alfie?'

Alfie ignored the heavy hint. 'Your old man, he didn't have anything to tell the cops, then?'

Exasperated, Rosie turned to face him. 'No. We don't know anything about Balaclava House.'

'You must know old Monty.'

'Yes, of course we know *Mr* Monty. But we don't know anything about the dead man, how should we?'

'You didn't see anyone hanging about?'

'*No! Why on earth—*' Rosie realised she'd raised her voice and

172

broke off. What did he want her to say? Perhaps the way to get rid of Alfie was to tell him something, anything. 'Pete told them about the burned-out car in the quarry, that's all.'

Immediately, she was sorry. She should just have told him to clear off, he was bothering her. Instead, she'd given way to his insistence. Blast Seb for not being here!

Alfie's expression had sharpened. 'What car is that, then?'

'Someone torched a car . . . a stolen car, I suppose. We've had stolen cars dumped on our land before now. Pete gets pretty fed up.' She replaced the nozzle of the petrol hose.

Alfie gave her a slow, chipped-tooth smile. 'You bought petrol here the other day; the day they found the dead bloke. You didn't need to stop by today, did you? Not really.'

But he'd overstepped the mark and Rosie had got his measure now.

'Excuse me, I have to go and pay.' She marched into the minimart and up to the counter. Maureen, who worked there, gave her a sympathetic look.

'Alfie bothering you? Don't worry, I'll put him right. He won't do it again.'

Rosie almost burst out, 'What's it got to do with you?' But she managed not to. 'He's interested in the murder,' she said instead. 'It's normal I suppose, at his age.'

'Alfie's interested in anything that's not to do with his work,' said Maureen sapiently. She passed Rosie's credit card and receipt to her. 'I'm his auntie,' she added.

'That's nice,' said Rosie, meaning the exact opposite.

Maureen read the true meaning and sighed. 'I know. Seb only gave him the job because I asked. I thought Alfie might buckle down and make something of himself.'

Fat chance, thought Rosie. Aloud, she only said, 'Thank you!'

She walked out of the shop. Alfie, thank goodness, had taken himself off. Rosie drove home, unsettled.

Jay Taylor had lived in a flat at the top of a very beautiful early nineteenth-century house in Cheltenham. The flat had been created from the former attics. This gave an eccentric form to the rooms, the ceilings slanted in parts steeply beneath the gables. The dormer windows let in restricted light. The living area, combined with the kitchen, was reasonable in size but the other rooms were tiny, token versions. So Carter and Jess found out after they had toiled up several flights of stairs.

'Living in a garret has come on a bit since writers were supposed to starve in them,' Carter puffed. 'But it's still living in a garret, just a very expensive one.'

They had wondered how they'd gain entry and if they'd need to force the door. But here Terri Hemmings had proved unexpectedly helpful.

About an hour after they had parted from Billy Hemmings, they had a call from him. He had broken the news to his wife, he said. She was very 'cut up' about it. He had mentioned to her that probably the police would want to take a look at Jay's place. Terri had told him Jay used the services of the same cleaning company as they did. 'Except Jay only had them come to his place once a month, Terri says,' Billy informed them. 'But

I got to thinking, if you haven't got his keys, the company keeps all the keys to the properties on their list.'

A visit to the office or the cleaning company in question had produced, after some little argument, the key to Jay Taylor's flat.

It was pretty obvious, when they went in, that Jay hadn't bothered much between the monthly visits of the cleaners. To say the flat was untidy hardly described it adequately. The tiny bathroom was a jungle of dried washing hung on a line strung across the bath. The kitchen area was scattered with an assortment of mismatched coffee mugs, all used, some on the draining board awaiting attention; others in wavering towers on top of the microwave oven. Yet more mugs, plates, sweet wrappers, crisp packets littered the flat. Presumably when Jay had run out of crockery completely, he did something about it but not before.

Central to the whole place was Jay's computer on its table and all around it, evidence of his work. They had found about twenty notebooks, all full of Taylor's near-indecipherable scrawl interspersed with pages of shorthand, before they stopped counting. There were boxes of taped conversations with his subjects. Then there were the scrapbooks filled with newspaper cuttings, mostly dealing with various well-known names in the world of sport or entertainment.

Jess thought it sad that everything seemed to be about other people, professional contacts past or perhaps future. There was a sterile impersonality about it all. The sole exception was a small scuffed black leather photograph album of family snaps, mostly showing an unsmiling, plain-looking woman and a small boy, also unsmiling. Jay and his mother? They were the usual mix of seaside holiday locations and school sports' days. Jay, if it were Jay, had been a Wolf Cub . . . but apparently hadn't progressed to the Scouts. Pity, thought Jess. He might have cheered up.

'Given time and a bigger house,' Carter remarked, sweeping an arm across the scene, 'Mr Taylor would have ended up living like Monty Bickerstaffe!'

But Jess had taken a seat on the sagging leather-covered sofa where she was sifting through the notebooks, stopping occasionally to make a cross-reference.

'This is his reference library,' she announced suddenly. 'It's not as chaotic as it looks. Each notebook only refers to one book, one subject. The scrapbooks are a different thing. Jay never knew when he might get a call from someone wanting him to ghost a book by a celebrity, someone in showbiz, perhaps, or a sports star. So he kept anything he found containing articles on well-known people's lifestyles or interests. It's his background material. He was obsessive about other people's lives – people who were successful, that is, and in the public eye. They were his raw material. Even his hanging round racecourses takes on a different aspect. He wasn't just there to watch the horses. He was people-watching, too.'

Carter looked round. 'So, who killed him? One of his clients, if that's the word for it? Did someone not like the version he gave of his or her life? Did a book not sell in expected numbers? Was he in dispute with anyone? Did he, in his researches, unearth something embarrassing?' He paused. 'Should we be looking for any sign that he was a blackmailer? We'll have to get permission to examine his bank accounts. Did he have an agent? Who's his next of kin?'

'Well,' Jess said slowly, 'it's all got to be here somewhere . . .'

But it quickly became obvious that it was going to take a very long time to go through everything. They packed up some of it in plastic bags and left the rest in the locked flat for later attention.

'This will keep Sergeant Nugent busy,' Carter said, shutting the haul of assorted paperwork into the boot of his car. Dave Nugent was their computer expert.

'Me, too,' muttered Jess, foreseeing endless new lines of enquiry opening. But something else had caught her eye. They were being observed. The twitch of a net curtain at the window of a downstairs flat betrayed the watcher.

'Downstairs left,' she murmured to Carter.

He glanced in that direction but the curtain now hung still. 'We need to talk to his neighbours, anyway.'

'I'll go,' Jess said.

She walked back to the house and rang the bell for the flat occupied by the watcher. For good measure, she stepped back and rapped on the pane. After a moment the curtain was twitched aside and a face appeared.

Surprise almost made Jess laugh aloud. The face was very much that of an elderly and angry baby. It was round and pink, surmounted by tufts of fairish hair and its small, rosebud mouth was pursed in disapproval. Jess held up her warrant card on the other side of the intervening pane of glass.

The baby scowled even more ferociously and let the curtain drop. Soon a rattle at the door revealed the body belonging to the head. Before them stood a short, podgy individual, wearing a ginger woolly cardigan, baggy brown corduroy trousers and slippers.

'What do you want?' he snapped.

'We've been investigating the top flat,' Jess began.

She was interrupted.

'*I* know that! You should have introduced yourselves first! I didn't know who you were! Stamping around up there, poking and prying. Where did you get the keys? You might have been thieves. I kept an eye open and I saw you had taken some things away. You were putting them in the boot of your car. I made a note of the registration. I was getting ready to ring the police.'

'We are the police,' said Jess patiently.

'I know that *now*. I didn't know it *then*. You didn't introduce yourselves. You should have done. I'm the house-owner. You should have rung my doorbell first. I need to know if the police are visiting one of my tenants, especially as he isn't there. Is he in trouble with the law? I can't have any tenant who's got a police record. It wouldn't do.'

'Mr Taylor has no police record . . .' Jess began.

The man hadn't finished his complaint. 'You were ferreting about in Mr Taylor's flat. If he's a law-abiding citizen, what were you doing up there? What would he have to say about it? He didn't say anything to me about you coming.'

Oh dear, thought Jess. He doesn't know Taylor is dead. Taylor must go away frequently and doesn't always bother to inform his landlord first.

'I'm sorry,' she said. 'You are Mr . . . ?'

'Hopkins!' said the man.

'Perhaps we could come in and talk to you for a moment, Mr Hopkins? This is Superintendent Carter.'

Carter had approached during the conversation and now stood by her side.

Hopkins looked Carter up and down, then scanned Jess again before finally inviting them in with a grudging, 'Well, all right then.'

He turned and shuffled back inside. They followed.

Hopkins's living room suited his personality. It was cluttered and claustrophobic, lined with bookshelves and knick-knacks of all kinds. A canary in a cage began to spring from perch to perch, alarmed at the entry of strangers.

'I'll cover up Osbert,' said Hopkins. 'He doesn't care for visitors.'

Like his owner, thought Jess, watching Hopkins drape what appeared to be an old curtain over the cage.

'Now then,' said Hopkins, returning. 'What's it all about, eh? What authority have you got to remove items from that flat? Where's your warrant. I want to see your warrant.'

'Mr Hopkins,' Carter spoke for the first time. 'Perhaps you'd like to sit down? We have some rather sad news for you.'

'What?' Hopkins glared at him. 'What news?'

'That looks a nice comfortable chair,' suggested Jess, indicating an armchair that looked, from its sagging state, as if it might be in regular use.

'It is a comfortable chair, what's that got to do with it?' demanded Hopkins. But he sat down.

'I'm afraid,' said Carter to him, 'that Mr Taylor has died.'

This silenced Hopkins for a minute; otherwise he reacted to the news, as he seemed to react to most things, with fury.

'Died? What do you mean *died*? He's a young man, well, fairly young. I don't know how old he is – was. He wasn't ill, or he wasn't the last time I saw him.'

'When was that?' asked Carter. 'When did you last see or speak to Mr Taylor?'

Hopkins's fat little hands gripped the arms of the chair as his forehead puckered in thought. 'Three days ago, early morning. He used to come and go at all hours. Didn't have anything of a proper, regular job that I could see. He told me, when he first moved in, that he wrote books. I asked him, what kind of books? He said he wrote autobiographies. I said, "You can only write one *auto*biography, your own. Have you written your own? What have you done that's so remarkable that you've written about it?" I asked him. No, he said, he wrote other people's autobiographies. I told him, in that case, they were *biographies* he wrote. You can't write another person's autobiography because they have to write it themselves. He would have it they were *auto*biographies because they were in the first person. We had an argument about it.' The landlord drew breath. 'But he paid his rent on time. What did he die of?'

'We're looking into that, Mr Hopkins,' Jess told him.

Hopkins put his head on one side and she was struck by how

bright his eyes were. It was as though Osbert had escaped his cage, grown in size, and now observed them.

'Did he smash himself up in that car?' the landlord asked.

'No, not exactly. When you saw him, three days ago, did you have any conversation with him?'

'No, not what you'd call conversation. He bid me good morning. I returned the same. That was about it. I never had conversations with him. I don't know where he went, what he got up to. If I'd thought he was into anything shady I'd have had it out with him. I'd have told him I couldn't be doing with it, not in a tenant of mine.'

'How was he dressed on that last occasion you saw him? Was he entering or leaving the house?'

'He was leaving. It was about ten thirty. He was dressed smart, but he was always a smart dresser,' Hopkins admitted grudgingly. 'I'll say that for him. I didn't think anything of it. I told you, he came and went a lot.'

'Who else lives in the house?' asked Jess, thinking that Hopkins probably had arguments with anyone about anything. His tenants quickly learned not to volunteer any information or get into conversation. They scuttled in and out, avoiding the landlord. Unfortunately this meant Taylor wouldn't have said where he was going. Nor, apparently, was his being smartly dressed unusual. But if Tom Palmer were right in his guess that someone had doctored Taylor's last lunch, then it made sense to suppose that Taylor had been going out on his way to meet someone for lunch. Where though?

Hopkins pointed at the ceiling. 'Miss Jeffrey lives on the first floor. She's always reckoned he had a raffish look. That's her word, "raffish". She wouldn't have any conversation with him. She's very religious. She doesn't speak to anyone who isn't a member of her church. She don't speak to many who are, I reckon. It'd surprise me if any of them speak to her.'

Hopkins jabbed a finger upward again. 'Mr and Mrs Simpson live on the second floor. They're in New Zealand visiting relatives, been gone for a month now. Taylor had the top flat. It used to be the attics. I had it converted. It's my income, leasing the flats in this house. Are you clearing Taylor's flat? Because he's paid up to the end of the month and after that, I'll have to lease it again. I can't afford to have it standing empty. I'll be out of pocket. I'll have to decorate it, too, I dare say. He's probably left it all knocked about. I'll use his deposit to repaint it. I always ask for a deposit against damages when I lease. You wouldn't believe what people do. I've had people knock cup hooks through kitchen tiles.' Seamlessly, Hopkins added, in a change of subject, 'He used to go to the races, I know that, horse racing.'

'Mr Taylor used to go to the races a lot?'

Hopkins nodded. 'There's a lot of racing goes on round here. People come in from all over the country for the Cheltenham meetings. Lot of Irish people come. Miss Jeffrey told me Taylor must be a gambler and it's a sin. Well, she would say that.'

'Thank you, Mr Hopkins,' said Carter to him. 'Do you hold a key to the top flat?'

Hopkins gave him a sour look. 'I have all the keys. I have to have them. Suppose there was a plumbing emergency when the tenant is out?'

'I am afraid,' said Carter firmly, 'we'll have to ask you for your key to the top flat.'

'It's my flat!' Hopkins was outraged. His baby features glowed scarlet. 'I'm not giving you the key.'

'I am afraid the flat must be regarded as sealed pending our investigations,' Carter went on inexorably. 'We'll be sending someone over to put a tape over the door and also to talk to Miss Jeffrey. In the meantime, no one must go into the flat. Can I have the key, please? It will be returned to you as soon as we've finished.'

Grumbling, Hopkins hauled himself out of his chair and went to hunt in the drawer of a sideboard. He returned with a key attached to a luggage label. 'It's this one.' He held it up. 'And sealed for your investigations or not, his rent is only paid until the end of the month. You'll have to get the place cleared out by then – and clear out yourselves!'

'What do you think?' Carter asked Jess as they set off again. 'He was going out to lunch?'

'Yes, I was thinking that when talking to Hopkins back there. I was remembering what Tom Palmer said about his last meal. Do we trawl the restaurants?'

Carter considered this briefly and shook his head. 'There are any number of them in the city and outside of it. It would take all the manpower we've got available and there's only a slim chance we'd turn up anything. If Palmer's right about his last meal containing crushed pills, that's unlikely to have happened in a restaurant setting. How would the murderer manage it? No, it's far more likely he met someone in a private setting somewhere. That could be anywhere.'

Jess sighed. It seemed they were not much further forward, after all.

'Perhaps Nugent will strike lucky with Taylor's computer,' she said.

Carter grunted.

The thing about a secret is not simply that you don't tell anyone. It's that you have no way of knowing whether it's exclusive to you; or whether any others are hugging the same secret to their chests, having found it out by a totally different route. If that's so, it isn't a secret at all; that's the desperate irony of the whole thing. It's just something everyone knows but no one mentions. Unknown to yourself, you are part of a great conspiracy to hide an unpalatable truth.

Monty worked all this out later in life, much too late for the knowledge to be any use to him. Meantime, the secret of what he'd seen that fateful day in Shooter's Wood, like all the things no one mentions, continued to fester like a hidden sore. The answer, logically, would be to share the horror, drag it kicking and screaming into the light of day and hang the consequences.

'But that's it, ain't it, Hamlet?' muttered Monty into the darkness, lying sleepless in the comfortable bed Bridget had given him. He tossed about and wondered why he didn't sleep as well here as he had done back on the unyielding chaise longue at Balaclava House.

It was the fear of the consequences that kept you silent, stopped you taking the way out with all that revelation would mean. To speak or not to speak. Either way, concluded Monty with the wisdom that comes to you in the middle of the night, either way you're trapped. Treacherous things, secrets.

He wondered why events that were associated with his family home, and ought to stay there when he walked away from it, had followed him to Bridget's. He screwed up his eyes, as if that would make any difference, and faced them again.

The realisation that he wasn't the only one to know or guess what went on in Shooter's Wood also came to him far too late. For years, growing up, he tried to forget what he'd seen and couldn't. Things that won't go away come to the surface, sooner or later.

It was Christmas and Monty had begun the seasonal celebrations by breaking his ankle. People asked him if he'd done it skiing. But he had to admit he'd only done it jumping off a bus before it stopped at Piccadilly Circus. He'd sprawled on the wet pavement surrounded by Christmas shoppers, with an irate bus conductor yelling from his platform, 'Serve you right, mate!'

It was his last year at school and he'd been offered an opportunity to train as a draughtsman the next summer, if he could avoid the looming period of National Service first. He still hadn't really decided what to do with the rest of his life. The decision had been complicated by a change in the lives of his family, a change that ought to have been entirely for the better. In fact it caused that festering wound, spreading its poison for such a long time, finally to burst out and triumph.

The good news, the positive change in the Bickerstaffe fortunes, had been when a multinational monster came along and gobbled up the brand name and associated ailing family business. Bickerstaffe's Cakes and Biscuits still counted for something in the national psyche. They were a quality name. The surviving Bickerstaffes, including Monty, suddenly found that they should have a modest income for life, if they were sensible with the windfall. For the first time his mother had planned a turkey for Christmas Day. In other, leaner, years they'd made do with a cheap leg of pork, courtesy of the Colleys. Now they'd eat the pork at New Year in place of the usual stringy fowl obtained from the same source. They always had a Bickerstaffe's boiled fruit cake in lieu of a Christmas cake, even though so few had been produced in latter years. Probably the famous delicacy would be the first product to be discontinued; now the new bosses had their hands on the tiller.

'It'll be a damn shame, of course,' said Monty's father. 'After all these years, well . . .' But he couldn't make his voice sound as if he really cared.

Monty didn't fret over the demise of the cake. He'd always disliked it, anyway. So he hobbled home with his ankle in plaster and into Balaclava House. Its normal gloomy welcome was only slightly alleviated by his mother's annual effort at Christmas decorations. That meant the same few tatty paper chains and a wreath that had lost a few more of its berries and leaves each year it was brought out, and now resembled nothing so much as a funeral offering. It annoyed Monty that no one had thought to replace these sad apologies for festive cheer. But he understood that his mother had begrudged paying out any of the new wealth on paper lanterns and artificial swags of nameless greenery. Economy was bred into her heart and soul now. Even so, the sight of it all brought home the full horror of their family Christmases. Monty gritted his teeth and prepared to enter into the awful pretence of merriment; and his mother's mince pies that had hardly any mincemeat in them.

It was a rainy winter and bad for coughs, colds and influenza. The first thing Monty discovered, once he got past the hall and into the drawing room, was that his father had gone down with a cold some ten days previously. Then he had developed a persistent cough, wheezing and struggling for breath. He sat over the meagre fire with an old plaid travelling rug wrapped round him. It was the same rug with which the twelve-year-old Monty had toiled uphill carrying it on his shoulder, with Penny alongside him, issuing directions. When his father extended his hand in greeting it looked an old man's hand, thin-skinned, brown-spotted and thick-veined. But he wasn't an old man, only forty-nine.

Despite all this, his father hadn't given up smoking, as an ashtray of squashed remains testified.

'Perhaps you ought to pack this up for a bit, Dad,' suggested Monty, indicating the evidence. 'Help your chest.'

'Won't do me any ruddy harm,' wheezed his father. Seeing that Monty was really concerned, he added, 'I'll be all right for Christmas Day.' But he didn't look all right.

As for Monty's broken ankle, his parents' reaction was much the same as the bus conductor's.

'Bad luck, old chap,' gasped his father. 'Daft thing to do, wasn't it?'

'Honestly, Monty,' complained his mother, 'why on earth did you have to do it *now*?'

The Bickerstaffes were not ones for seeking a doctor's advice. Monty hobbled painfully down the lane with the aid of a crutch and asked Jed Colley, elderly but still active, if any of his clan was going into town and, if so, could he or she bring back a bottle of whisky. Jed had promptly produced one from his own stock of booze, and pressed it into Monty's hands.

Monty had tried to pay for it. They had the money now. But Jed wouldn't hear of it.

'Merry Christmas, you tell your dad and mum,' he said.

So Monty hobbled back with the bottle in his jacket pocket and his mother began brewing up hot toddies.

'That'll see me right,' wheezed his father.

Two days before the Day, he took to his bed, something unheard of, and the doctor was finally called.

He said it was influenza, complicated by a chest infection, and he wanted to send Edward Bickerstaffe into hospital.

Edward and his wife reacted with horror and refused. Well, said the doctor reluctantly, the hospitals were all filling up with the victims of seasonal ailments. Edward could stay at home provided he slept in a separate room, in which a fire had been lit, and received only essential visitors. But they must let him, the doctor, know immediately if things got worse. 'And don't forget about the fire!' repeated the doctor on leaving. The temperature in the bedrooms at Balaclava was always arctic.

'That means you stay away from your father, Monty,' ordered his mother, when the required fire had been lit, causing a downfall of soot and bits of bird's nest into the hearth. It made the sick man cough more and, as the room dried out, you could feel the dampness evaporating on the walls.

'I don't want you catching it. It's bad enough you had to go and break your ankle.' She was busy polishing up the remnants of the family silver, brought out for the annual Christmas display, as she spoke. She sat at the kitchen table, rubbing away with wadding soaked in some cleaning fluid that turned her fingers black.

Monty painfully hauled himself upstairs and along the corridor to stand outside his father's door.

'How's it going, Dad?' he called.

'Bloody awful!' croaked the invalid. 'Go away!'

So Monty went away.

Late on Christmas Eve, he awoke with a start to hear his father coughing hideously. Then came his mother's footsteps hurrying along the corridor. He got out of bed and hopped to his door, opening it a crack and peeping through. His mother was coming back from the sickroom, wrapped in her old towelling dressing gown. She didn't see Monty and went downstairs.

Monty disobeyed orders and made his way to the sickroom. It was lit by a single bedside lamp, with a dusty and faded pleated pink silk shade. Monty could see it clearly now, in his mind's eye, with its china base of a girl, a twenties 'flapper', holding the leash of a couple of greyhounds. Lending a little more light were the glowing coals of the fire lit in the vain hope of encouraging the sick man's recovery. His father sat up in bed, propped on damp pillows, sweat pouring down his face. He was drawing great painful breaths, only to expel them in a splutter and with a groan.

'I feel a bit strange, old chap,' he managed to gasp.

Monty, frightened, said, 'I'll go down and phone the doc to come out at once – or an ambulance. Perhaps that would be best.'

'No need,' returned his father. 'Your mother's gone downstairs to phone. He'll be here soon. You get back to your room. You'll catch this bloody thing.' He stretched out a hand and gestured feebly. 'Go . . .' he managed before another coughing fit overtook him.

So Monty, to his everlasting shame, hobbled back to his room.

The doctor didn't arrive until nine on Christmas morning, but by that time Edward Bickerstaffe was dead.

'Why the hell didn't you come at once?' Monty demanded angrily, trapping the doctor on the first-floor landing beneath the stained-glass window of Jezebel. 'I know it's ruddy Christmas, but he was your patient. You knew he was ill. You should have come when my mother phoned!'

'I did come at once!' snapped the doctor. 'Your father should have been in hospital! Of course, I knew how ill he was! He'd been ill for years, a physical wreck. I tried to get him to cut down on the cigarettes and see a heart specialist.

He wouldn't. He couldn't fight the influenza; his body didn't have the weapons any longer. When your mother rang, I realised what it meant. I just grabbed my bag and came! I haven't even had my breakfast!'

'But she—' began Monty.

Then he broke off. Of course, she hadn't. She hadn't rung the doctor in the middle of the night. She'd gone downstairs – but she hadn't phoned. If he, Monty, hadn't meekly returned to his bed, but had made his awkward injured way down to the hall, he'd have made sure she rang. But she had waited until she knew it was too late.

With a sick feeling in his stomach, he realised at once why she'd done it. She'd known all along about the affair with Penny's mother. How could he, Monty, have been so naïve as to think she – the deceived wife – hadn't found out – hadn't known by some instinct? That she hadn't read all the little signs like an archaeologist deciphering some ancient runes? All the time they had been poor, the affair hadn't threatened her own position, because neither she nor his father had any choice but to live on together, husband and wife, in this cold, cheerless, loveless house. But now that their financial position had changed his father might have begun to think of divorce; to dream of beginning anew with the woman he loved. But this was all his mother's life held: Balaclava House and her position as its mistress, as Mrs Bickerstaffe. She'd skimped and toiled here without proper domestic help or a decent household budget for years. Was her reward for all that to be cast aside? No, she wasn't the sort of woman to let that happen.

So now Monty said to the doctor apologetically, 'Yes, of course you came at once, and it's Christmas Day, too. I'm sorry I snapped your head off like that. I'm upset. My mother and I appreciate all you've done.'

'Naturally you're shocked and upset, old fellow,' said the doctor, patting his shoulder. 'I'm very sorry it ended like this.'

But it didn't. How could it? Life had to go on. His life, his mother's life, their lives together as parent and child, how could they lead these now that he knew? What was he going to do? Was there never to be any end to it?

Chapter 11

Jess was driving out to Weston St Ambrose for a second time, but this time alone. They had been optimistic, after finding Taylor's flat, of tracing his family, friends and business acquaintances.

They were having reasonable success in doing this, but so far had not turned up anything significant enough to give them a lead as to who might have wanted the man dead, or where he had been setting out to when Hopkins saw him leave the house on the fatal morning.

Taylor had been a networker of experience, a racing man, with a wide range of acquaintances, a party animal. Yet Jay Taylor had also been a highly professional writer, dissecting the minutiae of celebrities' lives and lifestyles, admittedly at their request in a joint enterprise, but getting uncomfortably close to them in doing so. Perhaps that had made a lot of people wary of him.

The celebs whose confessions he'd ghosted had not been the hardest to track down; but trying to make an appointment to see any of them was another matter. They had full diaries and travelled widely. One was in the USA promoting a music album. Another, nearer to home, was in the Priory Clinic. But Carter and Jess managed it. Interviewed face to face or down a phone line between engagements (sporting, television or photo shoots), all of them were decently shocked to hear of his murder. But they shrugged their shoulders when asked about the man. They agreed he had interviewed them. He had got them to talk about themselves and their lives in detail. Jess's impression was that, in most cases, that wouldn't have been difficult. In other cases it must have meant hours of patient and skilled coaxing. Just as some presented themselves to the public in airbrushed pictures, others would have liked to present airbrushed lives. To Taylor's credit, he hadn't allowed them to do that. Whatever he found, he promised to handle 'tactfully' and generally they agreed he had kept his word.

They – the stars – had not encouraged Jay to talk about himself. There was no necessity. That had not been the purpose of the exercise. It had been a business arrangement.

His publishers were kinder about him and regretted his loss to his profession. One of them, interviewed by Carter, summed it up.

'Jay was one of the best, a damn good writer. Yes, he earned pretty good money; but he was a bit of a bon viveur, that's the impression we all got. It wouldn't surprise anyone here to learn he spent it as fast as he earned it. He wasn't one of those chaps who turn up for lunch wearing jeans and a scruffy old jacket. He had a fondness for designer suits. We didn't know anything about his private life, apart from that. We'll miss him, certainly. You could always rely on Jay. He always did a thorough job and turned in a manuscript on time.'

So Carter and Jess ended up knowing little more about the man himself than they had at the outset. They had decided that Taylor, like many people, was neither popular nor unpopular, hovering somewhere in between. He had been generally liked, or at least not actively disliked. (The exception being by Miss Jeffrey.) Hopkins had perhaps not quite approved of his tenant's way of earning a living; but Taylor had paid his rent on time, and Jess imagined that was all that really mattered to the landlord. For others with whom Taylor had come into contact it had been a social or work-related kind of liking, not an emotional one.

Billy and Terri Hemmings, on the other hand, had considered him a friend and appeared genuinely upset. But they still insisted they knew little about his background. Other racing acquaintances said 'they hadn't really known him that well'. No one admitted to having disliked him. 'Very pleasant sort', they said of him. They were all quite clear about that. After all, the poor guy had been murdered, hadn't he?

Had the motive for murder stemmed from Taylor's financial situation? Although Hemmings told them Jay was good at picking winners, Jess and Carter soon found out their man had had lean days too, when the money had vanished on the heels of losing nags. This raised the possibility that he had owed money within the betting world. So far there was no evidence of this. His bank account was in the black, if not generously so. It had rarely gone into the red, his bank manager told them, though it had teetered on the brink a few times. Mr Taylor compared favourably with some other of the bank's clients. So the dead man had been a gambler, but not a reckless one. Taylor hadn't fallen into the debt trap. But had he fallen into another? That was the question.

Jess had imagined that, if they ever tracked down any relatives, these would show more grief. But it was not to be so. Gerald 'Jay' Taylor's medical records contained the fact that his next of kin was a Miss Bryant. She was, it turned out, his only surviving relation, an aunt and retired civil servant. She lived in an aggressively tidy bungalow just outside Bristol. Jess visited her there to bring her the sad news and, with luck, learn something more personal about the dead man.

She need not have worried Miss Bryant would be too distraught to be interviewed. She was a stocky, bespectacled, grey-haired woman wearing a pleated tartan skirt and a crisp white blouse under a beige woollen gilet. Sitting bolt upright in a chintz-covered armchair without a crease in it, she eyed Jess with disapproval and announced, 'Naturally it's a pity my nephew has died. But I'm not surprised to see the police involved. Even as a child he was secretive . . . *pah*!'

The elderly, overweight dachshund with which Miss Bryant shared her home looked as if it might also have shared its mistress's opinions. Curled in a dog basket, it kept its baleful stare on Jess and twitched its greying muzzle from time to time in a canine sneer.

Miss Bryant, for all her disapproval, was more than willing to talk but, from Jess's viewpoint, had little to tell – and nothing about her nephew's recent movements. She had last seen him ten to twelve months earlier, when he'd turned up 'out of the blue, showing no consideration, as usual. He sat there where you are, in that chair, and started reminiscing in a maudlin sort of way, about his mother and father and his childhood. I thought it quite possible he'd been drinking.'

Miss Bryant leaned forward. 'He borrowed a photograph album of mine. He had no early photographs of himself, he said, and he wanted to make some copies. He didn't return it. If it's among his effects, I want it back immediately.'

'I think there was one,' Jess told her, 'I'll look into it.'

Other than that, Miss Bryant had received an annual Christmas card and, very occasionally, a brief phone call. Gerald, as she continued to call him, had been a 'bright little boy and really, quite a good student'. But then things had rather fallen apart, in her view. She described his lifestyle as rackety, and confirmed he had never married.

'A wife wouldn't have put up with it!' she said grimly.

She had never known anything about his girlfriends.

'All rather a waste. Deirdre would have been disappointed.' The grimness was still in her voice but also a touch of satisfaction. Miss Bryant had been proved right.

'Deirdre?' enquired Jess.

'My late sister, Gerald's mother.'

'I see, what about his father?' There had been, as Jess recalled, no male figure constant in the family snaps album they'd found in Taylor's flat.

At this question, Miss Bryant's eyes flashed. 'Lionel? He took himself off when the baby was still in its cradle. I wasn't surprised. He was a rackety sort, too. I suppose Gerald took after him.

I warned Deirdre when she married him, but she wouldn't listen to me. Lionel was what they used to call a charmer. Deirdre never heard from him again; and she didn't know where to begin to look for him. He'd quitted his job. He had no family she could contact. He'd been brought up by some people called Taylor; that was where he got his surname. They'd adopted him as a baby and were both dead by the time Deirdre met Lionel. He had no other relatives, or so he told her. Certainly no one turned up at the wedding. It was a registry office affair with about six people present, all on Deirdre's side. His whole background may have been a complete fabrication. It wouldn't surprise me. So there you are. Or rather, there poor Deirdre was, with a babe in arms and no man to support her. Lionel Taylor might just as well have been a will-o-the-wisp. He probably had half a dozen wives up and down the country.'

Miss Bryant leaned back and surveyed Jess thoughtfully. 'I suppose I'll be Gerald's heir, then? To his estate, I mean?'

'I can't give you legal advice, Miss Bryant, I'm afraid. I'd see a solicitor about that, if I were you. All I can say is that, so far, we've found no will.'

'Then it's mine. There's no one else. I suppose it's modest,' said Miss Bryant discontentedly. She brightened. 'There's a flat in Cheltenham, you say?'

'Only rented, I'm afraid. The landlord is anxious for it to be cleared so he can decorate the place and relet it.'

'Huh!' exclaimed Miss Bryant. 'Typical of Gerald. No provision made for his future!'

Or for Miss Bryant's future, either.

'I suppose,' she said discontentedly, as Jess left, 'I'll be expected to pay for his funeral out of whatever he's left . . . and I'll have the inconvenience of clearing that flat, as well. It's Gerald all over. Like father, like son. Feckless!'

The dachshund uttered a canine rumble of confirmation.

Jess drove away with a feeling of relief.

But at least Miss Bryant was able later to give a positive identification of the dead man. She did so in a matter-of-fact way, showing no more distress than she had earlier. Jess felt relief at seeing her depart in a taxi. 'Awful woman,' she said unguardedly.

Phil Morton took an unexpectedly positive view. 'Look at it this way; it's a good job we've got a family member to identify him before the inquest opens. The coroner wouldn't be impressed if only given an assurance about identity by Billy Hemmings!'

In the event, the inquest, when it took place the next day, consisted of little else but the identification of the dead man and the circumstances of the discovery of the body. Few people attended, although Mr Hopkins had found his way there. He sat in the front row of seats, arms folded, staring belligerently at the coroner. In the back row sat a man in a well-worn anorak, holding a notebook. Probably the local press had sent along a representative, in case there was a story, although if there were it wouldn't come out now, at the preliminary hearing. The reporter might be freelance, taking a chance. The Hemmingses provided a more striking sight. Billy was crammed into a suit. Terri was dressed entirely in black: an eclectic outfit of a short fake fur jacket, brief skirt, sheer tights and very high fashion heels.

Monty had been persuaded to come to the court and describe his experience. He did this in few words.

'I walked in and there the bally fellow was. I didn't know him from Adam. Now you've told me his name, I still don't.'

'A very nasty shock for you, Mr Bickerstaffe,' said the coroner sympathetically.

'It was very inconvenient!' Monty replied loudly. 'And it still is. When can I go home?'

The coroner said it was largely a matter for the police to decide. The house was still a crime scene. He then adjourned proceedings until a later date, to allow the police to complete their enquiries. The man in the anorak got up and left. He hadn't written much in his notebook.

The Hemmingses were not called upon to give evidence. Billy sat with his arms folded throughout and seemed pleased that he was not required to make any official statements. Terri looked disappointed. She approached Jess after they had all left the court.

'You'd have thought,' she said crossly, 'considering how many of those celebrities Jay knew and all, that at least the local paper would have sent along a photographer.'

Jess decided it was probably best not to mention the man in the anorak, with the notebook. Terri would be even more upset to know any kind of pressman had been there, but not interviewed her and Billy.

'The press would know this is a preliminary inquest, only

a formality,' she explained. 'The inquest proper will be later. But I wouldn't count on a crowd of paparazzi even then.'

'We were only in there a few minutes,' moaned Terri. 'If I'd known it'd be so quick, I wouldn't have bothered.'

'Are you coming or what?' demanded her husband, surfacing at her side.

Terri teetered away on her spike heels, still complaining. They drove off immediately.

'Was she supposed to be in mourning or something?' asked Morton in some awe.

'Something, Phil,' retorted Jess.

Monty had now come out of the building accompanied by Bridget. He gave them a dispirited wave of greeting, at the same time shaking his head. He didn't want to talk to them. They respected his wish and watched him being driven away by Bridget, who had acknowledged their presence with a brief nod.

Hopkins scurried by, calling over his shoulder as he did, 'You've got until the end of the month. Then I'm going to advertise the flat. It'll go at once. You'd better get a move on!'

'So,' Jess said later to Carter, when she and Morton had returned from the inquest and reported back to the superintendent. 'Now what do we do?'

'We get to know our man,' Carter told her.

'We've tried that,' she reminded him. 'We've been through all his papers; Dave Nugent has searched his computer. We spoke to his landlord. Stubbs spoke to Miss Jeffrey and came away with a religious pamphlet. She pushed one under Taylor's door once, apparently, and he took it very badly. He and Miss Jeffrey had a stand-up row about it and she never spoke to him again. We've interviewed his publishers, the subjects of his books and his one surviving relative. I still don't feel I know him.'

She knew her frustration sounded in her voice. But the clock was running and they had hit a dead end. To hear the coroner speak of the police being given 'time to complete their enquiries' had echoed hollowly. Some chance . . . had been Jess's private reaction.

'We keep trying; because somewhere, at some time in his life, he made himself a candidate for murder,' Carter said patiently. 'Look at it this way: do we have so little sense of the inner man because he went to great pains to conceal it? If so, what is missing? What is there about Mr Taylor that he didn't want anyone to know?'

Jess looked unconvinced. 'Perhaps the reason we can't find anything else is just because there is nothing else? He was active professionally and socially but had put down no roots, owned no property, was in no relationship, depended on getting new writing commissions, hadn't got anything permanent in his life, really.' She warmed to her theme. 'If you think about it, he trod a fine line between success and failure. His publishers told you he was professional and painstaking in his work. He should have made enough from his writing to give him a comfortable lifestyle, in theory, anyway, and keep him in designer suits. He was a single man without dependants.'

'From what Miss Bryant told you about his father, Lionel, I wouldn't be surprised if Lionel didn't describe himself as "single without dependants" to the next woman he met after abandoning Deirdre and her baby,' said Carter. 'Lionel Taylor sounds to me to have all the earmarks of a bigamist. However, that's all long ago and not our concern. His son, Gerald, known as Jay, is our problem. We're very little further on in solving it.'

'Well,' Jess picked up her exposition cautiously. 'We know he had expensive tastes, inspired by the exotic lifestyles of the more successful and highly paid of the celebrities he wrote about, perhaps? These could, literally, have cost him dearly. He was making enough money to live well within reason, and to manage to stay in the black financially, but not to compete with the mega-earners.'

Carter was nodding slowly. 'Yes, those tastes rub off on someone who observes them from a less favoured background. They probably did on Taylor. You're right. He admired and respected their success and he wanted to live like them. Did that turn out to be a fatal weakness? When he was in funds, he splashed money around – as when he took the Hemmings duo out to dinner after his win at Cheltenham. What do you expect? If you hobnob with wealthy people, you have to keep up, look the part, spend your share. Someone like Billy Hemmings would be quick to spot a freeloader and ditch him.'

Jess felt uneasy. Did all this indicate that Taylor, secretly, had been a desperate man? Was that what they were missing? He had just turned forty at the time of his death. Had Miss Bryant put her finger on the moving force behind all this, when she said that her nephew had made no provision for his future? Had his recent birthday, perhaps, brought this home to Jay? Middle age was on the horizon, and he didn't even own his own home. Money had been frittered away. He possessed nothing of any substance to cling to if, for any reason, he couldn't write. Had he perhaps hoped that, among all the information so painstakingly amassed in that cluttered flat, he would find something that would prove a real winner? Something to earn him enough money to put his finances on an even keel, not just for a few months until the next writing job came in, but for ever, regardless of whether he wrote another book? It was hard to imagine what it could be. Why he should be found dead in Balaclava House seemed destined to remain as much of a mystery as ever.

'I'd like to talk to your friend, Monica Farrell,' she said to Carter, who raised his eyebrows enquiringly. 'I want to know more about Taylor's visits to Weston St Ambrose and his friendship with the Hemmingses. Did he go there to see them often? If he did, perhaps Mrs Farrell will recognise his photograph. I know it's grasping at straws,' she went on hurriedly. 'But right now, straws are all we have apart from a burned-out car and a dead body where it should never have been. Besides, Mrs Farrell knows Monty. I'd like to talk to her about him. Perhaps I could just drive over and chat to her for an hour, say, early this evening?'

It seemed to her that Carter hesitated but then nodded.

'I'll phone ahead and tell Monica to expect you. She'll be glad of a visitor.'

Jess understood the hesitation in his manner. Carter, she had realised, was a private man. In visiting his ex-wife's aunt, Jess was stepping on to sensitive territory.

* * *

It was drizzling with fine rain, badly needed by the dry soil, as she negotiated the winding minor roads to Weston St Ambrose. The windscreen wipers swished back and forth revealing an arc of newly damp landscape and little other sign of human habitation apart from the occasional signpost to a farm. The village itself first let the approaching traveller know of its existence by its church spire, piercing the leaves of surrounding chestnut trees. The church looked as if it ought to be disused, but it must have a congregation of sorts because a recently painted signboard outside informed passers-by that it was in urgent need of a new roof, and a fund had been set up. It even had a website. *Help us save this ancient church*, the noticeboard pleaded.

Jess drove past the Hemmingses' schoolhouse home – no sign of life there either, today, not even the dogs – and found Monica's cottage, described to her by Ian Carter in some detail.

'So you're Inspector Campbell!' a plump, grey-haired woman greeted her cheerfully. 'Come inside, you'll get wet standing out there. Not a nice day, unfortunately.'

The interior of the cottage was blessedly warm and cosy. Jess was ushered into the main living room and found herself settled in a comfortable chair and being plied with tea and rock cakes. A black cat was curled up on the windowsill, but after lifting its head to give the newcomer a cursory stare, it tucked itself into a ball again and went back to sleep.

'He's been out all night,' said Monica Farrell, indicating the cat. 'He goes mousing over in the churchyard. Sometimes he brings his trophies home, not always dead. I have to catch them and release them back where they came from.'

'I see your church has an appeal going, for a new roof,' Jess said.

Monica pulled a face. 'It's such a lot of money. I doubt they can raise it. The diocese will help a bit and we've tried all the various historic building trusts. But the shortfall is massive. The congregation can't do it. There are only a dozen of us on the best of Sundays.'

'Do you have your own vicar?'

'Goodness, no!' Monica chuckled. 'We have whoever is willing to come and tend our souls. It's a pity because it's an interesting old church. We keep it locked most of the time but I have a key. I'm a churchwarden. If you're interested, we can walk over there and take a look at it.'

'I'd like that,' said Jess. It was time to tackle the business that had brought her. 'You know that we're investigating a murder and that the victim was found at Balaclava House?'

'Oh, Ian told me all about that,' said Monica. 'He told me you were in charge of it and he's got every confidence in your being able to ferret out the truth, nail the guilty party!'

'He said that?' Jess asked, startled.

'More or less, words to that effect, anyway. More tea?'

'Not just at the moment, thanks. You were able to tell Superintendent Carter quite a bit about Monty Bickerstaffe, who lives at Balaclava House.'

'Yes, poor old Monty, I have to feel sorry for him, although truth to tell, he was always an awkward blighter. He brought nearly all his troubles on himself. It was a great pity, you know, that some big company bought out the family biscuit business.

It gave them enough money to live on, at the time, and it hindered Monty having to make a real effort to have a proper career. If only he'd had to earn enough to look after his mother and, eventually, his wife. It would have been much better if Bickerstaffe's had just gone bust; and Monty had had to buckle down to real life and a nine-to-five existence. I always felt,' Monica concluded, 'that Monty had problems with reality. His mind always seemed to be somewhere else. I knew his late wife quite well. I don't know how she stuck him for so long. I wouldn't have done so!'

She surveyed Jess. 'It's an odd thing, but you do look a lot like Penny, when she was a younger woman.'

'So people keep telling me,' Jess confessed. 'Tell me, would you say that Monty was a devious person?'

'He was good at hiding his bottles of booze from Penny,' said Monica. 'He used to sneak out and bury them around the garden. She kept digging them up.'

'I suppose,' Jess explained, 'what I really mean is, how is he with facts? You said he always had trouble with reality? He insists, you see, that he'd never seen the dead man before that day. Could he have forgotten? Or could he just not be bothered to tell us? It would help if we knew.'

'Monty wouldn't lie!' Monica Farrell said firmly. 'Certainly not intentionally. If he says he doesn't know him, hasn't ever seen him, hasn't got a clue about him, I'd say he's telling you what he believes to be the truth. How good his memory is, now, that's another matter. I suppose he could have forgotten him. But, on the whole, I'd say it was unlikely. Not many people have bothered with Monty over the last few years. A stranger would be remembered.'

'That's something, anyway,' said Jess. 'It's quite a relief to hear, actually. I have wondered if Monty was just keeping his head down – not wanting us to bother him – and was holding something back.'

'Well, just remember those buried whisky bottles,' Monica warned her. 'I don't say he couldn't be artful. But I don't think he'd mislead the police.' She paused and surveyed Jess again in that slightly unsettling way. 'And he wouldn't lie to *you*. You look like Penny. He wouldn't lie to you, any more than he'd have lied to her.'

'No, but he did hide evidence of his drinking from her,' Jess said.

'Exactly. There's a difference. I think you understand it. If you want to know something from Monty, just ask him a direct question. That's the best.'

'Right, I'll remember that!' Jess grinned. 'If we could move on to another subject, the Hemmingses, who live at the schoolhouse—'

'Are they involved?' interrupted Monica, brightening. 'Do say they are. I'd love to see them carted away in chains.'

'No, not involved exactly, but they did know the dead man. He was expected at their house for a dinner party the day he died. When Superintendent Carter stopped outside their house, Mrs Hemmings thought at first it was Jay Taylor, the dead man, because he also drove a Lexus.'

Jess fished in her pocket and took out the snapshot Hemmings had given her. 'I wonder if you recognise the man in this photograph – if you've seen him around Weston St Ambrose.'

Monica reached across the tea things to take the photo and study it. 'This is he, I take it, your corpse? Only in life, as it were, and what life, eh? At the races, are they? Good Lord, look at the hat the Hemmings woman is wearing. She looks like a standard lamp.'

Jess tried not to laugh and urged, 'The man?'

'Oh, yes.' Monica pursed her lips. 'Can't be sure. But, yes, I did see him once – I think. It was a few weeks ago. He and Hemmings strolled past here together, going to our one and only surviving pub, probably. I remember thinking they looked birds of a feather. If it wasn't this fellow, it was someone who looked very like this.'

'Were they talking, when you saw them go past the cottage?'

'What? Oh, yes, well, one of them was. Not Hemmings, the other one, this one in the photo – if it is the same one. He was holding forth about something and seemed very pleased with himself.'

'He may just have had another good win at the races,' Jess said, taking back the photo. 'But it does help to know about it.'

Were they up to something, Hemmings and Taylor? she wondered. If they were, how am I going to find out about it?

She thanked her hostess for the information and her time, and for the tea and cakes. Monica asked again if she wanted to view the interior of the church. It seemed rude not to accept the offer, so Monica fetched a key. Then she put on a voluminous plastic raincoat and led Jess out of the cottage. They tramped across the road and through the leaf-strewn churchyard with its tombstones mostly at an angle, their lichen-encrusted inscriptions now illegible, and into the porch sheltering the north door.

The key was enormous and must have been nearly as old as the heavy oak door it opened. They descended a short flight of steps on to the flagged floor. The exterior of St Ambrose might be dilapidated but the inside had obviously been lovingly dusted and polished by a band of loyal workers. There were war memorials on its walls to the sons of families that no longer had any members in the village. An elaborate pair of sculpted figures topped a fine early seventeenth-century tomb. Husband and wife, finely dressed and painted in now-faded colours, lay side by side in death, accompanied by a tiny infant wrapped in black, but smiling cheerfully.

'She died in childbirth, you see,' said Monica, pointing to the inscription on the side of the tomb. 'So many women did. The baby died too. He must have had the monument built for her and their child and then lived out the rest of his life, waiting to join her in it. He lived another fifty years after her, as you can see.' She patted the black-shrouded baby. 'Whenever Millie has visited me, she's always insisted we come over here and see the baby. Children are funny.'

'Millie?' Jess asked.

For a moment, Monica looked embarrassed. 'Oh, dear. Yes, Ian's daughter. She must have turned eleven now. She hasn't been down for a while. Sophie, her mother, has remarried and there's been a lot of reorganisation going on in her life and Millie's. But I mean to persuade Sophie to let Millie come and stay with me for a week some time soon, now that Ian is living nearby. Then he can come over and spend some time with her. But perhaps you didn't know he was divorced?' She peered anxiously at Jess.

'I knew he was divorced,' Jess told her. 'But not that he has a daughter.'

'I see,' Monica said. 'Well, you know now and I can't see that there's any secret about it. I'm sure Ian wouldn't mind.'

Outside the rain had stopped but had released a pungent odour.

'Foxes,' said Monica, seeing Jess sniff and pull a face. 'I do worry about Henry, the black cat, mousing here at night, in case he meets one. They might just ignore one another but I can't be sure. He's quite an old cat now. But I can't keep Henry in. He just yowls until he's let out. His brother, Mickey, on the other hand, hardly goes out at all and never at night. Besides, those terriers of the Hemmingses are let loose in here on their so-called walks, and if they met Henry I'm afraid he'd have little chance. I've told the Hemmings female, she ought not to let her terriers run loose around the churchyard, and not just because of my cats. If there is a fox's earth somewhere, the terriers will go straight down the hole and might get stuck. She didn't believe me. She said her dogs aren't interested in foxes. It the sort of daft thing she does say. I pointed out her dogs are Jack Russells and bred for digging out foxes, it's in their blood. But no good, she just goggled at me.'

They parted outside Monica's cottage. Jess climbed back into her car and began to drive slowly back through the village, her mind very much on what she had just learned. If Carter had feared Monica might start chatting about private matters, then his misgivings had been well grounded. But, after all, the existence of an eleven-year-old daughter was hardly something he should mind being known.

She rolled sedately past the old schoolhouse. There were no lights on. Had the Hemmingses already left for the holiday in Marbella of which Terri had spoken? Jess hoped not. They might want to speak to Billy again. She had nearly reached the village boundary when, without warning, she came upon an unexpected sight. There was a disturbance. She wasn't the only police presence in Weston St Ambrose.

The first thing to attract her attention was the police car. It was parked outside a brick-built house surrounded by an unkempt garden. The wooden garden gate was open and on the garden path two uniformed officers struggled with a young man with a shaven head. They were hauling him towards the patrol car and he was resisting vigorously.

Jess stopped and got out. As she approached the scene, she could hear the young man abusing his captors and shouting out it was 'a plant'.

'What's going on?' Jess called, holding up her ID so that the two uniformed men could see it.

'Who's she?' demanded the shaven-headed young man, pausing in his struggle and glaring at her.

'Inspector Campbell,' she told him.

'Sending ruddy inspectors to pick me up now, is it?' he demanded of one of the officers holding him.

'Alfie Darrow, ma'am,' the same officer called out to Jess. 'He's Weston St Ambrose's local drugs pusher, a regular Mr Big, aren't you, Alfie?'

'They framed me!' Darrow yelled at Jess.

The other officer produced a small plastic bag containing a heap of pills from her jacket. 'Under the floorboards upstairs, ma'am.'

'Do you need any back-up?' Jess asked.

'No, ma'am, Alfie knows he's coming with us. He's just going through the motions.'

'It's only bloody Ecstasy!' yelled Darrow.

'How do you know, if it's not yours?' asked the officer.

Darrow hung ludicrously between his captors like a disjointed marionette. He was staring thoughtfully at Jess. 'You're plain clothes, that mean you're CID?'

'Yes,' she told him.

'You investigating that murder at Balaclava House?'

The hair on the back of Jess's neck prickled. 'Yes.'

'I got a bit of information for you, maybe,' Darrow said. 'How about they –' he glanced up at the officers who held his arms – 'let me off with a caution and I tell you what I know?'

'How about I charge you with withholding information from a murder inquiry?'

Darrow looked crestfallen. 'You don't know what gratitude is, you lot,' he said bitterly.

Chapter 12

'I'm doing you a favour,' declared Alfie Darrow.

He sat on the uncomfortable wooden chair on one side of the interview room table. Jess and Morton sat on the other.

'I know you,' said Morton to him. 'You work for Seb Pascal.'

'That's right – and I remember you, and all!' retorted Alfie. 'You came asking questions of old Pascal and you were in the right place.'

'Suppose you tell us . . .' Jess began.

But Alfie's mind was on a track of its own, pursuing his many grievances. 'He's a miserable old git, Seb. He's a ruddy slave driver. He keeps on about me learning a trade; but all I do is the rotten boring or dirty jobs he doesn't want. I don't owe him nothing!' He glared fiercely at the other two, defying them to argue the point.

'What's this got to do with what happened at Balaclava House, Alfie?' Jess asked patiently.

'I don't owe him *nothing*!' Alfie repeated with greater emphasis. 'I'm not ratting on him like I was grassing up a mate. He's not a mate. I told you, he's a bad-tempered old sod, always finding fault.'

'All right,' Morton said wearily. 'So now we know what you

think of your employer. What's all this got to do with us? What's Pascal done that you're going to grass – tell us about?'

Alfie leaned across the wooden table, looking earnest. 'I got form,' he said.

'We know, Alfie,' they chorused.

'You cops have picked me up lots of times. I reckon it's persecution. I don't sell anything heavy, only Ecstasy and grass. I ain't a Colombian drug baron. To hear them talk, you'd think I was. They said I might go to jail this time. It ain't fair.'

'You mean,' Morton observed, 'that you've only been caught with those two substances in your possession with intent to supply. How do we know what else you've peddled?'

'See?' said Alfie. 'You're all the ruddy same.'

'We're not going to bargain with you,' Jess told him. 'But cooperating with us in our investigation would go in your favour. That is, if you've really got something to tell us?' she added sceptically. 'You're not going to tell us a load of fairy stories, I hope? This is going to be something that checks out, when we look into it?'

'Course it will,' said Alfie virtuously.

'Go on, then!' ordered Morton.

But Alfie was determined to enjoy his moment of being in charge of the situation. 'How about another cup of tea?'

Eventually, he began talking. 'He's an old misery—'

Morton groaned and put his head in his hands.

Hastily Alfie continued, 'Like I told you. But he's got some funny old ways with him too, has Seb. After I'd been working there for a while, I noticed that quite often he'd slip out, mid-morning, and go walking up the road towards Toby's Gutter.'

His listeners sat up.

'Then . . .' Alfie smirked, pleased at their reaction. 'Then I began to make a note of it, exactly what time he went, how long he was gone, when he came back. I also noticed something else. He always seemed to leave after old Monty Bickerstaffe had walked past the garage on his way into town. I thought to myself, "There's a connection there!" You know,' added Alfie, 'I reckon I'd make a good detective.'

'Get on with it!' Morton told him.

'So, one morning when things were really slack, I told Auntie Maureen, who works behind the till in the shop, that I'd got a hangover and I was going to sit down, behind the car wash, for a while. Then I slipped across the road and followed old Seb. I could see him up ahead of me, walking really fast. He never looked back once to see me following. He turned into Toby's Gutter and just about two minutes later, so did I. But I couldn't see him! It was like he'd vanished. I'd no idea where he'd gone; there's nothing in Toby's Gutter except that creepy old house. Well, not until you get to the Colleys' place and I didn't think Seb had had time to get that far.

'Then I saw someone was coming down the lane towards me and I jumped into the ditch, quick. It was a woman. I peered out and saw her go into the gates to the house. I got a closer look at her, too. It was Rosie Sneddon, old Pete Sneddon's missus. She buys petrol regular at our place. "Hello!" I said to myself. "I'm beginning to get the picture here! So that's where Seb gets to."' Alfie sniggered. 'They were having it off behind old Pete's back. It made me laugh. Pete is nearly as big a misery as Seb.

'I crept out of the ditch and went real carefully after her. I saw her push open the door to the house. It wasn't locked. I thought that was strange, but it wasn't. I don't know if Seb has a key and he opened it and left it for her. Anyway, she went inside and I heard her call out, "Seb! Are you there?"'

Alfie smiled in a singularly unpleasant way. 'I followed after a couple of minutes. I stood in that gloomy old hallway and listened. Cor, that's a funny old place, it really is. It's like something outa one of them horror films. You don't know what might come creeping out of one of the corners. I'd like to have taken a good look round. But I could hear voices upstairs, so I went up, really slow and careful, and followed the sound. They were in one of the bedrooms.' Alfie gave a snort. 'She must be desperate for it, that's all I can say! He ain't no pin-up, Seb. Anyhow, they'd closed the door so I couldn't see them; but I could hear them and the bed creaking.'

There was a silence.

'And?' asked Morton.

'And I came away, went back to the garage, before Auntie Maureen got suspicious and went looking for me.' Alfie leaned back in his chair and folded his arms. 'I reckon that's worth something, in't it? It's information, that's what that is.'

'You never saw anyone else in or around Balaclava House, or Toby's Gutter Lane?' Jess asked him. 'A stranger?'

'No,' admitted Alfie. 'But you could always go and arrest old Seb, couldn't you?' He grinned hopefully.

'One other thing,' Jess said. 'You haven't taken a car and done a spot of joyriding lately, have you?'

Alfie's smile vanished. He looked horrified and insulted. 'What? Trying to pin something else on me? I haven't done anything like that since I was a nipper, about fourteen. I work with cars. I don't need to go hotwiring one and driving around. That's kid's stuff.'

'You haven't heard of anyone else doing it, lately?'

Alfie eyed her. 'No,' he said shortly. 'How would I know?'

'How reliable do you judge Darrow?' asked Ian Carter.

'As a human being, not reliable at all,' returned Jess promptly. 'But as an informant in this case, I'm inclined to believe him. He could just be taking revenge because of some grudge against a boss he doesn't like. It's a pity we couldn't get any usable DNA from the blanket on the bed in the room. But the lab thinks another cover was thrown over it. That cover is missing and it suggests whoever used the room took it away with them. It could have been a sheet, quite lightweight and easy to fold up into a small package. Whoever used the room, Pascal and Rosie Sneddon or anyone else, was very, very careful.'

'As far as I'm concerned, Darrow's a horrible little yob,' growled Morton. 'He doesn't know the difference between truth and fiction. He could have driven that car into the quarry, no matter what he says now. I can imagine him torching it and dancing round the flames, whooping with joy. On the other hand, he does work with cars all the time and probably has plenty of opportunity to take one of them out for a spin. Remind me never to leave my car at Seb Pascal's garage for any reason. The thought of Alfie Darrow tinkering with it makes my hair stand on end. Admittedly, joyriders are generally kids. Alfie's getting too old for it, just like he said.'

He paused. 'He's probably telling the truth about the occasion he followed Pascal to Balaclava House. It's the sneaky sort of thing he'd do. That bit about jumping down into the ditch when he saw a woman coming, that rings true as well. And he described the interior of the house. Of course, he might have been in there before. He isn't admitting he knew the front door was left unlocked but he could've known. How do we know he wasn't the one using that bedroom?'

'I think he's telling the truth. He followed Pascal.' Jess smiled. 'I don't see Alfie cleaning the room so thoroughly. He'd have left his fingerprints all over it and probably other traces of his presence.'

'Fair enough,' said Carter. 'So, he's telling us the truth and not just trying to get himself out of trouble and his employer into it. We have to explain the use of one of the rooms upstairs at Balaclava. If this means we can, and it should turn out it's nothing to do with the murder, we'll be making progress by eliminating a diversion from the main inquiry. If, on the other hand, it plays a part . . . You'll have to speak to Pascal again, Phil. Jess, you tackle the woman. You'll have to get her away from her husband somehow. It'll look less suspicious if a woman officer goes to the farm; but Sneddon will still want to know what you're doing there, if he spots you.'

Jess heaved a sigh. 'I'll have to think up some story on my

way over. I really hope Alfie isn't spinning us a tale here. It would be helpful if we could eliminate the mystery of the phantom visitor to Balaclava from enquiries, if nothing else.'

'But what about Taylor?' Morton asked. 'Could this solve part of that mystery too? How he got to be slumped on Monty's sofa when found, I mean.' Morton's manner grew enthusiastic. 'Perhaps it doesn't eliminate Pascal and Rosie Sneddon but instead drops them right in it. Let's say Rosie and Seb have had their usual fun upstairs and are setting off home. She leaves first. They don't want to risk being seen together.

'Rosie finds Taylor collapsed over the wheel of his car in the lane outside the house. Or he's managed to get out of the car and is lying in the road unconscious. She runs back in to tell Pascal. Yes, that's the most likely.' Morton was warming to his theory. 'They panic. They're not supposed to be there, not supposed to be together. Between them they drag Taylor inside – leaving the scuffmarks we found – and leave him in the room downstairs. They know Monty will find him when he gets back from his daily walk into town. They hope Taylor will still be alive and Monty will summon help. They were behaving callously but their first concern was to keep their secret from being found out. It blotted out any other consideration in their minds. But, when they'd got him inside and propped him up on the sofa there, they realised he'd died on them. They had a dead body on their hands, not a sick man. That,' concluded Morton, 'sounds pretty feasible to me.'

'Yes, it does, Phil.' Carter nodded. 'But what about Taylor's burned-out Lexus? We know from Pete Sneddon's account that it was driven down to the quarry during the night following the discovery of the body and torched. Where was it during the entire day when the body was found and we were all running around the house? If Pascal and Rosie found Jay Taylor dying, took him indoors and left him there, they must have done something with his car immediately because it had gone by the time Monty got home. I'm accepting, for argument's sake, the hypothesis that Taylor drove himself to Toby's Gutter Lane and then felt so unwell he stopped the car, got out and lurched towards the first house he came to – Balaclava.'

'They hid the car during the day, sir. Pascal could have driven it back to his garage and parked it up behind the place. They didn't want us to examine it in case either of them had left prints on it. Neither of them could retrieve nor move it while SOCO and a search team were at the house and in the grounds. Pascal went back at night, drove it to the quarry and torched it,' Morton offered.

'If it were parked on or near the petrol station premises, Alfie would've seen it,' argued Jess. 'Alfie doesn't miss anything going on around that garage, we've discovered that!'

'So they parked it somewhere else. There have to be plenty of places to hide a car round there.' Morton was not going to give up his cherished deductions without a fight.

Carter still looked unconvinced. 'We won't find out until you've spoken again to both parties. There is another flaw in your idea, Sergeant, I'm sorry to point out. Why was Jay Taylor driving up Toby's Gutter Lane in the first place? If he was on the main road and felt ill, why didn't he just pull over and try to flag down the next car to come along?'

'He was confused . . . he was looking for a human habitation and first aid . . .' Morton shrugged.

'So, who slipped him the fatal overdose?' Carter asked. 'Who doctored his last meal? It wasn't Pascal or his lady love.'

'We know we've got two separate events,' Morton persisted. 'One person stuffed his last meal with crushed pills. We don't know who that person was. But we do know Taylor found his way to Balaclava House. I reckon it happened the way I said. Pascal and Mrs S took him inside and dumped him there.'

But that's all wrong! thought Jess. Phil thinks he's cracked it, but I'm sure it didn't happen that way. Seb and Rosie wouldn't have emptied Taylor's pockets. Why should they try and slow identification of the dead man? Phil's theory is plausible but it depends on too much speculation about what two other people did. She moved slightly to her right, which brought her to the window. She glanced down at the unlovely spectacle of the car park with its rows of cars, all sorts of cars, even a Lexus that she knew belonged to Carter. The pale late-afternoon sun of this time of year was sinking already. A ray beamed through the window and struck her face with an unexpected warm caress. It also dazzled her and made her turn quickly back to face the room. She saw that both men were looking at her, waiting for some comment. Morton looked like a man who had just pulled off a difficult conjuring trick. Carter's green-brown eyes, fixed on her, were harder to read.

'I don't buy it.' She spoke up firmly; and Morton gave her

a reproachful look. He was a conjuror not receiving the expected round of applause, and she was a colleague not giving support. 'Sorry, Phil,' she added because she felt she'd let him down. But she didn't agree with him and she couldn't just let it go unchallenged.

Carter, observing them and probably reading both their minds, raised his eyebrows and asked, 'Yes?'

'It's that house, sir. It's the key somehow. Taylor didn't just stumble into it by chance. Nor was he helped indoors by Pascal and Rosie Sneddon, just because they happened to be there – and to be leaving as he collapsed outside. Taylor was there because he wanted to be there, or someone else wanted him there. Balaclava House holds secrets.'

Chapter 13

Jess had no idea, when she began her drive to the Sneddons' farm, how she was going to explain her wish to speak to Rosie Sneddon alone. Morton was to tackle Pascal. Already the rain had settled in, breaking the long dry spell. The drizzle had turned to a heavy fall overnight. A brief but violent shower had deluged them again this morning at breakfast-time. The road surface glittered with a myriad bright spots dancing along it before her as she drove. Sometimes they were bright enough momentarily to dazzle her. She put up a hand and pulled down the sun visor, hoping the recent downpour wouldn't have kept Sneddon near to his house. It would suit her best if the farmer was well out of the way, working on his land a good distance from the farmyard, and she'd find Rosie at home alone.

She turned into Toby's Gutter Lane. Here the rain had filled the many dips in the road producing puddles that sent up muddy sprays as she lurched over them. This would leave her car in a terrible mess, patterned like an army vehicle with khaki patches. She'd have to take it along to the car wash. But not Pascal's.

She'd reached Balaclava House and slowed to a crawl to look across at it. It presented a desolate aspect, lonely and deserted. The sadness sprang from so many sources. It represented the failure of what must once have been confidence and hope for the future, built on the success of a business enterprise. Ironically, if Monica Farrell's history of the Bickerstaffe biscuit factory was correct, that confidence and prosperity had itself been built on a failed enterprise, bogged down in the bloody mud of the Crimea. She felt a pang of pity for the wretched soldiers, betrayed by the ineptitude of their leaders and the government of the day, and with nothing but an army-issue Bickerstaffe dry biscuit to console them.

Yet that ill wind had blown good fortune the way of the Bickerstaffes. With what pride must the first of them have taken possession of their new home, have crossed its threshold. How splendid those cavernous rooms must have looked with their brand-new furniture and carpets, all kept in sparkling condition by a small army of maidservants. How were the mighty fallen . . .

Strips of blue and white tape marking a police crime scene still hung dispiritedly from its gates. Jess made a mental note to stop here, on her way back, and check the exterior of the house to make sure no one had broken in. The discovery of a body there had been well reported in the local press and could have attracted a ghoulish interest from sightseers and others, some taking the opportunity of an abandoned building to indulge in a spot of housebreaking. Monty might not have much money; but that house was stuffed with good Victorian furniture and decorative objects.

There was no sign of life when she passed by the Colleys' gate, either. It was as if the recent rain had washed the landscape clean of human life and activity.

At that moment a car suddenly appeared ahead of her, breaking into the empty landscape with an almost physical impact, shattering its calm. It shot out of the entry to the farm track ahead and began to career wildly towards her. There was barely room for the two vehicles side by side; but the other car was determined to get by and by some miracle it did, flying past. Jess reacted, wrenching the wheel to avoid what had seemed like an inevitable collision; and nearly hit a dry stone wall. She just had time to establish that the driver was male and wore a cap. She had not met Sneddon so couldn't say if it was the farmer; but whoever he was, he was driving like a maniac. Presumably he didn't normally encounter another vehicle at this point in the lane. No one lived further down Toby's Gutter than the Sneddons. He was still an idiot. She wished she'd taken the car registration. She'd have called in to Traffic Division.

She turned on to the track and parked in the farmyard. The only living thing to be seen here was a sheep dog, a collie. It had been tied up near the front door and was running round in fretful little circles, risking entanglement in its tether. Seeing Jess's car rattle into the yard, it looked up hopefully and wagged its plumed tail.

Jess got out of the car and as she approached, the dog ran to greet her, as far as the rope allowed, crouching in abasement, still wagging its tail furiously and whimpering.

'You want me to untie you, old fellow, don't you?' Jess stooped to pat its head. 'But you've been tied up for some purpose.'

She stood up and looked about. The dog whined again. It

was deeply worried about something and Jess was beginning to feel very uneasy. If the driver of the car had been Sneddon, where was he going in such a hurry? Should she have turned round and gone after him? She had had good reason. She could have forced him to pull over and warned him about his erratic driving. Jess walked up to the front door and rapped with the metal knocker. The sound echoed inside but no one answered the summons. The dog gave a nervous, impatient yelp.

With an increasing sense that something was terribly wrong, Jess began to make a tour of the outside of the building. There was no one in the yard at the rear. Washing hung, dripping, on a line, but there was no sign of Rosie who had presumably pegged it up. It had been pinned there before the breakfast rain shower and no one had bothered to bring it indoors. Jess didn't need to feel it to know it was sodden.

She went up to the back door and knocked again. Then she put her ear against it and listened. It seemed to her there was an answering knock, like an echo, from within. She rapped harder.

Thump – thump – thump came from inside in response.

Someone was trying to communicate, someone who couldn't get to the door. Jess rattled at the handle but the door was locked. If there's anyone as aware of the basics of breaking and entering as a burglar, it's a police officer. Jess inspected the kitchen window, often a weak point. Bingo! It was ajar, unlatched, and held in position by a metal arm punctured with holes that dropped over a peg on the window frame. She hunted round and found a length of narrow stick, used to tie up some fuchsias in a flowerbed by the door. A further hunt turned up a wooden crate with wilting greens in it. She tipped them out, lugged the crate back to the window and upturned it beneath it.

Then she climbed carefully on to the crate and reached through the crack of the window with the stick. A couple of awkward attempts and she succeeded. The pierced arm jumped free of the peg and flew upward. Released, the window was easily pulled open. Jess set about hauling herself up and scrambling over the ledge inside.

Like many a kitchen window, it was located over the sink. Jess slithered over the sill and down into a big old-fashioned glazed stoneware sink with a couple of inches of cold, sudsy water in it.

'Faugh!' she muttered. She swung herself over the edge to the tiled floor and attempted to brush off the worst of the wet stains from her clothes. Then she heard the noise again, coming from above her head, the pounding of a fist on wood and a rattling.

Jess hurried out into the narrow hallway and shouted up the staircase, 'Is someone up there? This is the police!'

Thump – thump! It came again and was followed by a muffled shout, a woman's voice. 'Help, help me, please!'

Jess ran up the staircase. The voice and sound of a fist on wood came from behind the closed door of a large cupboard at the top of the stairs. As Jess reached it, the door began to rattle and shake as someone inside tried to force it open.

'Mrs Sneddon?' Jess called.

'Yes! He's locked me in – Pete's locked me in!'

Thankfully the key was still in the outside of the door. Jess

229

turned it. The door flew open and a dishevelled, wild-eyed woman was catapulted into her arms.

She clung to Jess, gasping and uttering incoherent words. Jess gripped her arms tightly. 'Rosie? Calm down, come on, take a deep breath – now, another! Your husband passed me in the lane. Where is he going?' But even as she asked, she knew the answer and felt her heart give a painful leap.

'Gone – gone down to Seb's garage!' Rosie drew a deep ragged breath. 'He's taken his gun!'

Jess was aghast. '*What?* When did he leave? What kind of gun is it?'

'It's a shotgun. He's going to shoot Seb and it's all my fault!' Rosie Sneddon's voice rose in a desperate wail.

'Morton!' exclaimed Jess. Damn and blast, Phil Morton was on his way, unaware of any danger, to Pascal's garage to interview him again in the light of Alfie's story . . . also to find out if his cherished theory was correct and Pascal and Rosie had dragged a dying man into the house. But Phil wouldn't get the opportunity. If Sneddon got there first, Phil would walk in on the situation. If Phil had got there first, Sneddon would burst in, armed, on Phil.

Jess scrabbled at her mobile phone and tried in vain to get a reply from Morton. He might already be at the garage and anything could be happening. There was no time to lose. Jess rang through to HQ and shouted, 'Man armed with a shotgun, Peter Sneddon, at Pascal's garage on the ring road, near turning to Toby's Gutter Lane. Sergeant Morton may be there. I need an armed response team, urgently!'

Rosie gripped her sleeve. 'They won't shoot Pete? It's all my fault! Pete wouldn't harm a fly normally! I told him – I told him about me and Seb and our meetings at Balaclava House. I thought it would all come out now you're investigating that murder and I wanted to tell Pete myself. He flew into a rage. I've never seen him like it . . .'

Jess shook herself free and ran down the stairs, then along the hall and out of the front door. The dog leaped to its feet and jumped up at her. She managed to avoid it and reached her car. She scrambled in; only then realising to her dismay that Rosie Sneddon had followed on her heels and had got into the passenger seat beside her. The collie was barking wildly and pulling at its tether, desperate to be free and come with them.

'Mrs Sneddon! Get out, please! Stay here! This is a dangerous situation,' Jess ordered as she switched on the ignition.

'I'm coming with you!' Rosie shouted. 'He's my husband! He'll listen to me! He's angry, but he won't do anything if I'm there!'

There wasn't time to argue or waste precious minutes trying to eject Rosie from the car by force. Jess wrenched at the wheel; they skidded round in a circle in a shower of grit and set off back the way she had come to the farm.

The car rattled and bumped over the uneven surface, and splashed through the puddles sending up showers of spray. Beside her, Rosie was still lamenting and pleading that no one shoot her husband.

Just so long as he doesn't shoot Morton, thought Jess furiously. Or anyone else! Even if Sneddon was not normally a violent man, just now he was seeing the world in a sudden red mist of fury. With all sense of judgement gone and holding a loaded shotgun, he could easily go berserk and loose off the weapon at anyone.

But Pascal's garage, when they reached it, appeared deserted. Jess parked well away, pulling the car up on to the grass verge behind a large clump of spiny blackthorn bushes.

'Stay in the car!' she ordered Rosie Sneddon. 'I mean that!'

She got out and using the blackthorn as shield peered in the direction of the garage. Sneddon must be inside – and there was Morton's car parked outside. Phil was in there, too.

'Come on, come on!' muttered Jess to the approaching back-up team. It was going to be a good five minutes longer before they got here.

There was a deep ditch running behind the blackthorn towards the garage, with high grass and wild plants at its edge. Jess jumped into it, cold muddy water swilling round her ankles and seeping into her footwear. She crept, crouched nearly double, as near to the garage as she reckoned she could safely go.

She stopped when she had a good view of the plate-glass window at the front of the building. Something moved behind it. It looked like the outline of a woman. That must be Alfie's aunt, Maureen, who worked at the till. The female figure held up her hands at shoulder height. Sneddon was in there all right. But was Pascal? Had Sneddon arrived to find his quarry not at home? Was he holding Maureen and Sergeant Morton as hostages until Pascal returned? Jess prayed no driver decided he needed to stop by the garage and fill up with petrol.

She crept back to her car and checked that Rosie was still sitting obediently inside, although the woman was so jittery there was no guarantee she'd remain there. Then, seeing a car approaching, Jess stepped out into the road and flagged it down.

'I'm sorry,' she told the driver, showing her ID, 'but there's an incident taking place at the garage down there. You'll have to turn back.'

'What sort of incident?' grumbled the driver. 'I'm in a hurry.'

'Armed man!' snapped Jess.

'What about her, then?' asked the driver belligerently, pointing past Jess.

Jess turned her head and saw to her dismay that Rosie Sneddon had taken the opportunity afforded by Jess's distraction to scramble out of the car. She was racing down the grass verge towards the garage.

'Rosie!' Jess yelled. 'Come back! You'll make things worse! You'll give Pete an extra hostage! There's a specially trained team on its way! They'll deal with it!'

But Rosie took no notice, still running and, now that she was near the building, beginning to shout. 'Pete! Peter! Put the gun down and come outside! The police are on their way, armed police! Peter! They'll shoot you!'

'They won't shoot him if he throws the gun out first!' yelled Jess.

She wasn't sure Rosie could hear her, intent on her own mission. But it seemed she had because she repeated what Jess had just said.

'Throw the gun out of the door, Pete! Then they'll know you're not armed any longer and they won't shoot!'

Jess saw the figure of Maureen turn her head. She had heard Rosie's shouts. At that moment, Jess heard the wail of the approaching sirens. At the same time, there came a deafening explosion from within the garage building and the sound of a woman screaming.

Earlier, Phil Morton had arrived at the garage and parked in the forecourt. He went into the minimart and was greeted by the till operator. He seemed to remember her name was Maureen.

'Seb's not here,' Maureen told him, in reply to his query. 'He's gone into town.'

'When's he expected back?' Morton glanced at his watch. 'Has he been gone long?'

'He went about half an hour ago. He should be back soon. Are you going to wait? You can go and sit in the office, or wait in your car. I'll make you a coffee if you like.'

And that was when it all went pear-shaped and bloody bedlam broke out, as Morton later described it.

The automatic doors to the minimart flew apart and an apocalyptic figure appeared: Pete Sneddon, wild-eyed, twitching and grasping a shotgun. He ran up to the desk and yelled, 'Where is he? I'm going to blow his head off his shoulders, the scum!'

Maureen let out a banshee screech and the shotgun leaped about in Sneddon's hands.

'All right, Maureen!' Morton ordered quickly. 'Keep calm.

234

You, too, Mr Sneddon. What's all this about? Why don't you throw down the gun? It's not necessary. Seb Pascal isn't here.'

'What do you mean, not here?' Sneddon's feverish glance took in the office door. He darted over to it. Morton made a snap judgement as to whether he could reach the doors to the outside while the man was distracted, and decided it was too risky and would mean leaving Maureen alone in here with the man. Sneddon had kicked open the office door with his earth-caked boot and seeing the tiny room empty, whirled round again to face the other two.

For a moment he looked perplexed, unsure what to do now his original plan had been thwarted. 'You –' the shotgun indicated Morton and then the petrified Maureen who threw up her hands to shoulder level in approved manner. 'You two are my hostages. That's it, yes, hostages.' He seemed pleased at remembering the word.

'Why do you want to see Pascal, Pete?' Morton asked as calmly as he could. 'You don't really want to harm him.'

'Yes, I do!' yelled Sneddon. 'He's been knocking off my wife!'

Oh-oh . . . thought Morton. Aloud he began, 'This still isn't the way to settle it, Pete. Now then, before anyone gets hurt, just throw down the gun and we can discuss how to go about it.'

Sneddon was still looking very jumpy but now undecided too. He had not planned this part of things. He scowled in thought. 'No, we do it my way. I wait here for Pascal and you two just – just keep quiet. Shut up, right?'

A frozen silence descended on the minimart. Sneddon paced up and down and the other two watched him. Maureen was trembling and silent tears ran down her cheeks. Morton was aware of the anger towards Sneddon building within him. Bloody man, who did he think he was, rushing in here like Butch Cassidy, waving a – they had to assume – loaded firearm? He was terrifying an elderly woman. It was only by chance no customers were here and some might arrive at any moment. He held Maureen and Morton, and could yet end up with half a roomful of hostages.

He knows Maureen, reasoned Morton to himself, and he won't shoot her. If he takes a pot shot at anyone, before Pascal gets here, it will be me. Morton edged a little closer to the nearest stacked shelves standing mid-aisle. If Sneddon made a threatening move, he could throw himself behind the shelves and hope they'd protect him.

'Stay where you are, copper!' Sneddon rasped. 'I can see what you're up to. You do like Maureen's done. That's it, put your hands up! Now, you keep your hands in the air, do you hear me? And you keep absolutely bloody still and right there, on that spot, where I can see you!'

More fraught minutes passed. Sneddon paced up and down, occasionally muttering to himself. Maureen whimpered. Morton debated again whether it was worth diving down behind the shelves, but what then? He wasn't alone with Sneddon. There was Maureen to consider. If any firing started, there was a strong risk of a stray shot hitting her.

Then, faintly, outside the building and coming nearer, they heard a woman's voice, shouting.

Sneddon gave a convulsive twitch and looked, if possible, even more wild-eyed. 'Rosie?'

'Pete! Pete! Throw the gun out of the door!'

They could all hear the words now.

'That's my wife!' Sneddon looked flabbergasted. He stared at the other two helplessly. 'What's she doing here? How did she get out of that cupboard? I locked her in.'

Morton turned his head and to his horror saw the dishevelled figure of Rosie Sneddon running past the window towards the automatic doors. They opened and she burst in. Pete swung round to face her; the shotgun jerked upwards and there was a deafening blast. A large lump of the ceiling fell down and crashed to the floor, leaving a gaping hole above their heads.

Morton and Maureen had both flung themselves to the floor. Sneddon looked up at the hole in the ceiling as if stunned, unable to believe he was the cause of it.

'Pete!' Rosie's voice was high-pitched but crisp. 'What on earth do you think you're doing? This isn't the Wild West. Don't be stupid. How could you shoot anyone? Throw the gun down, *now*!'

As a technique for dealing with a gunman it might have left much to be desired, but it worked.

Sneddon obediently dropped the weapon to the floor with a clatter.

'Thank God!' muttered Morton, scrambling to his feet.

Maureen, on the other hand, decided it was time to start screaming again.

Chapter 14

'I'm sorry she managed to slip out of the car, sir. It shouldn't have happened. She went tearing off down the verge towards the garage like an Olympic sprinter, yelling out her husband's name,' Jess explained ruefully to Carter. 'Then the armed back-up arrived. Phil threw the gun out of the door and shouted that it was all under control. It was over pretty quickly after that. Maureen, Mrs Wilson, has been taken back to her home in Weston St Ambrose to recover. I'll arrange for her to make a statement later.'

'You'd better take the rest of the day off and go home as well, Phil,' Carter said. 'I'll interview Sneddon. Where's his wife now, Jess?'

'In an interview room downstairs. Bennison is with her. I was on my way to get her version of Alfie's story when Pete Sneddon passed me in Toby's Gutter Lane. He was driving wildly but I didn't then know for sure that it *was* Sneddon, nor that he'd taken off for the garage.' Jess grimaced. 'Rosie had decided confession was good for the soul and told him about her affair with Pascal. It set the whole thing in motion.'

Rosie sat huddled on a wooden chair with an untouched cup of tea in front of her and DC Bennison for company. When

Jess appeared, Bennison switched on the tape recorder and announced, for its benefit, 'Inspector Campbell has just come in.' Bennison glanced at her wristwatch and added the time.

'All right, Rosie,' said Jess, taking a seat. 'Do you feel up to telling me in detail exactly what happened?'

The woman looked at her wretchedly. 'What will they do with Pete?'

'I can't tell you that yet. Why don't you just tell me all about the events leading up to it?'

'It was like I told you already,' Rosie said nearly inaudibly.

'Why don't you drink some of your tea?' suggested Bennison, leaning forward, braids bobbing. 'You'll feel better. A cup of tea always bucks you up.'

Rosie obediently sipped at the cup and then set it down again. But when she spoke, her voice was louder and firmer.

'It was really stupid of Seb and me to think we could keep it secret for ever.'

'What do you mean by "it"?' Jess asked.

'The affair, I suppose you'd call it.' Rosie looked bewildered. 'Funny thing, when you say "affair" it sounds sort of glamorous, doesn't it? But this wasn't. It was quite ordinary, really. Not at all romantic.'

'How did the affair start?' Jess asked sympathetically.

Rosie gave a despairing shrug. 'I don't really know. It was about six months ago. Pete's a good man and a good husband. Good father, too. We've got two girls, both married now. How am I going to tell them?' She spread her hands. 'I didn't want to hurt Pete, or the girls. I don't love Seb. I love my husband.

It's just that it's lonely at the farm, now the girls have gone. Pete's out all day in the fields or doing something away from the house; and when he gets indoors of an evening he's tired out and you can't have any kind of conversation with him. I wanted company. That's all it was, really. It wasn't about sex; it was about company and a bit of excitement. Getting away from the farm for an hour from time to time, kicking over the traces. I suppose you'd call it a bit of middle-aged madness. I'd never done anything like that before. I never thought I would. But then it – it just happened and it was so easy.'

Rosie snuffled and wiped away the tears that had started to roll down her cheeks with the heel of her palm. Bennison handed her a fistful of paper tissues. Rosie took them and mopped her tears.

'I'd got to know Seb quite well over the years I've bought my petrol at his place,' she whispered.

'Can you speak up a little, Rosie?' Jess asked.

Rosie nodded. She cleared her throat and began again, 'He's fixed my car a couple of times, too. We always exchanged a few words, just sociable, you know. I got chatting to him one day, much as usual. I'd been into the minimart to pay for the fuel I'd filled up with. When I came out, Seb was standing there just watching the road. That horrible boy, Alfie, wasn't around. Seb and I got into conversation. While we were talking, Mr Monty lurched past on his way to town, poor old chap. Seb drew attention to him and said he'd offered to drive Mr Monty in, from time to time. But Mr Monty wouldn't have it. He was an obstinate old bugger, that's what Seb said.

'I said, we all worried about Mr Monty – Pete and me and the Colleys. We'd known him all our lives. He lived all on his own in that great rambling house and he never bothered to lock the front door during the day.' She drew a deep breath. 'Then Seb said, we could meet at Balaclava House, while Mr Monty was in town. It shook me when Seb suggested it. I hadn't thought about any such thing. I refused. I was really indignant. I'd never given Seb any encouragement. Or I didn't think I had. Seb said, well, think it over.

'That evening at home, Pete came in dog-tired from working all day. He just sat there, eating his evening meal and not saying a word. I tried to talk to him a bit but he just grunted and nodded. I thought, "Is this it? Is this the rest of my life? I deserve better than this!"' She looked up in sudden defiance.

Bennison was nodding in a way that indicated Rosie had touched on some shared experience.

Rosie fell silent and drank some of the tea. She put the cup in the saucer and sat staring at it for a minute or two. 'It must have been a week or two after that, I told Seb, well, all right. But we'd have to be very careful. I'd given it a lot of thought. It would be as easy as anything for someone to burgle Balaclava House one day and it had always worried me that would happen. There's lots of old stuff in there and antiques fetch a good price these days, don't they? I watch those television programmes about it. Some of the values they put on old stuff, really ugly old vases and grandfather clocks that don't work, it's a real shock. But it made me think that, if Seb and I used the place and left our fingerprints everywhere, and if one day the place was burgled and the police came . . .' Rosie looked at them helplessly. 'Well, they'd find our fingerprints and think it was us who did it!' She raised her eyebrows in enquiry.

'You'd certainly have put yourselves in a very awkward situation,' Jess agreed. 'So you were careful to wipe all surfaces in that room before you and Seb left. You did do a pretty good job cleaning up after you. It puzzled us and, I can tell you, you gave us quite a headache. We didn't know who'd been using the room. We didn't know when the clean-up took place.'

Rosie nodded vigorously. 'I used to take an old sheet down with me . . .' She blushed. 'You know . . . I'd read about DNA. We put a blanket – Seb brought that – on one of the beds and then I put the sheet over it before we – you know. I took the sheet home with me, folded up small under my coat, and washed it, every time.' She looked down at the cooling cup of tea. 'Every time I did that, I thought how sleazy the whole thing was. Like I said, it wasn't romantic. It wasn't even much fun. I began to think I really must get out of it, tell Seb it was too risky. I was always scared we'd be caught; that Mr Monty would come home early, or that someone else would show up. One day, someone did. We nearly did get caught.'

Jess sat bolt upright. 'What? When did this happen? Who came?'

'It was about two months ago,' Rosie said, frowning. 'I can't give you a date, but it was about then. You can ask Seb. We heard a car draw up outside and a door slam. Then we heard footsteps outside. The room we used looks out over the gardens, at the back. Whoever it was had walked right round the house to the back and was under our window.' Rosie swallowed. 'I was near petrified, I can tell you. But Seb went to the window and peered out, really carefully, from behind the curtain. He said there was a bloke outside, a stranger. He was acting very oddly, so Seb reckoned. He was looking through the window of the kitchen downstairs. You know, his face pressed up against the glass and his hand shielding his eyes to cut out the sun, like you do when you're trying to see into a place from outside.'

Jess and Bennison both nodded.

'The next thing was, Seb said, the man had left the window and was exploring the grounds, that's what it looked like. So I got up the courage to take a peek myself. Sure enough, there was this fellow I'd never seen before, any more than Seb had. He was a biggish chap, in his forties perhaps, or a little bit younger, very well dressed and set up. Not someone who'd come to do a manual job of some sort, that was for sure. I did wonder, just briefly, if he was an estate agent. Perhaps Mr Monty was thinking of selling up?'

'Do you remember how he was dressed?' Jess asked.

She nodded. 'Oh, he was quite a gent in a nice brown jacket and pale-coloured trousers. The jacket looked like leather. He was taking a really good look round. The gardens are overgrown, a really terrible mess, like a jungle. You've seen them. So we'd keep losing sight of him among the trees and bushes. Then he'd reappear. He was a good fifteen minutes hunting round out there. Goodness knows what he was looking for.

'I whispered to Seb . . .' Rosie gave a sheepish little smile. 'I don't know why I whispered but I remember I did. It was knowing we shouldn't be there, I suppose. I said, "What do we do if he comes into the house?" Seb said, "We ask him what the hell he thinks he's playing at?"

'I said, well, he could ask *us* that! But Seb said no, he wouldn't. Because Seb reckoned this fellow was up to no good. He believed the house was empty and he was unobserved. "If he finds us," Seb said, "it'll give him a bigger fright than it'll give you or me, Rosie!"

'I wasn't convinced and I still thought the man might try and get in. I remembered my old fear about burglars. Perhaps this was a burglar, even though he didn't look it. There was something really furtive about the way he was snooping round out there. Or a dodgy dealer? There are people who go round looking in the windows of empty houses and so on, checking out any antiques, aren't there? Then they turn up at the door and badger old people into selling them things cheap. It happened to Pete's auntie. This bloke could be one of those.

'Well, anyway, eventually he came back and walked round the house to the front. We heard the car door slam again and then the sound of the car leaving. I was so relieved, my legs turned to jelly. I couldn't stand up. I just sat there on the bed, shaking like a leaf.'

'Did you ever see this man around Balaclava again?' Jess asked. 'Or did you see him anywhere else? Did Seb see him anywhere else? Did he ever call at Seb's place for petrol, perhaps?'

Rosie was shaking her head vigorously. 'No, I never saw him again. No more did Seb, because I asked him about that. Seb was sure the bloke hadn't been to the garage because he had been looking out for him. It was a couple of weeks before we met again at the house. The whole thing had given me such a fright I couldn't go back there straight away. I think the incident had shaken Seb, too. He tried to act casual but he was jumpy and kept looking out of the window. We should have called it a day, then, stopped meeting like we were. It was a warning. We should have heeded it.'

Rosie was growing distressed and near to tears.

'All right, Rosie,' Jess said soothingly. 'I know how difficult this is. But try and take it easy and just tell us what happened next.'

'Sorry . . .' muttered Rosie, fumbling for more tissues from the box on the table.

'You're doing fine. Now, I want you to think about the day the body was found at Balaclava House.' This was the question that, if any, was going to send Rosie into a blind panic. Jess held her breath.

Rosie looked terrified and half rose to her feet. 'Seb and I never had anything to do with that!'

'All right, I'm not saying you did. But were you and Seb at Balaclava House that day? Did you meet there, as you had before?'

'No, no, we didn't, and thank goodness. We'd have got caught up in it all.' She leaned across the desk. 'It would have served us right if we did. It was all wrong, what we were doing. When I heard about the dead man my first thought was that we were being punished, somehow. It's a silly thing to have thought and selfish, but I was feeling so guilty. It was Seb told me. I'd gone down for petrol as usual and I saw, when I drove past Balaclava, that there was a police car there. I told Seb and asked if he knew what was going on. He told me all he knew, how he'd seen Mr Monty drive past in Mrs Harwell's little car. How he'd rung Gary Colley and been told about a body being found there. I nearly went all to pieces! I said to Seb that the police were bound to find out all about us. Seb told me to keep my head. There was no reason the police should find out. We'd been careful to clean up the place after us. Even if they found a fingerprint or two, they didn't have Seb's prints or mine to compare them with – and there was no reason why they – I mean, you,' Rosie nodded apologetically to Jess, 'why you should ask for our prints. We were quite safe.

'But I wasn't sure. I just kept thinking how horrible it was, the body being found, and how we could so easily have been there, Seb and I, when it happened, whatever it was. When that poor man died, I mean. I knew we couldn't ever meet there again. Truth to tell, I didn't want to meet Seb again anywhere else, ever! I think Seb knew it, too. We'd sailed very close to the wind and we'd nearly got mixed up in something really bad.

'Then there was the boy, Alfie. I was sure he was on to us. He came up to talk to me one morning when I was at the garage and Seb not there. I didn't need more petrol, but I went down just hoping to see Seb and find out if he knew anything more. Alfie was trying to find out what I knew, too. He wouldn't go away. He kept grinning at me, like he already knew something and thought it was funny. He more or less said he knew I'd only come to see Seb. I knew there was only one thing to do, besides put a stop to the affair. I had to tell Pete about it, confess the lot. It would be hard to do and Pete would be so upset. But it would be worse if he found out from someone else. That Alfie, he might make trouble. The more I thought about it, the surer I became that Alfie *had* found out. He might try and blackmail Seb or me. I know he's been in quite a lot of trouble. Maureen told me about it. Alfie is her nephew. Even she says Alfie is a bad lot.'

Rosie sighed, 'So, I did tell Pete . . .' she finished her story lamely. 'I knew he'd be angry and hurt – hurt more than angry – but I didn't know he'd go crazy and grab the old shotgun.'

A girl with straggling blond hair and a metal pin through one eyebrow was operating the till for the petrol station/minimart when Carter walked in. She was taking money from a motorist and there was no sign of Pascal. Carter stared up at the plastic sheet taped over the hole in the ceiling while he waited for the customer to leave. He wondered if Pascal was there or if he was too afraid now to step into his own place of business, even though they still had Pete Sneddon in a cell. The farmer would appear before a magistrate later and the case would certainly be referred to a Crown Court. Whether Sneddon would later be given bail was another matter. Given his responsibilities to his farm and the animals, he might. They'd confiscated his shotgun. At the moment the unfortunate Rosie Sneddon had to run the place alone with the help of a retired farmer who lived in the area. Nobly he had creaked out of his comfortable bungalow and peaceful retirement to take up a working life again, plodding about in mud.

The motorist left at last and Carter approached the counter to show his ID and enquire if Pascal was there. The girl first stared at the ID blankly and then, just as unresponsively, at him. At last, with great effort, she said Seb was in his office.

'I'll just go and find him, then,' said Carter, thinking that Pascal must be desperate to put this girl in charge of anything, let alone a till.

Mild panic crossed her face. 'It's private,' she said.

'I'm on police business,' said Carter as clearly as he could.

'I dunno about that,' said the girl.

'I do,' said Carter.

Pascal received his visit with a look of doleful resignation touched with not a little nervousness.

And well you might be nervous! thought Carter. It's no thanks to you that Phil Morton isn't gravely wounded or even dead.

As if he read Carter's mind, Pascal asked, 'How's the other chap, the sergeant?'

'He's OK,' Carter told him briefly.

'I didn't know Pete was going to come storming down here looking for me with a ruddy shotgun!' Pascal's nervousness gave way to whining defiance. 'I don't know whether the insurance company's going to pay for that hole in the ceiling out there, either.'

Carter ignored this and, indicating the girl outside in the minimart with a jerk of his head, asked, 'That young woman isn't Mrs Wilson, I take it?'

Pascal looked even glummer. 'No, Maureen's handed in her notice. She says she can't imagine ever working here again. She wouldn't feel safe. I told her, look, Pete's locked up at the moment and the cops have taken away his gun – and it's not like he was trying to rob the place. It was purely personal. But she wouldn't have it. I've had to take on someone else – in a hurry,' he added, in justification for any poor opinion Carter might have formed of his new staff member.

'I'm not surprised,' said Carter. 'It was a very hairy moment. We're fortunate no one was hurt.'

Pascal, his mind still running on his staff shortage problems, observed wistfully, 'Perhaps Maureen will change her mind when she's had a bit of time to get over her fright.' He didn't look as if he had much faith in his optimistic forecast.

Carter, in any case, had no interest in Pascal's staffing problem. 'You and Mrs Sneddon,' he said briskly, 'have been using Balaclava House for a series of meetings while the owner, Mr Bickerstaffe, was away from the place.'

'Yes – and I'd like to know who put you on to us!' Pascal rallied, prepared to defend his actions.

'Information received,' said Carter expressionlessly.

Pascal glowered at him. 'Who from? Nobody knew. Well, one of the Colleys might have seen us, but they wouldn't go to the police.' He chewed his lower lip. 'It was that bloody useless nephew of Maureen's, young Alfie, wasn't it?'

When Carter made no reply, Pascal went on. 'You don't have to tell me. It had to be him, spying on me most likely. I only took him on because Maureen asked me. She told me he'd been in trouble and she thought if he had a steady job, he'd mend his ways and make something of himself. But you've picked him up again, haven't you, for selling his happy pills and hash? He hasn't dared to show his face here again. Still, I'll catch up with him. He lives in Weston St Ambrose, same as me. He can't avoid me for ever!'

'If you're thinking of violence, Mr Pascal, I advise you strongly against it,' Carter warned him.

'Much as I'd like to beat the little sod to a pulp, I won't,' said Pascal. 'But I can still make his life a misery.' He stared at Carter. 'We weren't guilty of breaking and entering, you know, at Balaclava House. Monty leaves the front door unlocked. Anyone could walk in. And we didn't take anything. We were trespassing, admittedly, but that's all.'

'You've been giving it some thought,' said Carter drily. 'Had some legal advice, have you? The day the dead man was found in the house, it was searched and we found the room you'd been using.'

Pascal sighed. 'Yeah, I know. Rosie realised you must have done and got on the phone to me about it at once. She was dead scared you'd trace us somehow. She wanted me to go back to the house and get in there and check out the room to make sure we'd not left anything – and give the place another clean round. I told you, she was out of her mind. I couldn't get back in, even if I wanted to, not with police all over it. Even if I could, I couldn't move anything in that room not one inch. You'd have photographed it, right? You'd notice the slightest thing out of place.' Pascal shook his head. 'She was panicking, you see. I was worried about it myself, honest truth.'

'I'm afraid you'd left it all rather late to be worried, Mr Pascal.

However, I'm not here about your affair with Mrs Sneddon. I'm here about a visitor whom, she claims, you saw in the grounds of Balaclava House one day when you were both there. He was a stranger, she said.'

Pascal nodded and looked relieved that he hadn't to defend his activities at Balaclava House any more for the moment. 'Yes, that's right. We heard a car draw up and my first thought was it might be Mrs Harwell. She does drive over from time to time to check on Monty. I don't know why she bothers, except that I suppose the old chap has got to leave his estate to someone. He's stony broke, of course, but there are antiques, stacks of them, in that house. Must be worth something.'

'Mrs Sneddon has made the same observation.'

'We didn't take anything, I've told you that once!' Pascal snapped. 'We could've done, anyone could've. It's a miracle that place hasn't been burgled. But Rosie and I never even picked up anything to look at it.'

Because you didn't want to leave prints . . . Carter thought sourly.

'Mrs Sneddon was afraid of a burglary and of being blamed for it,' he said aloud to the garage owner. 'And when you saw a stranger apparently casing the place, she feared that was his intention.'

'So did I.' Pascal nodded. 'He was up to no good, creeping around. I don't know if he tried the front door. I reckon he didn't, because, if he had, he'd have found it was unlocked and walked in. When I looked out of the window upstairs, I could see him below me, peering in the kitchen window. But then he started off walking all over that jungle of a garden. It's a pretty big area and it took him twenty minutes at least. He kept appearing among the bushes and disappearing again. Rosie was freaking out. I didn't know whether to worry more about her than about him! I thought she might have hysterics or something. Thank goodness he eventually took himself off.'

'You never saw him again?'

'No, never. He didn't call in here and if I had seen him at the house again, I might have gone downstairs and asked him what he was doing.'

Carter raised his eyebrows. 'You were hardly in a position to do that.'

'If I walked round the corner of the building and confronted him, he wouldn't have known I'd come out of the house,' Pascal said. 'He might have assumed I had, but he wouldn't have seen me. He was at the back. Rosie and I used the front door.'

Carter put a hand to his inside jacket pocket and produced the photograph taken at the races, showing Taylor and Terri Hemmings. Silently he handed it to Pascal.

Pascal hesitated but took it and stared at it frowningly. 'That's the bloke,' he said at last. 'He was dressed a bit differently, but that's him. I took the trouble to remember his face because I thought he might turn up again or stop by my place here.' He returned the photo and looked thoughtfully at Carter. 'So, is he the dead 'un? That's why you're carrying his photo round with you?'

'Yes,' Carter said. 'It would appear so.'

Pascal thought again. 'Funny, that,' he observed.

Funny meaning 'peculiar', thought Carter, observing Pascal. Not funny meaning 'comical', I suppose. Though he's got a sort of grin on his face now. He thinks he's away clear, but we'll see about that . . .

'Did you, with or without the help of Mrs Sneddon, take the victim, this man in the photograph, alive or dead, into Balaclava House and leave him there on a sofa?'

Pascal's grin vanished. He gaped foolishly, staring at Carter first in surprise and then in horror.

'Me? Us? No, we weren't there that day! We had nothing to do with any dead body!'

'Let me ask you again. Think carefully, Mr Pascal. You didn't find him outside the house as you were leaving? You might only have thought him very ill. You were chiefly concerned with protecting your reputation and that of the lady. So you took him inside and left him there for the owner to find on his return.'

'*No!*' Pascal almost shrieked the word. 'We weren't there that day!'

Carter believed him. So much for Morton's theory. Jess had never gone along with it but Carter himself had thought Phil's idea a possibility. But it hadn't happened that way.

'Thank you, Mr Pascal,' he said. 'We may be in touch again – or Mr Bickerstaffe may be.' Carter smiled. 'Or more likely, Mrs Harwell, on Mr Bickerstaffe's behalf.'

Pascal put his hands over his face. 'Oh, Gawd . . .' he moaned.

Chapter 15

Carter sat in his car outside the petrol station for a few moments, pondering his next course of action. He was only a couple of minutes' drive away from Balaclava House, and was curious to retrace Jay Taylor's steps, the day Pascal and Rosie Sneddon had seen him from the window, wandering about the former gardens. It also occurred to him – as it had done earlier to Jess – that he should check that no one had tried tampering with the scene in any way or done any damage to the building. Empty premises attracted vandalism.

He drove off towards Toby's Gutter Lane, watched, he knew, by a miserable Seb Pascal through the window of the minimart.

The house stood in lonely crumbling decay and yet today, when Carter got there, it was not quite deserted. An elderly Ford Fiesta was parked outside. There was no sign of its occupants.

Carter got out of his car, pushed his way through the rusted gates and approached the house, hoping he wasn't about to discover another body on a sofa. The front door was ajar. It should have been locked and sealed with a strip of blue and white tape, but the plastic ribbon lay tangled on the ground. Was he too late? Had the place already been ransacked? There would be hell to pay if it had. He pushed the door open and listened. Within, all was quiet.

He stepped into the hall, pausing to glance round its gloomy splendour and up the staircase, to where the dull light still made patches of colour play across the landing from the stained-glass window. The silence was oppressive but he wasn't alone. He could sense another presence. He stood still, waiting, ears straining. Then he heard, from the direction of the kitchen, the chink of china or glass and the scrape of a chair.

'Police!' Carter called out loudly.

He fancied he heard an inrush of breath but possibly that was imagination. The kitchen door, at the far end of the hallway, opened and a woman stepped into the hall. The light was behind her and she was only a dim outline, slim, with long hair and some kind of loose, coat-like garment.

'Who are you?' Her voice was loud, confident and educated. It was also young.

'Superintendent Carter,' he replied, and reached for his ID. He held it up, open towards her.

She came briskly towards him and now he could see her clearly. She was no more than twenty. The hair was fair and very straight so that it lay on her shoulders in a pale gold waterfall. As for features, he thought her pretty in a sharp-faced kind of way. The coat-like garment was a long knitted cardigan with geometric patterns. Carter still held up his ID and when she reached him, she studied it carefully.

'Doesn't do you justice,' she commented. It was a simple observation, delivered in a matter-of-fact tone.

'It isn't meant to be flattering.' He put the ID away, obscurely nettled.

As he did, she asked, in that same cool, disconcerting way, 'What are you doing here?'

'This is the wrong way round,' Carter told her mildly. 'That's what I ask you.'

'It's my uncle's home. I'm checking everything's OK.'

'Ah,' said Carter, 'you're Tansy Harwell.'

'No,' her voice was colder. 'I'm Tansy Peterson.'

Damn, yes, of course. Bridget Harwell was much married. 'I apologise,' he said.

'There's no need for you to apologise. It's my mother's fault for having so many husbands.' She pulled a wry grin. 'Uncle Monty is at our house, but you know that. Mum's concerned about Balaclava standing empty, so I drove over to take a look at it. I've got Uncle Monty's keys.' She took them from a pocket of the knitted coat and jangled them. 'Mum got them off him.'

'You didn't bring Mr Bickerstaffe with you, to see his home for himself and that everything's OK?' Carter asked. 'How is he coping, by the way?'

'Come off it. If I brought him here I'd never get him to leave again. He'd just move straight back in. He's coping well enough with the thought of finding a dead body. It wouldn't put him off returning here. It's staying at our house that he's not coping so well with. To be frank, he hates it.' Tansy raised her eyebrows questioningly. 'I was just making a cup of tea. Would you like one?'

'Thank you, that would be very nice.'

Minutes later, they were seated in the kitchen, either side of the table, and Tansy was pouring tea from a chipped brown glazed earthenware teapot into a couple of cups with odd saucers.

'Do you take sugar? If so, I haven't found any yet, but I dare say there is some – somewhere . . .' She gazed round at the untidy, cluttered dresser and array of cupboards.

'I don't take sugar, thanks.'

She was prettier, now that he had a chance to view her better, and she was more relaxed, than he'd first judged. The sharp look had probably been due to tension and perhaps the chill temperature. She had cupped her hands round her teacup as if using the hot liquid to warm them. They were small hands, with neat, clean, well-polished nails and looked more like a child's than an adult's. But she was nineteen, or almost nineteen. He knew that because Jess had told him.

'Have you checked upstairs?' he asked.

'Not yet. Downstairs is fine. It's a mess but it's always a mess. Uncle Monty lives like that.'

'It must have been a fine house once,' Carter said, making conversation.

Her reaction was unexpectedly vigorous. 'It's still a fine house! It's beautiful. It needs some repair and decoration and a good clean through, but it's a wonderful place! I've always loved it. Uncle Monty loves it, too, and I understand just how he feels. Mum doesn't. She thinks it's a ruin. But there's real history in here.'

There is some friction between mother and daughter, thought Carter. Jess Campbell witnessed that.

'You came here a lot as a child, I think?'

She nodded, steam from the hot drink spiralling upward before her nose. Her eyes lost that combative shine and became misty in memory. 'Oh, yes, during the school holidays. That was when Aunt Penny was alive and Uncle Monty was not nearly so decrepit. Aunt Penny kept him in order. But in the end, it got too much even for her – and she went away. Mum was fond of Aunt Penny and furious with Uncle Monty. They had a blazing row about it and that put an end to our visits to Balaclava for a long time. Uncle Monty sort of turned inward after that. He missed Aunt Penny and wanted her back but he knew that wouldn't happen.' Tansy's voice was sad.

There was an awkward pause. Did Sophie leave me because I was impossible to live with? Carter wondered. I wasn't the best of husbands and the police work got in the way. It always seemed to have first call on my attention. But, in the end, Sophie met someone else. In a funny way, if Penny Bickerstaffe had met someone else, Monty wouldn't have been left feeling it was his entire fault. But she didn't; and Monty's been living with the thought that he'd driven away the woman he loved.

He was glad when Tansy, who also seemed to have drifted away on a line of thought private to her, broke the silence.

'When Aunt Penny died, Mum tried to get Uncle Monty to come to the funeral, but he wouldn't,' she went on more briskly. 'I don't think she went about persuading him very tactfully. Mum has the knack of rubbing Uncle Monty the wrong way. He gets very cross with her. It's easy to do,' added Tansy disloyally but probably truthfully. 'So they had another blazing row.'

'The house would have been in a much better state during the time Mrs Bickerstaffe was alive and living there,' remarked Carter.

She pursed her lips. 'To be honest, it wasn't in a wonderful condition, even then. Of course, it was a bit better than this!' Tansy indicated their surroundings with a wave of her hand. 'But it was much too big for them and I think Aunt Penny lost heart. She only had the help of a local woman who came in to mop the floors and push a vacuum cleaner round downstairs, that was all. They only lived in part of it, you see. Here –' she nodded at the kitchen – 'and the drawing room and dining room, one of the bedrooms upstairs and the smaller bathroom up there. The rest was just shut away and left to rot. I used to go up and explore, with Gary.'

Carter blinked, surprised. 'Gary Colley?'

She flushed. 'Yes. He was older than I was but he was still a child, then. We were great pals. He kept a couple of ponies down at their place. I used to go there with him and he let me ride round their paddock. He always walked or ran alongside in case I fell off. Mum is snooty about the Colleys, but I like them. They're very kind, you know, in their way.'

'What about the Sneddons? Didn't they have two daughters?'

She nodded. 'Yes, but I didn't know them very well. Their girls were older than me and didn't want a little kid tagging along. Mrs Sneddon was nice. I remember going to the farm once with my mother about something to do with Balaclava. I think Mum was worried about Aunt Penny. Mrs Sneddon gave us tea and cupcakes with different colour icing on them. I remember them because I thought they were wonderful. My mother didn't bake – still doesn't.' Tansy's lips twitched in the barest smile. 'I didn't like Pete Sneddon much. He was always a bit dour. He came into the kitchen while we were having our tea and cupcakes and told Mum to leave "the poor old bugger and his missis alone". He meant Uncle Monty and Aunt Penny. Mrs Sneddon told him off for using language like that in front of a child. It put an end to our visit, anyway. Mum spoke to him sharply and dragged me away. We didn't go back.'

Carter put down his empty cup. 'Perhaps I should take a look round upstairs?' he suggested, getting to his feet.

'I'll come with you.' Tansy jumped up, perhaps glad to put a stop to the childhood reminiscences.

They climbed the wide staircase and paused to gaze up at the Jezebel window.

'Isn't it great?' said Tansy. 'That one, over there . . .' She turned and pointed to the boarded-up companion window across the landing. 'That one showed Jael and Sisera – before a branch broke off a tree in a storm one night, about two years ago, and smashed it. In the original scene he was asleep and she was creeping up on him with a tent peg and a mallet, one in each hand. I always preferred poor Jezebel; but Gary liked the Sisera one better. He was really sorry when it got smashed and came over and did his best to repair the damage.'

'Both violent subjects,' Carter commented, thinking that Gary's 'best' carpentry skills were limited. He had secured the broken window as he might have fixed the hole in the pig compound fence he'd told Jess of. 'A pity murder at Balaclava didn't remain contained in a coloured glass picture.'

Tansy flinched and he was sorry he'd added that. The recent events at the house must have upset her. She walked away quickly down one corridor. Carter followed and, one after the other, they checked the rooms. At the room used by Pascal and Rosie, Tansy paused. Then she pushed open the door and they both looked in.

'Someone had been using this room, hadn't they? Without poor Uncle Monty knowing?' Tansy's voice sounded muffled. 'Your Inspector Campbell told us.' She looked around. 'You can tell someone's been here.'

'Yes, they did use this one.'

'Do you know who it was?' she demanded with a sudden return to her usual belligerent style.

'We do now know,' Carter told her cautiously. 'We think it's unconnected with – the later event.'

'Well,' Tansy said fiercely, 'whoever it was, they had no right!'

'No, they didn't. But your uncle had a habit of leaving the front door unlocked when he went out. It's fortunate no one came in and vandalised the place, or stole anything. The people who used this room at least left it tidy.'

'It doesn't excuse them!' Tansy was having none of it. If she found out it was Seb Pascal, Carter could imagine her going down to the garage and haranguing the hapless owner. She'd probably have a go at Mrs Sneddon, too. A distant memory of cupcakes wouldn't save Rosie.

At the moment he, Carter, was there and Tansy, lacking any other target, had decided to have a go at him. 'You should tell us who it was. Isn't it a crime? Are you doing anything about it, now you know who they are? Aren't you charging anyone?'

'We'll inform the owner, Mr Bickerstaffe, of the intruder's identity, in due course,' Carter said firmly. 'What action is taken, if any, will rather depend on him, the householder. He habitually left the door open when he left the house, so there was no forced entry. There was apparently no vandalism and, as yet, no items have been reported missing, so no theft.' Tansy hissed in exasperation and opened her mouth, but Carter continued inexorably, 'So at the moment we are left with trespass and that is a civil matter, rather than a criminal one.'

'You mean it's OK for whoever it was to waltz in here and make use of a bedroom?' Incredulity replaced the arrogance.

'Not OK, but difficult to prosecute through the courts. There was no confrontation between Mr Bickerstaffe and the person or persons concerned, no threats were made, no violence offered and even if there had been . . .'

Tansy dismissed all this legal quibbling with a sweeping gesture. 'My mother will sort it out!' she said firmly.

Carter had already forewarned Pascal of that possibility, but he said nothing. It was better to let Tansy think she had had the last word.

They retreated downstairs.

'I'm just going to walk around the garden,' Carter told her.

She nodded and fell into step alongside him, although, truth to tell, he'd rather have searched out there alone. He briefly

263

considered telling her so. On the other hand, she could act as his guide and he soon realised he needed one.

'Whew!' he exclaimed when he realised what a tangled mass of neglected and unchecked growth the garden had become. 'We could do with a machete!'

'There is a path down here . . .' Tansy led the way, pushing aside undergrowth that tumbled and sprawled across the route forward.

Sure enough, the remains of a crumbling brick-paved walk lay beneath their feet. An arched pergola had once spanned it but most of that had fallen, rotted away, and only a few mossy uprights remained. It was no longer possible to tell where flower-beds had been. The lawns, too, were muddy, weed-infested patches fighting a losing battle with encroaching undergrowth. At the edges of one such patch Carter noticed fresh-looking footprints – a male shoe. Monty's? Or could Taylor have made them during his surreptitious visit? But if the prints had been here when the search team combed the grounds, their presence would have been marked for investigation. Most likely one of the search team was responsible.

Tansy squeaked and Carter was startled to see a mocking face leering at them from between damp foliage. Then he saw it belonged to a statue trapped in a prison of interwoven branches. It was lichen-covered and its scabby, bearded features grinned evilly at them.

'It's poor old Pan,' said Tansy with a little laugh. 'I'd forgotten him. So he's still here. There are some other statues about the place. They're probably hidden now, just as poor Pan is.'

'Garden statuary, particularly Victorian examples, fetch a good price now,' Carter remarked.

It was the wrong thing to have said. Tansy rounded on him. 'Why must everything have a price? Uncle Monty wouldn't sell Pan or any of the others. I wouldn't sell them! They belong here. People now are – are horrid. Everything must have a price tag. It's sordid.'

'Not everyone can afford such high-minded principles,' Carter told her.

Her face reddened. 'And I'm a spoiled wealthy brat, is that it?'

'I certainly didn't suggest that, nor would I,' he protested. 'I don't think it.'

'Your Inspector Campbell thinks it.'

Surprised, Carter protested, 'I'm sure she doesn't.'

Tansy's ire subsided. 'I wouldn't blame either of you. I'm not poor. My father's a rich man. He makes me a generous allowance.' There was a pause. Then she added sadly, 'It's not always a blessing, you know.'

'I don't suppose it is,' he said sincerely. 'Tell me, I know you said the house wasn't all that well maintained, but was it still a beautiful garden when you came here as a child? When you could see all the statues and plants in all their glory?'

She shook her head. 'No, it had run pretty wild, even then. It must have been stunning in Victorian times, even for quite a long time after that. I think the rot set in about the nineteen fifties. By the time I came here with my mother to visit it had long gone to rack and ruin. Uncle Monty and Aunt Penny kept just the bit round the house tidy. Uncle Monty pushed a squeaky old mower up and down the lawn. If I were here I'd help, scooping up the cuttings to add to the compost heap. Mummy always grumbled because I'd get green grass stains on my clothes. Aunt Penny had a few vegetables growing in the kitchen garden – behind that wall.'

Tansy pointed. They had reached a tall mellow red-brick wall, pierced by an arched gateway. The wrought-iron or wooden gate that must once have stood in it had gone, leaving only its hinges to mark its presence.

Carter went through the arch and stopped in surprise. This had once been a real kitchen garden, a Victorian gardener's pride and joy. There were even the collapsed, ivy-grown remains of a hothouse, with a brick-built furnace room attached. Add this area to the area of the other garden, he thought, and you've got quite a bit of land here. But who could possibly restore it all to its former glory? The cost, the work involved, and the maintenance afterwards . . . it was prohibitive. An idea occurred to him.

'Aren't there two fields belonging to the estate? Between here and the road, I think.'

Tansy shrugged. 'They're pretty small and not much use. Gary sometimes grazes his horses in them – or Pete moves his sheep down there.'

'Mr Bickerstaffe might not want to sell the house and gardens, but he could raise some cash selling the fields . . .'

Tansy expelled breath in a hiss and glared at him. 'Are you thick or what?' she asked. 'Uncle Monty *wouldn't sell*. He's right.'

'No, of course he wouldn't,' Carter agreed. 'It would let the outside world in and your Uncle Monty is determined to keep it out. I'm sorry I suggested it. I don't admit to being thick, as you put it, but my mind was wandering for a moment there.'

Tansy blushed. 'No, you're not thick and I was very rude to say that. Sorry. You are probably quite horrifyingly intelligent. I'm not, you know. I am rather dopey. Always have been.'

'Now then,' he said severely, 'don't put yourself down. Perhaps you haven't yet tackled the right sort of challenges. You may surprise yourself at how well you'd manage.'

'I'll have to manage when my mother goes to New York.' She gave him a wicked grin. 'But I have a let-out, you see. If the worst comes to the worst, I can go and live in Jersey with my father.' She frowned. 'Although that might give him a shock, cramp his style a bit. He has glamorous girlfriends.'

Poor kid, thought Carter. She's been made to feel an inconvenience, probably when she was quite young. It's stayed with her. I don't suppose either of her parents intended it. I hope Millie never feels this way about her mother and me. I don't think she will. But I can't say now, after listening to Tansy Peterson, that it won't be on my mind.

He looked down at the earth. There were more footprints here. If they had been left by the late Jay Taylor, he'd certainly covered every inch of this place. But the marks were too fresh to be Taylor's. Pascal and Rosie Sneddon had seen him here during the long dry spell when the earth had been baked hard. They might be Gary Colley's footprints as he spied on the police. Carter told himself they must have been left by the search team. But then he dismissed this conclusion, feeling annoyed with himself. His mind really must be wandering. Both Colley's prints and those of the search team would have been made *before* the recent rain. These, pressed clearly into the mud, had been made *post-rain*. Some later visitor had been taking a look at the place now it was in the news. There was nothing like a suspicious death for attracting sightseers. Or was someone else still interested in Balaclava House for whatever reason had brought the late Jay Taylor here?

He didn't want Tansy to notice the prints. She was sharp enough to draw the same conclusion he had. The idea that even more interlopers had trespassed on the hallowed soil of her beloved Balaclava House would send her ballistic. He moved away from the incriminating evidence.

They left the garden and returned to the front of the house. 'Are you going back inside?' Carter asked Tansy.

She shook her head. 'No, I'll lock up now and go home. Unless you want to go indoors again?'

'No, I have to get back to my office.'

They walked to her car. Tansy patted the roof and said, 'People wonder why I don't buy a new one. But I like this one. I told Inspector Campbell so.'

Carter glanced back at Balaclava House and then at the ageing car. 'This isn't a joke – I'm quite serious – have you ever thought of working in the antiques world?'

She looked surprised. 'I'm not bright enough.'

'I've told you,' he reminded her, 'not to put yourself down.'

Tansy studied him for a moment. 'I think it's possible,' she said slowly, 'that you are a nice man.'

'Don't run away with that idea,' Carter advised her. 'Remember, I'm a policeman.'

'One who doesn't do anything about whoever has been walking in and out of my uncle's house, using one of the rooms.' She wasn't going to let him get away with that.

'I explained that,' he said patiently. 'We will discuss with Mr Bickerstaffe what he wants to do.'

'Then, are you close to arresting anyone for anything? For killing that man who was found here?'

'Not yet, but we'll get there.'

'Really?' Tansy stared at him.

'Oh, yes, really,' Carter assured her.

She didn't look reassured.

Chapter 16

Bridget and her daughter were quarrelling again. Monty had retreated to his bedroom, out of the way, and lay in the semi-darkness, listening to the rise and fall of their increasingly strident voices. It wasn't the first clash he'd overheard since coming to the Old Lodge. The two women seemed to be constantly at loggerheads. This time they were really going at it, hammer and tongs. He gathered Tansy had been over to Balaclava to check out the place and had encountered a senior police officer there. Tansy was upset that the police were taking no action over someone having used one of the bedrooms. He thought he heard her say that the police now knew who it had been. Monty didn't want to know the identity of the intruders. Just so long as they didn't come back; that was all he cared about.

Then Tansy and Bridget must have realised Monty could hear them, because they'd lowered their voices and hissed at each other like a pair of venomous snakes. So he'd missed all the next bit. Not that he was interested. All new information threatened to disturb his peace of mind. Gradually their voices had risen and now they were back to storm force and yelling again.

Penny and I didn't row like that, noisily, thought Monty. She would get annoyed with me and say a few sharp words. She knew how to pick 'em. She didn't need to shout. I used to ignore her. It seemed the easiest way and eventually she'd give up. One day, after so many long and acrimonious years together, she'd really given up and walked out.

'Serve you right,' Monty told himself aloud.

He was sorry Penny hadn't lived on long in her new life, free of him, after that, but had gone early to her grave. He hoped he hadn't driven her there, but accepted he'd done his bit. She'd deserved a few decent years after all the time spent with him. All those things that had gone wrong and for which he felt responsible to a bigger or lesser degree; all of them stood like ghosts at his bedside, pointing accusing fingers.

A violent slam of a door signalled one of the quarrelling pair, probably Tansy, had stormed out and gone to her room. His mother and father hadn't argued loudly like that, either. They would have considered it ill bred, a vulgar way of carrying on. Theirs had been a cold, bitter silence of things unsaid. Perhaps it would have been better if they'd yelled a bit more instead of letting resentment simmer. Perhaps then his mother wouldn't have taken her revenge in so deadly a way.

Monty had said nothing to his mother on that grim Christmas Day, after the doctor's departure. Nor had he spoken during the days that followed, or even after the ghastly funeral lunch, when the small band of mourners had sat down to eat the Christmas turkey. Not having been cooked when intended, due to events, the turkey had lingered ripely in the fridge until the day of the burial. It was a wonder they hadn't all got food poisoning.

It wasn't until the following spring that Monty broached the subject. He was home again, this time for the Easter holiday. He came upon his mother on her knees at the flowerbed by the front door. She was energetically digging out weeds. He looked down at her, wondering at the ferocity of her attack on the groundsel and couch grass.

'You didn't call the doctor during the night, last Christmas,' he said. 'Dad thought you were phoning him. I went into his room and spoke to him and he told me so. But you didn't call the doc until the next morning.'

He didn't say it accusingly. He hadn't even intended consciously to say it at all. He had added it to the list of secrets, never to be spoken of. But it came out, just like that, as a simple statement.

She paused in her onslaught on the weeds, sat back on her heels and wiped a gardening glove over her brow, leaving a dirty smear. She didn't look up.

'Nonsense,' she said. 'Of course I called him.'

'I spoke to the doctor, too. He said he came as soon as you called him, before breakfast on Christmas Day.'

'I called him!' she said sharply. 'You were confused, Monty. It was a very stressful time.'

There was a silence. She still had not looked up at him. Now she indicated the bed with her trowel. 'I thought geraniums might do all right in here. It gets very dry but they don't mind.'

Monty didn't mention the subject again. There was nothing

to be gained. Didn't he carry his own burden of guilt for that night? He had gone back to bed so tamely; instead of going downstairs and waiting for the doctor to arrive. He could have hopped and hobbled down to the hallway where the phone was, then he would have known, he would have called the doc again himself . . . But no, back to bed he'd gone and – he couldn't understand this even now – he'd fallen asleep again until early morning. He'd woken to the grey light and the figure of his mother standing over him, still in her dressing gown, to inform him his father had passed away.

'Your father's just gone,' she'd said, as if Edward Bickerstaffe had decided to get up, dress, and take himself off for a short time to attend to some business.

'Gone where?' Monty had asked foolishly.

But she had already turned and was leaving the room.

He'd married Penny six years later.

'Congratulations, Monty,' his mother said to him drily at the wedding breakfast. 'You couldn't have done better.'

He understood the true meaning of her words. She believed he had married Penny to be revenged on her. He had foisted on her, as a daughter-in-law, the flame-haired daughter of her old rival. They were all in the wedding group photo. His mother stood stone-faced, in a tweed suit and sensible shoes, at one end of the line-up; Penny's mother, faded but still pretty and wearing a feathery hat, at the other. The spirit of his father seemed to lurk somewhere above their heads. No, he couldn't have taken a better revenge.

But his mother was wrong. He'd married Penny because he

loved her. He really did. Later, he found that loving someone and being a halfway decent husband were two different things.

Later that day, when he and Penny studied the photos alone, Penny said, 'Your mother doesn't look very happy in any of them. She must be sad at losing you.'

He wanted to speak the truth for once and say, 'No, she doesn't give a damn about me. It's having to hear you called "Mrs Bickerstaffe" that bugs her.'

What he actually said was, 'She probably drank a couple of gins too many before the ceremony, and she never liked having her photo taken.'

Thus he discovered, right at the start of his marriage, that he would have to keep on telling little white lies, adding to the cairn of secrets of which the first stone had been laid so many years before, on a sunny summer's day when the lark sang.

Footsteps tapped along the passageway past his room. He heard a sharp tap at a door and Bridget's voice. 'Tansy! We can't just leave it like that. You have to be sensible.'

There must have been some reply missed by Monty because the next thing he heard was Bridget saying, 'We'll talk again in the morning.'

She tapped past his door again. The Old Lodge was silent.

The following morning the sun was shining and Jess came in to find a note on her desk, informing her that Tom Palmer had phoned and asked that she call him back. She picked up the scrap of paper and sighed. She supposed he wanted to go out again that evening and eat somewhere or have a drink. She wasn't sure she wanted to. She liked Tom's company but she didn't want these outings to take on a regular pattern. She even felt mildly resentful that Tom should assume she had nothing else to do in her evenings, no one else to meet. For that reason, she decided not to phone him back at once but to wait until later. She had more important things to do than discuss the pros and cons of various spaghetti houses or country pubs.

Also, Phil Morton walked in at that moment and said, 'The super wants us in his office.'

Tom would have to wait now. Jess sighed. Ian Carter no doubt wanted them to thrash out some plan of action. A case conference was inevitable, with all that had happened. But the fact was, the mystery of the ultra-clean bedroom at Balaclava and its secret visitors had now been cleared up. That left them back at square one, with very little to go on by way of new leads.

Carter was waiting for them, standing behind his desk and aligning pens and other desktop items with concentrated care. He looked up when they came in and said, 'Glad you've both got a minute.'

Is he being sarcastic? Jess wondered briefly. Probably not but it did sound a little like it. Beside her, she sensed Phil bridle.

'I called in at Balaclava House yesterday,' Carter went on. 'Tansy Peterson was there.' He gave them a résumé of his conversation with Tansy. 'There are fresh male footprints in the gardens. I think someone has been wandering around up there within the last day or two, certainly since it rained. It could just be a sightseer. Or even the local press, I suppose, gone to take a photo or two. But if anyone is taking an interest in Balaclava House, I want to know who it is.'

'I can phone the local rag and ask if they've sent anyone over there,' Morton offered.

Carter nodded his approval. 'It's made me think rather more about that place, the house and the land. The fact both are in a dismal state of neglect doesn't mean the whole estate isn't worth quite a bit. Monty could be a rich man if he sold up.'

'Who'd want it?' Morton asked gloomily.

'A developer would,' Carter told him briskly. 'And by coincidence, or not, Billy Hemmings is a property developer. We ought not to overlook any little bit of knowledge we have, even if it seems unrelated to the inquiry. Jay Taylor is altogether too much of a man of mystery. I don't believe Taylor being expected at Hemmings's house for a dinner party on the day of his death *is* a coincidence. You told me, Jess, that you believed Balaclava House is at the centre of this business. I think you could be on to something. They haven't left for Marbella, as you feared, Jess. I'm going to talk to Hemmings today. I rang his home. He wasn't there but I spoke to his wife. He's got an office in Gloucester and will be there all day. I'm driving over there shortly and if he's been hanging round Balaclava House, I intend to get it out of him.'

'Monty wouldn't sell to a developer!' Jess said promptly.

'Neither would Tansy,' Carter said with a brief smile. 'She made that very clear to me!'

Phil Morton, his hands jammed in his jacket pockets said moodily, 'She thinks she's the old bloke's heir, does she? That it's going to be up to her to sell or not? Or it should be "heiress", I suppose, if you want to be picky.'

He was unprepared for the silence that followed his suggestion, and looked up, taking his hands from his pockets as if he expected to be reproved.

Jess said slowly, 'It's a distinct possibility. Monty's fond of Tansy. He's got to leave Balaclava to someone.'

'He might not have made a will,' said Morton quickly, preempting any objections to his new idea. The last time he'd produced a theory, they'd knocked it down, after all. 'Look at the people who don't make wills, even people with plenty to leave.'

'Oh, I think Mr Bickerstaffe will have made a will,' Carter decided. 'He's an educated man of middle-class upbringing and professional background. The Bickerstaffe family must always have made wills. They owned property and used to own a business. Of course, any will Monty made during his wife's lifetime will have needed to be redrafted after her death. Monica Farrell made no mention of a divorce. I think Penny Bickerstaffe just packed her bags and left. She may still have been in the old will. I'm fairly sure he would have made a new will when she died or, if there was a divorce, after that. That property has been in his family since it was built in the eighteen sixties. He'd make arrangements for it in the event of his death. He'd be very conscious of the necessity and see it as a duty. What's more he'd be very keen to leave it to a family member who might, who knows, one day restore it. Bridget Harwell sees the place as a burden to be unloaded. But Tansy doesn't. Tansy loves the old place. She's the obvious person to inherit it.'

Jess said slowly, 'I'm remembering something he said to me, when I drove over to Bridget Harwell's house to talk to him. He said something about not having any *money* to leave Tansy. That's true. He doesn't have cash but he does have the house and property. The fact that he talked about leaving anything at all to Tansy shows he does have the situation after his death in mind; and he wants to leave something to her. He can't stand Bridget Harwell. But Tansy is a different kettle of fish.' Excitement was growing in her voice. 'Yes, I bet he has left Balaclava to Tansy. What's more, I believe she knows it. That's why she was there, checking the place out, when you met her, sir. That's why she spoke so strongly about it in her conversation with you. She already regards it as hers!'

'But she wouldn't sell it and the land for development,' Carter reminded her. 'She made that clear to me.'

'She might have no choice,' contributed Morton. 'I know she's got money and her dad is rolling in it, but just think of trying to put that crumbling old ruin in order and the cost of its upkeep afterwards! It's huge. She couldn't live in it. So, she's got a sentimental attachment to the place. If she owned it, she'd have to face facts, be practical. I mean, she's not much more than a kid now. She might have all sorts of dreams about fixing the place up and so on. But real life—'

'All the more reason for me to talk to Billy Hemmings,' Carter interrupted him. 'To find out if he does have any interest in Balaclava House and whether he's approached any family member about it. Not Monty himself, perhaps, but what about Bridget Harwell? Mrs Harwell is not the sentimental sort. She'd see

Balaclava as a liability to be unloaded as soon as possible. I think you'd better talk to Bridget again, Jess. I'll tackle Hemmings.'

'Where does Taylor come into it?' Morton asked.

There was another silence. 'Blowed if I know,' said Carter at last. 'But it's high time we found out!'

Chapter 17

As Jess walked back to her office, her mobile phone chirruped, letting her know she had received a text message. It was from Tom Palmer, following up his earlier missed phone call. Restored to conventional spelling it read: *Call by my office. Something here you might like to see.*

She needed to drive over to The Old Lodge and see Bridget again, but she could make it to Tom's office first. It would stop him bombarding her with messages. Besides, she was curious. She had assumed that he'd wanted to make an arrangement about going out to eat tonight. Apparently this wasn't the case. She puzzled over the few words on the screen. What had Tom found now? Surely he hadn't conducted a second post-mortem. There had been no request for one. If he had done so, and found something he called 'interesting', Jess hoped it wasn't now in a glass jar and she would be required to study some gory section of human internal organ. Tom had the blessed ability to distance himself as a human being from the remains he dissected. 'A lung is a lung . . .' he'd once cheerily informed her. 'Doesn't matter if it's human or animal. You cook, don't you? Well, sometimes you do, anyway. You've chopped up meat?'

Jess had viewed enough corpses not to be squeamish in general. But she had never managed the trick of dissociating her own mortality from the sad remains on the slab. 'What I cut up comes neatly cling-film wrapped in a polystyrene tray!' had been her reply. 'And it never looked like me or you.'

At least Tom wasn't in the morgue itself, when she got there. He was, as he'd said he'd be, in his office. That lessened the possibility of bits in jars considerably.

'Ah!' said Tom smugly, when she walked in. 'Bet you don't know what all this is about? It took me three-quarters of an hour to find it. My time is valuable, I'll have you know. I ought to send you a bill.'

'What are you on about?' Jess asked. 'All I've got is a cryptic message. My time is valuable, too. You're not wasting it, I hope? I've got an important interview to conduct.'

Tom looked hurt at this less than gracious reply. 'You can't expect me to spoil my surprise by putting it all in a text message? Anyway, it would be too long.'

'*What is it?*' Jess burst out.

Tom pulled open a drawer in his desk and pulled out a very tattered copy of a glossy magazine. 'Ta-ra!' he heralded this unpromising object. 'I told you; it took me three-quarters of an hour to find it. You're lucky. She was just about to throw them all out.'

'Who was? Throw what? Stop talking in riddles, Tom. OK, I'm surprised, if that's what you want. I am, actually, I didn't have you down as reading that sort of stuff. But what about that one am I expected to be surprised at?'

'The receptionist at the dental surgery was going to throw them out. Now then, you remember I told you I thought I'd seen the corpse you sent me recently before? In life, I mean, not on a slab.'

Jess's impatience turned to eagerness. 'Yes, I do. Have you remembered?'

'Now you want to know, don't you?' Tom smiled happily at her. 'It bugged me, you see, that I couldn't place the chap. You asked about newspapers and I knew it hadn't been in a newspaper. Then, last night, I remembered. I went for my annual dental check-up a couple of weeks ago. I had to sit around in the waiting room for a while and, as you know, they always have piles of ancient magazines. So I started looking through them. That's where I'd seen Taylor, in a magazine, one of those topical gossip glossies – showing us what glamorous lives some people have, unlike our humdrum daily toil. So I went back this morning first thing, straight through the door as they opened up. The receptionist thought I had an emergency tooth problem. I explained I needed to look through the magazines and might want to take one away. "Take the lot," she said. "They're so out of date no one wants to look at them. I'm going to put them out for recycling today." So I had to sit down there and then and leaf through them. Blooming boring it was too, I can tell you. But I found it. Here it is.'

Tom opened the magazine in question and turned it on the desk surface so that it faced Jess right way up. 'See? That's him. That's Taylor. Full of life and grinning away, I grant you, but that's the joker I autopsied for you.'

He tapped the well-thumbed page. Jess bent over the desk to study the photograph. It had been taken in a well-known nightclub. It showed a party of revellers. They were, the text said, celebrating the success of a racehorse belonging to one of them. Certainly champagne bottles were much in evidence. The horse's owner – and his female companion – were well enough known to the readers of this kind of gossip machine to be of interest. The caption stated the celebrity pair was having a night out 'with friends'. One of the friends was clearly and unmistakably Jay Taylor.

Poor Jay, thought Jess. There he is, as Tom said, full of life and hobnobbing with the sort of people he wrote about and longed to be like. Also just a little flushed and the worse for drink, grinning his head off at the paparazzo who had snapped this shot. He had a proprietorial arm around the shoulders of a girl who was leaning against him. She, also, looked rather the worse for champagne. Her face shone and one strap of her party dress had slipped off her shoulder and rested on her upper arm.

'Any use to you?' asked Tom hopefully. 'Probably doesn't tell you anything you don't already know. But I thought you'd like to see it.'

'I would, I am interested, very much indeed,' Jess told him. 'Thanks for this, Tom, really very, very much! Yes, that's Jay Taylor . . . and I know her, too, the girl he's very pally with.'

Jess tapped the image of the girl with the slipped bodice strap. 'Tansy Peterson! Well, well, well . . . I'm just on my way to talk to her mother. Now I need to talk to her, too, and urgently.'

*　　*　　*

But neither Bridget nor Tansy were at home when Jess reached The Old Lodge. Monty was wandering around the garden, whisky glass in hand. He looked quite happy.

'Both gone out!' he announced. 'Marvellous! They left me here all alone and Bridget didn't remember to lock the drinks cabinet.'

'Did they say where they were going?' Jess asked.

'No and I didn't ask. They didn't go together. They went separately.'

Jess frowned. That sounded as though mother and daughter had set off in different directions.

Monty had noted her frown and interpreted it as disbelief. 'I know it sounds potty. But first Tansy shot off in her old banger of a car and then Bridget went chasing after her in that little blue job she drives.'

So the two women may have been heading in the same direction, after all. Something had happened.

'Monty,' Jess said, 'please try and remember anything at all. I must find them. What about last night? Did either of them mention last night they might be going out this morning?'

'Oh, last night,' returned Monty with a sniff of disapproval. 'Last night they had a bally awful row, a real ding-dong battle. They row all the time, mind you, so it probably meant nothing.'

'What were they rowing about?'

'Dunno,' mumbled Monty. 'Tried not to listen. I was in my bedroom. I could still hear them, though, when they didn't remember to whisper.'

'Monty!' Jess urged. 'Do try! It is important. I think it's important to Tansy. I know you don't care about Bridget, but you do care about Tansy, don't you?' Jess took a plunge. 'Is she your heir?'

Monty blinked at her, astounded. 'Blimey,' he said. 'You're sharp, you are. Yes, she is, for what it's worth. I haven't got any money. She knows that. I've left Balaclava to her in my will and that's likely to be more of a burden to her than a blessing.'

'Does she know? Have you told her you've left her Balaclava?'

Monty shrugged. 'I did say something or other to her. She seemed pleased at the time, poor kid.' He eyed Jess thoughtfully. 'Tansy in trouble of some sort?'

'I need to talk to her urgently, Monty, that's all.'

'Mm . . .' Monty gazed into the now-empty glass in his hand. Perhaps the need to refill it before Bridget got back decided him. 'They might have gone over to Balaclava. I think that's what they were arguing about. You cops know who's been using that bedroom upstairs there, don't you? Well, it's got Tansy's goat that you're not doing anything about it. Don't explain it to me. I don't bloody care.'

Billy Hemmings ran his business from a small first-floor office in the area of Gloucester Docks. A modest brass plate gave no indication of what kind of business it was, but presumably people who wanted to conduct it with Billy knew all about it. A secretary, a small dark woman radiating energy, presided over a cramped outer office at the top of the steep flight of stairs. She appeared to be the only staff.

'Superintendent Carter!' she said briskly. 'He's been expecting you. Go on through.'

Carter smiled wryly. The phone line between Weston St Ambrose and this office had been busy. Unfortunately, though unavoidably, Terri had had plenty of time to forewarn her husband and Billy had had plenty of time to prepare for his visit. But perhaps Billy had been waiting for this interview from the beginning . . . if he indeed had an interest in Balaclava House, that is. He must be shrewd enough to have realised the police would make a link, sooner or later. It was going to be interesting to hear him explain his lack of frankness on the subject.

The brisk receptionist/secretary was still indicating the narrow door with a frosted glazed panel in it.

'Thank you,' Carter said to her and 'went through', as directed.

Beyond it Hemmings was waiting for him with a smile fixed in place on his fleshy lips. It didn't quite reach his eyes.

'Hello, then, we meet again!' he hailed his visitor with false jocularity. He was rising to his feet as he spoke and holding out his hand.

'Thank you for seeing me so promptly,' Carter returned, not to be outdone in the matter of civilities. He shook the proffered hand as briefly as he could.

'Oh, well, as soon as Terri rang here to say you'd been on to her, I was waiting for your call. I'll get Amanda to bring us in some coffee.' He leaned forward and called into the intercom on his desk, 'Coffee, Amanda!' He leaned back again. 'What can I do for you this time? Found out who did for poor old Jay yet?'

'No, not yet, not quite yet,' Carter admitted, lowering himself into a shiny new armchair of modern design, all tubular steel and black plastic. It looked like an ejector seat and felt about as comfortable. He was reminded of scenes in James Bond films; and wondered if Hemmings had a button under his desk to get rid of unwanted callers. They were in the former docks here, after all. Perhaps, he thought with a moment's amusement, a trapdoor would open and he, Carter, would plummet neatly down into the water.

His suppressed smile had been noted by the other man and interpreted differently.

'That's a designer piece,' said Hemmings proudly, indicating the chair with a wave. 'I paid good money for that chair. That cost me more than all the rest of the office furniture put together.'

Carter hastily murmured something to indicate he was impressed. Then he got to the subject that had brought him.

'Actually,' he began, 'I'd like to talk to you about Balaclava House.'

Amanda chose that moment to appear with the coffee. From her boss's point of view, she couldn't have timed it better. Carter wondered if she were listening over the intercom, out there in her cubbyhole office.

'Ah, coffee!' Hemmings beamed, as if he hadn't just asked for it. He opened a lower drawer in his desk and took something out. 'Would you like a drop of something in that, Superintendent?' He held up a brandy bottle.

'I'm on duty, I'm afraid,' Carter refused the offer with a smile.

'Of course you are.' Hemmings returned the bottle to its hiding place and sat back again. 'Balaclava House, you say?

Where Jay was found? I think I remember you telling me that.'

'Yes, I did tell you that. Had you heard of the place before?'

For the barest second Hemmings was tempted to lie. His face didn't tell it but his body language did. He seemed to hold his breath and stiffen. Then he relaxed.

'Yes, I did remember – after I'd seen you – that I had heard of it before. Well, it's local to us in Weston St Ambrose, isn't it? Or almost.'

He had realised that if Carter were here to talk about it, the superintendent already knew or had guessed something. Now Hemmings would try to find out just how much. But two could play at that game.

'It's a big place, lots of land,' Carter said conversationally, reaching for his coffee cup.

'So I believe,' said Hemmings, watchful.

'House is in a terrible state, of course.'

The developer nodded. 'So I've been told.'

'Oh?' Carter asked, setting down his cup. 'Who told you?'

'Damn!' said Hemmings, 'This coffee is a bit too hot for me!' He put down his own cup hurriedly.

But not quickly enough, old son! Carter allowed himself an inner smile. It's not burning your tongue you're regretting, it's falling into such an easy trap.

'I asked around about it, after you told us about Jay being found there . . .' Hemmings's excuse sounded feeble and he knew it. 'It made me curious.'

'You haven't been over there to visit the place, quite recently, since Jay's death and since the owner, Monty Bickerstaffe, has been staying with relatives?'

There was a silence. Hemmings stared at him moodily. 'All right, Superintendent,' he said at last. 'Cards on the table.'

'I'd appreciate it,' Carter told him.

'You're a man who likes to come to the point, so am I.' Hemmings cleared his throat. 'Jay told me about the house. He'd got to know about it. He thought there was land for development there. I'm in that line of business, so he came to me with a proposition. He knew me as a racing acquaintance. A lot of business is done, or started at least, on the social network. You meet up with someone and get chatting . . . Well, that's what happened. He suggested he and I could develop the land together, form a partnership. My first question was, how likely was it the land and house would become available and when? You've got to be practical. I've heard people float all kinds of wild ideas to make a cartload of money – if only this or that big problem can be overcome. "First things first, Jay, old chap," I told him. "Who owns this land and the house? Is he putting it on the market? Who else knows about it?"

'He told me the present owner had no plans to sell, wouldn't want to sell it. But he was elderly and not too fit, a bit of a drinker, it seems. Circumstances could change rapidly. The next owners might think differently. If we got in now, we'd be the first. No one else was on to it. I told him I was definitely interested.'

'You weren't concerned you might not get planning permission?' Carter asked him.

Hemmings had the answer to that one. 'The house is old but it's not listed. I checked. A sympathetic development scheme would go down well in the planning office. After all, once it's vacant, once the present owner is – has passed on – it'll stand empty and that'll suit no one. It'll soon be in a dangerous state. Already doesn't look too safe to me at the moment. I – I made a few general enquiries of the council.'

'It might make a hotel, or a nursing home . . .' Carter suggested.

But Hemmings was shaking his head. 'No, too far gone and not suitable. Believe me, the only thing you could do with Balaclava House is pull it down.'

'You've seen it yourself, then. You've viewed the property, as they say?'

Hemmings was no longer bothering to pretend. 'Yes, of course. First thing I did, after Jay came to me with his big idea, was go over there and take a look at it for myself. Second thing was to approach the planning department, like I told you. Balaclava House –' he nodded knowingly at Carter – 'is a very good business prospect, take it from me. Ripe for development.'

'Been over there again recently?' Carter asked again. 'I don't think you quite answered that question.'

Hemmings grimaced. Then he shrugged in defeat.

'Yes, as it happens, a couple of days ago. Just to see if there was any sign of anything happening. There wasn't. I was pleased about that. There's been quite a bit in the local press about the place since the – since Jay's body was found there. Some other developer might be getting ideas. I might have to move quick.'

Hemmings's small dark eyes flickered at him. 'I was seen, was I? You appear to know all about it.'

'Something like that,' murmured Carter. 'So, you and Taylor were about to form a business partnership to develop the land in the future – and you were prepared to wait for Mr Bickerstaffe to die for you to get ownership? That could be years. He's only seventy-six and, far from being frail, as Taylor would have had you believe, my understanding is that he's remarkably robust.'

'Yeah, well, things can change fast, can't they? It's not like old Bickerstaffe has a car and can drive himself around. He's isolated out there in that house, high and dry like he was on a desert island, almost. He can't live there alone much longer, no matter how spry you reckon he is,' said Hemmings confidently. 'He'll have to sell up within the next year or so – or the next owner will.'

He hesitated briefly. 'Jay reckoned we wouldn't have to wait for the old man to die. He thought, if the old fellow found he couldn't live there any longer, he might gift the place to someone, a family member. It's been in the family for over a century and a half and he'd want it to stay that way. Jay seemed sure about that.'

'A family member? A woman, perhaps?' Carter waited.

Hemmings considered that carefully. 'I can't tell you,' he said at last, 'because I don't know. That's the truth. It's a thought, though, I'll give you that. It just seemed to me Jay might have some card up his sleeve. I've no idea what kind – a bird or anything else – and I could be wrong. Whether *he* was right to be so certain about it is another matter, and I can't help you there, either.

I was just satisfied, from my own observation of the place, that the old man couldn't reside there himself for very much longer. That house, take it from me, is coming on the market very soon now. All the indications are there and I know how to read 'em!'

Carter put the tips of his fingers together, a gesture that seemed to dent Hemmings's last confident statement. 'Right, let's see if I've got this straight. You and Taylor would be partners. You'd oversee the development from your office here. But what would be Taylor's input, other than telling you about the house? He didn't have access to large amounts of cash. What would qualify him to be your *partner*?'

Hemmings took a deep breath, his gaze fixed on Carter's hands. 'That's why I reckoned Jay had some card up his sleeve, an ace.' Hemmings looked up, squinting at his visitor. 'Jay had found out something; something that would help him get his hands on that land. He kept hinting heavily that if things worked out, we wouldn't have to pay a penny for it. "You've got to be joking," I said to him. But he grinned and told me to trust him. Don't ask me any more. Jay was playing his cards *very* close to his chest until he was sure I'd come in with him. I don't blame him for that. I'd do the same. You never give away any information until you have to, do you?'

Carter suspected this was an appeal to him to overlook Hemmings's failure to tell the investigating officers any of this before now. If so, it fell on stony ground.

'Keeping back information isn't always a good idea. If Jay had been more open about what he'd discovered, he might be here to tell us about it himself, now.'

Hemmings looked uneasy. 'Perhaps I should have asked him, should have made him tell me all about it. Well, I was going to, soon. We'd got to that point where I was ready to sign on the line but to do that, I would have insisted on knowing what trick he'd got tucked away – whether it was a woman, as you seem to be suggesting, or what. But I didn't know he was going to get himself killed, did I? When you told me he'd turned up dead in that ruddy house, it gave me a helluva shock, I can tell you.'

Hemmings ran his fingers nervously over his mouth. 'This whatever-it-was he found out, you reckon it killed him, then?'

'I don't think his murder was motiveless,' Carter told him. 'I think, Mr Hemmings, it's not a good idea in the present circumstances for you to go wandering about Balaclava House and grounds. Whoever killed Taylor might also see you as a threat.'

Billy Hemmings had been looking uncomfortable. Now he began to look worried.

Chapter 18

Balaclava house, when Jess reached it, was deserted. To make sure, she toured the building on foot, peering in windows. This is what Jay Taylor had done, she thought. But then Seb and Rosie were watching him from above. If anyone is watching me, he or she is keeping very quiet. She rattled the front door handle but now it was locked. She walked back slowly down the drive to the lane and scoured the ground for signs of a car having parked here, fresh footprints other than her own, anything that would have indicated a recent presence. There were marks of tyres outside the gates, but both Carter and Tansy Peterson had parked there the day before and had probably left the traces. If either Bridget or Tansy had been intending to drive here this morning, there was no sign of either. Footprints in the garden were those seen by Carter and already no longer fresh.

Jess returned to her car and thought desperately. Monty might deliberately have put her on a false scent. But she remembered Monica Farrell telling her that Monty wouldn't tell an out and out lie, not to Jess who so resembled his late wife. If Monica was right, Monty might have been telling the truth about the previous evening's argument; but he could still have drawn the wrong conclusion when he saw the two women drive off in such a panic and in separate cars that morning.

No, decided Jess. Monty didn't think it out wrongly. The women had argued violently about Balaclava House only the night before. The quarrel or dispute, whatever it was, was left unresolved. They would have picked it up again this morning. When they did, it resulted in Tansy running out of the house, closely followed by her mother. They were coming here. So, where are they?

She looked around. This was a benighted spot. Everything was in need of repair: the potholed surface of the lane, the collapsing sign at the entrance to it, poor Balaclava House sinking into ruin, a shadow of its once-proud self. Jess drummed her fingers on the steering wheel. Tansy had left The Old Lodge first. Bridget had followed her. Therefore it was a question of where Tansy had been heading. The assumption by Monty and by Jess herself was that the destination was Toby's Gutter Lane. But if not to Balaclava itself, then where?

The Colleys! Jess gave the steering wheel a little slap of triumph. Bridget would not have any time for the Colleys but Tansy told Ian Carter that she and Gary Colley had been pals when children. Tansy used to go to the Colley homestead and ride Gary's pony round the field there.

'And Tansy's gone there again,' said Jess aloud. 'I knew those Colleys were mixed up in this somehow!'

She drove the short distance to the Colley pig farm. Leaving her car outside, she pushed open the gate and walked through. As she did so, she remembered Morton telling her about the dogs. To walk boldly up the drive unannounced might not be the best idea. She turned back to her car, drove through the opened gate, got out and closed it as Morton had done on his visit. She then continued down to the complex of buildings Phil had described to her.

There it all was, just as Phil had said, house, old stable block, pigsties and dog run . . . and she was not the first, nor even the second, visitor today. Two cars were parked in the muddy yard: Bridget's little two-seater and, in front of it, Tansy's Fiesta.

Bingo! thought Jess, allowing herself a moment's satisfaction at having found her quarry. She looked across towards the dog run to check it was safe to get out.

This influx of visitors seemed to have thrown the dogs into some confusion. Probably they had been ordered sternly not to bark at the previous arrivals and so did not know what to do about Jess. They crowded to the wire to stare at her suspiciously but didn't bark, not even when Jess got out of her car.

Others had heard her, however. Both Dave and Gary emerged from the former stable block and stood watching her.

Jess walked towards them and they watched her approach with the same mix of hostility and caution as shown by their dogs. Gary obviously recognised her, but this was the first time she'd met Dave, his father. She took out her ID and held it up so that he could see it.

'My lad's told me about you,' said Dave.

Jess wasn't going to waste time. 'Where are they?' she asked briskly. 'Where are Mrs Harwell and her daughter, Tansy Peterson?'

'Gone walking up over Shooter's Hill,' said Dave. 'Nice day like it is, after all that rain. They decided to stretch their legs.'

'I don't think so,' Jess said curtly. Tansy might ramble over Shooter's Hill for the fun of it. Bridget was not the hiking type. 'Don't waste my time, Mr Colley. That's obstruction and an offence. I want to speak to both women and I want to know where they are right now.'

Both men stayed silent, hostile, watchful and wary. Dangerous, too? Should she have waited for Phil to join her before tackling them? The Colleys stood shoulder to shoulder in the open entrance to the former stables. It was as if they blocked it. They *are* blocking it, she thought.

She addressed Dave Colley. 'Mr Colley, I don't have a search warrant, but I can get one very easily. I don't have to leave, I just have to phone through to my superintendent with a request; and he'll be here within the hour with one.'

'We can ask you to leave our property meantime,' growled Dave.

'Sure, why don't you? And I'll just wait outside your gate back there, blocking the way in and out, just as you are both blocking my view of that barn or stable or whatever you call it now. Neither woman will be able to drive away. Neither woman can get very far without transport. I can stay around for as long as it takes and, sooner or later, one of them if not both will have to come out and face me.'

'What do you want them for?' Gary asked truculently.

'That's police business.' She paused. 'I'd like to look around the barn now, please. I'd be obliged if you would give your permission. Mr Colley?'

The Colleys exchanged glances. Gary looked as if he would still object. Unexpectedly, Dave shrugged. 'Go and look, then, if it makes you any happier. It's nothing to do with either of us, is it, Gary?' A minatory note sounded in his voice.

Gary hesitated. 'No, right . . .' he said unwillingly.

'That's very sensible of you, Mr Colley. If you are already in any trouble, you don't want to make things worse, do you?'

They parted barely enough to allow her through. Jess stepped into the former stable block and into a lost age. She was surrounded by signs of its former, as well as present, use. One end was still divided into stalls. Dusty harness items hung from pegs on the wall, the leather dried and cracking. Touchingly, a painted sign still hung above one stall. It read 'Brutus'. If Brutus had been a carriage horse, what had been the name of his pair? Caesar? Modern times had come. The elegance of a carriage and pair had gone and been replaced by a mud-splashed truck garaged at the other end of the open floor area. Against the rear wall a flight of wooden stairs rose into the loft above. The air was musty and made her nose itch.

'Mrs Harwell? Tansy?' Jess called. 'It's Inspector Campbell. If you are up there in the loft, come down, please. I need to talk to you both.'

There was silence. She sensed a collective holding of breath. A slight movement behind her, telegraphed by the disappearance of one part of the shadow falling through the open entry, caused her to turn her head. Dave Colley was still there, watching her sullenly from the doorway. Gary, however, had vanished. Now, where had he gone? Jess felt uneasy, not having him in sight. Her ear caught the faintest creak above her head.

'I'm coming up there!' she called out.

She started slowly up the wooden stairs. They creaked ominously beneath her feet and she reached for the handrail. She could feel the intense gaze of Dave Colley's eyes watching her every move. He himself had not moved, thank goodness. But where was the wretched Gary?

Jess had reached the top and the loft. The shadowy rafters, strung with ancient cobwebs, loomed high above her head. The place was packed with every kind of junk, ancient and modern, old tools, furniture, tea chests, some of it looking as if it had been there many years. Even wisps of Edwardian hay still lay in corners. What the Colleys planned to do with all this rubbish she couldn't imagine. Perhaps they just didn't bother to throw any of it away, keeping it as they had kept the old harness, useless but part of the place. The loft was brightly lit, more so than the floor below. The light streamed through one of the floor-length openings through which hay had been brought up so many years ago to feed Brutus and his companions.

Bridget Harwell stood on the far side of the loft, away from the head of the stairs, and framed by the opening behind her. She was standing too close to the edge for Jess's liking; but she guessed it was a deliberate ploy on Bridget's part to prevent Jess moving towards her.

'Where's Tansy?' Jess asked.

'We had another row,' Bridget told her in her brittle voice.

'She stormed out and has gone off walking over Shooter's Hill somewhere to cool off.'

So perhaps Dave had almost been telling the truth.

'We don't need Tansy, in any case,' Bridget went on. 'I can tell you what happened. I suppose that's what you want to ask.'

'Yes, I do. I was at your home earlier and spoke to Monty. He said you and Tansy had a violent quarrel last night. You continued it this morning and first Tansy drove off and then you followed. I guessed the quarrel was about Jay Taylor. I do now know that Tansy was well acquainted with him. Was he her boyfriend?'

Bridget uttered an expression of disgust and waved a hand to dismiss this outlandish idea.

'Come off it,' Jess told her. 'I've seen a photo of them at a nightclub, very pally. I thought at first you were making for Balaclava House, but when I didn't find you there, I guessed you'd come here. Tansy was friendly with Gary Colley when they were children, wasn't she?'

'My daughter,' Bridget said coldly, 'has a talent for picking unsuitable friends.' After a moment's hesitation, she added, 'Perhaps she inherited it from me. I pick unsuitable men, too. But a mother always does blame herself when things go wrong for her child, as if that child were still a schoolgirl. Tansy is a woman. She'll be nineteen in two weeks' time. But she is still a child in her attitude. She has no idea of the world, no knowledge that men like Taylor exist. I think she met him at a party somewhere in London. I won't dignify the emotion she felt towards him as falling in love. As far as I was concerned, it was just a massive schoolgirl crush. She thought he was wonderful. He told her a load of nonsense about loving her and she believed every word.'

'You met Taylor?'

'Oh, yes, I met him. As soon as I got wind of what was going on, I sought him out. I wanted to see who this fellow was she was talking of marrying. Marrying! She was supposed to be going to university, spreading her wings, finding out a little about life. When I met Taylor, all my worst fears were confirmed. He was much too old for her, very experienced in the world, and an out and out chancer. I didn't know what he wanted from Tansy – apart from the obvious and he didn't need to offer her marriage to get that! She was falling into his arms! I told him to stay away and he told me, as cool as a cucumber, that it was between him and Tansy, and nothing to do with me. Her mother! I was supposed to stand back and let him ruin her life?'

'So when you looked at his dead body in Balaclava House, you recognised him. You said at the time you didn't.'

'Of course I recognised him. I was responsible for his being there.'

There was a silence.

'Perhaps you could explain that?' Jess prompted.

'Why not?' Bridget returned coolly. 'It's pretty straightforward. I got Tansy out of the way for the day and invited the wretched Taylor to come down to The Old Lodge for lunch with me, to talk things over. I made the invitation the day before, when I went up to London.'

'You were confident he'd accept your invitation? He knew you disapproved of his friendship with your daughter?' Jess asked.

Bridget gave a knowing smile. 'I knew he'd accept. His vanity made him do that. He thought he'd won. He thought I was going to give up my opposition and I had invited him down to talk terms. He didn't know me if he thought I would just throw in the towel like that. I wasn't about to let him have Tansy and I had to do something to stop that happening, stop it for good! I'm going to the States soon to get married myself.' She grimaced. 'I suppose I ought now to say that I *was* going. At any rate, I wouldn't be here to protect her. So I did what I had to do. I would make her safe from him.'

'And remove an obstacle from your own life, too? If you wanted to keep to your schedule in travelling to the USA.'

Bridget gave a satisfied nod. 'Of course. He had to go, however you look at it. The wretched man had just made himself a complete inconvenience. It was stupid of him. But I counted on his being stupid. So he came down to The Old Lodge and I cooked him a first-rate lunch, if I say so myself.'

Jess didn't want to interrupt Bridget but she was worried about how close the woman still stood to the edge of the hayloft and the open hatch behind her.

'Perhaps,' she suggested as calmly as she could, 'we could talk more comfortably. There's an old sofa over there. It doesn't look too dirty.'

'We're quite all right as we are!' Bridget snapped. 'I'll stay here and you stay right there and we'll be fine.'

'OK.' Jess didn't think it was fine at all, but the other woman's nervous tension fairly crackled through the air between them. I need to calm her down, Jess thought. If I let her go on with her story, she might relax a bit. Then I'll have another go at persuading her to come with me, or at least move away from that opening.

'I crushed up a bottleful of sleeping tablets and mixed them in with the wine sauce,' Bridget said. 'It was coq au vin. I usually do that for lunch parties. We'd had a couple of drinks before we ate and a bottle of decent red with the meal.'

'You thought that would kill him?'

'No!' Bridget grew irritable. 'Of course that wouldn't *kill* him. Or it wasn't likely. I couldn't have relied on it and I didn't. I knew it would make him very sleepy and then I could make my next move. I thought it would be an hour or a bit more before the pills and booze had any real effect. My idea was to have him leave before that, drive away. I thought he'd crash on the way home, just another drunk driver cut from the wreckage. Add him to the statistics.'

'He could have killed other people, innocent people!' Jess broke in angrily, unable to stop herself.

Bridget shrugged. 'I didn't think of that. I was only thinking of Tansy. I told you, I did it for my daughter. That was all that mattered to me; the only thing I had on my mind. I had to kill the bastard – or arrange for him to kill himself – because he'd left me no other choice. Blame him!'

'So how did he end up on a sofa in Balaclava House?'

'I'm coming to that!' Bridget was beginning to sound exasperated. 'Stop interrupting.'

I'm not doing a very good job calming her down, Jess told herself. Shut up, Jess, whatever she says. Let her finish. But I've got to get her away from that opening.

Bridget looked discontented. 'It was a good idea but it started to go wrong at once. The pills and wine worked more quickly than I'd judged they would. We hadn't even finished our meal and he was already dozing off over the cheese. I'd misjudged how powerful they'd been. I began to be afraid he'd pass out right there in my house, flat out on the carpet. He mumbled he didn't feel well. I told him I'd drive him home. He was confused and clumsy but I managed to get him to his feet and out of the house, into his car. He slumped in the passenger seat and hardly appeared to be breathing. He closed his eyes and I thought he'd gone to sleep. Fine, that suited me. I'd planned for him to crash and he was still going to, only I'd have to organise it differently.

'First of all, we had to get away from my house. I remembered Shooter's Hill. That would be ideal, steep, lonely, no one to see what happened. I'd stop at the top of the hill and manhandle him somehow into the driver's seat. Then I'd release the brake, give the car a bit of a push, and off he'd go, rattling down Shooter's Hill to pile up at the bottom. Sooner or later someone would find the wreck, either Pete Sneddon or a walker. But I'd be long gone, well away.'

'How?' asked Jess crisply. There were more holes in this story than a sieve. 'You didn't have any transport to get home.'

'I knew I could come here, to the Colleys' place. Don't forget . . .' Bridget's tense features were unexpectedly softened by a brief smile. 'I'm a Bickerstaffe. I've known the Colleys all my life. I'd tell them I'd been on my way to Balaclava House intending to check the place over. My car had broken down. I'd say I'd phoned Seb Pascal and he'd come with his tow-truck to take my car away. I'd ask Dave to drive me home, or Gary. Even if they didn't quite believe me, I could trust the Colleys not to ask questions. It's all quite feudal really, Bickerstaffes and Colleys. It always has been. It's really weird in this day and age. But once you step into the world of Balaclava House, you're not in the present day, you know. You're stuck in some benighted past.'

'So that's what you did?'

'Not quite. You see the blighter died on me just as I turned into Toby's Gutter Lane.' Bridget's voice grew vicious. 'He just coughed up a load of vomit and pitched forward as far as the seat belt would allow and stayed like that. I nearly did crash the car, with both of us inside it! It was quite disgusting. I nearly threw up myself. I pulled over and got out of the car for fresh air. Then I began to think, I could still carry on with most of the plan. I could still crash the car at the bottom of Shooter's Hill. But the experts are so damn clever these days and they'd realise, at a post-mortem, he was already dead when he crashed. My fingerprints were all over that car, too. I only then thought about that. Something so elementary and I'd forgotten that, can you believe it? It was because I was in such a panic to get him away from my house. Then I had a bit of luck. There's a field there, where the lane starts, and as I stood by the car, Gary Colley came towards me over the open land with a shotgun broken over his arm. The Colleys always did shoot anything with fur or feathers.

'I called out to him. I told him the basic truth: my passenger had died in the car. I wanted to get rid of the car and the body because I didn't want to get involved in a court case. Gary appreciated that argument. I also remembered that Balaclava House was never locked in the daytime and there was a good chance Uncle Monty hadn't got back from his daily walk into town.'

'You suggested putting the dead man in your uncle's house, for the poor old man to find?' Jess asked incredulously, forgetting her resolution not to interrupt. 'The shock might have given him a heart attack!'

'Uncle Monty? Not likely, he's as tough as old boots. Don't waste your sympathy on him. He led Aunt Penny a dreadful life. She adored him, too. In the end even she couldn't take any more and left. Do you know? The miserable old brute wouldn't even attend her funeral! If you want to know the truth, the image of him stumbling in with his shopping bag full of clinking bottles and finding a stiff, well, it would serve him right. It even amused me and I needed a laugh after all I'd gone through that day.' Bridget scowled.

Jess stared at her nonplussed. There was something wrong with all this but she couldn't put her finger on it. It made sense with a dreadful logic, except that . . .

'You drove the car to Balaclava House, I take it, with Gary as passenger?'

'Gary drove. I didn't fancy getting back into the driver's seat beside Taylor so I got into the rear seat. We actually drove past Balaclava to the Colleys' and parked here. Gary fetched his father. Dave and Gary partly carried and partly dragged Taylor through the grounds to the house and left him inside. Then they came back and put Taylor's car in this barn.' Bridget pointed down at the wooden floor beneath their feet. 'Out of sight, in case Pete Sneddon decided to call by. He does, from time to time, usually to complain about something to do with the pigs.'

Damn! thought Jess furiously. I should have got a search warrant that first day and come here to the Colleys' with it. I'd have found the car in this barn before they ditched it later that night.

'The Colleys drove the car down to the quarry that night and torched it?' she asked.

Bridget nodded. 'Yes, they said they'd do that. It would take care of any fingerprints or DNA, linking me with it.' She drew a deep breath. 'I'll come with you now and make a statement, if you like.'

'Not quite yet,' Jess said. 'First I'll wait for Tansy to come back.'

'We don't need Tansy!' Bridget said furiously. 'Leave her out of it.'

'I can't, Mrs Harwell. I need a statement from her, too.'

'She wasn't *there*!' Bridget almost howled at her.

'But, you see, I think she was,' Jess said. 'I think you and she cooked this up together. You may have gone to London the day before, as you said you did, but I doubt you saw Taylor there. He lived in Cheltenham and only went to London on business.

You'd have arranged to meet him in Cheltenham if anywhere. Why didn't you say all you had to say while in Cheltenham? Why invite the man to lunch at your house the very next day? What's more, I don't think he'd have accepted such an invitation so easily, without smelling a rat. He may have suspected he'd arrive to find every man in the family you could round up there to confront him. But he *would* accept an invitation from Tansy. The only reason he'd accept would be if Tansy were going to be there.

'Besides, it took two of you to manhandle him into the car. He was a big, heavy guy. I might have been able to do it alone because I'm a police officer and very fit. I've had training in how to get a recalcitrant detainee, possibly drunk into the bargain, into a squad car. But you alone, Bridget? No way. You didn't meet him in London or anywhere else. Tansy rang him up. What did Tansy say to him? That you'd given in and wanted to discuss it all, just a cosy threesome?'

'Yes, that's what I did say to him,' said a new voice.

There was a movement to Jess's left and Tansy Peterson stepped out from behind a stack of crates.

'No, Tansy!' Bridget cried out. 'Leave this to me! We agreed!'

'There's no point,' Tansy said bleakly. 'She isn't buying the explanation the way you told it, Mum. Even if I went along with it and said I was away from The Old Lodge that lunchtime, Inspector Campbell here would ask me for witnesses who could put me elsewhere at the time, an alibi, wouldn't you?' She looked full at Jess.

'Yes,' Jess confirmed, 'I certainly would, because you've been lying to us all along. The only moment you nearly betrayed yourself was when I told you that someone had been using one of the upstairs bedrooms at Balaclava. You were extremely distressed. You realised that person or persons might have been there when you, your mother and the Colleys were putting Taylor's body in the drawing room. You could have been seen.'

'I wasn't there for that,' Tansy objected. 'Dave and Gary did it between them. I'd helped get Jay into the car at The Old Lodge, as you guessed, but my mother drove off with him alone. She wouldn't let me come along. I thought it had all gone according to plan, with the car crashing at the bottom of Shooter's Hill, as we decided it should. I didn't know the plan had had to be changed until my mother came back. I wouldn't have let Gary and his father put Jay in Balaclava for Uncle Monty to find. I was furious when I found out what they'd done. I love Uncle Monty. He's a wonderful old man! But after my mother drove off I didn't know what happened until she returned and told me. It was too late to do anything about it then. I didn't want Jay near Balaclava House dead or alive, much less actually *in* it!'

'But why,' Jess couldn't help but ask curiously, 'did you want to kill Jay Taylor? You were in love with him. Your mother was in a blind panic over it. You spoke of marrying him. You and Mrs Harwell fought over it.'

'Oh, yes,' Tansy said bitterly. 'Jay and I discussed marriage. I'm over eighteen and, whatever my mother thought about it, I'd have married him. Then I found out that it wasn't me he wanted. He wanted Balaclava House. I'll be Uncle Monty's heir and had stupidly let Jay know it, all about Balaclava and how

Uncle Monty lived there all on his own and the place was falling down. But it would be mine one day and I planned to restore it. It would be beautiful and I'd live there.

'Jay had checked the place out, just from curiosity. When he saw the size of it and how much land was attached, it gave him his big idea. He thought he'd marry me; Uncle Monty wouldn't last much longer, and wow! He'd get his hands on Balaclava.' Tansy voice grew incredulous. 'Do you know what he planned to do with the house? He and some developer pal of his were going to pull it down! Raze Balaclava to the ground and put a lot of brick boxes all over the land!'

'How did you find that out?'

'The developer he was going in with, I think he's called Hemmings, went to the local planning office to see if there would be any objection, any difficulty getting permission. He mentioned to them that he would be in partnership with someone called Taylor. Well, a friend of mine works in that office. He shouldn't have done it, I suppose, but he got in touch with me at once to warn me. He knew about me and that I stood to inherit Balaclava, and that my relative was the owner and still living in it. So alarm bells had rung when a complete stranger turned up talking about developing the site. As soon as I heard the name "Taylor" mentioned, I just felt cold all over. I knew in my guts it was Jay. I thought I would be sick. How could he do that to me? Everything he'd said about loving me was a lie. I faced him with it, demanded to know if he was the Taylor in partnership with this man Hemmings. I was furious, screaming at him. He didn't bat an eyelid, just listened to me with a smirk on his face. It made me even madder, he was so – so cool. He didn't even try to deny it. He admitted he was in cahoots with Hemmings, and told me what a good idea it was. I should be pleased because I'd be part of it, too, and we could both make a mint.

'For a minute or two I couldn't speak, I was so angry. The words piled up in my throat and choked me. When I could speak, I told him to get out of my life. I said he was a sneaky, treacherous snake in the grass. He'd tried to use me. I wasn't going to stand for that. I assured him I'd scotch any chance he and Hemmings had of developing the land. Over my dead body, I said. He was never going to get Balaclava House.'

Tansy drew a deep breath. 'Then he said he had a right to Balaclava. *A right! Because he was a Bickerstaffe, too!*'

This astounding statement had barely left Tansy's lips when there was a sudden loud crack from the hayloft hatch. Bridget gave a stifled shriek. Both Jess and Tansy whirled round. But the window frame was empty. Bridget had disappeared.

Chapter 19

Tansy let out a piercing scream and started towards the empty window frame. Jess grabbed her arm and wrestled with her to prevent her going closer.

'No, Tansy! The floor is rotten! Look!' She pointed to the broken board that had given way under Bridget's foot, unbalancing her and toppling her backwards. 'Stay here!'

Jess turned and raced back down the flight of wooden stairs to the ground floor. Tansy, ignoring the order to stay where she was, panted along on her heels. Jess dashed across the barn floor and out into the yard.

Dave and Gary stood in frozen horror above the sprawled motionless form of Bridget Harwell. The remaining members of the Colley family were running from their cottage towards the spot. The oldest woman was waving her arms above her head. The youngest, overweight, lumbered beside her, mouth gaping and badly dyed scarlet hair flying. Between the two extremes of age came a middle-aged third who must be Maggie Colley. She was shouting a string of obscenities. The words tumbling from her lips were not, Jess was able to realise despite her own shock, aimed specifically at her. They were Maggie's automatic reaction to the horror of the moment; the only

313

vocabulary at her disposal in which to express her dismay. At the same time, in her ear, Jess could hear Tansy screaming, *'Mummy, Mummy!'*

The dogs were loose and milled about excitedly. *That's where Gary went, to let the dogs out!* The realisation flashed through Jess's mind. *What did the idiot think? That the animals would keep me penned in while the women made some kind of escape?* The dogs crept closer and began to circle the inert form. Gary moved at last, swearing and kicking out at them to drive them back. Into Jess's head leaped the image from the stained-glass window at Balaclava House. Jezebel: the treacherous woman . . .

'I've spoken to the hospital this morning,' Ian Carter told Jess the following day. 'Bridget has been very fortunate. The recent heavy rain helped. It turned the Colleys' yard into a sea of soft mud and she landed on that rather than on hard ground. She has a broken leg and broken pelvis, concussion and of course considerable bruising. But she's escaped internal injury. She will recover and eventually, we trust, be fit enough to stand trial. Her fiancé is on his way from America. We don't know what the outcome of that will be but I doubt she'll be getting married to him now, not if he wants to see his wife other than on visiting days.'

'I feel responsible,' Jess said dully. 'She was being interviewed by me when she fell out of that opening. I saw she was in danger. When I couldn't get her to move away from it and sit on that old sofa to talk, I should have made a grab for her and dragged her away.'

'There will have to be an inquiry, of course,' Carter told her. 'But I am quite confident you'll be cleared of any responsibility, Jess. It wasn't your fault she fell. She was in a highly excitable frame of mind. You tried to persuade her to move away from the open window and she wouldn't. She wanted to keep your attention on her so that you wouldn't realise her daughter was hiding up there in that loft. You were quite right not to move towards her. She might have stepped backwards automatically and then fallen. That's a hundred-and-fifty-year-old floor up there and it's not been well maintained. It gave way under her weight. If you and she had both been standing on it, you'd both have fallen. No one can be surprised at what happened; or put it down to anything you did or didn't do.'

'I still feel I screwed up somehow,' Jess argued. 'If I'd got a search warrant for the Colleys' pig farm on the day of the murder, we'd have found Taylor's car, complete with his fingerprints and DNA and Bridget's.'

He interrupted her briskly. 'On what grounds would you have requested a search warrant then? As far as we were concerned, the Colleys were neighbours of Balaclava House and that was all. There was no indication at that time they'd been involved.'

Jess was still unconvinced. 'Phil and I both realised at the scene that at least two people had carried the dead man into the house; and that they'd come through the shrubbery. That means they came from the general direction of the pig farm. At least one of those two people must have known that Monty would be absent in town and would have left the door unsecured.'

'Not necessarily. Given the state of the place, anyone could be excused thinking it was empty, and decided to dump the body there for that reason. It's easy to be wise after the event, Jess. Come on, let it go . . . I wouldn't have put you down as someone given to wallowing in self-reproach!' was the severe reproof.

'I'm not!' said Jess indignantly.

Carter grinned. 'Good. That's more like it. Now, let's go and get the rest of the story from Miss Peterson. It should be very interesting listening.'

'I always thought,' said Tansy with muted fury, 'that Jay and I met for the first time by accident at that party. But it wasn't like that. He had been seeking me out. He got me to talk about myself. I was such a fool, prattling away to him about my family . . . I should have realised he was pumping me for information. The more he learned, the more his big idea grew. He thought he could get Balaclava House through me and he had a crackpot belief that he was somehow *entitled* to get his hands on it!'

She sat with her solicitor on one side of the table in the interview room. Carter and Jess faced them. Phil Morton lurked by the door. Above their heads the fluorescent strip emitted a faint hiss. Tansy's fair skin looked bleached in this light. Her fair hair resembled a tangled sweep of drift weed. It all lent her the appearance of a marble angel above a Victorian tomb, albeit an avenging one.

'OK, Tansy, take it easy,' Jess advised. 'Why don't you explain to us why Taylor thought he was entitled to get hold of Balaclava House?'

Tansy stopped scowling down at the table top, sat up, pushed back her curtain of hair and turned to her solicitor. She fixed him with a minatory glare very like her mother's and demanded, 'I have to tell them all this or what?'

'You'd better tell them about Taylor's claim,' said the unfortunate young man whose job it was to give this simmering time bomb of a client advice. 'But that's all you need to say at this moment.'

He clutched his briefcase against his chest with both hands as if it were a shield. Tansy's father, Peterson, had arranged his presence. He represented an old and well-respected legal partnership. However, they might have done better thought Jess, to give the job to a senior partner. Perhaps they had mistakenly reckoned there would be more empathy between legal adviser and client if there were less of an age difference.

'Right, then.' Tansy turned back to Carter and Jess. 'This is the family dirty linen I'm going to flap in front of you now. Everything they got up to.' She gave a wicked grin. 'How they would all have hated to know I was telling anyone this and to think I'd be telling the *police* – they'd all have had fits!

'It's hard to know where to begin because it all goes back donkey's years, to the late nineteen forties, just after the end of World War Two. Edward Bickerstaffe was living at Balaclava House with his wife and their son, Monty – that's Uncle Monty, who was only a schoolboy then. They sent him away to boarding school so he was only there in the holidays. They didn't have any other kids and I don't know the name of Edward's wife. Funny thing . . .' Tansy frowned. 'No one in the family ever uses it

317

when talking of family history. She's always referred to as "Edward's wife" or as "Monty's mother". The poor wretched woman might never have had a name or any individual existence.

'Anyhow, as I was saying, they were living at Balaclava, mostly just Edward and Mrs Edward, she-of-no-name, all on their own. A war widow called Elizabeth Henderson lived nearby in a cottage belonging to Sneddon's Farm. That cottage is just a ruin now but then it was still habitable, if a bit primitive. I suppose it was the cheapest place she could find. She lived there with her young daughter, Penny, and supported the pair of them writing little stories for children's magazines. There were a lot more mags of that sort around then, I believe. She educated Penny at home herself, no money for school fees. I know all this because Aunt Penny told me about her childhood. She said it had been very happy with a lot of freedom.'

'Aunt Penny?' interrupted Jess, surprised. 'That wouldn't be—'

'Yes, it would!' snapped Tansy. 'That's the real irony of the whole thing. Little Penny Henderson and young Monty Bickerstaffe grew up and got married. It was really unfortunate because long before that, Elizabeth and Edward had a fling, well, an *affair*, I suppose you'd call it, and a pretty hot-blooded one. It must have gone on for quite a long time.'

Tansy paused and grew thoughtful. 'They were all so bloody hypocritical in those days. They really were. They were dead set on respectability. That didn't mean they behaved themselves, just that they buried any bad news, any scandal, as they saw it. It turned out later some of Elizabeth's friends knew about it, but said nothing. If any of the Bickerstaffes got wind of it, they all kept quiet. No one ever spoke of it freely, the most they did was whisper together in corners, but everybody knew. That's where the hypocrisy lay. They hoped that in time when their generation, the ones who knew, had gone, the whole thing would be written out of history. The younger generation wouldn't ever have known about it and so couldn't pass it on.'

Tansy's gaze, as she spoke, had been fixed on the opposite wall. Now, unexpectedly, she turned her large pale blue eyes directly towards Carter and Jess.

'I don't know whether Edward and Elizabeth were in love. Perhaps they were just bored to tears out there in the sticks; Elizabeth in that tiny cottage with a little child for company and Edward rattling around Balaclava with a dull wife whose name no one could remember.'

The frown briefly puckered her brow again. 'When you think about it, it's quite possible Edward's nameless wife knew her husband was fooling around. I'd have realised it, if I'd been her. Not that anyone seems to have cared what she thought about it. They would just have wanted to be sure she'd shut up and not make waves.'

'Perhaps she had little choice,' Carter said quietly. 'It wasn't easy to get a divorce back then. She could have cited adultery on her husband's part, but would have had to prove it; and there would have been a lot of unwanted publicity. Edward's wife would have feared that, as much as the rest of the family. Divorced women, even if they were the injured party, still faced a mountain of criticism. They risked being social outcasts. It took guts to go through divorce.'

Tansy shrugged. 'Well, whatever the reason, no one spoke about it. It was a big secret, one they all shared in their tight little circle, but still a secret from public knowledge. Of course, the children, Penny and Monty, wouldn't have known anything. No one would tell a child a thing like that and little kids were innocent back then. They wouldn't have twigged what was going on. It seems to me, from what my mother's told me, that no one told children anything on principle. They drummed it into them that their parents represented the ultimate authority and were never to be questioned. Our great-grandparents were a pretty mouldy lot, if you ask me.'

'So where does Jay Taylor come in?' asked Jess, dragging Tansy back to the story. 'How do you know so much about it and how do you know it really happened at all, if everyone was so secretive and never spoke of it?'

Tansy tossed her hair. 'Finding it all out was down to Jay. A generation had passed away. No one knew the truth. Our ancestors had got what they wanted: an event just written out of history. It took Jay and his decision to research his family tree to dig it all up.'

'Quite an achievement on his part, too,' Carter remarked.

'He was very good at research,' Tansy told them. 'It was part and parcel of what he had to do to write his books. You know, look up people's family trees and try and ferret out any scandal, because scandal helps sell those sorts of books. The people in whose name he was ghosting them generally didn't mind. The idea is to sell books, as many books as possible, and if a connection with a well-known name of any kind turns up so much the better. They don't worry about skeletons in cupboards, not nearly so much, anyway. It would have to be something really bad to make them want to hide it. A love affair, well, they'd see that as sad and romantic. People don't try and hide that now, and a good thing, too!' Tansy opined fiercely.

'So, Jay?' prompted Jess.

'Oh, yes . . . Jay had a quiet period work-wise, a window between jobs. He'd turned in one completed manuscript. Happy celebrity, happy publisher. Another commission was on the cards but only at discussion stage. So he had a bit of time on his hands. He decided to research his own ancestry. He'd been wanting to do it for ages because he only had one living relative he knew of. She's an oldish woman, retired and unmarried, who lives in Bristol.'

'Miss Bryant. We've spoken to her,' Jess told Tansy.

Tansy looked startled. 'How on earth did you get on to her? Jay told me she was a miserable old biddy who'd never liked him; but she was all Jay had or knew about. His mother was dead. He'd no siblings. His father bunked off when he was a baby and no one had heard of him since. He wanted to try and find some other relatives, anyone at all. He thought there must be some. He began by visiting the aunt about a year ago, and quizzing her. She came out with a real bombshell. Jay's father, Lionel Taylor, had been adopted as a baby. Taylor was the name of the people who had adopted him. Jay said that when the aunt told him about it, she had a really spiteful look on her face. "You wanted to know, so now you do!" she'd said.

'Well, he was glad she'd told him because otherwise he'd have wasted time researching the Taylor family tree; and they were nothing to do with him, not blood kin, anyway. But he really had something to go for in finding Lionel's birth mother. He managed to get hold of a copy of his father's original birth certificate; the one issued when his birth was first registered. Not long after that he was adopted and got a new birth certificate. But on the original one Lionel's mother's name was Elizabeth Henderson. She lived at Sneddon Farm Cottage. In the column headed "Father" was only the one word, "unknown". It was an illegitimate birth. But the informant on the certificate, the person who'd actually gone to the registry and registered the birth was Edward Bickerstaffe of Balaclava House.

'Jay scented he was on to something, but he needed a lot more to put it all together. He tried tracing Elizabeth Henderson but she was long dead, sadly, and information scarce. So he turned to her war hero husband's family. It was a shot in the dark, but it turned up trumps. He actually found a Mrs Edmonton, née Henderson, a much younger cousin of Elizabeth's husband, and still alive. Jay went to see her. She was really ancient, terribly upper crust and very frosty. He explained who he was and why he was searching for information. Elizabeth Henderson was his grandmother. At first Mrs Edmonton wouldn't admit a thing; said it was all too long ago and she didn't remember. Luckily he persevered. Eventually she said she'd no knowledge of Elizabeth having any baby other than

Penny, who had unquestionably been legitimate. He wondered if she'd said that just to get rid of him because any scandal would've touched all the Hendersons. At any rate, he was afraid he'd reached a dead end. But then, quite unexpectedly, Mrs Edmonton phoned him a few days later. She'd been spending sleepless nights over his visit; and had decided he had a right to know the truth. She invited him back to see her and Jay went like a shot.

'She confessed that she knew Elizabeth had had another baby when she'd been a war widow for several years. All Elizabeth's friends, and even her late husband's family, had conspired to "protect" her and prevent the news getting public. The old lady had been one of those who had known all about it, but had kept quiet. "Not just for her sake," she said, "but for poor dear Penny's, too. Her childhood would have been blighted. She'd have lost all her little friends." A case of the sins of the fathers, or in this case, of the mothers, you know. Miserable bunch. As if it could have been the child Penny's fault in any way!

'Jay's informant told him she only knew for sure that the father of Elizabeth's baby had been a married man, a neighbour with whom she'd been conducting a long affair, an "unfortunate entanglement" as she called it. Otherwise, the neighbour was rumoured to be one of the Bickerstaffe biscuit family, but the old lady had no firm knowledge of that. She kept insisting that Elizabeth and her lover would have married, had he been free. "I don't want you to have the wrong idea about your grandmother," she told Jay. "She was a thoroughly decent but unlucky young woman. Her husband had been killed and she was all alone and vulnerable. She wasn't a floozy."

'Jay liked that word, "floozy". He said it made him think of girls wearing black-market nylons, jitterbugging in smoky cellars. He'd quite have liked to have had a grandmother like that; but the old lady was *most* anxious he didn't have that impression of Elizabeth. Anyway, whatever the truth, Elizabeth found she was pregnant and couldn't have been too pleased about it. It must have given Edward a bad moment, too.'

Tansy scowled. 'It was dealt with very efficiently. She was whisked away to a very private nursing home that specialised in unmarried mothers like her, and gave birth there to a boy. She called him Lionel. The Taylors, who were childless, adopted the baby. The nursing home ran a profitable little sideline as an adoption agency. It was all very informal, as it was back then. He was handed over at only a few weeks old. Elizabeth had already returned home, her reputation intact, and that was that.

'Jay had smelt a rat when he saw the name of Bickerstaffe on the birth certificate as informant; now he had his suspicions confirmed. Edward had avoided having to own up to being the father, but he'd gone along to register the birth – protecting Elizabeth from some clerk's disapproval, I suppose – and he must have paid the nursing home fees. Elizabeth was scraping along on a tiny war widow's pension and what she could earn from her books. She couldn't have afforded it. But it was neatly managed. Everyone carried on as before, secret well and truly buried! But Jay had successfully dug it up. His father,

Lionel, was that baby. Randy old Edward Bickerstaffe was his grandfather.'

From the doorway Morton gave a long low whistle that earned him a glare from Carter.

Quietly but in a voice trembling with remembered rage, Tansy added, 'I can't describe Jay's manner when he told me all this. Every sentence was – flung at me. It was as if he really was lobbing rocks at me. When he finished he looked so – so triumphant! I had no answer to any of it and he knew it.'

'If all this is true, Tansy,' the superintendent told her, 'whatever Jay Taylor's belief, it would still have to be proved. Until then it's a conjecture based on circumstantial evidence: rumour, an elderly person's memory, the name of someone, who might have been acting as no more than a good friend in need, registering a baby's birth . . . this wouldn't be enough in law. A DNA test would have settled it; if Monty, say, had agreed to participate. He might have been loath to do so. If it did prove it, it would make Lionel Taylor Monty's half-brother. Jay would be right.'

Tansy nodded. 'I think he was right. I sort of feel it in my bones. My mother says the Bickerstaffes were always very cagey about Edward, even though the poor chap died before he was fifty. My grandfather Harry – Monty's cousin – remembered his Uncle Edward smoking like a chimney; and told us some chest complaint took him off, not surprisingly. Mummy later got the impression from Grandpa that Edward had blotted his copybook somehow, although she'd no idea how or when. Neither of us did until Jay starting digging and presented us with his findings.'

Tansy leaned forward earnestly. 'But Uncle Monty never knew *anything* about Elizabeth's baby, or the affair or any of it. He was only a schoolboy himself at the time. I told you, it was all hush-hush and "we don't speak of it". So when poor Uncle Monty found a dead man on his sofa and told you, the police, he didn't have a clue who he was, he was telling you the truth. He *didn't* know and he still doesn't.'

Tansy stared at them disconsolately. 'I suppose the poor old chap will have to be told now. He'll have to be told everything. About Mum and me feeding Jay that—'

The solicitor coughed loudly and leaned towards her. 'The prosecution will have to establish that. I advise you not to say anything about it now.'

'Yes,' Carter said to Tansy. 'He will have to be told everything, I'm afraid.'

'It will be such an awful shock for him. And it's all Jay's fault!' Tansy burst out furiously.

'Miss Peterson—' began the solicitor again.

'Oh, shut up!' snapped Tansy, rounding on him.

The unfortunate young man subsided into a depressed huddle, still clutching his briefcase to him, and probably contemplating the premature end of a promising career.

She turned back to Jess and Carter. 'Jay traced all the surviving Bickerstaffes and collateral descendants. That was easy enough because the Bickerstaffe family were once well known in the biscuit world. There are all sorts of references to us. You can even still find the odd packet of biscuits with the name on it. The family don't own the firm any longer, of course. They sold that ages ago. But you can trace the Bickerstaffes, every last remote branch of the tree, with no problem. Jay even found *me*. He also went off to see if Sneddon Farm Cottage, where his grandmother had lived, and Balaclava House, where his grandfather hung out, were still there. The cottage had fallen down and had obviously always been a dump. But Balaclava was a different matter. It was also pretty much a ruin, but it sat on a big piece of land. It belonged to Monty Bickerstaffe, who was childless and old. It was then Jay got his crazy idea that he was morally entitled to inherit Balaclava. Of course, his father had been born illegitimate, and no Bickerstaffe had ever recognised him, but Jay still thought Balaclava should be his; and he meant to get his grubby paws on it somehow or other. So, you see, it *was* all his fault.

'He started plotting and planning and snooping round in the way he did so well, and decided to use me. He'd seek me out and chat me up. That would be easy for him to do. He was good at interviewing people and getting the "real" story from them. That was the journalist's training he'd had. I was stupid enough to be flattered he liked me, as I thought. I believed for a while that he *loved* me. I was even ready to marry him at that point, although I dare say I only really wanted to spite my mother. She was so dead against him from the start. I should have been sharper, too. I'm not normally that thick when judging men.

'Well, he got from me that I was Uncle Monty's heir in his will. Jay thought he'd hit the jackpot. He'd marry me. This was when I was still obviously dewy-eyed over him! I'd

327

inherit the house and he'd persuade me to pull it down. When I told him I'd found out what he was up to, and he could forget any idea of marrying me, he said he'd press his own claim to Balaclava. He said he was a closer blood relative than I was to Uncle Monty. We all call Monty "Uncle", but he was my grandfather's cousin. So, I'm a cousin's granddaughter, that's my relationship to Monty. But Jay was his nephew, his nephew! I wasn't sure Jay couldn't persuade Monty to alter his will. Jay could be very persuasive and who knew? Monty might be tickled pink to find out he had a nephew. So I talked it over with Mum and we decided that we had to kill him—'

'Miss Peterson!' pleaded her distraught solicitor.

'I wasn't going to let him think he could use me and get away with it – and I wasn't going to let him get his hands on Balaclava, pull it down, and cover the whole place with horrid little starter homes, so there.'

Tansy turned her attention to Jess. 'I told you once I'd never had an aim, any goal in life. That wasn't quite true. I've always had a secret dream, since I was a kid. It was to make Balaclava beautiful again. I wasn't going to let Jay kill that dream, although I suppose now he pretty well has. That's my real punishment, you know. I don't care about being sent to gaol. I thought if I killed him, my dream would live on. Now it's gone. I've got nothing left – and that includes nothing more to say,' Tansy finished.

'Yes!' agreed her solicitor fervently. 'Say absolutely nothing more, please!'

Chapter 20

'So,' said Jess into the phone, 'I owe you a dinner, Tom. That magazine photo you remembered and dug out for us, gave us the link that took us to Tansy, and then to her mother.'

'You don't owe me dinner,' said Tom's voice in her ear. 'Glad to have been of some use. You can buy me a drink, if you like. Are you free this evening? We could drive out into the country and find a decent pub, one that does steak and chips. I have a hankering for steak.'

'That would be fine,' Jess told him.

'Then I'll stop by your flat and pick you up at, say, seven thirty tonight?'

Jess confirmed that would suit her perfectly, as Morton appeared in the doorway. 'See you later,' she told Tom in farewell.

'One of us,' Morton said gloomily, 'has to go and see the old fellow at Balaclava House and give him all the lurid news about his family. What's he going to make of it all? He's already had to be told two of his family are murderers. Now we've got to add in to the mix his father's fling with a neighbour – and a neighbour who ended up as Monty's own mother-in-law. Then you've got a brother and a nephew, neither of whom he had the slightest idea existed. The nephew was the man he found dead on his sofa. What's poor old Monty going to make of all that? His head will be spinning. They talk about dysfunctional families nowadays. What was that Bickerstaffe bunch like, if not dysfunctional? It's like a blooming soap opera; they ought to put it on the telly.'

'It's going to be a lot for Monty to take in,' Jess agreed. 'And it's a real tragedy, however you look at it.'

Morton shook his head and then looked at her desperately. 'It's not going to be my job, is it? To go and tell him? Not only does that house give me the creeps, but I can't play the agony aunt. There's a load of other work on my desk, as well.'

'I'll go,' Jess said briskly and Morton looked relieved. 'I'm not an agony aunt, either, but I agree he has to be told as soon as possible. As you say, he knows Tansy's under arrest and Bridget, too, even if she's still in hospital. He's got to be bewildered and wondering why on earth it's happened. He'll have to be told exactly why and what the motive for it all was. I'll go there now, this morning. I'll ask the superintendent if he wants to come with me.'

'Good idea,' agreed Morton and took himself off before Jess could change her mind.

'No, I don't think so, Jess,' said Carter when she relayed her question. 'The old chap likes you and I think you'll handle it better than I would. I'd be in the way. Besides, there's a mountain of paperwork to do and get off to the Crown Prosecution Service. I haven't the time.'

'Men!' muttered Jess to herself, as she drove to Balaclava

House. 'As soon as it's got to do with emotions and love affairs and babies, they're suddenly all too busy!'

It was a fine, bright day, if a little chilly. As she passed Pascal's garage, she saw Seb standing by the petrol pumps talking to a spindly youth in overalls. Alfie's replacement, Jess supposed. At least Pascal had got over his fear of reappearing at his place of business, even though Pete Sneddon was now out on bail, awaiting his trial date at the Crown Court. Pete no longer had a gun, and his licence to own one had been revoked, but there were plenty of other objects around a farmyard that would make a weapon. Sneddon, however, was banned by court order from approaching Pascal or his garage. He had given assurances that he wouldn't and seemed to have lost the urge to take any action. The police were confident there would be no repeat of the earlier drama. Jess hoped they'd judged it right. Sneddon was busy working about his farm and Rosie was coping somehow. One of her married daughters had come to stay and lend a hand keeping an eye on her father.

Balaclava House, however, had a visitor. A yellow Renault Megane hatchback was parked outside the gates. Jess parked alongside it, and walked up the drive to the front door. It was ajar. Now that Monty was back in residence, it seemed he had reverted to his old bad habit. She walked in and stood for a moment, listening and looking up the staircase to where the sun threw patches of red and yellow across the wall from the stained-glass Jezebel window. She could hear voices in the drawing room. The driver of the Megane. Now, who could that be? Jess set off towards the sound.

The drawing room was in an even greater state of disarray than it had been originally, difficult though that would have been to imagine when Jess first saw it. Now it looked as though a whirlwind had hit it. The air was full of the disturbed dust of years and Jess had to pinch the bridge of her nose to stop herself sneezing. Cupboards and drawers were open, their contents spilled on to the faded carpet. What on earth was going on? Was a desperate robber ransacking the place?

Then she saw that, in the middle of this chaos, Monty was sitting in an armchair, gripping the arms so fiercely that the veins on the backs of his hands stood out like cords. He was glaring at an unknown, middle-aged woman who looked reassuringly normal and non-threatening. Nor was Monty exhibiting alarm, just simmering resentment. His visitor was moving around, picking up items and putting each into whichever she considered appropriate of several wooden crates. As she did so, she carried on a one-sided conversation with Monty under the guise of consulting him.

'What about these?' She held up a pair of china shepherdesses. 'Would you like to take these, keep them to remind you? They're very pretty and would look nice in your new home.'

'Chuck them out!' growled Monty.

'Nonsense, of course not! I'll put them in the box going to the auction rooms. They're too good for Oxfam and probably worth quite a bit. They should be valued properly.'

She became aware of Jess, standing by the door, and paused in her activity. 'Hello?' she said, managing to make the word both a greeting and a question.

'Inspector Campbell,' Jess told her, taking out her ID. 'I've just called by to see how Monty's doing.'

'I'm not doing at all,' said Monty loudly before the woman could answer. He pointed at his helper. 'Her name is Hilda and she's married to someone in the family.'

'I'm Hilda Potter,' explained the woman. 'My husband's mother was a Bickerstaffe.' She made this claim with pride.

'You'd think it was something special, wouldn't you?' snarled Monty. 'Well, it is, in its way. It's specially awful – a curse!'

'Now, Monty,' began Hilda. 'You don't mean—'

'What would you know about it?' Monty interrupted her rudely. He turned back to Jess. 'They're packing me up, too. Packing off, more like it! I'm going to some damn sheltered flat.'

'You'll be very comfy there,' said Hilda, undaunted. 'Do you want to keep some of those books over there?'

'No,' snapped Monty. 'No one's opened any of them for fifty years. I'm not going to start reading them now!'

'I think we'll get an antiquarian bookseller in to look them over. You never know.'

Monty hauled himself up out of his armchair. 'Come into the kitchen,' he invited Jess. 'She's driving me barmy.'

'Oh, I can take a hint!' said Hilda breezily. 'You stay here and have a nice chat with the inspector. I'll go upstairs and see about making a start up there.'

'You see what it's come to?' Monty asked Jess, when Hilda had gone. He sank back into his armchair and gestured at another.

'Sit down, m'dear. Like a drop of whisky? The bottle's hidden in that coal scuttle there. She hasn't found it yet.'

'I won't have a drink, thanks, Monty.' Jess took a seat facing him. 'I am very sorry for everything that's happened. I deeply regret Mrs Harwell is so badly hurt. But the hospital says she should recover in due course. There are thankfully no significant internal injuries. As for Tansy, I do understand how you must feel. I know how fond of her you were—'

'Still am!' snapped Monty.

'Oh, good.' There didn't seem to be much more Jess could say about that. She indicated their surroundings and went on, 'I'm particularly sorry you're leaving Balaclava. I know you don't want to go. But the new flat will be warm and comfortable and I dare say you'll be much nearer the shops. You won't have to walk all that way to buy – er – groceries.'

'Yes, yes,' Monty mumbled. 'I know I've got to go. In a way I'm not sorry to be rid of the place. It's caused nothing but trouble. Truth is, I should have sold it years ago. I can't think why I was so keen on staying on here. It's not as if it holds any happy memories. The whole place is jinxed.'

'Is it to be sold, then?' Jess asked him.

'Yes, and there's already a buyer, believe it or not. Some property developer by the name of Hemmings. Good luck to him. I don't care if he pulls it down. He's paying a fair price. There'll be enough money to set me up in the new flat; and there will be a nice little bit left over in the bank for young Tansy, when she gets out of gaol.' He looked up at Jess. 'She will go to gaol, I suppose?'

'I can't second-guess the verdict, Monty, but it was a cold-blooded, carefully planned murder, carried out by both women. Bridget may be in hospital now, but she'll stand trial too, eventually. Tansy didn't have anything to do with the dead man being left here on your sofa. You should know that. But she plotted together with her mother, was present at the fatal lunch, even gave a hand helping prepare it, and she watched her mother drive away with the dying man. She could have rung the police, rung an ambulance, anything, if she'd wanted to save Taylor. She didn't.'

'Of course she didn't,' Monty said calmly. 'He betrayed her. Bickerstaffe women don't take kindly to being betrayed. Bickerstaffe women kill.'

This seemed an over-the-top statement to Jess but she let it go. She had to tackle the duty that had brought her.

'I've come to explain some things, Monty, things you might not know about. Some of it may come as a shock. But you need to know because, among other reasons, you'll understand why Bridget and Tansy plotted together as they did. You must be wondering. Not that anything can excuse them, murder can never be excused, but they had what they considered a motive.'

Monty said nothing, avoiding Jess's gaze, and staring meditatively into space. He was listening; Jess knew that. Tentatively she began to unfold the details of that old doomed love affair and its consequences. She told him of his father and Elizabeth Henderson, of Lionel's birth, the adoption, Jay's discovery of the truth and his belief he had a claim on Balaclava. She went on to explain how he hoped to use Tansy, once he'd learned

335

she was to inherit the house, by marrying her and in time persuading her to sell off the whole estate. When Tansy indignantly refused to go along with his plan, he had been prepared to tackle Monty directly, claiming to be a nephew. Not knowing how this would play with Monty, the two women had panicked.

At this point, Monty muttered, 'No, no . . . Wouldn't have changed my will in favour of a complete stranger!' Otherwise he made no comment.

When she had finished, they sat again in silence for a while. In the quietness she heard Hilda Potter come down the main staircase, go out of the front door and almost at once re-enter. She began to puff her way up the staircase again. What had she taken out to her car, wondered Jess, that couldn't be put in one of the waiting crates?

Monty stirred in his chair. 'Secrets are buggers,' he said. There was another long pause, before he went on, 'The only place for them is out in the open where they can't muck up anyone's life. There was I, all those years thinking I was the only one who knew. The truth was they all knew, but they thought *I* didn't.'

'You knew about this?' Jess asked incredulously.

'What?' Monty looked at her as if he'd forgotten she was there and the words he'd spoken had been an observation made to himself. 'Oh, no, not *all* of it, not by a long chalk. I didn't know Mrs Henderson, Penny's mamma, had a baby. Lionel, you say his name was? I had no idea that fellow sprawled on my sofa over there . . .' Monty pointed at the piece of furniture in question. 'Was in any way related to me. But I knew about the affair between my father and Penny's mother. I came across them

336

in Shooter's Wood, in flagrante delicto. I was twelve at the time. They didn't see me. They were too busy! I crept away. But there was no disguising what was going on. Young as I was, I knew what it must be. I went to a boys' boarding school, you see. We eavesdropped on the older boys and they seemed to talk of almost nothing else. It fired our curiosity and made us precocious little brats. But I never told my friends at school about Shooter's Wood. I couldn't speak to *anyone* of what I'd seen. It was my secret and I've kept it for over sixty years.'

'Oh, Monty . . .' Jess said sadly.

He sighed too. 'Later on, I had reason to believe my mother knew of the affair, though possibly not about the baby. There's no way of finding out now, but if she had known it might have been enough to push her – but there's no use in speaking of that now, either. Nothing can be changed about any of *that*. It's all water under the bridge, as they say, ancient history. The main thing is, *I* never spoke of it. I think that drove the first wedge between Penny and me. It wasn't the only reason our marriage hit the rocks. There were plenty of others and most of them down to me. But Penny was shrewd and knew me well. She realised I was keeping something from her and it rankled with her. As the years went by and I still didn't speak, she became angry. "I never know what you're thinking, Monty!" she would say to me. "But whatever it is, it always comes from the same place. You've got something on your mind, worrying you, and you don't trust me enough to share it." So she kept tapping at that wedge, and eventually the tree trunk that was our relationship split clean in two, right down the middle. Of course,

I couldn't ever have shared it, not with her. I couldn't have told the poor girl the truth, could I?'

Monty turned his head sharply in Jess's direction and stared at her. 'Could I?'

'No, Monty,' Jess said quietly. 'No, you couldn't.'

Monty looked relieved. 'Thank you for that, I'm glad to hear you say it.' He made to struggle up out of the chair. 'You may not want a drink, I certainly do.'

'I'll get it,' Jess said quickly. She got up and opened the brass lid of the coal scuttle. The whisky bottle lay in it, nestling in ancient coal dust. She found a glass in the sideboard and poured a generous measure. The poor old fellow deserved it.

'Monty,' she said when she had retaken her seat. 'There is one thing that may not have occurred to you but I must warn you about.'

'What's that, then?' asked Monty over the rim of his glass.

'It is quite possible that Lionel could still be alive somewhere. He would be younger than you, a good eleven or twelve years younger. He turned out a bit of a rotter, I'm sorry to say, deserted his wife and baby and disappeared. He would have been afraid of being found for a long time after that. He might have left the country or at least moved hundreds of miles away; he might have changed his name by deed poll. But, well, after all this time he may think there's nothing to fear any more. Jay tracked you down and who knows? One day Lionel may turn up. I don't want you to worry about it but you should be prepared. There will be a lot about all this in the newspapers, I'm afraid. All of the story will get out. Wherever he is now, and whoever he is now, Lionel may read it.'

Monty scratched his ear. 'I suppose so. Can't be helped. Much good it would do him, anyway.' Monty looked at her quite mischievously. 'It'll be too late for him to get his hands on Balaclava!' He grew sober again, shaking his head. 'Not, I repeat, that I'd ever allow that.' He gave a sad smile. 'Funny thing, when I was a youngster I'd have quite liked to have a brother. But not now, I couldn't be doing with complications now.'

He brightened. 'See here, the fellow has never tried to find me yet. He may have popped his clogs. If he's alive he could be living anywhere in the world. He may know nothing about his true parentage or Balaclava. He's a happier man for it, if so. It would have been better for his son if he'd learned nothing, poor devil. If this Lionel chap reads the newspapers, he might be more afraid I'd find him, than I'm afraid he'd try and find me. He deserted a wife and kid, you said. He'll still be lying low.'

Monty waved a hand at their surroundings. 'By this time next year, Hemmings will have pulled this place down, every last damn brick. That'll be the end of it, at last . . .' His voice trailed away into a whisper. 'Yes, at long, long last, it will be an end to it *all*.'

This was true, thought Jess. What Jay Taylor had discovered had led inexorably to his death. Lionel had his own guilty secret to keep, wherever he was. He might not even know his abandoned wife, Deirdre, was long dead. He might just be frightened of her sister, the acid Miss Bryant.

'One other matter, Monty,' she began.

'What?' asked Monty, eyeing her warily. 'You're not going to produce any more of my wrong-side-of-the-blanket kin? I can't be doing with any *more*.'

'I wasn't thinking of your family. I was about to mention Seb Pascal and Mrs Sneddon who were using the room upstairs . . .'

'Your Superintendent Carter told me about that,' Monty said crossly. 'It doesn't matter a damn now, does it? They're not going to be using it again. Any problems arising from that are all theirs, nothing to do with me! You've taken Pete Sneddon's gun away, I assume? Silly bugger, why did he have to go blasting it off at Pascal's petrol station?'

'Yes, we have his gun and he won't be getting it back. His licence has been revoked. Nevertheless, we're keeping a close eye on him until his trial. However, without wanting to harp on about it, Seb and Rosie were trespassing, Monty, and you may want to consider bringing some civil charges . . .'

'No, I don't,' snapped Monty. 'I'm just glad I never walked in on the blighters. I walked in on my father and Penny's mother and that was enough. I wouldn't have wanted a second experience like that, thank you! They kept the place tidy up there, I'm told?'

'Very tidy,' Jess agreed. Tidier than Monty had kept the rest of the house.

'Oh well, then,' said Monty. 'They didn't cause me any trouble. They only caused trouble for one another. I don't want to talk about it any more.'

The door opened and Hilda looked into the room, smiling brightly. 'I'm just about to make some coffee. Would you both like a cup?'

'Oh, for pity's sake . . .' groaned Monty.

'Yes, please,' Jess said hastily. 'That would be very nice.'

'Don't encourage the woman,' begged Monty.

Hilda, ever resolute under fire, beamed at them. 'I won't be a tick.'

'Monty,' Jess said when Hilda had gone, 'that was a bit unkind. She's being very helpful.'

'You should know me well enough by now, my dear,' said Monty stiffly, 'to have learned I don't like being *helped*.'

'I like being helped,' argued Jess. 'I'm always grateful for help.'

'That,' Monty said, 'is because you're young and can still do things for yourself. Help isn't a necessity for you. When you're as old and as decrepit as I am – though I hope you never are such an old ruin as me – you won't be able to do things and you will hate other people drawing your attention to it.'

He pushed himself up out of his chair and ambled towards the sideboard. 'I've got something for you. I don't want it and I don't know what to do with it. You might as well have it.'

'I can't accept a gift, Monty!' Jess protested in alarm.

'You haven't seen what it is, yet.' Monty stooped awkwardly and rummaged in the cupboard. He emerged backwards clasping something to his chest. Returning, he set it down on an ancient bridge table near Jess's chair.

It was a round tin, very old and scratched, still sealed with yellowing tape. On the lid was an illustration showing a coat of arms similar to the one above the door of Balaclava House, but here flanked by a smug lion and a palm tree.

'It's Bickerstaffe's boiled fruit cake,' said Monty, indicating it with a wave of his hand. 'It's probably the last one in existence.

Must be fifty years old or very nearly. It's an historical artefact.
I can't throw it out. You take it. Only for heaven's sake, don't
try and eat it.'

Jess, Detective Sergeants Morton and Nugent, with Detective
Constables Stubbs and Bennison, all stood together with Ian
Carter in a circle round the cake tin. They looked, Jess thought
with amusement, as if they were all going to break into some
sort of New Age ceremonial dance. There was something very
totem-like about the ancient sealed tin.

'Blimey,' said Stubbs, breaking the silence at last. 'Are you
going to open it? I don't mean eat it. Just to look at it, make
sure it's really in there?'

'It'll be all horrible and manky!' protested Bennison. 'It'll
probably smell, too.'

'Don't see why,' argued Stubbs. 'My mum's still got a bit of
her wedding cake in a tin. It's dried out and crumbled and you
wouldn't eat it, but it's not smelly.'

'Why's she kept it?' demanded Bennison. 'What is she going
to do with it?'

'What are we going to do with *this*?' Carter interrupted.

There was a moment's silence while they all gazed at the tin
again.

'Chuck it out,' suggested Morton. 'The old bloke should have
got rid of it years ago.'

'It's an antique, you can't just bung it . . .' protested Stubbs,
in his role of upholder of tradition. 'There are museums with
that kind of stuff in them. We were all taken on a school trip to

one, when I was a kid. It was arranged like a Victorian grocer's shop. It had rusty old tins just like that on the shelves.'

'Can you remember where this museum was?' asked Bennison. 'We could send it to them.'

'I did have one thought . . .' Jess ventured. They all looked at her expectantly. 'It's rather on the lines of what DC Stubbs was saying. The company that bought out Bickerstaffe's business may have some kind of an archive, documents, biscuit tins and packaging and so on, to do with their company history. We could write to their head office and ask them if they'd like it.'

'That's a very good idea,' Carter said approvingly. 'I'll do it.'

The others drifted away, leaving him with Jess.

'You've done very well in this case,' Carter said.

'We had a bit of luck, sir, in Tom Palmer remembering he'd seen a photo of Taylor in the magazine at his dentist's. Any thanks is due to him.'

'It still had to be put together. You moved very quickly to catch the two women at Colleys' pig farm. Well done.'

'Thank you,' Jess said, reddening.

Carter, too, looked awkward. 'I was wondering if, by way of celebration, you might like to go out for a drink tonight.'

Jess reddened even more. 'I would, sir, but I've made an arrangement to meet up with Tom Palmer. Of course, we'd be delighted if you'd join us . . .'

Carter looked horrified. 'No, no, wouldn't dream of it . . . It was just an idea. Enjoy your evening and give my regards to Palmer.'

He took himself off at such speed, the phrase 'fled the scene' came irresistibly to Jess's mind.

'Listen!' she wanted to shout after him. 'Tom and I are just friends!' But he probably wouldn't believe her.

'All I'm saying, Billy,' protested Terri Hemmings, 'is that you ought to think about what you'll do when you retire.'

'I'm not retiring, not bloody yet, anyway,' retorted her spouse.

Terri took up a combative stance. 'So, when are we going to go and live in Spain as you've always said we would one day? What day? You're nearly at pension age. You'll be sixty-four next birthday – you could have a bus pass, if you wanted!'

Billy glowered at her.

'Of course you don't look it,' she added in a mollifying tone. 'No one would think you were nearly an OAP – senior citizen. But you've got to think of your health, sweetie. You hardly ever take time off, just a few days at the races now and again. It's always business with you. Now it's this Balaclava House deal. All right, it's going to make lots of money. It'll also mean loads of work for you and I'll be lucky to see you. You know we were off to the Spanish villa for a nice break in the sun. I've already started packing.'

'You can still go, can't you?' was the reply. 'I'll come out and join you when I've got this deal all sewn up. It's at a very tricky stage.'

'You'll have a heart attack or something,' his wife warned. 'You work too hard for a man of your age.'

'Will you stop going on about my age!' shouted Billy. More calmly he went on, 'I won't have a heart attack. Why the heck should I? I'm as fit as a fiddle. Go and pack for Marbella.'

Terri clattered out, muttering furiously.

Billy moved over to the window and took out of his pocket the photograph showing Terri with Jay Taylor at the races. The police had just returned it, with their thanks for his help. He moved so that the sunlight fell on it.

'I intend to push this deal through for you,' he told the grinning image of Jay Taylor. 'It meant a lot to me that you and I were going to develop this bit of land together. And I'll see it through, Jay, don't you worry. A signature on the dotted line and Balaclava House and its land are mine.'

He contemplated the photograph for a few minutes more and continued to address it, this time mentally.

Fate brought us together, that's the truth. If I never believed in Fate before that day at the races, when we met up, I started to believe in it then. After all those years, eh? And you none the wiser.

He gave a little laugh.

Well, I couldn't tell you the real truth, could I? I couldn't tell you why I agreed to come into this deal so quickly, was so keen to work with you. You might have asked yourself why I wanted to tie myself to working with a complete novice. Fair enough, I did think it was a good project, developing that land. There was money to be made and if I was able to steer some your way, it might make up for pretending you didn't exist all those years. Not that you knew anything about that. Nor was I going to tell you. The last thing I wanted was to have you start calling me "Dad". I walked away from being Lionel Taylor long, long ago. There was no point in telling you *now* who I was back *then*. I'm Billy Hemmings now, Gerald – sorry, Jay! I've been

345

Billy Hemmings so long, I can't believe I was ever that other chap. Besides, there's Terri to consider, you know. She wouldn't have understood. She'd have kicked up a hell of a fuss. So I had to keep it all a secret.